Exposure

Exposure

INCANDESCENT SERIES

BOOK 3

SYLVIE PARIZEAU

Library and Archives Canada Cataloging-in-Publication Data:

Parizeau, Sylvie

Exposure: Book 3 of the Incandescent Series / Sylvie Parizeau

ISBN print : 978-0-9953240-7-7

Interior Design and Formatting by:

www.emtippettsbookdesigns.com

To Melleny, for the pure joy.

Prologue

Olivier,

I'm so sorry.

I knew this would come. I ignored it too long, liking it too much.

Mea culpa a thousand times over. If only...

No. I can't do this to you.

I can't talk to you over the phone, ever.

I can't write to you again.

I can't meet with you.

I'm not who you think I am.

I wish.

Lost in a world quilted by silence is who I am.

A world in which I remember the sounds of life, echoes of the distant past.

A world in which I was whole; perfect for a short while.

A world now passing me by, soundlessly.

I've fallen in love with you.

Forgive me. I didn't mean to.

—*unsent email*

One

P.O.

Val-David (Québec), seven months earlier...

A rivulet of hot water streams down my neck, trickling down my chest. Of course, the bar of soap I've been chasing slips away from my fingers for the zillionth time. Goddammit!

Wait.

This can't be right.

There's no hot water at Leo's old farmstead, just cold-as-fuck showers.

I crack my eyes open, my glance hitting the slanted ceiling with its peeling paint in an ugly-ass shade of... Whatever the heck that puke color's called.

It's as I thought, too good to be true.

Fucking hell, I curse, waking up more fully. I'm drenched, sweating like a pig roasting on a pit.

I flip onto my back, rubbing at my eyes.

It's only midmorning, my wristwatch confirms, but the couple of hours of sleep I managed to catch will have to do for now. There's just no way in hell I'll be able to snag any more zzzzs in this oven.

I roll out of bed, eyeing balefully the useless window duct taped to death.

If this unusual heat wave hitting Québec's Hautes-Laurentides this late in August goes on much longer, I'll probably do something drastic. Like switch bedrooms behind Zac's back the minute he stays over at Magali's place for the night. A window in working condition letting in the cool night breeze is at a premium around here, and I have no compunction in doing so, either. After all, Zac switched bedrooms on us first, the little shit, just before Yann and I flew in from Boston a month ago for our summer break.

Coming out of the sweltering bedroom tucked under the eaves, I wipe my forehead with the back of my hand, missing MIT's air-conditioned computer labs for a minute. Who knows, though, this might be just what I need to grow a brand-new fondness for icy cold showers.

Eyes shrivelled to the size of raisins, I shuffle down the stairs in dire need of a few shots of caffeine after pulling another all-nighter debugging new lines of code on the firewall program I'm developing. Probably the reason why my body considers coffee a food group by now.

Absently swiping beads of sweat dotting my chest with the tee I picked up off my bedroom floor, I yawn on my way to the kitchen in my boxer shorts.

Hitting the last step, I sigh with relief at the summer breeze coming in from all the opened windows downstairs. It instantly washes over me and cools my skin. Makes me briefly wonder if it would be worth waking up with yet another sharpie-drawn goatee, or worse—like it's been known to happen before—to hitch a hammock in between the staircase newel posts, tonight.

I stop by Liam and Éolie's closed door, noticing that the whimsical blackboard tied to their bedroom doorknob reads: **Twin Feeding in Progress. Do not disturb**.

That explains why the house is so quiet at the moment.

My chest expands, filling with warmth as I think of the twin babies that belong to Liam and Éolie. Those two little guys pull at my heart strings like nothing else.

Even with my lack of experience with kids, I'm not surprised I took to being an uncle so quickly. And I'm not the only one. We all have.

Fascinating phenomena.

It's not like the six of us guys growing up at a Swiss boarding school had a lot of hands-on experience with family life... "And tiny infants at that?" I scoff underneath my breath. "Might as well have been talking foreign species from another planet altogether."

I flick the sign with my index finger in passing, chuckling low. Before that little blackboard came into being, we all had a hard time letting our twin baby boys have a little peace and quiet, always bickering about whose turn it was to hold them. Now, we're more disciplined, waiting for the flip side to appear. **Twin Fix Inside. Come and get it.**

Guess for now coffee it is. I keep moving, shaking my head at Magali—the mastermind behind it—and her creative thoughtfulness. The love of Zac's life is a midwife through and through.

I stop short in the kitchen's doorway, inwardly groaning. *Aw, man.*

The other reason the house is quiet. Zac and Magali are making out like oversexed teenagers, hogging the counter space and blocking access to the stove. Not that shit tasting instant coffee made from a pot of boiling water is worth all that much, but still. Caffeine is caffeine and beggars can't be choosers, as Leo would say.

With two couples madly in love living here for now, Leo's place no longer qualifies as a quack farm as much as a remake of *The Love Boat*. Theo's the only one missing in on the fun, stuck at his uppity law firm in Boston for the summer and grumbling weekly about it. But sometimes, like now, I'm not so sure Theo isn't the one better off. Leo, Yann, and I literally trip on one, or both couples, either cuddling, gazing into each other's eyes endlessly to the oblivion of everything else, or making out ad nauseam pretty much everywhere we turn.

Not that I'm envious or anything.

"Hey, you two," I say to Zac and Magali, eliciting zero reaction and no refraining on the action.

"Mind if I step in for a minute?" I ask drily. "You're standing between me and coffee and that might be hazardous to your health," I say, only half-jesting.

Their lips on lock down, their hands all over, they don't even acknowledge me, lost to the world around them. Surprise. Surprise.

"Okay, well, guess that's my cue to go hunt coffee elsewhere."

Still nothing.

I double back to the stifling bedroom upstairs and pull on the first pair of passable cargo shorts I can find on the floor, not bothering to shower first nor hunt down a clean shirt.

I. Need. Caffeine. Try, yesterday.

It's as urgent as my dampened, wrinkled tee implies with the text. **COFFEE.**

EXE not found: (A)bort, (R)etry, (F)all asleep.

I shove my other half, Lucie, into my computer bag and make a beeline for the front door.

"Later!" I shout, grabbing from the peg a set of car keys from our Volvo Cross Country station wagon fleet of cars on my way out.

No answer. Go figure.

As I stumble over the threshold, I spot Yann comfortably sprawled in one of the Adirondacks spread out on the front porch. He's reading some sort of quantum physics textbook like, say, a normal person would a novel. When he sees me, his brows shoot up above his classic tortoise-shell glasses.

"Let me guess? You've been cut out from your usual caffeine supply by the ongoing kissing fest?" he asks.

I stop in my tracks. "They've been at it that long?" I shake my head, wondering what that would be like. To kiss someone for that long. To want to.

"Longer."

I grunt in reply, "Christ, maybe we need to check if they're turning blue from lack of oxygen." Yeah, and maybe I need a bit more breathlessness in my own life. I feel a tad depressed by my lack of a love life all of a sudden.

"Been there. Done that," Yann says, making a big production of swiping clean his eyeglasses with the hem of his dark-green polo shirt before shoving them back on his nose. "Do so at your own peril, man. Some images cannot be unseen once they're burned on your retinas."

"Did they fog up your lenses with the applied physics, Math Man?" I rib him, and right on cue he turns red, the flush spreading like wild fire from his neck up to the roots of his mahogany-brown hair.

"Something like that," he mumbles under his breath, and I take pity on him. The guys and I aren't even sure he ever kissed a girl. Hard to tell with him, but out of our band of intellectual misfits he's the geekiest, so, not improbable. And considering I've known him since I was a kid and we tell each other everything, the fact he's never divulged anything remotely physical with a woman speaks volume.

Not that I can talk. I can count on the fingers of one hand the number of brief encounters of the girl kind I've had. A few weeks at the most is my record. But it never bothered me before tripping all over Liam's and Zac's brand-new kind of happiness.

"I'm going down to the village for a shot of espresso. Want to come with?" I ask him, hobbling down the front porch stairs into the hazy morning sun.

"I'm good nerding it over here but feel free to bring one up."

"Will do."

On my way to the woodshed in the back where our herd of station wagons is corralled, I spot the sixth member of our little guy-tribe taking measurements by his ruin of a barn with its roof caved in.

I hail him. "Hey Leo, want to go down to the village for coffee?"

His shoulder-length, ash-brown hair is half undone from its usual leather tie, blowing in the wind and lending him an air of mad scientist. Not entirely a lie.

"Thanks, but no," Leo shouts back, hyped by whatever he sees in this pile of barn crap. "I need to get back to my architect with some more ideas I came up with during the night for my greenhouse."

I eye the mess and snort, shaking my head at him. Guess experimental farm means just that, experimental. With the ink still wet on his PhD in agronomy research, he wants to integrate into his projected, state-of-the-art laboratory greenhouse the remains of the old barn, salvaging it. But the rotten thing is so far gone that even his architect is scratching his head over that piece of the puzzle.

"Looks good to me," I snicker before cupping my hands on either side of my mouth to yell, "Maybe you'll breed a new species of magical mushrooms out of it."

"You wish!" he yells back. "Get out of here, you arse, and bring back coffee while at it."

"Looks like it's you and me, Lucie." I unlock Volvo Cross Country number three, the silver-colored one we all chipped in to buy, dropping Lucie's bag onto the passenger seat.

Sliding in, I adjust the driver's seat forward by rote. When you're surrounded by guys over six feet tall it kind of goes with the territory when you're barely topping five feet six.

I cut the engine in front of C'est la Vie Café alongside the linear park, Le P'tit Train du Nord—a two-hundred-kilometers-long ancient railway reclaimed as a cycling and cross-country skiing venue bisecting the village, hopping from one to the next. The village boasting dozens of bistros and cafés, but I haven't tried this one yet. My eyes cut to the display easel standing at the foot of the stairs, advertising an in-house blend blacker than black. And just like that, I'm sold on the place.

"Come on, Lucie, let's hit the terrace and get some work done," I mumble into the empty car, my sleep-deprived brain salivating over the vision of a double shot of espresso.

Stepping out, I'm greeted by an old '40s French song, *La Mer*. A popular classic the guys and I heard many a time on weekends in Paris in our A-level years, the lyrics of which are a poem in itself. The music spilling onto the terrace from the open door of the café transports me in the space of an instant to La Place du Tertre sur la butte Montmartre and its quaint sidewalk cafés. Well, minus the sidewalks, the sheer masses of gawking tourists and the blasé attitude we used to wear around us like a scarf. I chuckle low, remembering. Yeah, when we hit eighteen we thought we were the shit for a little while. Thank the fuck it passed quickly.

I follow the coffee aromas inside, my mouth watering at the smell of roasted beans permeating the place.

On my way over to the counter at the back, I shake my head at the barista who dries some cups as he sings along in a pleasant, baritone voice.

To be heard, I practically have to shout over the loud music. "Nice voice you got there, but I never thought I'd hear a Charles Trenet's soft ballad blasting the speakers at a nightclub's volume level," I joke.

Chuckling, the tall, skinny guy, not much older than me, dabs a few beads of sweat from his temples with the corner of his black apron with the bright-white C'est la Vie logo written across his lean chest. "Yeah, sorry about that. We're not allowed speakers on the terrace but at *la belle saison* everyone's outside and it's kind of our trademark, coffee and French oldies. What can I get you?" he asks over the sink, washing his hands.

I place my order, my French no longer so choppy now that I get to practice it daily. *"Un double espresso allongé, s'il-vous-plaît."*

You'd think that with my Swiss Romande origins I'd be organically more fluent in French, but I grew up with the guys in English at Berlinger Academy, a Cambridge International boarding school—a Swiss boarding school as ironic as it is, given the size of a country that rivals the size of the city of Montréal. But what's left of my family wasn't into the whole commuting daily thing. Nor communicating for that matter, I inwardly snort. So my French is pretty much as fluent as what I learned in school, and not much else.

The dark-haired barista nods once. *"Installez-vous où vous voulez et je vous l'apporte à l'instant,"* he says with a knowing look at my half-awake, rumpled appearance as he enjoins me to sit where I want, my espresso coming right up.

Magic words if I ever heard them.

I step out into a blast of humid air that makes my tee stick to my back. "Great," I grumble, faced with either having my eardrums splintered by sitting inside or have my brain cells liquefied by sitting outside.

Thankfully, it's too late for the breakfast crowd and too early for the lunch crowd. So, apart from a few tourists pouring over activity pamphlets, I have the deck overlooking the linear park pretty much to myself. And the only table on the side shaded by a bouquet of mature apple trees grown wild, their gnarly branches reaching to the sky some forty feet up.

You won't hear me complaining.

I swipe the sweat pearling on my forehead with the back of my hand, waiting for Lucie to boot up.

"Merci beaucoup," I thank the barista when he arrives with a full tray and begins setting items in front of me. First, the steaming coffee he places just so. A water glass and a small bowl with lemon wedges and what looks like fresh mint leaves by smell alone, follow. I fight the urge to roll my eyes and hurry him along. As he fills my water glass, I slurp my coffee and scald my tongue in the process.

He makes a face before turning on his heels like I just made the worst faux pas ever by not taking the time to savour the heavenly concoction.

I don't give a damn by now; I'll savour the next one. I let the shot of caffeine spread through my veins, sighing in quiet bliss even though my tongue stings like crazy. All that matters is that I may survive the day with eyes wide open after all.

On my fourth cup, pleased by the yield results of my latest lines of code, I look up from my screen and stretch my arms over my head, ready for a break.

At this rate, I'll be able to present on schedule the final version of my firewall app in a marketable form by the end of this upcoming year at MIT, my last before I earn my double Master degrees in software engineering and computer science. The beta version is already attracting interest from the big five but, for now, I'm happy to go solo and do my own thing.

The air is still thick with heat and kind of soggy. Sunlight filters through the branches of the apple trees covered in shiny leaves and ripening fruits, which reminds me I haven't eaten anything since last night. Right on cue, my stomach growls loudly. I should probably order some kind of croissant sandwich to go with my liquid diet or fold and grab something at the farmstead. Undecided, I stretch my neck to the side to work out the kinks in it. That's when I see her.

I still mid-motion, eyes locked on the woman on the lawn below me.

My heart starts to beat in a weird staccato rhythm.

I could blame one too many hits of caffeine on an empty stomach, but that's not it. A pair of toned legs stretched out on the grassy area bordering the park overlooking the deck is to blame. The legs are attached to the most beautiful girl I've ever seen. The breeze has kicked up from earlier, and the wind is playing peek-a-boo with her pale yellow sundress, showcasing her perfect backside and white lacy boy shorts underneath. If she notices, she doesn't care enough to stop it.

But I care.

I definitely care.

Unable to help myself, I stare.

She bends low and then sprawls flat across the grass, facing me now. Wonder brightens up her exquisite face as her bent legs swing charmingly to and fro, and she talks to. . .a dragonfly cupped in her hands?

Not that I can judge since I regularly have long chats with Lucie, my trusty laptop. Still. A beautiful girl like that deserves better company than a bug. And coming from someone who used to hack into computers to plant them, it's quite the admission.

For the first time in my life, I'm seriously contemplating debugging a flesh-and-blood female. Slowly, and oh, so pleasurably...

Two

P.O.

Staring at the interesting girl from my vantage point, high up on the café's balcony, I have the distinct impression, in that moment, that I know her, that we've met before, which is ludicrous. Even from here, I can see the girl is stop-the-traffic gorgeous with her toned body and strawberry-blonde hair haphazardly held in a messy bun, complete with wind-tousled tendrils framing her delicate features, high cheekbones, and plump, kissable lips. Not even a reformatted C: drive wiped clean could erase her memory, I'm pretty sure of that.

With nothing else to do, I continue to watch her—and tell myself that it's not at all creepy.

The dragonfly takes off seconds or minutes later, I can't tell anymore, and she sits on her heels, her eyes tracking its flight. I'm almost sorry the previous show's over. Almost. But not quite.

Mesmerized, I watch a dreamy look etching on her face as, lo and behold, the bug comes back to her, hovering by her side and landing once more in her cupped hands. Up until she extends willowy fingers, blowing it a sweet kiss...

An image comes to me. That intriguing girl is blowing me a kiss in the exact same way. The dreamlike feel tightens my guts, my befuddled mind screaming in the background that it's not wishful thinking. And more than that, it's true.

A frisson runs up my spine, jolting me. Energy courses through my veins and electrifies my nerve endings. In the pit of my heart, a dull glow fires up, whispering into the deepest recesses of my soul that this girl is meant to be mine. That I'm meant to be hers.

Man, what is that shit?

Is this weird sense of déjà vu what Liam and Zac talked about experiencing upon meeting Éolie and Magali? Could it be my turn to fall in love at first sight?

As insane as it sounds, I can't stop the stupid smile stealing across my face.

A tremor spreads beneath my skin. My breath catches in my throat, my pulse picking up at the possibility that it could be, and all the *what if's* it brings to mind... Nothing else computes for the next little while, my CPU stuck in overdrive.

"Are we destined for each other?" I can't help but ask under my breath, infected by that thought gone viral, curse it all.

I stare at her ethereal beauty for a beat longer.

No, can't be, man. My brows pinch together. *Look at her, she's so far out of your league it's not even funny.* I slump in my chair, my head falling back over my shoulders.

Get over yourself.

What was it Zac said on the night he met Magali at the ski resort? Nothing. He said nothing, man, just flipped his gourd. No shit. *Love at first sight?* I inwardly scoff. Thanks to them now I'm expecting it to happen to me as well, I suppose. This is only me envying both Liam's and Zac's brand of happiness and getting all worked up over nothing, here. Must be.

I straighten from my slouch, eyes narrowing on two twenty-something guys walking the path along the grass below me. They both notice the girl at the same time and stop short at the sight of her. Not that I blame them. Still. An unexplainable jealousy courses through me.

One of the blokes calls out to her, his flirty come-on floating up to me. Tall, square-jawed, sporting all the chiseled features of gym-droids, I'm fairly certain I know how this is going to end.

My hands grip the edge of the small table, white-knuckled, and I make a concerted effort not to jog down the stairs and lay claim.

Whoa, what's with that?

"Need a refill?" the well-timed barista offers, interrupting me mid-divagations and I decline, mumbling to his retreating back, "What I need is a reboot."

When he's gone, I look back down to the grass.

My stomach drops to my shoes as the taller of the two dudes calls out to her, insisting when she doesn't react. "Hey, *chérie*, you from around here? We could use a tour guide!"

Bloody hell.

"I just bet you do," I say, pushing away from my table before I can stop myself, a weird protective instinct surging forth. She doesn't say a word to them, but it's too late. I'm already on my feet. Listening in as they switch to butchered French, my breathing grows erratic and I ball my hands into fists at my side.

But no matter what they say, she doesn't pay them any attention. None whatsoever.

Somehow, it makes me breathe easier and my fists unclench.

She stays oblivious to her immediate surroundings, her forehead wrinkling in concentration as she leans forward, solely focused on something in the grass before her. I watch as she picks it up carefully with her index finger. Some type of fat bug she gives free reign to run from one hand to the other, her movements slow and graceful.

Oh, the irony.

I plop my ass back down, one hell of a raging boner now tenting my shorts.

"Watch out!" The shout, yelled by a cyclist racing by on the gravel track used by pedestrians and cyclists alike, startles the two guys into stepping aside. The girl doesn't even look up and the biker swooshes by, his bright-orange performance shirt fast disappearing down the lane.

The two dudes exchange a look and a dismissive shrug, rating her as a lost cause, no doubt. I'm not sure how to feel about this. On one hand, it makes me happy, strangely, or not strangely enough. On the other hand, well. . .if those two didn't make the cut—judging by her total disinterest as they walk by her with one last look behind—it dashes any hopes I may have entertained, despite myself, of catching her attention.

Reality check, man. Not happening. Short, geeky types like you and runway models like her do not mix, I remind myself sternly. Different species. They speak trendy; I speak computer.

So, even if she gave me the time of day, then what? I'm not anti-social exactly, just not user-friendly.

I sigh and resume my one-sided binary convo with Lucie, something solid and familiar, refusing to dwell any longer on the tantalizing girl down below.

After ten minutes of staring at lines of code and expecting them to mean something, I flip Lucie's lid closed, annoyed that I've ruined my concentration. "What the fuck is wrong with me?" I grouse.

Out of nowhere, a dragonfly lands on my laptop. I swear its bulbous eyes give me the once-over as though taking my measure, translucent wings flapping on a slow beat, before it takes off in a sweeping arc. I wonder if it's the same one my girl cupped in her hands earlier, then snort at my flight of fancy. *My* girl, now?

I stare down at my cup. A dark-brown stain on the bottom, dry-baked from the sun, is all that's left of my coffee. With no other choice left, I guzzle down my glass of water, untouched until now, and refill it twice. Theo would be so proud. He thinks there's something in the drinking water up here that makes us sit up and take notice.

Unable to help myself, I check the linear park down below for a sight of her. A part of me, albeit small, wishes I won't find what my eyes are searching for so that I can chalk the whole thing up on too much caffeine and not enough sleep.

I swallow hard.

She's still there, and I still get the impression I know her from somewhere, no hallucination. I narrow my eyes, torn between letting go and never letting go.

A slight frown mars her delicate features as she thumbs a quick text on an outdated flip phone, the likes of which I haven't seen in at least a decade or so, before shoving it back into a front pocket. For a moment, she looks so young and vulnerable that my heart pings out of my chest, wanting nothing more than to keep her safe by my side.

She blows out a long breath as though shoring up her courage before putting in earbuds. She stands up, brushing the back of her dress as she makes her way toward the path, but she hesitates. She cranes her neck, one hand shielding her eyes from the sun. Using the same relentless focus she gave the bugs earlier, she searches the path long and hard, right, then left, letting a group of four cyclists go by, then another two. She lets one more fly by, before she squares her shoulders and walks down the path, keeping to the very edge.

She's getting away, man. I sigh. Guess letting go won.

For now. The two words, unbidden, whisper through my mind and I ruthlessly stomp on the fire they ignite in my soul.

As she disappears from sight, the wind flirting with her butter-yellow sundress, her shapely figure imprints on my brain, and other parts of me.

I shift in my bistro chair, groaning.

Great.

Just great.

Now I'll fantasize, mooning over some unattainable girl I'll probably never see again. But on that last thought, my chest compresses in a painful vise, an unfamiliar weight pressing down on my breastbone.

And won't Zac have a field day with this one? Yeah, and I'll never hear the end of it. Payback's a bitch, he'll point out, full of it, and I won't even have a good come back for this one. Last winter, I did rib him mercilessly over Magali...

Boy, if I knew then what I know now.

Awesome.

Looks like I've been bitten by the love bug and it's gone viral, same as Zac and Liam before him. But unlike them, I've got zero moves to put on that girl.

None.

Access denied.

No source code.

And for once, I don't know what the fuck to do with this virus.

Three

AURÈLE

I sigh happily. *I made it!*

I feel giddy and a little awed at myself upon sighting Val-David's old train station crossing the village center, today's destination I set out for. The one-hour walk from my newly rented lake cottage may look like nothing, but to me, it opens up the world. One in which I'm proclaiming my independence. No small feat.

I plop down on the grassy area bordering the groomed cycling and walking path, smoothing down my light cotton sundress over my knees as I take in my surroundings.

A few tourists take pictures, others read the colorful art exhibit and concert notices on the public bulletin boards cleverly scattered throughout this part of the park. I'd like to take a look too, but I'll wait my turn. Hoofing it down here is one thing. Rubbing elbows with people casually interacting with one another as a natural way of life and taking it for granted—like I used to when I was an unblemished, perfect little girl according to my father—is something else altogether. They understand each other. I no longer do.

One challenge at a time, Aurèle.

Drawing my knees to my chest, I wrap my arms tightly around my legs. I rest my chin atop them, looking down, before brushing my hand over the blades of grass in a gentle back-and-forth motion. No surprise. Not a sound. All is quiet around me. *But then, when isn't it for me, now?* I inwardly sigh.

It's unseasonably hot for the last week of August and the midmorning sun darts its rays over my bended head, dotting my skin with a fine sheen of perspiration. It makes me glad I had the foresight to pack a few summer clothes in my getaway suitcase.

I fiddle with the tip of my red Vichy canvas shoes. *My getaway...* Was it just last week? Seems like a lifetime ago.

Maybe it was.

I close my eyes and take a deep breath, sighing. I must admit, I enjoy this newfound freedom and the accompanying lightweight feel buoying my chest.

A soft breeze ruffles my untidy hair and I retie it in a top knot, the warm air rippling over my skin cools the back of my neck some. I promised myself I'd stay put for one hour before trekking back, but if I don't find a bit of shade, sunscreen or not, my pale complexion will burn to a crisp.

A dragonfly hovers by me, following my every move as I retreat underneath the canopy of one of the maple trees. We sidestep each other in a strange little dance before it lands less than a foot away from me.

I sprawl on my stomach, cupping the winged creature delicately in my hands. Surprisingly, it lets me.

I grin.

The object of so much legend and lore, surely, it's a sign. *"Libellule,"* I whisper the French name for it, remembering its musicality. "You are by far the most beautiful sight I've seen today," I mouth, staring at its iridescent hues, from the brightest turquoise to the deepest blue. Never mind that I'm surrounded by the majestic beauty of these lush green hills and panoramic vistas I remember from my youth.

"But you know I'm not really talking about your elegance and grace, right?" I pursue my muted conversation, and the spherical midnight-blue eyes of this gorgeous *libellule* stare back at me.

In that moment, I swear it sees me beyond what's on the surface. Not as damaged goods, something my father and Laurent, his designated son-in-law and successor, were prone to remind me over and over again, but as me.

Just me.

And Laurent be damned, I will find *me* now that my father's gone if it's the last thing I do. And my chances are better here, I remind myself, far away from the mansion in Westmount, now up for sale along with everything I've ever known, on my own for the first time.

"Easier said than done, I know, finding the real *me* now that I'm rid of them both," I silently confide to my dragonfly. "But you know what? Relocating here in Val-David is the first step in the right direction."

I feel it.

I watch, entranced by the power and poise behind its slow wing beat, and wish I could capture the moment in picture. Maybe I'll take up photography.

I continue with my silent conversation, the graceful insect seemingly catching on. "You know that in almost every part of the world you're considered to be an agent of change and self-realization. Don't you?"

For an answer, the dragonfly hovers over my hands for an instant, then, quick as lightning, flies straight up, zipping backward and on either side of me.

I smile up to it as it stays nearby, flying every which way, almost as if showing off.

I straighten from my stomach sprawl on the grass and sit on my heels.

"Is this what I'll find here, self-realization? Is that what you're telling me?" I inwardly muse.

To my delight, the dragonfly lands back in my hands the space of an instant, bobbing its torso. The tail end of its body curves upwards like an exclamation mark punctuating the end of its resounding, *Oui!*

I unfurl my fingers, palms wide open to the world, blowing it a gentle kiss goodbye.

"I'll take it," I murmur to myself, my gaze tracking its flight. "Starting now."

I watch it disappear from my sight, and sigh up to the sky. *Those are brave words with not much substance to back them up yet, Aurèle.* I lower my eyes, starkly reminded that I'm unused to being so out in the open, vulnerable. "Starting now," I repeat under my breath. *You made it here, and that's progress.* I refuse to go back to the shell of a life planned for me, my only escape found in the extensive collection of books our personal library held, thanks to my mother.

Stay out of sight, my father would sneer if I ventured downstairs while he was in residence. "No need to flaunt in everyone's face that you're now irreversibly damaged and of no real use," he liked to point out. Meaning, you should have had the good taste to die from the illness like your mother did instead, not linger on with a permanent brain lesion to boot like a blemish on my perfect escutcheon.

I shiver as a familiar ribbon of ice mushrooms in my veins, pumping frozen bleakness straight to my heart, isolation almost choking me in that moment.

Focusing on the play of sunlight dappling the blades of grass in front of me, I take a few deep breaths, willing the unwelcomed sensation of frost to melt away.

Brushing my fingers over the warm sod, I inhale a lungful of the earthy smell of freshly mowed grass baking in the sun. The sunny aroma, as comforting as a warm cup of cocoa on a winter day, thaws the ice-cold vise squeezing my chest, speaking of lazy summer days happily reading in the backyard.

A scurrying beetle catches my attention as it forges its way ahead, undeterred by obstacles more than twice its height. Reflecting on it, I pick it up on my index finger. His black shell and long antennas appear shot with streaks of midnight blue under the harsh light of the darting sun.

The fat June bug runs up my arm, tickling my skin. I bring it back down on my finger over and again, admiring its determination. Energized by it, I let go of the scarab watching it clear pebbles, scurrying from one blade of grass to the other, determined to climb and conquer any obstacles put in my way just as well.

With that in mind, I glance over my shoulder up to the nearest café's wraparound balcony some twenty feet away and some eight steps above me.

Fitting.

I feel like everyone is eight steps ahead of me. Or more accurately that I'm eight years behind.

My gaze skims over the few scattered patrons of C'est la Vie, wondering if I can blend in somehow. But the more I look, the less inclined I am to brave the coffee-drinking crowd today, even as thin as it is.

I'll stick out like a sore thumb without a good book to hide behind.

I sigh, resigned.

My earlier and uncharacteristic show of pluck fizzles out.

I don't belong.

Not today.

Everyone sits back, features relaxed into laid-back grins, easy conversations flowing among them while they sip cups of brewed happiness, enjoying one another and the late morning sun.

No. Not everyone.

A lone guy catches my attention.

I straighten my shoulders back and tilt my head to the side for a better look.

He's about my age I'd say, so early to mid-twenties. But with his scruffy jaw locked tight, his stern features and hooded eyes solely focused on his laptop screen, he wears a certain air of aloofness as though wisened beyond his years. If I go by his detached expression, he appears to be as alone as I am, isolated in a bubble of his own making.

A small smile curls at the corner of my mouth. I can so relate.

Maybe it's the reason why I notice how handsome he is in a cute boyish way with his rumpled T-shirt and his shaggy mane of golden-brown hair the gentle breeze ruffles and messes with, even though I have no business noticing it.

My pocket vibrates, distracting me away from my quiet perusal.

I whip out my phone before I can stop myself, the acrid taste of aversion on my tongue following close behind.

I blame years of conditioning turning me into this well-bred automaton for even reading Laurent's text.

L: Are you done rebelling yet? It's been five days. You need me. Just admit it.

I frown in disbelief then roll my eyes. His gall is on par with his overblown ego. So why am I surprised?

Pulse beating in my throat, my thumbs fly out, texting a reply:

Contrary to what you think, I'm deaf. Not dumb.

But I feel stupid for having believed him to be different when all along I was just a price he had to pay to fulfill his unending thirst for money and power. He had a good teacher. He is nothing more, nothing less, than my father's creature, and I, on the other hand, am no longer.

Or getting there, anyway...

I exhale on a long breath, knowing the notarized renunciation I signed yesterday is about to set me free for good and make my father roll in his grave.

Maybe.

Probably.

I almost grin.

A brand-new sense of accomplishment settles over me as I send my very last message to Laurent. Ever.

> Me: Expect the executor to transfer all the shares into your name. I do not want anything to do with you or the company. Have a nice life! Over and out.

I don't wait for a reply, blocking his name, shutting down my phone. Something I never thought of but should have done a long time ago. Stupid me, indeed.

I shove my summon-the-dumb-and-deaf-girl phone back into my dress pocket, vowing to switch it for a laptop to widen my horizons.

Feeling better already for having made the decision, I put my earbuds on.

I hide behind the visual prop, but it helps me feel somewhat normal, just like everyone else. One of the many things I took for granted before and something I now crave despite being locked into my quilted silence. So much the better if it gives me back a small degree of self-confidence, I argue with myself, feeling a bit foolish nonetheless.

But then again, I've had enough pitying looks or scoffing and scathing sneers from my late father's household staff in the last eight years to last me three lifetimes.

Looking right and left, I square my shoulders and start the long trek back to the lake cottage, walking as close to the edge of the path as I can, half afraid I'll be mowed over by a speeding cyclist I won't see. . .or *hear*.

Four

P.O.

arking by the woodshed, I swing Lucie's backpack over my shoulder, juggling my six cups to go, thankful Éolie's nursing the twins and not drinking any. Seven would be just over my legal limit as Theo would undoubtedly joke.

"Well, well. The prodigal son has returned," Leo states upon spotting me rounding the corner of the house.

"And bearing gifts," Zac says as I step onto the front porch where everyone's gathered over lunch, or what's left of it.

"Beware of geeks bearing GIFs," Yann quotes another one of my shirts, and everyone snickers.

"Would be wise on any other day, but it's real coffee for now, believe it or not." I slide the wobbling cardboard tray onto the rustic kitchen table they brought out. "A much-needed reminder, living here, of what it's supposed to taste like," I add with just a side order of sarcasm percolating like a rich blend of coffee lacing through my tone of voice.

"True dat," Yann agrees, picking one up.

"Are you disparaging my house?" Leo arches a telling brow.

I snort. "Absolutely."

His fixer-upper is holding up with duct tape and a prayer with no faith left in the antediluvian plumbing and electrical wiring. Rustic charm doesn't even begin to describe Leo's decrepit place. So no one dares disrupt the fragile equilibrium we reached between supply and demand by adding small kitchen appliances to the load.

"O ye, of little faith." Leo takes the lid off a cup and breathes in the dark brew's heady aroma, aaahing on a long exhale of contentment. "You're forgiven."

"You're welcome," I say drily.

"Here," I say to Liam, holding out my hands for Nicolas cuddled up on his lap—a white-yellow-and-blue-striped onesie identifying him at a glance. Sébastien wears solid colors. Minus the cherubic cuteness all their own, the dark-haired identical twins are Liam's spitting image but for their unusual light-turquoise eyes, the exact same shade of sea-green as Éolie's, and like hers, always observing, missing nothing. "Give over my twin fix and have a coffee; it's on the house."

Liam scowls instead of diving for a coffee cup, like I expected. "No way, man. This one's clean. Shower first. You stink almost as bad as Sébastien five minutes ago." He moves Nicolas away from me, his arms shielding him protectively.

I take a sniff of eau de armpits. My eyes water. He may have a point.

A quiet smile playing on her lips, one of Éolie's hands rubs Sébastien's tiny back in soothing circles, holding him in the crook of her neck. "Don't listen to him," she croons softly in his ear before kissing his soft-as-a-rose-petal baby cheek. "You don't stink, ever. Even when you do," she reassures Sébastien while a few chuckled "beg to differ" comments fuse all around.

It's now a well-known fact among us. Nothing quite compares to an overflowing, squishy, and smelly diaper. They should come with a warning: **Hazardous Waste. Open at your own risk**.

I lean over Yann to filch a few chips. "Man, go reek elsewhere," he says, jerking back on a scowl. "Preferably upwind." He waves me off.

I scoop a corn chip an inch high with guacamole. "Wasn't my turn so I haven't showered yet," I state the evidence, leaning my back on one of the porch pillars, crunching on my loot. With only one bathroom still in working condition, and I use the term loosely, we're on a rotating schedule tacked to the door. Our Swiss precision displayed at its finest. Man, single beds, one bathroom, I shake my head. Does it ever bring back Berlinger International

Academy's memories, big time?

"Now that you mention it, isn't that yesterday's shirt?" Éolie quirks a brow in question, shaking her head at me. "That won't do." Her eyes twinkle, belying her stern tone. Or what passes for one. My lips curl in a small grin and I shake my head at her in turn. That girl is too sweet for words, she just can't pull off authoritarian. Then again, after Herr Vorberger, our former dorm supervisor, the bar is set pretty high.

She shrugs one shoulder with an answering grin before replying, "I'm cheated out of my computer nerd quote du jour, just saying."

Éolie's highly entertained by my tees, all sporting one-line computer nerd humor. Reminds her of her formal wedding day when we all wore one-liner shirts. Liam's idea in order to keep it light and informal just for her, and it worked. Her nerves no longer got the better of her as she glided down the austere courtroom of Le Palais de Justice de Sainte-Agathe-des-Monts last winter. I have tons of those. Guess laundry is not really high on my list of priorities at MIT. Or anywhere else for that matter.

I chuckle, wiping off my salty, grease-stained fingers on my wrinkled shirt for good measure. Might as well dirty it some more and make it really worth my while doing a wash.

"Blame them." I jerk my thumb toward Zac and Magali sitting side by side on the baluster.

"Us?" Magali's eyes pop wide, hands coming over her chest in an overdramatic gesture. "What have we done?"

"The usual. Making out like a couple of Bonobo monkeys let loose in the wilds after a year in captivity," Yann says drily. "Spent in separate cages."

"I couldn't shower. Couldn't get to the coffee. It was a miserable wake-up, and coming from me, that's saying something."

"Oops." Magali claps a hand over her mouth and her cheeks redden.

Leo swallows a laugh along with the last dregs of coffee from his cup. "Man, that's good coffee. You should go at it in front of the stove more often for all our sakes."

"That could be arranged." Zac laughs as Magali backhands him on the arm.

"Sorry we ran you down to the village in such dire straits, but truly, I didn't hear you," Magali says somewhat sheepishly.

"Means I'm doing it right." Zac angles a brow, his flirtatious tone altogether too smug, giving her the once-over.

"Oh, definitely," Magali assures, and he hugs her to him, nuzzling her neck. "Do it some more."

"We'll all pretend we didn't hear that," Yann coughs out.

"Whoa there, Math Man. Count us out of that one." Liam drops a kiss on Éolie's temple before murmuring in her ear something that makes her honeyed complexion turn scarlet, signaling a code red alert. Nap time. Typical. "And on that note..." Liam pushes away from the table, bringing Éolie and Sébastien up with him, Nicolas secured in the crook of his arm. "We're getting a room."

Éolie's flushed expression blooms a deeper shade of crimson. "Liam!"

"What? They nap, we nap." Dark-blue eyes aglow, he points his chin towards Zac. "Doctor's orders, remember?" One of his brows arching, he tips his head to the side, inviting her to follow him. Not that he leaves her the choice really with his hand tugging on hers, towing her along.

Zac stifles a laugh at Liam's mention, the suggestive tone behind it unmistakable. "You're welcome," he says to him. "Just don't overdo it."

"Is there such a thing?" Magali deadpans.

Zac cocks his head at her, the slow grin spreading on his lips more than telling. "Daring me?" he asks, and I swear the heated look they exchange hikes up the temperature on the porch by a scorching ten degrees. Which is saying a lot.

I tug at my shirt collar, looking away, not as unaffected as I'd like to be. A persistent image of my palms curving on the alluring girl's shapely backside showcased in cute boy short underwear edged with white cotton lace sticks out in my mind, making me itch to claim her. All of her. Sending jolts of electricity across my skin.

Éolie settles closer to Liam's side as they amble round the table, eyes twinkling. "We'll practice *sleeping* then, until we get it right and don't overdo it."

"One, sleep's overrated," Liam replies without missing a beat, strutting over to the front door. "And two, we need to practice some more for the boys' siblings; we're a bit behind schedule." And Éolie melts on his side.

Looking down, I wonder what this kind of intimacy feels like? I try to ignore the stab of sheer envy that lances through my heart.

"Get out of here!" Leo throws a bunched up napkin at them, which lands harmlessly on the edge of the table.

Magali waves playfully at their retreating back. "So long. Have fun, you four," she says, having picked up Zac's typical rejoinder to a code red as her own, adding, "Practice makes perfect. Get to it."

"Count on it," Liam says over his shoulder.

"TMI, man," Yann playfully groans the warning.

"Oh, Math Man, if only these walls could talk..." Liam shuts the door behind him.

What would they say about me? A vision of the girl's silky hair spread on my pillow like poured honey shot with cinnamon comes to mind. I would pull her across me. "Nap time. Come here you," I would say, my lips brushing the shell of her ear. She would dip her head into my neck, whispering over my ear, "I'm not ready to go to sleep yet."

I rub a hand down my face.

Bloody everlasting hell.

It's like I'm obsessing, here. And the worse of it all is that I'll probably never see her ever again.

Did I just groan loud enough to wake the dead?

The guys shoot me looks.

Guess I did.

Awesome.

It does not lessen the uncontrollable effect of her.

Jesus, man. Get a grip.

"There, there. Don't despair on us." Magali pats my arm consolingly, misinterpreting the reason behind my heartfelt groan. "Maybe next time we're blocking your access to coffee, you can just shove us aside and go for the kill," she says.

I perk up, only too happy to deflect everyone away from my useless musings. Myself included. And hell, who am I really to tell her she got that wrong, right?

Zac gives me a look over her head, mouthing one of our old gaming calls to arms, "Try it, and prepare to die."

I arch a brow, challenging him right back, suddenly amused. "Will do," I answer her, looking him in the eye.

He grunts.

I smirk, gloating.

I cross my arms over my chest, watching his reaction with something akin to relish.

Or is it envy?

He takes making out with Magali every chance he gets so seriously that his legendary laid-back persona is now officially listed as missing in action. Something unheard of in all of our twenty-odd years of shared history.

Not that I blame him. Last winter on our ski vacation, after a stormy encounter with Magali at Mont Saint-Sauveur that left him reeling and decidedly off-kilter, our footloose Zac surprised us all by moving into the old farmstead. Admittedly to look after Éolie and the twins as their personal in-house obstetrician, but really, to look for *her*. Thing is, Zee Man for the Impossible didn't even have to go looking, our old BIA days' nicknames proving accurate once more.

Only Zac, I inwardly shake my head, swallowing down a laugh.

Magali landed him on his ass when she walked in as his midwife intern a few weeks back. And just in case he didn't get the memo, she also happens to be the daughter of our closest neighbors and good friends a few kilometers down the road, Vie and Grégoire, he learned last month on the day the twins were born. And ever since they hit it off, he can't get enough of her. Like he can't believe his luck.

Definitely envy.

Yann snorts, mumbling back to me, "Good luck with that, Byte Man."

"He'll need it," Zac avows, a sharp brow lifted in warning.

Yeah, probably, who's saying I'll ever see her again?

No longer so amused, now I'm wishing for luck too, but not in the way they meant.

Not one bit.

I'm so screwed.

Magali's glance, inquisitive as ever, bounces between us all, effectively bringing me out of my messed up thoughts. One of her eyebrows rises in question. "How so?"

In so many ways it's not even funny, I almost laugh out loud.

"It's your boyfriend's not-so-subtle way to warn me not to mess with your kissing under any circumstances, ever."

"Damn straight, I am. You've lost all sense of self-preservation if you think you can get away with it."

"Are you daring me?"

"No. Are you?" Zac smirks.

"Oh, man. Now, you've done it." I waggle my brows at Magali. "The stories we could tell."

"Oh?" Magali's face brightens as she hops down from her seat on the balustrade, all ears. "Ditch the dirt."

"Please, don't ask." Zac smothers a groan, knowing a gang up on him is coming.

Leo, Yann, and I share a too-good-to-pass-let's-get-him look and I've never been more grateful for a distraction.

Zac's not too keen on her becoming cognizant of all the wild, asinine dares he agreed to in our teenaged years, his rap sheet a mile long. Again, can't fault him there. Last winter, Magali, then a ski patroller, wasn't too keen herself on the stunt he pulled on her that got him blacklisted for all eternity at Mont Saint-Sauveur faster than a melting snow cone in Hell. Really went downhill for him indeed and it was a mild one, compared.

The corners of my eyes crinkle with suppressed mirth and I shake my head.

Yanking Zac's chain is too easy nowadays but, hey, it keeps him on his toes. He never knows what little gem we'll drop on Magali. Or not.

We recount the time he gave Frau Engelmeyer a stroke as he streaked in the buff past her hors d'oeuvres through a crowd of prospective students visiting on parents' week, Herr Vonberger, our dorm supervisor, hot on his heels.

"I was nine, I didn't want to shower, get over it."

"Don't mind Zac; he's not fully house-trained." Yann leans back in his chair, crossing his feet at the ankle.

Laughter rips from her.

"It's part of his wild charm and how he got his impossible nickname." I can't help but grin evilly at Zac, high-fiving Yann. Better a gang up on him than me.

Leo rubs his chin as though contemplating the notion. "Remind me again, what was it that clinched the deal? The bungee jump or—"

"You're dead."

Leo leans over the table and picks up Liam's cup, left untouched, ignoring Zac's empty threat.

"What bungee jump?"

"So many jumps so little time," Yann snickers.

"Depends." Leo takes a sip, pondering the matter. "Are we talking about the ones before or after the stupendous bare-ass one, because I can't recall any after—"

"No way!" Magali exclaims.

"And you wondered why I wanted you to myself these past few weeks?" Zac grunts.

"Is that what it's called, now?" Leo smirks into his cup, knowing full well Zac purposely kept Magali away using sex as an excuse. Zac stayed pretty much at her place for the past few weeks, effectively distracting his favorite midwife intern away from meeting us before the twins were born, unwilling to risk exposing Éolie's preternatural abilities, like self-healing at warp speed, until she's ready to share on her own, if ever. Not that going on a sex binge as a distraction was such a hardship on him.

Zac shoots daggers my way over Magali's head as though it's all on me.

"Hey, Leo brought it up. Look elsewhere, man." I tell him, hard pressed not to laugh. "I'm not touching this one."

"Why?" Magali pouts, crossing her arms.

Zac leans his face close to her ear, eyeing me balefully over her shoulder. "He knows I know where he sleeps."

"And?" Magali's glance darts between us, probably questioning our sanity by now.

"*And* a word to the wise is enough," Zac says drily, using Leo's predilection for proverbs and corny sayings against us. "Remember payback's a bitch, boys, and it will come back to bite you in the arse."

"*And* we used to think he was so laid-back." I tsk, fighting to keep it straight-faced.

"By all means. . .bring it on," Leo snickers, saluting Magali with his cup. He leans in closer to me and adds, "He's toast."

"Done for." I clap him on the back.

"Game over." Yann and I bump fists.

"No better way to go, boys," Zac replies, totally unfazed by our ribbing. He nudges Magali's back flush to his front, enfolding her in his arms, his overlapping hands coming to rest over her abdomen. It's unbelievable, really. We thought he would be the very last one of us to settle down. If ever.

Magali shakes her head at us. "You guys are weird sometimes but strangely enough, I mean it as a compliment."

"I'll take it." Zac drops a kiss on her temple, his lips lingering there. "And you."

Swaying in his arms from side to side, she hums contentedly. Her head drops on his chest, her fingers brushing over his interlocked hands in a gentle back-and-forth gesture.

I almost smirk.

Almost.

Instead, another shit ton of yearning hits me in the chest, knocking me sideways.

I stuff my hands in my pockets, fighting the urge to rub at the unfamiliar tightness now constricting my ribs in pulsating waves to the point of pain.

What in the bloody everlasting hell is this shit?

"You never witnessed P.O. going viral before his first shot of caffeine in the morning, I gather?" Leo says on a laugh to Magali in answer to something I missed. "His rabid dog syndrome is worse than Theo's on a good day."

"He's got a point," I say, picking up the thread. Maybe I should just drop by the café for real coffee first thing in the morning and bypass the usual early kissing fest in the kitchen altogether? *Yeah, man, keep telling yourself it's for the sake of good coffee and not to go looking for her.*

I inwardly snort. Like I need convincing.

"Not pretty," Yann concurs.

"Entertaining, though." Zac smirks.

Leo nods. "But definitely not pretty."

"Oh, well, in that case," Magali says impishly. "No more kissing downstairs should cover it," she vows to us. "See, simple." She shrugs one shoulder.

"Ha!" Yann rolls his eyes to the ceiling. "Probabilities of that happening are nil—"

Yeah, that pretty much sums up the probabilities of that girl and I happening. So, why does the concept of never seeing her again scares the unholy fuck out of me exactly?

"No way!" Zac and Leo exclaim over each other and above Yann.

"Just not in the kitchen, then?" she asks, pretending to muse it over.

I plaster a smirk on my face before they notice just how rattled I am.

"Hey, no can do." Leo salutes them with his disposable cup, pointing the obvious. "As you were. You made P.O. hunt down a better fix. I'm all for that."

A better fix? Man, if you only knew how down for that I am.

Magali chuckles airily.

Zac murmurs something in her ear and she turns in his arms. Balancing on his shoulders, she stretches on the tip of her toes, dropping a tender kiss at the corner of his mouth. Zac's arms lock her into place.

Holding her firm to his chest, his hands splay on the small of her back. "I'm addicted to you too," she says softly, her index finger tracing down his jaw. "There's no better fix; best high ever."

Yann face palms. "Guys, you're over your quota of mush for the day, just so you know."

"Speak for yourself, Math Man." Leo stretches out his legs, crossing his hands behind his head. "I'm taking notes."

"What for? It's like watching a video clip on a loop, man," Yann grumbles good-naturedly and the two lovebirds laugh it off, quips flying high and low for the next little while.

The usual.

Zoning out for a few, my dream addled mind conjures up images of the girl looking at me with love and wonder brightening up her features like Magali looks at Zac more often than not. Like now.

I feel the tip of my ears burn as I picture the girl once more, just as she was. An exquisite sight, sprawled on her stomach, her bent legs crossed at the ankles, rocking in a gentle sway as she conversed with the dragonfly cupped in her hands—wishing it could be me she talked to, nose to nose, instead.

"No sweat. I'll make all the coffee runs in the mornings," I volunteer out of the blue, out of sync with the ongoing convo, sounding like an over eager Boy Scout interested in earning a merit badge. Even to my ears.

Great.

My shoulder propped against the post, hands in my pockets, I cross my ankles in a bid for nonchalance.

"Sweet," Leo says. "He fell for it, hook, line, and sinker."

"Nice. Wait. Are his ears turning red?" Yann asks.

Another flush of heat spreads like wildfire in my veins, and I bolt. "And on that note," I say, taking a leaf out of Liam's book. "I'm off to shower."

I rush inside, suddenly thankful for the only option here.

Cold-as-fuck showers.

Five

P.O.

It's my fourth morning spent at C'est la Vie Café, same time, no sighting. And to top it off, I can't concentrate for shit so, for once in my life, Lucie's just a prop ranking lower than the cups to go I'll collect when I leave. They, at least, serve a dual purpose. I've gotten zero work done since the day I saw her here.

Clément, the barista, chuckles under his breath, shaking his head as he hands over my cup of espresso over the counter. "Nice shirt!" he shouts over the music.

Looking down at my red tee, I smooth the inscription over my chest, reading today's selection I didn't even check before donning. **My attitude isn't bad, it's in beta.**

And I'm left wondering if it will need a tweak or two for me to get the guys off the scent or get the girl out of my system, whichever comes first.

"Yeah, for a random pick this morning, this one's a winner," I say deprecatingly, handing him some change while Aznavour belts the song *For Me, Formidable* in my ears, the chorus about unrequited love decidedly apropos.

"Ah. Girl problems," Clément states like evidence. An overly loud one, in more ways than one.

Man, he'll probably be deaf by the time he hits his thirties exposed to that level of decibels on a daily basis, even if just for the short weeks *la belle saison* lasts over here.

"Something like that," I reply instead. *Yeah, enough to cloud my head and stir up my heart.* "But nothing a few shots of espresso won't cure." I give him a tight nod on my way out to the terrace, effectively closing a subject I'm not ready to discuss with anyone yet, least of all the barista.

What's to discuss about a mirage, anyway?

But as I step outside, anticipation hardens every inch of my body, nonetheless. That emotion zings through the air like bolts of lightning, my heart thundering in my chest. And the hope I know I should discourage reignites.

No two ways about it. She's infected my brain. Gone viral. And here I am, berating myself for being so foolish. "And just where's a foolproof firewall when you need one?" I mutter, yet again, the irony certainly not lost on me.

My cup clicks against the saucer as I saunter over to my favorite table, the shady one overlooking the park. My black engineer boots thud on the freshly stained boards and a few small birds picking at crumbs scatter in my wake into the nearby apple trees. The seasonal temperatures are back to normal so it's nicely cool now, the furled umbrellas letting the few patrons dispersed on the other side of the deck lap up the midmorning sun.

Perfect.

Means I won't have to devise any bloody excuse to walk over to the railing at regular intervals and check on the park below, my view unobstructed.

I plop my ass down and boot up Lucie, determined to get some shit done today.

Twenty minutes later, I stare at my blinking cursor on a blank screen.

Did I just delete twelve bloody fucking lines of code over an associative array not meant to be trashed?

Slouching back in my chair, I pinch the bridge of my nose, exasperated with myself. Cursing underneath my breath, I squint at the blinding sunrays darting through the dense foliage of the wild apple trees. I blow a breath through my cheeks, running a hand through my hair. This shit is going nowhere fast, and I wonder if I should take it as sign.

I straighten in my chair, ready to call it quits for today, and probably the whole thing just as well, when a dragonfly zips by my table, a second one following in hot pursuit. The two dance in the sky, frolicking for a brief moment in front of me, before disappearing beyond the tree line.

I hardly dare breathe.

No way, man. I shake my head, snorting at my flight of fancy. *Don't go reading into it.*

Fuck me, but on the thought, an involuntary shiver ripples down my spine, lodging deep in my gut.

I glance to the right.

Unsteady and irregular, my heart hammers.

The girl I can't shake out of my thoughts is sitting cross-legged underneath the same maple tree down below—seemingly out of nowhere, like an apparition my delusional brain came up with.

The air leaving my lungs hitches while giving her the once-over.

No way.

Bundled up in an Irish cable-knit sweater dress hitting her mid-thigh, dove gray leggings, and flat-heeled ankle boots showcasing toned legs I remember a tad too well and wouldn't mind wrapped around my waist, *sexy as all hell* is the first thing that comes to mind.

A given.

The girl is effortlessly gorgeous.

But this is not what has me staring at her profile, transfixed.

No.

Hunched over a laptop, her forehead puckers in concentration while her pointer fingers hesitantly peck their way, her intent gaze searching the keyboard. By the time she squints back up at her screen, her face scrunches up in bafflement before her shoulders slump in defeat. She thumps the back of her head on the tree trunk, eyes turned skyward. I get the impression she's one second away from launching the computer as far as she can throw it.

I couldn't ask for a better intro now, could I?

"Cue me in," I say, pumped by what I see.

I take a deep breath, adjusting the cuffs of my long-sleeved tee over my wrists.

Man, if you ever had one, now is the time to channel your inner Zac.

My chair scrapes on the wood plank deck as I shove away from the table. I rub my palms on my jeans a couple of times and square my shoulders, all the while keeping her in my sights.

She blows out a determined breath before returning her undivided attention to whatever she's trying to figure out, hesitant, as though her laptop needs coaxing to do her bidding.

I take the stairs fast and stride quickly across the lawn toward where she sits.

"Computers are not intelligent. They only think they are," I call out gamely from the lane.

I don't want her to feel threatened so I stay at a safe distance a few feet away, facing her from the edge of the groomed lane where it meets the turf.

She doesn't even flinch, either completely zoned into whatever she's working on or. . . purposely ignoring me.

I clear my throat so loudly I end up choking on my saliva, coughing up a lung.

Still no reaction.

Well, unless you count plump lips flat lining as one, and I'd rather not.

If at first you don't succeed, call it version 1.0.

I take a deep breath and go for broke.

I crouch at eye level.

"Computer trouble? I can be of help, there."

She scowls at her screen intently but never makes eye contact, nor does she say anything.

Well, that went well.

I stand up and roll on the balls of my feet, shoving my hands in my pockets. "Try me?"

I inwardly cringe.

Try me? Real suave, man. There goes my inner Zac.

Heat creeps up the back of my neck, shooting up to the roots of my hair.

Bloody hell.

Now I'm channeling Yann of all people, blushing quicker than a thirteen-year-old faced with his first crush.

Great.

Just great.

"By try me, I mean, I'm good at debugging computers, not, you know..." I rub the back of my neck.

"Christ," I mumble under my breath. Guess I should have worn my shirt that reads: **ASCII stupid question, get a stupid ANCI.** At the very least, we could have had a good laugh at my expense out of it.

But no, she stays irritatingly composed, eyes on her screen.

"Right, so... I'll be up there. At the café."

I tug at my collar, letting the nip in the air cool me some, wondering if I can blame it on sunburn if I'm caught sporting a face probably the ruby color of a good Merlot by now, matching my shirt.

But she doesn't even look up, lowered eyes staying stubbornly glued to her keyboard.

Oookay.

Well, so much for that.

Disappointment slams me like a punch to the gut. I blow out a regretful sigh and rough a hand over the top of my head, trudging my way back up to the café.

I turn to look at her flawless features over my shoulder one last time before plopping my sorry ass back down on my chair. Down on the grass below me, she continues to struggle with her laptop.

Confusion pinches up her face just before her eyes grow wide and she starts pressing down on the escape key repeatedly like the safe landing of the Mars probe depends on it.

No shit. Whether she wants to or not, she needs my help.

Fuck it all. I'm coming in.

I grab Lucie and start typing.

Six

AURÈLE

*W*hat *happened to instruction manuals?*

None came with the laptop I ordered online, and I've since discovered that it's pretty much useless on its own without an internet connection, which the small lake cottage doesn't have.

Yet another thing to deal with, I inwardly groan, unsure if I can meet all the new challenges of living on my own that are piling on.

But for now, I take advantage once more of the café's wireless signal spilling over to where I sit underneath my favorite maple tree, and click on the help button.

I'm giving up on figuring out by myself how to configure the thousand or so Google preferences and whatnots the computer keeps on requiring. Maybe I'm not meant to have access to technology after all. Maybe it'll be more peaceful this way.

I thump my head against the tree's smooth trunk as another video tutorial appears on my screen. Another one I can't make heads or tails of. What happened to *written* instructions?

I sigh heavily up to the sky.

Closed-captioning services are complicated to set up, cumbersome, the translations not all that smooth—besides, it's not a viable option anyway without a regular connection. I can't follow on the instructor's lips with the rapid-fire instructions delivered as she speaks in English, the tutorial only translated in French not made in French. I'm fluent in English but not in lip reading in English. Moot point anyway, as even if I could follow the fast-paced talking, the camera zooms in on her face only once in a while, never mind when her commentaries run over a snapshot menu I've no idea how to reach. Do I really need a Gmail account to get started? I have no one to correspond with! The only living person who wants to speak to me is now blocked—for good reason.

Unnerved, I resist the urge to shove my brand-new laptop aside, or throw it as far as I can.

My shoulders sag in defeat. I haven't been near a computer for nearly a decade and nothing is the same. What possessed me to get one now?

I stare up at the canopy of emerald-green leaves fluttering in the breeze and can almost hear them rustling in the wind in a soft, swishy symphony rising from the past. The soundtrack of life I took for granted and never paid much attention to up until it was no longer there.

For the space of an instant, I close my eyes and will the caress of the wind on my face to sing to me and push aside this unrelenting silence.

A faint echo answers back, fleeting, evanescent, until only quiet remains.

Will I lose those remembered sounds too, over time?

I pop my eyes open before I get any more maudlin.

Your five minutes of self-pity are over, I remind myself caustically. You don't have time for this.

I blow out a determined breath.

Surely I can get up to speed, even as fast-paced as everything seems to be nowadays, *non?* Like I told Laurent, I'm deaf. Not dumb. Keeping that in mind, I peck my way through yet a few more awkward tries but it yields no results. I stare at my keyboard and stifle a sigh. Clearly, I have no idea what I'm doing but I forge ahead, absently pressing down on the upper F keys, one after the other. Something is bound to happen.

The back of my neck prickles suddenly, sending goosebumps racing down my arms. My fingers halt mid-motion. I stifle a shiver as I feel someone's intent gaze slicing through me.

I chance a quick peek underneath my lashes, all the while praying I'm wrong. The last thing I want is to catch someone's attention, and so far so good; by keeping my head down, I stayed invisible. I'd like to keep it that way.

My breath lodges in my throat.

The cute guy I took a brief notice of the other day is stopped dead in his tracks a few feet away from me by the graveled pathway, staring hard.

A confident expression spreads all over his handsome face as I catch a few words on his lips. Is that. . .a *try me* he just said?

Lovely.

My stomach bottoms out.

I know what he's seeing. It's what they all see. A perfect outer shell. Right before my disability no one sees past once it's put out there, hits them. And for once, I'm enjoying a reprieve, feeling almost normal again, and my fledging self-confidence is not ready yet to be poked or messed with.

With unseeing eyes, I stare down at my fingers, which lay twisting nervously over my keyboard.

He's still there.

I feel it.

And I thought him shy, aloof, introverted, a kindred spirit of a sort.

Aggrieved, I feel a twinge of disappointment I can't even begin to explain. Freed from my father and Laurent, I'm here on a self-discovery journey, not to be burned anew by someone else's expectations. Most of which I wouldn't want to meet anyway, let alone achieve. Even if I wanted to, I couldn't. Not anymore.

Please go away, there's nothing to see in shallow beauty only skin deep, I'd like to say, but I haven't spoken out loud for the past eight years. I'm likely to croak unintelligibly.

My stomach knots.

Please don't stare.

Please don't stare.

Please don't stare.

Finally, after no less than infinity times ten, I see his jeans-clad legs skirt by me from the corner of my eye. He's leaving.

I release my pent-up breath and, by doing so, inadvertently swipe my fingers over the silky smooth surface of the central mouse pad, a sidebar menu sliding out to the right of my screen as a result.

My brows dipping, my fingertip retakes possession of the mouse pointer, or so I think. This mouse is possessed, and it's not by me.

I don't know what I do exactly as I wrestle with option menus appearing in rapid succession just by hovering over them. I click in a bid to get rid of them, but instead it grants permission—without my permission—to download an obscene amount of Windows updates.

How did that happen? And critical updates, really? So soon?

I'm left staring stupidly at an indicator showing a steady zero percent progress and a dire warning not to shut down my computer while in progress. Understatement of the year. Progress, what progress?!

Downloading now. Please wait. Time remaining eight hours forty-seven minutes.

I shake my head in disbelief, staring at the remaining hours. It's the only change occurring on my screen every second or so, going up, going down, while the rest of my computer stubbornly sticks at the zero percent progress mark.

When the hours hit a new high of thirteen, an annoyed buzz swarms inside my body. I know I only get a flickering two bars of signal sitting this far out from the café, but this is ridiculous.

I press the escape key over and again, growing frantic when nothing aborts.

This computer has gone rogue on me.

Now what? Camp outside the café all night?

Just then, my screen blacks out and lights up again on a bright-blue backdrop. Long lines of indecipherable codes scroll down for what seems like a millennium, give or take a few seconds, as I sit immobile, staring wide-eyed, wondering if the thing is getting ready to implode on me.

I'm pondering if it would be wiser to snap it shut and never ever go near it again when a pop-up appears, stating: **As a computer, I find your faith in technology amusing.**

I blink.

A surprised peal of laughter escapes me. I slap my hand over my mouth. When was the last time I laughed out loud? I don't even know how it sounds, but right now, I don't care.

Meanwhile, what looks like a private chat window opens on the bottom left corner of my screen, identified as coming from MIT Computer Science and Artificial Intelligence Lab. MIT as in the world-renowned Massachusetts Institute of Technology? I scrunch up my nose in confusion. What on earth...?

Mesmerized, I watch a row of five little dots prance in a wave before a text message appears.

Are you aware your laptop lacks in the most basic security protocol leaving it wide open to cyber-attacks?

My cursor blinks, and so do I. I hesitantly type a reply, because right now...

Is this a joke?

Not even close. Took me less than three minutes to target you and take over.

I'm either chatting live with an aggressive market research company, an innovative infomercial, or a computer lunatic. Not sure which.

And you're telling me (your target) this...?

Seriously?

I'll go with lunatic, but I kind of like his or her repartees, piquing my curiosity. And since I can't remember the last time I had this much fun, I go with the flow. Besides, whoever it is has effectively put a stop to the absurd amount of critical downloads my computer was trying to swallow, earning points with me already. The timer has frozen. I take that as a good sign.

Asked by the pirate upon hacking my laptop! Seriously.

Hey, I resent that. a) Not all hackers are pirates. b) Coming in was too easy to call it hacking per se. c) All the above.

I laugh softly, loving this quirky, anonymous exchange. It's freeing, being able to talk to someone who doesn't feel put out with my limitations.

> Which bears the question. What are you doing in my laptop?

Securing it! Any more questions?

I roll my eyes and shake my head as I type: **That would be a yes.**

Shoot.

> Are you really from MIT?

Yes. Really.

We're chatting in French, which would be awesome if it wasn't so bizarre coming from someone supposedly stateside.

> How did you know I am French speaking?

Your location.

My head jerks back in surprise.

> What...?

You're presently connected through C'est la Vie Café in Val-David, Québec. A Canadian province where 96.4% of the population either speaks or understands French. I took an educated guess.

He knows where I am. That's probably just this side of creepy, but for some unfathomable reason it doesn't freak me out. *Au contraire.* I'm even more curious now. Go figure. Still.

How...?

How do I know the stats or how do I know where you're at?

Both... Should I worry?

Nah. Your laptop is equipped with a GPS tracking device. Cool app. Want me to sync it with your phone?

What for?

I hate the thing and unless I need to send an SOS to 911, I won't be using it any time soon.

So it will ping back to you a location message if you ever lose it or, you know, if someone is trying to hack into it. ▢

Like now?

I can't help but tease, enjoying myself immensely.

Please. I didn't even have to break any laws in order to get in. What do you have to say to that?

That will teach me to leave my 'Windows' wide open!

(Hacking up a laugh.) No worries, I'm closing them now.

Why are you doing this?

I'm a nice guy?

Sure you are. Try again. What's the deal?

Truly. No big deal. Our computer lab servers systematically scan network servers across the web to find new types of vulnerabilities so that we can develop better firewalls. (See? Nice guy.)

Impressive. So, it means I'm helping all of mankind by using a café's WiFi connection?

More like MIT grad students wrapping up their thesis. We would love to change the world but they won't give us the source code.

a.)You're welcome? b.) Wonder why they won't give it to you (insert light sarcasm).

a.)Don't mention it. b.) I wonder the same (insert clueless shrug).

No surprise. Computer Science: solving today's problems tomorrow.

Hey, I can live with that.

I'm sure you can! So, Nice Guy (jury is still out; you could be a seventy-two-year-old sex offender luring me in). Student or professor or... Which one are you?

Which one do you want me to be?

Is that a trick question? Or are you trying to be creepy now?

Are you always answering critical updates with a question?

Virtually?

For real?

Yes. So?

So. Let's say my answer is grad student...

For real?

For real. Aren't you glad you asked me (out)?

Out of what? My laptop? :D

Harsh. Did you hear that sound? Me. Crashing and burning.

I swallow hard. The reality check crashes upon me, burning down my throat.

No... I didn't hear anything.

Seven

P.O.

urèle. Aurèle de Grandpré is her name... Well, according to her laptop online sales receipt.

Storm the ice princess's tower, fix whatever, then get the hell out is no longer an option.

Program not responding.

I'm in deep shit.

I laugh out loud as I read her cute commentary about computer science finding solutions for today's problems, tomorrow.

She's funny. And friendly.

Where's the insusceptible girl who couldn't be bothered to look my way or answer me back just a little while ago? She's taking me by storm with her witty comebacks, blowing out of the water all of my good intentions to leave her the fuck alone once I'm done fixing up her upgrades and settings.

Guess she's lucky her computer's practically a blank slate because right now I don't think I would be able to resist delving into it. And delving deeper and deeper still until I uncover all of her secrets.

I bounce my knee as I type a reply asking her if she can hear the sound of me, crashing and burning, and the funny thing is I'm only half-jesting. When I'm done typing, I look over to catch the expression as she reads my comment.

Fuck me. She reads it and her smile withers and dies like a twinkling star swallowed up by a black hole. It ushers in a cold that pumps directly through my veins and settles in my gut. Whatever she's thinking, it can't be good.

My heart sinks like a rock at the bottom of a pond because I can only imagine how badly she'll shut me down and I'm not ready to let whatever this is between us go. Not twice in one day.

I wait as she stares at her screen, unmoving.

And wait.

And wait.

My heart thudding in my throat, I start typing. **Never met anyone like you. Don't cut me off. I got caught in the moment**... Only to delete the corny lines one after the other.

I rub a palm down my face. *What have you done to me?*

Thirty seconds of waiting for a game over message on my screen feels like thirty minutes, and I'm about ready to come out of my skin when a line appears.

No... I didn't hear anything.

A giddy sense of relief dances in my chest as I read her reply, and it takes everything in me not to jump out of my seat and shout a few choice yeses, fist pumping over my head.

But instead, I keep my head in the game and my brain cells firing up, no caffeine required by some unforeseen miracle I'll eternally be grateful to.

Game on.

(A)bort, (R)etry, (P)retend this never happened... What crash and burn?

I look down, watching and waiting. I don't have long to wait. A gorgeous smile blooms on her face as she reads then starts typing.

Is this how you wipe out "memories"?

My lips quirk up.

She's enchanting, hooking me in, altering my operating system by the same token. I'd be lying by pretending I don't love her impertinent, cheeky, irreverent little commentaries.

> **Sad to say, there's nada to wipe here. Your laptop is about to expire from sheer boredom with nothing to crunch on. Who. Does. That?!!**

> I haven't been near a computer in the last eight years... Figuring everything out is giving me a rash!

Whoa. Eight years? *Why did she shut me down earlier when I offered to help her when, obviously, she needs some?*

Nope. Not going there, man, I silently berate myself. Not when this new channel of communication opened up for me unexpectedly.

Geek, zero. Computer, one.

Let's leave it at that.

"For now," I mumble under my breath while my fingers fly over the keyboard.

Even from up here, I can see her animated features as she waits on my reply, her eyes glued to her screen, her face glowing with anticipation.

Holy freaking hell. Witnessing it is giving *me* a rash, but one of pleasure as a shot of pure joy shoots up my spine.

> **Wait up. You haven't been near a computer for the last. . . (sorry, hacking up a lung choking and yes, before you ask, bad pun fully accounted for)... *eight* years? Impressive. I'd be dead by now from withdrawal symptoms alone. How'd you manage that?**

> I pressed escape! That's the key. ;)

I bark out a laugh, shaking my head. Fuck me if that girl isn't pulling me under that much more.

What are you, a unicorn or some other mythical creature? Who can resist computers? They have a cache full of cookies!

Move over dark side?

Exactly. A girl after my own heart. Where have you been all my life?

Sleepwalking through mine, and who says I'm a girl? I could be a three-hundred-pound hockey player or a ninety-something badass little old lady.

Don't shatter the last of my illusions. Please say it ain't so.

Why? Afraid to chat with a ninety-five-year-old lady?

Nope. That'd be cool. It's the whole jock thing that doesn't do it for me. You're too witty; it does not compute.

Are you profiling?

Yes, one too many shoves received, I suppose. My glance sweeps down over her lithe form under the tree, huddled over her laptop. She's so lovely with her face all lit up.

Absolutely. Take an IT geek for example. We're easy to identify as an extension of our computers, welded to them. Can't miss us. Well, you could. We're easy to like...

True enough (so it seems) =). Speaking of... Will you help me get up to speed? It doesn't have to be right now if you don't have time.

Get her up to speed? Man, there's nothing I'd like more, envisioning her huddling close to me as I show her all she needs to know over the next week or, better yet, the next forever. And isn't that the beauty of technology, always something new to show and tell?

Now, if I could just lead her to where I sit up here so that she can ask me in person, none the wiser.

It so happens I have loads of free time this week. BUT. . .I think it would be much easier if you get someone to sit beside you and talk you through it, show and tell style. Take a look around the café you're at. Chances are you'll find a computer nerd in there. We are notorious for hanging out in those. We live on coffee.

BUT... (Are you crazy?) I would NEVER do that, not in a million years. The last thing I need is to ask a random stranger at the café to help me with this!

She would never? The last thing she needs?

Bloody hell. Tell me how you feel already... But then again, I don't think I can take her rejection twice in one day, either. So, I hedge my bets.

Fair enough. But, uh... tell me. Curious, here. What am I but, you know, someone random and (crazy) strange on top of it? (Head scratching.)

You're a different sort of crazy, strange, and random. One that's easier to deal with knowing you're far from here in Boston. Besides, you're already in my computer and weird as it seems, I trust you (don't ask me why).

I trust you. . .to be in Boston. I rub a palm down my jaw a couple of times, resisting the urge to face-plant on the table.

How am I supposed to get her to come up here and ask me now? Without scaring the crap out of her with the truth that is.

Now what? Shut her down? Or worse yet, have another go at getting shut down. This time, permanently.

My lips press together in a slight grimace. I just can't do it. Too late. I want in. More than before, which is saying a lot.

Who am I to argue? Let me configure your microphone for an audio chat and we're good to go.

I type in, praying she won't walk into the café while I do, or I'll be screwed tighter than a laptop hard drive caddy.

I swallow down the kernel of unease at the deception I'm about to continue.

I'll be in Boston in less than eight days from now... It's not a complete lie, I reason with myself. I still have two semesters to complete over at MIT.

Meanwhile, I can't risk video chats. Not while hiding in plain sight at the café—which is also the only goddamn way I get to see her, *see her*, for now, come to think of it. Fuck me sideways. With no way to add video chats for the next week without risking giving away the gig too soon, Boston suddenly feels like infinity and beyond before it's behind me and I can come back, come clean, and meet in person. Well, meet again, I should say, and hope for the best.

The realization hits me hard in the chest.

> NO! no, no. No need to. Talking is overrated. Besides, I do MUCH better with written prompts. I have a photographic memory. You just have to show me on the screen slowly, and I'll catch on. Seriously. NO talking.

No talking, either? Christ above. I didn't think this through. Get in. Get out. Simple, right? Or so I thought not even forty minutes ago. But no, I just had to hack my way into her laptop and engage, didn't I? Then she replied, charming the holy hell out of me. And now that I've had a taste, it's no longer as simple.

My gaze arrows on her focused face as she attentively waits for my reply, her teeth gnashing at her plush bottom lip. What I'd give to soothe that little hurt away with a kiss? At this point, probably my left nut, which is not reassuring in the least.

Keep with the program here, man, and build on it. You're not ready to let her go. Not by a long shot. Play by her rules and take what you can get for now even if it's only texting once in a while.

"I want so much more, Aurèle de GrandPré," I confess ruefully, staring down at her.

So be it.

Game on. But this time, I'm playing for keeps.

NO talking? C://DOS RUN. RUN/DOS/RUN. (Hands up in surrender.) You ready for me to start your conversion?

Yes, thank you! :D You're nuts by the way.

In a nutshell. Yes.

Certifiably nuts about you.

You're in good company, then. My laptop turned nuts on me just before you came in.

Don't anthropomorphize computers—they hate that.

Then I'll be calling my laptop Harry from now on just to get even! I'm close to hating the perverse thing right back, just so you know.

Tsk. Tsk. Now who's being perverse? Repeat after me. Computers are (lovable) biddable creatures.

(*gasp*) Since when? Have you seen the insane amount of upgrades Harry wants to download on his own? He's out of control.

Not anymore. Lucie (who loves me to bits and follows my

every command) took over control of Harry, remember?

Lucie, huh? I see great potential here for the remake of an old classic. When Harry met Lucie!! But, really? (Insert eye roll.) Obeys your every command? Maybe Lucie's faking it? :D

I burst out laughing. That girl is too adorable for words. And it's not like I don't get the reference she alludes to. What guy hasn't seen the scene where the entire diner is listening in on Meg Ryan having a superb, albeit fake, orgasm in the movie *When Harry Met Sally* on YouTube at least once? If only to note the signs to be looking for... The character, Sally, is so good at driving her orgasmic point across that the scene ends with the lady sitting next to her asking the waiter to bring her whatever she's having.

Byte your tongue. Faking it (insert eye roll of my own)? Lucie, obey? More like follow attentively all of my instructions. Maybe *you* should have what she's having?

Her tinkling laugh rings out in the quiet buzz of the midmorning, and I upload the airy sound deep into my memory cache, transferring it on my soul.

All right. You got me. I'll have what she's having. ;) Ask Lucie to ask Harry why he needs to upgrade. He's brand new.

I got you? Not even close. But I'll get her if it's the last thing I do, I vow here and now, delighted to no end by this little chat we're having.

Your laptop is an end of the line model and it came with an older version of Windows. Lesson One. The definition of an upgrade: take old bugs out, put new ones in. Keeps us IT geeks on our toes, or in business, depending who you ask.

My heart goes in overdrive upon hearing her laughter drifting up to me once again. *Jesus, that mellifluous sound...* And knowing I'm the one responsible for it gets me high as a kite.

No shit. I'd like nothing better than to walk up to her, introduce myself, and come clean, but I can't risk my only link to her at this point. Not before I'm embedded so deep under her skin, her heart, her soul, she won't know where I start and where she ends.

Maybe then, she'll forgive me for the small deceit it started with... One can only hope. I chastise myself for acting so impulsively, but I can't shake her out of my thoughts. It's as if she permanently lodged herself inside my brain.

Shoving all misgivings aside, I push out a strained breath from my lungs, wondering again what the hell I got myself into, half afraid it will come back to bite me in the arse.

> Why does Windows require me to fill out all this personal info?

All the better to eat you with, I'm tempted to reply, feeling like a big bad wolf all of a sudden but type instead: **Many applications require personal information in order to function optimally and/or operate adequately**.

And it's not only Windows... So do I, Aurèle. So do I. Who are you?

No turning back.

Please don't let me fuck this up.

Eight

AURÈLE

Sipping the last of my hot cocoa, I stand on the rickety wooden dock watching the early morning tendrils of mist like ghostly fingers rising from the lake.

It's eerily beautiful.

A breeze ripples across, disrupting the dark blue surface of the still water. As it blows by me, the branches of the nearby trees sway back-and-forth as though waving hello. All around, the forest is dotted with new spots of red and gold leaves turning color overnight.

I breathe in the earthy aromas of decaying ferns that abound throughout the underbrush surrounding the chalet, mixed in with the vibrant fragrance of the evergreens.

When I was a little girl, we used to ski at Mont-Tremblant, enjoying the perks of an extended ski season—starting early in October and ending late in May. I had all but forgotten that the seasons in between the long winter months in Les Hautes-Laurentides are earlier, quicker, and sharper than in Montréal, and gone in the blink of an eye.

It's only the second day of September, marking the end of my second week away from Montréal, but it might as well be two light years away. Montréal feels like a lifetime ago. More like a place I visited once upon a time, leaving in its wake the blur of a memory frayed around the edges, and not somewhere I lived for most of my life. Which is more than likely true. Can existing be called living?

I curl my numbing fingers more tightly on the cobalt-blue earthenware mug in search of heat. Its tepid warmth seeping through my palms, I welcome the contrasting sensation, finding the nip in the air invigorating.

I've never felt more aware of each moment lived than here in this place.

Lifting my face to the sky, I watch the last play of rosy light from the rising sun painting the wispy clouds in spectacular pink and mauve hues until its darting rays dip the trees with golden highlights.

It is peaceful here with just nature and my thoughts to keep me company.

Not for the first time, I wish I could capture in pictures these moments of overwhelming beauty and gratefulness.

"And what's stopping me?" I ask in a circle with arms wide open, my eyes brimming with excitement.

And I decide here and there to do something about it. Now. Today.

I turn my wrist to check the time on my old-fashioned hand winding watch—a delicate pink-gold Tisserot with intricate pearl and diamond insets my mom gave me on the last birthday we shared. It belonged to my great-grandmother, passed down one generation to the next. It's the only thing of that other life I brought with me.

I shake myself out of the memory. Move on, Aurèle. A new life awaits you out there. Go. Get. It.

If I leave for the village in the next five minutes, I'll have just enough time for a quick online research on cameras before my fifth catchup session takes place with my favorite computer nerd, P.O.

Galvanized, I turn on my heels and walk up the stone path, watching the plumes of white smoke billowing out of the chimney. "I. Have. Fire," I whisper proudly, eyeing the neat wood pile I spent all afternoon yesterday stacking under the roofed portion of the back porch.

I refrain from thumping my chest but mentally pat myself on the back. I saw the lettered truck parked by Le P'tit Train du Nord Linear Park the other day and approached the driver to order a few cords of firewood. I can get the gist of simple conversations by reading lips and body language, but speaking out loud after staying mute for so many years? That's another challenge altogether, one that's on its way to be conquered on my to-do list.

I may have had to sit on the front porch for a couple of hours, waiting on the delivery, but when I declined politely the old-timer's offer to help me stack the firewood, he didn't flinch or look at me oddly, like I yelled or something. I still can't gauge my inflection accurately nor my pitch, but talking to myself out loud, practicing control of my voice for the past week or so, seems to be paying off.

"On to the village," I say, rinsing my cup and wiping my hands dry with the tea towel. Twirling on my toes all the way to the living room, I accidentally knock over the pile of books sitting by the coffee table, my current reading selection toppling over. "Oops, sorry," I apologize to the books as I gather them back, the unique smell of old paper and ink wafting up my nostrils. I inhale the distinctive fragrance, lovingly trailing my fingertips over their spines. So many books in here, so little time. I can't help but smile. "I'll be back soon and we'll spend the rest of the day together. How's that?" I playfully ask them. "A cup of tea and a good book." No two ways about it, they're my idea of a hot date. I sigh happily, stacking the dozen or so classics one on top of the other, old friends like *Jane Eyre* and new ones like *The Catcher in the Rye*.

Then I unplug my laptop left charging all night, and on a whim roll up the cord and stash it in my backpack. Who's to say I won't brave the café and conquer ordering out loud something else besides firewood today?

I set out at a brisk pace with a new spring in my step, energized by the prospect of widening my horizons even if only from behind a cup of coffee or the lens of a camera.

There's a definite shift in the air, and I breathe the moment in, committing it to deeper memory.

The lake cottage sits at the end of a private lane more than half a kilometer away from the main road, le Chemin de la Rivière, which intersects the linear park. I love the tranquility this place exudes, nestled deep into the forest. Here, I don't feel as acutely the relentless silence cocooning me from the outside, within. Not in the oppressive way I felt while in Montréal, leaving me dependent on others. Losing one of my main sensory perceptions used to leave my nerves in a constant state of high alertness, keeping me off-balance, and it's nice to be able to relax my guard from time to time, and go with the flow, carefree.

However, being so far out in the woods is also the reason why the local cable company is unable to supply my rented cottage with high-speed internet. Not unless the owners are ready to foot the bill for the heavy infrastructure required to bring cable up. And the signal for a satellite dish is close to nil at best, according to them, because of the small lake surrounded from all sides by woodsy mountains and granite cliffs.

I don't really mind, but I can't say the same for P.O. That guy almost had a stroke upon learning from the tech guy online that there was no internet connection to be had where I lived.

P.O.... Now there's an enigma.

I'll miss him once I'm all caught up, I'm sure. Strange as it seems, it's as though I've known him all my life and I've come to enjoy our daily online chats. Not that I've ever known a total geek before, but I kind of like his quirkiness and sharp wit. With no expectations whatsoever, this anonymity lying between us lets me be *me* and it makes me feel whole again. And that's addictive. Even his grumbles are endearing when he complains about yet again having to cut short one of our sessions as they can only last until all of Harry's battery power depletes and he shuts down.

Harry is high maintenance and power hungry, I wrote to P.O. during our last session, following the first time it happened less than an hour into it, shrugging it off as, **a male thing come to think of it.**

Unimpressive, was his reply.

> You almost earned a no comment from the peanut gallery with that one. Almost. But not quite. At the most, you get a free pass (just this once, mind you) for your *'male thing'* comment, but that's all. Let's not confuse high maintenance with high tech here, a marvel of computer engineering! Furthermore, may I point out that poor Harry is the antithesis of power hungry? Give him a break. He burns off energy trying to keep up with your demands while you leave him unplugged and unstable.

Ha! Good one. My demands? More like your (32 bits) bus loads of commands. C:\\ how well I learned? Aren't you proud?!

No comment from the peanut gallery. Well, other than this. FATAL SYSTEM ERROR: Press F13 to continue... Did I create a monster??!!

A cookie one I hope?

I did create a monster! (Awesome.)

I grin, remembering P.O. volunteering right after to pay for the cost of cable installation up at the cottage. I wouldn't mind paying for it, either, if only to thank my kindly landlords for renting me this slice of paradise. But the owners, a couple of university professors away on a sabbatical in Europe for a year, use it as a retreat from the hustle and bustle of modern life. No TV. No internet.

Felicity comes in the form of a loft upstairs under the eaves, filled with books and some more books. A secret reading nook only accessible by ladder. I can so relate to that. One of my very own definitions of a personal haven and, quite frankly, one pretty cool taste of Heaven for now. So, I'm not about to interfere with it by leaving a permanent mark behind me. Besides, limited access to WiFi connections down in the village more than does it for me.

Book nerd, one. Computer nerd, zero. Take that, P.O.

I chuckle, wondering if his ears are ringing right now all the way to Boston.

Upon reaching the end of the private lane, I look left, then right, and look again one last time before crossing le Chemin de la Rivière. From there, my hike down Le P'tit Train du Nord Linear Trail all the way to the village takes me a solid hour. I love every minute of it, though, as I don't have to worry about cars running me over if I get distracted by the breathtaking scenery unfolding at every turn. The path follows La Rivière-du-Nord flowing through the valley and it's easy to get lost in contemplation. Something that happens more and more, I can't help but notice.

It's as though I see beauty everywhere now. And maybe there is. And maybe I am.

I usually stop on my way down to sit on the flat boulders lining the river's banks and admire the white water rushing by and the swirls and funnels it creates. "But not today," I murmur, filled with purpose.

Today, I itch to get my hands on a camera and capture these moments instead, for all infinitude. Like these two dragonflies pursuing one another over a patch of wild grass growing by the side of the groomed trail. I see light, angles, transparencies, shapes, frames...

"Do you feel the change in the air?" I ask them while watching their antics. They hover over me for a brief instant. Enchanted, I take it as a good sign.

I could stay and watch for hours, losing myself in the moment, but I let them be. Soon though. I'm on a self-realization mission, I remind myself. And my record breaking fifty-minute walk over to the village reflects it.

From the park, I stare up at C'est la Vie's terrace undecided. Tourists no longer roam the linear trail in droves now that the school year started, and I can see that aside from a few patrons dispersed throughout, the place looks relatively quiet.

But then again when is it not quiet around you? I inwardly scoff. I let the words roll around in my head, shocking me both by the self-deprecating humor behind them and by the absence of an accompanying sting.

I look down, a soft smile playing at the corner of my lips, my chest filling with hope. Maybe, just maybe, a time will come when I won't feel so disconnected and feel like I belong, somehow, somewhere.

My fingers tighten on the straps of Harry's backpack, and I take a deep breath, encouraged. Before I can talk myself out of it, my feet climb the narrow staircase one step after the other, until I'm standing in the café's doorway. Out of the corner of my eye, I spot an empty table discreetly tucked away behind a column and make a note of it.

I draw a blank as a deep rumble vibrates through my torso as I walk into the café and over to the counter at the back, neither looking right nor left. Are those vibrations pulsing in some sort of music? I can't tell anymore. Music has been silent for so long, locked inside of me.

I swallow hard to wet my throat, awareness squeezing all the air around me.

A couple in their thirties wearing high-performance cycling gear stand next in line. While they put in their order, I study the items listed on the blackboard lining the wall behind the counter. So many coffees from all over the world to choose from. How am I to decide on the spot?

When the couple steps aside and it's my turn, I tamp down on my panic coming face-to-face with the dark-haired barista who wears an expectant look.

My lungs trip over my breath. Did he ask me a question while I wasn't looking?

I breathe in, breathe out, calming my racing heart. I give him a tight-lipped smile before taking a chance on saying, *"Un café mocha au chocolat noir, s'il-vous-plaît."*

His angular, clean-shaven face scrunches up indecisive, leaning in. "Huh… the music, sorry. You'll need to speak up, I didn't get that," he seems to be saying, gesturing around at who knows what. I need to concentrate on his mouth more.

"J'aimerais commander un moitié moitié? Chocolat noir?" I ask hesitantly.

I focus on his mouth, waiting for him to acknowledge my request, suddenly insecure.

His lips tighten in a straight line, then part. "Do you mind repeating that… huh…out loud?"

Did I whisper, or worse, mangle the words? I look down. Chills scamper down my spine and I stand frozen on the spot. Maybe practicing by myself wasn't such a good idea. Maybe I'm nowhere near as ready as I thought and that wood delivery guy understanding me was just a fluke.

My eyes glance back up. The barista blinks, staring for a minute past awkward before wiping the corner of his lips, discreetly looking over his fingers.

I stared at his mouth too hard. My chest inflates on a stuttered heave. I take a step back, hunching my shoulders, my arms involuntarily circling my middle.

"Do you want regular coffee or chocolate?" he asks me with just as much discomfort as I am drowning in. I nod, gesturing with my chin toward the coffee maker dribbling the last drops of a full pot into a glass carafe behind him, not trusting myself to speak.

He taps one of his ears then points to mine. My hands come up both sides, touching my earbuds with twitchy fingers, now remembering I have them in, but refusing to take them out.

I sigh a small sigh of consolation. They're my saving grace. I'd rather pass for rude than not all there.

I take a deep breath and this time do my best to add volume to my request. "Oh. *Désolée. J'aimerais—*"

To my consternation, the tall guy jerks his head back, visibly flinching in surprise, one of his hands coming over his chest. *Mon Dieu.* Did I just shout out the words? I slap my hands over my mouth, wincing apologetically.

"It's all or nothing with you." His face dissolves into laugh lines as he shakes his head. "Must be good music you're tuned into if it beats Edith Piaf. What would you like?"

I'm one minute away from running out of here, that's what I'd like. The only thing keeping me rooted there is the fact I want to call this village home for the next year without being pointed at as the village idiot. I wet my throat, by now as dry as a melba toast, trying my voice out again, praying I won't bellow but strike the right inflection. *"J'aimerais un chocolat noir chaud,"* I say, dropping any form of complicated coffee order, sticking with hot cocoa instead.

"Got it," he says with twinkling eyes and my shoulders sag in unabridged relief.

"Pour emporter ou pour—?" I read on his lips before the rest of what he says is lost to me as he bends at the waist to select a block of dark chocolate from one of the containers lining the refrigerated shelves underneath the counter. He drops it in a small pot warming on a stove top at his back.

"Pour ici," I say, guessing he wants to know if it's to go or not, and hope that's the extent of it, my previous relief dying a swift death. With his back to me, there's no way I can follow through any thread of conversation if he wants to strike one. What possessed me to think I could do this with none being the wiser exactly?

Embarrassment has me gnawing at my bottom lip.

I stay quiet, which, let's face it, isn't very hard for me. My newly discovered deprecating side is in splendid form today so it seems. I inwardly roll my eyes at myself, wondering if I can get away with the label taciturn instead of rude.

I watch the barista's quick efficient moves as he whips the melted chocolate square into warm milk, until it dissolves into a thick beverage he then pours in a cute latté ceramic coffee bowl.

He gives me a questioning look over his shoulder I decipher in all probability as the tail end of a *will that be all?* I nod, hoping I'm right, second guessing following close behind.

What if he ran a monologue beforehand and I just now acquiesced to giving him my firstborn? Which, of course, will never happen. Neither the giving, nor the firstborn. I can't let it happen. Not to me. Falling in love in my condition wouldn't be fair to anyone—not now that I'm damaged goods, my father's voice insidiously and persistently sneers in my mind—least of all vulnerable, tiny babies I can't be held responsible for. It would crush what's left of my spirit, and I just can't risk it.

Unbidden, the intense stare of the handsome golden-brown haired guy from last week flits through my mind, making me yearn for something I know I can never have in a way I never did before. Worse yet, now his face superimposes on P.O.'s faceless one.

No. Don't even go there. But of course, now that the seed's been planted, I do anyway. I sigh, rolling my eyes.

Great, now I'll fantasize over P.O. with another guy's face to put on him.

The barista gives me a weird look over the counter. Did I say that out loud? On the possibility, my eyes grow wide as he hands over my hot chocolate latté bowl in a rich garnet color that probably matches my complexion.

"Enjoy."

I look down, my eyes unseeing. A familiar prick of fiery heat stings me to my toes, blushing at the drop of a hat the curse of my strawberry-blonde too pale complexion.

"Merci," is all I can say, by now flustered beyond redemption. I give him a ten with a quick please-keep-the-change look that brooks no argument before hurrying over to the inconspicuous table I spotted earlier.

I drop on the chair, my gaze lowered, my heart hammering in equal parts exhilaration and mortification, holding my prized latté bowl in my hands. I concentrate on the smooth texture of my first sip of liquid decadence in the form of rich, melted dark chocolate, and it calms my galloping heart. I relish the bittersweet, nutty flavors bursting on my tongue. A delicious proof I made it here, in this exact moment, all by myself.

Buoyed by that last thought, I push the ceramic bowl aside and boot up Harry.

It's time for me to focus on attainable things, like finding a good camera, not chimeras. Like, let's say, hearing again, love. . .and a family of my own.

.

Nine

P.O.

I spot her as soon as I walk into C'est la Vie and stop in my tracks.

I have a moment of exhilaration followed by a desire to disappear in a puff of smoke.

Shit, now what?

I shove my beanie farther down on my forehead and look the other way, praying she won't notice me.

Not only is Aurèle earlier than usual, but it's the first time since we started our daily chat sessions four days ago that she's actually at the café, sitting at a table and not underneath her maple tree.

It's much too soon to show my hand, and too late to hightail it out of here as the barista, Clément, hails me from across the empty room. Well, apart from Aurèle, that is.

What in the hell is she doing inside, anyway? Not only is it a gorgeous day out, even if a bit chilly, but the few other patrons are all scattered outside enjoying the warmth of the sun on one's face while we still can. As usual, music blasts my ears to a quasi-uncomfortable level as I make my way over to the counter.

A discreet peek over my shoulder confirms she's totally into Harry right now, unconcerned by her surroundings, meaning me, or the loud music. I wonder how she does it. Well, the latter not the former. She's been very good at ignoring me.

I scratch the back of my neck, pondering her incredible ability to focus. I wouldn't be able to concentrate for shit in here, already sucked into the Jean Ferrat song blowing the speakers. The meaningful lyrics of this one seep into my soul, celebrating the beauty of life and love. *Que c'est beau la vie*, Ferrat's velvety, deep baritone voice sings. And I have to admit that right now, seeing her, it is. Life *is* beautiful. Not as beautiful as it will be once I sit across from her, our fingers entwined, our gaze lost on one another over our cups...

Jesus. My heart stutters and a rush of blood pulses in my ears. I can almost taste that moment in time, and just the concept of it almost brings me to my knees.

I sigh, sounding as forlorn as a lovesick calf, I'm sure, taking another peek at Aurèle over my shoulder. Her eyes—the color of bluebells in the English countryside at spring—stay glued to her screen.

"It will happen," I murmur, feeling equal parts mellowed out and frustrated. I don't know yet how and when, but it will. Failure is not an option.

Clément hands me my regular cup of espresso, leaning over the counter. "Quite stunning, isn't she?"

I put my hands on my hips, giving him a blank look, like I have no idea what in the fuck he's talking about. He motions with his head toward Aurèle like I'm an idiot. I take a deep breath and grind my molars together for a brief moment.

"Can't blame you for looking, but don't go there, man. She's taken."

What the...? My eyes narrow. Does he know if she's married or already has a boyfriend? And what does it say for me exactly that I don't give a shit, either way. She's mine. I feel it to the very marrow of my bones.

"What are you talking about?" My fingers dig into my sides, and I make a concerted effort to ease my white-knuckled grip.

"That." He sends me a knowing look, pointing at the heather-gray shirt my unzipped fleece jacket uncovered. **Don't byte off more than you can view**, it reads. "You can look all you want, but that one will chew you up and spit you out without looking twice. Trust me. She's taken, and it's not by you nor me. That one's been wrapped in a bubble of her own doing for the past hour. Not even an offer of a refill of hot cocoa or Joe Dassin songs could entice her away from her laptop and whatever she's listening to with those earbuds of hers."

"Really?" I perk up, perversely enough. Happy, somehow, she didn't give him the time of day—just like she didn't with me. But then another thought strikes me.

Bloody hell.

She's been here for an hour or so? "Fuck," I groan under my breath. She probably used up most of Harry's autonomy already. And it's not like I have that many sessions left I can get away with. She's all caught up and has been since day three. I kind of had to be creative in letting her believe she's not quite there yet and she still needs me.

"Really." Clément shakes his head like he can't believe it either. And I can't tell if it's him, dark-chocolate cocoa, or Joe Dassin he finds unbelievable anyone can resist, but I'm not about to ask him.

"Got it." I take my cup and scuttle out. For now, I have an in with her and I'm not about to fuck with that. Time to get to work.

Choosing just the right table outside proves to be trickier than I thought. I try a few, feeling like I'm starring in a bad remake of Goldilocks, but uncaring of the weird looks coming my way. At last, finding one that's halfway decent for my stealth operation—the farther away I can possibly get from any of the bay windows overlooking the café's balcony while still keeping her in my sights—I plop my ass down and boot up Lucie.

I make a discreet run through Harry's log history. I know it's an unfair advantage I have on her, but I can't help myself. At least my snooping is something I can own. For how much longer though?

She's been busy all right. I grin, scrolling down. She caught on so well, I feel like a proud father or some shit. No, scratch that, too disturbing. I want so much more from her. I purposely kept our chats computer-related. I want her to be the one to ask for more. More of me. More of anything and everything. Just. . .more.

Well, well, well. Internet browsing? Photography? Cameras? Shopping online? Subscribing to websites right and left? You're giving me (at last) some interesting info (Yes, Virginia,

There Is A Santa Claus...) worth hacking for!!!

I type instead of bemoaning the fact Harry's already down at the forty-two percent mark power wise, abstaining from berating her for it like I'd like to.

> Hi, P.O.! =) A direct reference to Francis Pharcellus? Impressive. Thank you for helping me out. I think I'm all caught up. As you can see, I can now: a.) Browse to my heart's content, b.) Use my newly configured email to receive freely dispensed spam when subscribing right and left, c.) Have no one to correspond with and/or discuss the latest breasts or penis enhancements techniques, and d.) All the above. I'm in business!

Damn. I sigh. Guess she figured out yesterday I've been stretching it thin. I drum my fingers on the table, deciding how to reply so she's stays hooked. Although, the fact she seems happy to chat nonetheless gives me all the encouragement I need for now.

> **I've been known to read a book or three... But blessed is the end-user who expects nothing, for *she* shall not be disappointed. May I remind you that you have the coolest firewall to protect Harry from catching any infectious disease spreading far and wide? Like spam, the cyber scourge of the earth, in case you've forgotten Lesson Two. In which case, I'd be happy to give you a refresher course. Besides, what am I in *your* book? Just some random IP address you're kicking to the curb now that you're all caught up, unworthy of corresponding with (enhancements discussions need not apply)?**

I hit send and glance over at her table. From this angle, I see her whole face brighten with a blinding smile and it sends little spasms of pleasure ricocheting through my gut.

Of course not! Random hacker v. 0.5 upgrading to friend v. 1.0, processing now. Please wait. Side note: I've always wanted a pen pal. So? What name shall I put on the stamped envelopes? P.O., Hacker Extraordinaire?

I shake my head, laughing quietly at her quick comeback, fighting the urge to get up and throw my hands up in victory. I've been upgraded to friend, yes! Progress, at last. But. . .letters? She's got to be kidding me... Not what I have in mind.

Cute.

But true. So? Name?

So she can Google me the hell out now that she knows how? Maybe even add one plus one when she sees pictures of me and the guys skiing at local resorts or all over this village as backdrop? Or all of my other nerdy shortcomings beforehand while at it and form her opinion of me based on what's outside? No way.

I'd tell you but then I'd have to kill you. I'm (almost) afraid to ask (blame it on the stamped envelopes comment): In this digital revolutionary era, what have you been reading these past ten years?

Real books. You should try them.

I do. Regularly. I'm sending you a wafer-thin tablet filled with them.

Digital? The horror! I meant real books printed on paper. Luring me in to the other side?

I consider it my duty as a computer nerd to ease you into

the digital world in all things.

I consider it my duty to acquaint you with the unique charm of ink and paper. Besides, there's a certain *je ne sais quoi* to the feel and smell of an old book. (And for your info, a nerd is a nerd is a nerd)!

Snail mail? Horrified look stamped all over my face. Pentium wise; pen and paper foolish. And for your info, my library of hundreds weighs less than a hundred thirty grams and follows me everywhere. How's yours doing?

Very well, thank you for asking. And with that, you're hereby put on notice. I challenge your nerdity to correspond with mine, using pen and paper. Warning: May lend to a state of nerdvana and become addictive.

Warning: Unholy experiment in progress. May lend to foul language and mood swings. Avoid at all cost.

Duly warned and ready. So, *pen* pal, give over. What's your name and address?

youvegottobejoking@gmail.com

Postal!!!

Agreed!!!

I grin, watching her screen display on mine. She delights me as I follow her configuring, then adding a new Gmail address on her own, in response.

So funny. Not. not.even.alittle@gmail.com

You're out of your bloody mind! Not kidding: not.even. alittle. And don't think I won't be using that address, I will. Just watch me. By the way, look into your contacts. You'll find *my* brand new email address (configured just for you, I might add). Fitting, don't you think?

I'm sure *you* will. Me, not so much. My notebook is open. My pen is waiting.

Christ. She's not even joking. She picked up a hardcover notebook and pen from her backpack.

You do realize that by the time I read one of your outdated parchments, the news it will impart will either be, out of sequence (which for a programmer is a nightmare), or worse...(choking here) obsolete by at least a week or four? Don't you know how old that is in computer years?

And how old does that make you in computer years?

Young enough to know better than to use snail mail and old enough not to go there! So? What about you? How old are you exactly? Ninety-five or ninety-six?

Nice try. Tell me what your initials stand for, and maybe, just maybe, I'll tell you my age. In a letter. Signed, sealed, and delivered via Postes Canada. We'll play twenty questions. =)

Yes! There it is. More. "Thank you, God," I say under my breath, looking up to the sky. Now if I could just convince her to do it via email.

Twenty questions? I'm all for it, but 1988 called, and it wants its pen back!

You must unlearn what you have learned.

You did not just quote Yoda to me. Emails, chats... Where did I fail you in my teachings, my little grasshopper?

(And you're mixing up your movie quotes.)

To err is human (and to blame it on a computer is even more so)! Come on, friends don't let friends play twenty questions via postal letters. Instant gratification rules! Haven't you learned anything these past few days?

I learned tons, actually. Anticipation rules!

My mission statement is to bring you up to speed—as in *data* speed—or have you forgotten (already)?

You do realize I don't drive and winter is coming at the forty-sixth degree latitude north where I'm at, and I might not be able to walk down to the village every day and access WiFi, right?

I straighten in my chair, leaning over my screen, rereading twice. Bloody everlasting hell.

She doesn't drive? Should I worry? *Winter* is coming up here in a couple of weeks at the most, with snow accumulations up to your eyeballs in the blink of an eye. I blow out a breath and lean back in my chair.

Why did she rent a place without internet again? Who the hell does that nowadays? I'll probably go out of my mind with worry and miss her like crazy if I don't hear from her every day.

I thump my forehead on the top of Lucie's lid. Kill me now.

No wonder Liam went bonkers, missing Éolie for all those years, preternatural link or not. If I had some inkling before, now I know. I slump back, shoulders drooping. Because there's not a damn thing I can say or do now.

Snow shoeing and cross country skiing are really popular in your neck of the woods (I may or may not have read somewhere). Try it.

Do or do not, there is no try.

You're killing me, here. Stop bringing Yoda into this chat will you? I'm not finished complaining. You do realize that you could type a draft email for days on end whenever the mood strikes you just as easily?

I glance back to see if I'm any closer at convincing her now. But she just stares at her screen with an unreadable look, no reply coming forth.

A new sort of terror grips me, constricting my chest. What if I'm losing her over my stupid shit? If I divulge my name, I'm sure to give up the gig too soon, the evidence stacked against me. And besides which, if I can't convince her to correspond via email instead of snail mail, I'll die a slow death waiting for her letters. Either way, I'm screwed.

My brows snap together as I hit reply over and again.

Instant (unless it's coffee), is so, so cool...
You still there?
Hello?
I know you're there.
Lucie can see Harry's still connected.
What gives?

She looks up at the ceiling, rolling her eyes.
She. Rolled. Her. Eyes. At me.

(Are you rolling your eyes?)   ← I bet you are, by now.
You are, aren't you? I'm on to you.
Can't ignore me forever.

She crosses her arms, arching a brow at her screen on a *oh, wanna bet* kind of move I've seen Magali use a few times on Zac with an alarming rate of success. Clearly time for me to change tactics.

Out of arguments to plead your case?

Is that a snort?

Come. On. Just hit reply already. It's been over seventy-eight seconds and counting.

She taps the tips of her fingers in a steeple, staring at her screen as though waiting me out, her face giving away nothing. Well, nothing good anyway, and it scares the unholy fuck out of me.

What if she's getting ready to cut me loose?

I bite my lip, knowing I have to do something. Fast.

White flag waving.
We'll do it your way.
We good?

After what feels like eternity, she starts typing, a small smile playing on her lips. Only when I see her response do I release the pent-up breath I've been holding and flop back on my chair.

This is a public service announcement: Instant gratification at all times, all the time, kills anticipation.

She got me good.

What's your name and address again, didn't quite catch it.

All right (hands up in surrender). I can do this. Challenge accepted. I'll email you my postal address (just as soon as I figure it out).

I'll wait for it. And while I wait, I'll start a letter. *'Write'* now.

All right, smartass. You win this round (under protest). But I want you to put it on record that Lucie considers this a downgrade. You can write me at: 91 Sidney Street, Unit 3605, Cambridge, MA 02139. And even though Harry squealed on you and I've got yours, I'll reply via email, thank you very much...

Missing a critical update. Under what name should I send my missives? I have to warn you beforehand that otherwise, you might end up with a Dear Cyber Pirate mention. Or an MIT Genius In The Making. Or a Monsieur X. Or à l'Occupant du 3605. Or worse...

I hesitate.

Her suggestions are cute, and I'd love to just let her run away with them. But I share a flat with Yann, and he'll either open her letters before I do (and I'll have to kill him), or he'll throw them away thinking it is some junk mail (and I'll have to kill him for that too).

I'm walking a very fine line here, between half-truths and lies by omission. Should I keep piling them on though? I don't like it. Not one bit. Then again, I want to know every little detail that makes her, her. The playful banter, the sharing of tidbits, I love it all. But I want more. I want it all. What will happen to this budding friendship of ours if I give her my real name and she digs me out? Will she flush me down the loo before I have a chance to plead my case in the spring when I can return with months of solid friendship under my belt to back me up?

I look her over in the glass reflection, so near and yet so far. My heart clenches with a pang of longing I try to ignore. Maybe I can get away with being totally truthful moving forward, under certain conditions that would ensure that my original deception is strictly contained within a no-need-to-go-there zone until I'm ready to open that particular can of worms in person.

When I look down at my screen, I have two unanswered replies waiting, and I can't help but laugh.

P.O. as in Put Out? Purchase Order? Program Officer? Pacific Ocean? No, I know...Postal Office.

I shake my head, smiling. Oh, man. I'm done for. She's delightful.

No reply? Should I worry you're wanted for cybercrimes? Are you a ninety-six-year-old woman??

Nope, not even close. Been thinking... This no talking rule still applies, or no?

Absolutely! It is the essence of pen paling. Why?

I have a few rules of my own to put out there before I cache in my microchips and get real.

By all means. Let's get real. Bring it on.

So, no talking means no video chats or phone calls. I'm cool with it, but can we add phone texting to emailing? And no Google search. No selfies. No social media. I'd really like for us to know what's on the inside without outside influences for once. You with me?

I bounce my knee, rattling my cup, and quit abruptly as Aurèle's electric-blue eyes meet mine through the space of a nanosecond or an eon, not sure which. Either way, I'm utterly frozen, my breath suspended. For the second Aurèle and I stare at each other, the buzz of voices around me recedes and everyone else in the café disappears, every cell in my body aware of her, and her alone.

She looks away first, back down to her keyboard, and the spell is broken. Still, I watch her, biting on her bottom lip as she types.

My heart hammers hard enough to feel as if it's about to explode. Did I just imagine the glint of surprised recognition in her gaze? Is the gig up? That's a long-ass reply she's typing. I have no idea if it's a good sign, or a bad sign. I wipe my sweaty palms on my jeans as I wait for the damn dots to stop hopping in front of my eyes already. When they do and I see the message that's come through, I'm almost afraid to read.

I blink a few times, making sure I got it right.

> No texting possible for two reasons: a.) No cell signal where I live (I have to walk a kilometer down the lane to get one)— Did I mention no internet, either? ;-) b.) I hate texting.
> Moving on...
> Let me get this straight. No social media stalking or Google delving nor selfies either? Meaning no preconceived notion of one another judging by outside appearances alone? And the launch of a thousand words on paper instead? I'm so IN. Deal! So, pen pal, you have an unfair advantage over me. Get me up to speed. Name?

When I get pass the texting issue, pass her questions that had my stomach just about to drop to the floor, all I can read over and again, is the last part. She's in.

I almost knock over my cup punching the air as I whoop, "Yes," startling into silence the middle-aged couple sitting at the table next to mine, their coffee almost spilling onto the saucers.

I lift my shoulder in a half-shrug, feeling sheepish. "Sorry, just received good news."

"She must have said, yes." They just nod in agreement before resuming their own convo, and I'm not about to ask what gave me away. In fact, I don't even dare look back at Aurèle through the window to see if she's noticed my outburst. Or worse, if it made her suspicious.

Instead, I sit back down. This is it. *Point of no return, man.*

I take a deep breath, then start typing.

Have you considered moving closer to civilization? Something to think on while you're hibernating. To put you

up to speed, my real name is Philippe-Olivier Tisserot. And before you ask, forget about calling me anything resembling Philippe; a name I share with my two brothers, Philippe, the elder, and Jean-Philippe, the middle one. I know, I know, original much? But hey, such is life. So, everyone calls me P.O. (I may have grown tired of being called Olive by default in my anglophile world).

Olivier fast became Olive for short when all the other boys at BIA started shooting up to the ceiling, growing faster than weeds on crack. Short, being the operative word in my case. I finally caught up though barely.

I'll take your suggestion under consideration when my current lease is up in a year or so ☺. I like the name Olivier, just saying. Wait. Get out. Philippe Tisserot, like the famed Swiss watches? Es-tu Suisse?

A year or so... Damn. This is going to be one long-ass winter without even texting and with only the occasional email or letter. I almost shudder on that last one. I'm not ready to give in on that one. She can write me letters; I'll reply through emails, thank you very much. But as I read the rest, a flush of heat spreads in my veins, raising goosebumps on my arms, my toes curling in my black engineer boots.

She likes my name.

It's ridiculous, really, but I can't help the pleasure I get from that.

My gut tightens upon imagining her whispering *Olivier* in my ear with just the right French accent, her voice sultry and languorous. Or better yet, screaming it as she comes apart in my arms. *Olivier* is a name no one ever uses in my world. But one I wouldn't mind at all hearing from her kissable lips.

I shift in my seat, my dick now as solid as a steel pipe filled with poured cement. Get your mind out of the gutter, man, and keep with the program here. Sporting an unshakable boner from Hell, leaving you with a bad case of blue balls and no brain cells left to work with, is not on today's agenda. Check back again in a few months.

Yeah, like that's helping my case.

I'll concede to your liking the name. *You* **can call me Olivier, all rights reserved. And yes, Tisserot just like the watches, which makes for another yes. One hundred percent Swiss-made but bred English at an all-boys international boarding school on the outskirts of Sion near the Italian border.**

Forgotten there by my two elder brothers. Both having more than three decades on me, and a guardianship they didn't know what the fuck to do with at the time, busy with families of their own. Can't really blame them though. I'm the oddball in a family legacy going all the way back to 1770. A legacy I have zero interest in perpetuating. Reason enough to love my brothers from a distance—and my thirty-something nephews. Some families do better with thousands of miles between them.

> *Merci,* Olivier, I will. =) So ... *that's* where your excellent French comes from? I did wonder. Did you attend Berlinger? I did a year and a half at Meier in Montreux at the start of my *secondaire!* And I received a vintage pink-gold Philippe-Tisserot on my thirteenth birthday! Small world. =D

I arch a brow, tilting my head up to look at her. What are the odds? Meier is the all-girls equivalent of Berlinger. And she owns an original Tisserot on top of it.

Small world indeed...

Ten

P.O.

"No shit, Leo. If you're not ready in five, you'll be riding to C'est la Vie squeezed within an inch of your life into Zac's backseat," I say, popping my head back in the front door, ready to take off in his dirt-brown Volvo by myself if need be.

"And if you don't get off my back, you'll be riding to the airport in Zac's Jeep sitting on top of your luggage," he replies, unperturbed, taking his sweet fucking time tying up the laces of his hiking boots. "Cool your jets, will you?"

Cool my jets? It's already half an hour later than my usual drop at the café. Liam and Éolie already said their goodbyes to both Yann and me earlier on before crashing back into bed. In desperate need of a power nap to offset an all-nighter pacing with the twins down with the sniffles, they declined joining the caffeine brigade. And managing the rest of the crew is like herding cats. Now, by the time we make it down to the village for a last cup of coffee before I fly out of here, I'll probably have missed most of my Aurèle time. Goddammit. What if she leaves before we get there?

I check my phone again. No. Can't happen. Harry still isn't connected which is another cause for alarm.

I pinch the bridge of my nose. Christ. What if she can't make it down to the village before we have to leave for the Mont-Tremblant Airport?

The next eight months or so without once seeing her exquisite face brightening up as she reads some of my chat replies loom ahead of me. And I wonder if it was such a good idea to ban pictures or video chats altogether. Maybe I can sneak in a photo of her before I leave for good? Something subtle that no one else notices...

"Too risky. Stick with the program."

"What was that?" Leo calls.

My eyes widen. *Shit.* I inwardly groan. I have to stop talking to myself out loud. "Nothing," I call back.

I'm nowhere near ready to share her with the guys. Not only will I never hear the end of it, but knowing them, they'll butt in left and right, asking for progress reports. We're too close not to. Thirteen years rooming together will do that. And this thing with Aurèle is different, too important to fuck with. Can't risk jinxing it.

Leo rolls his eyes. "What's too risky?"

"Trying to steal the car and leave you here," I lie.

His brow shoots up and I know I've let on too much. "What's the big rush?"

"Nothing. We're late as it is, and I really *need* to get to C'est la Vie one last time before I do without for the next eight months one week and two days."

"What will you do if we don't get you to coffee in the next fifteen minutes?"

"Have you ever seen a rabid dog bite?"

He shrugs it off. "I like to live dangerously."

"Good for you, you're about to," I grunt in reply, never more serious.

He pulls a forest-green beanie on his head before he leisurely picks up his gloves and keys, stuffing them in his coat pockets. It's colder out than normal for this early in September. "Relax. Your flight is in three hours."

"Exactly. Move it, will you," I say, turning on my heels, annoyed. Mont-Tremblant International is at least a forty-minute drive from Val-David and it doesn't leave that much leeway.

Leo keeps pace with me as I round the house at a fast clip, headed for the woodshed and the parked Volvo fleet. He spreads his arms wide, breathing in the decisive nip in the late morning air. I can see his breath fan out in front of me. "It's Sunday."

"That's a total non sequitur, man." I give him a look that says *poor sod, the gates are down and the lights are flashing but the train isn't coming.* "What's that got to do with coffee and hurrying the hell up?"

I roll my eyes behind his back before turning to Yann slouched against Leo's car. "Zac and Magali left already?" I ask him accusingly, hands on my hips. Zac's Jeep is nowhere to be seen.

Great. Should have sent Yann to corral Leo. I'd probably be sitting at the café by now.

"They went ahead to get us a table for five," Yann says distractedly, typing an entry into his phone's agenda in all likelihood. He tosses it back into his messenger bag and tucks the strap over his chest before bending his tall frame, buckling up in the front passenger seat.

"Awesome," I grit through my teeth. Not only is Yann riding shotgun, but now I won't even have a say in choosing tables, and odds are I won't have a good enough, unobtrusive angle to spy on Aurèle.

The corner of Leo's mouth twitches as if a smile is trying to form, but he's doing his best to suppress it. "Like I said, it's Sunday." He fucking starts singing, *"Don't worry, be happy."*

If looks could kill, Leo would be dead by now.

"Let's get this show on the road," I mutter sullenly. Opening the rear passenger door, I shove aside three bags of soil and an impressive number of brand-new seed trays—thank God for small favors or I would have been left holding Leo's sprouts— buckle in, and slam it shut.

"Chill, man," Leo says, giving me an amused look in the rearview mirror as he cranks the engine. "I'll make it quick and painless. Caffeine injection coming in ten."

"Make it five. You're not the one who'll be sitting next to him on the longest forty-nine minutes flight from Tremblant to Boston in recent history," Yann says with a smirk in his voice. "I'd like to keep all of my fingers if you don't mind."

"Hilarious," I grumble. I may or may not have snapped shut the lid of his laptop over his hands to reach a cup offered to him by a stewardess on a long-ago flight from Zurich. In my defense, I'd been deprived of my elixir of choice for thirteen hours straight at the time, due to unforeseen delays and missed connections and nary a coffee shop opened in the dead of night. Very uncivilized. Them. Not me.

I check my phone, but still no Harry. *Bloody hell.*

I'm out the door before Leo even cuts the engine and take C'est la Vie's stairs two at a time. My glance flits around the terrace, but I can't readily spot any strawberry-blonde heads. Then again, everyone's bundled up in heavy coats, wearing woolen hats and gloves. And everyone's sitting outside, enjoying cups, nevertheless. I shake my head. Only in Les Laurentides would anyone take a sunny day as balmy weather.

I spin in a slow circle searching. It's the weekend, and with the weekly invasion of day-trippers and chalet owners, the place is more crowded than usual. Over the sea of heads, Magali waves me over before I can do a more thorough search. Unlike yesterday, Aurèle could be sitting inside like she did on Friday.

Zac motions with his head for me to join them, brandishing a metal carafe like a prized possession. Giving him a disgusted look, I put my index finger in my open mouth, fake gagging. The whole point of being here is supposedly to savor one last cup of this particular café's specialty espresso. I made such a fuss, I'm not about to ruin my perfectly good excuse with a regular-blend coffee industrially brewed. I thumb in the general direction of the front counter. He rolls his eyes and waves me off as Yann and Leo make their way over to them.

A quick sweep through confirms that fuck, she's not inside, either. I check my phone again while waiting for my order. Yes! Harry's now connected to *this* WiFi, and she's surfing the net.

Where the hell are you, Aurèle? I'd like to ask but quickly type in one big-ass pop-up bloom, instead: **Hi! Are you and Harry having a good time?**

> Olivier! *Bonjour* to you too. Harry and I are now having a lovely time together, thanks to you. What are you doing all over my screen (not sure if it's creepy or not, having you drop in on us out of nowhere)?

I check out the terrace through the bay windows, looking for someone on a hot date with a computer. There is a god after all. I locate her four tables down in a straight line from ours, her back to us, facing the park. She wears an oversized black woolen hat pulled low over her ears and a glacier-blue fleece scarf wrapped a few times around her neck, but the long strands of hair escaping from underneath are definitely strawberry-blonde.

And already, I breathe easier.

I open our regular private chat window.

I'm not out of nowhere. I'm from somewhere. Big difference.

Clément hands over my alibi and I step out, cup in one hand, phone in the other, hard pressed not to detour and stare at her, face to face.

Better the back of her head than nothing at all, I suppose.

"Would one of you mind switching places?" I ask Magali and Zac, sitting side by side. That is, if we can call arms and other body parts all over each other sitting.

I almost feel sorry. Almost. But not quite. Desperation will do that to me.

Zac raises a brow in disbelief. "Why?"

Bloody hell. Why, indeed. I'd scratch my jaw but my hands are full.

"I'd like to face forward and drink in the view. You know, before I'm cooped up in a flying can of sardines hurtling through the sky at three hundred fifty kilometers per hour." Brilliant, convincing, and somewhat truthful, if I do say so myself.

"This should be interesting," Leo mutters into his mug, and Yann's green eyes widen behind his lenses.

"Never bothered you before," Zac argues, unmoving.

"Sure," Magali says, talking over him while trying to wiggle out from under his arm, but Zac keeps her firmly by his side, effectively putting a stop to her efforts.

"You're not going anywhere," he says to her. "Don't mind him. It's just his caffeine withdrawal symptoms talking. Besides, his eyes are always glued to a screen anyway, so he can't possibly miss any view."

Well, shit. He has a point. My eyes beseech Magali in a last-ditch effort.

"But look at those sad puppy eyes," Magali says, her head darting between the two of us. I knew she'd bite. She's my new favorite person.

Zac shoots me a glare all Theo-like over Magali's head. Ask me if I care, I'm ready to beg if I have to. I stare, unflinching.

Leo puffs out his cheeks in exasperation. "He's been a pain in the arse all morning." He rolls his eyes, crossing his arms over his chest. "Want mine?" he asks me pointedly from his perch at one end of the two little round bistro tables tucked together. Sandwiched as Leo is, in between three tables full, I won't see a thing.

"Nope. Same difference." I slide my tiny cup of dark ambrosia onto the table and tip my chin towards Zac. "So?"

"Here," Yann offers them, getting up with alacrity before Zac can open his mouth and tell me to shove it where the sun never shines. "Take both our seats. Problem solved."

Magali beams a smile, pulling Zac up by the hand. "See? Everyone's happy," she says to him and he follows without a single complaint, shaking his head at her before dropping a kiss on her temple.

I fist bump Yann before plopping down on the bistro chair vacated by Zac. "Thanks, man."

Yann snorts, pushing his tortoise-shell glasses up his nose. "No need. I should be the one thanking Zac."

"Really? If I didn't mention today that you guys are weird, consider it done," Magali deadpans.

"And I owe you two a solid." Yann salutes them with his cup. "Otherwise, I'd have been stuck on a regional flight from Hell with his grouchy arse."

"Nothing caffeine can't cure." Leo practically shoves my cup up under my nose. "Come on, man. Do *us* a solid and be done with it."

"Appreciate your concern." I salute them before swallowing my first sip, smacking my lips to a chorus of relieved sighs. Go figure. But then again, my addiction has been such a catchall excuse, you won't see me complaining.

I stretch my legs out diagonal to the table, sighing contentedly, the view so much better from where I sit. Now if only Zac could move his newly appointed seat six inches or so to the left, it'd be a perfect one. As he's whispering something in Magali's ear with a wolfish grin tacked on his face, I wisely decide not to push the issue.

I crane my neck to the side instead and take a discreet peek at Aurèle. Hunched over Harry, she's totally focused on her screen, as usual, unaware of her surroundings. And to be perfectly honest, I love that, for now, I'm the only one seemingly having an in with her... I pick up my phone, a slow grin crawling up my face as I read her latest comment.

I've been here for ages. Lost somewhere at the lab?

Nope. Not in the lab today. A lazy Sunday is to blame.

"With a little help from my friends," I mumble under my breath, totally ignoring Zac pointing out to Magali that, as predicted, I don't give a shit about the view.

Will wonders never cease? =) If not holed up in your lab, what are you up to on this lazy Sunday? Writing a letter, perhaps, like someone you know?

Writing a letter... It explains her lateness in booting up Harry, my only direct link to her, but not the electrifying flood of warmth those three little words of hers light up in me. I swallow back the smile that threatens.

Nope. Just chilling on a café's terrace with some of my mates.

Cool! With a side order of (much too) early frost in the air, I'm chilling myself on a café's terrace. But like any good natives, loving it. How's the weather in Boston?

I have abso-fucking-lutely no idea. *Christ.* That really makes me wish to be over there already, if only to stop fudging around the truth at the drop of a dime, giving me less rope to hang myself with. Not taking any chances, I open a browser to go check on the weather channel but it takes forever, the café's internet slower than slow right fucking now. My phone, unfortunately, doesn't pack Lucie's giga power and Lucie, unfortunately, doesn't do compact like my phone and had to stay put in the car. I curse under my breath as I stare at my frozen screen, my palms growing sweaty. I should be typing a fluid reply to this innocuous question, like I'd normally do if I were in Boston.

"Hey, Yann? What's the temp in Boston right now?" I ask him with some urgency, talking over their convo about Porter Airline and the fifteen-passenger regional jets used for our direct flight.

"Overcast and a balmy twenty-two degrees Celsius, or seventy-one point six degrees Fahrenheit, with a sixteen percent probability of precipitation upon time of landing."

"Thanks, man. I owe you," I say with heartfelt relief, my thumbs already flying over the keys.

"Since when does he need reassuring?" Zac says, completely misreading the reason for my question, but I don't look up, too busy typing my reply.

"Since you're not flying us back," Yann deadpans.

With that one, Yann singlehandedly launches a discussion they all get engrossed into without requiring any input from me. I owe him another one. At this rate, I'll owe him a kidney by the time we land.

Zac pilots his own twin-engine Piper Comanche, which is a pretty damn cool six-seater plane, and he used to fly us all over. But now, he's more often than not talking house plans and home decor with Magali, both feet firmly on the ground.

> Twenty-two Celsius, Olivier?!! They've let you out of the lab on such a gorgeous day to boot!!!!!! Program not responding... Get out from behind your screen this instant and get back to your other friends. And whatever is your *sujet de l'heure* under discussion. Enjoy the tropics for me! Ctrl-Alt-Del. @ *bientôt*.

Ctrl-Alt-Del? Shit. With her program not responding comment, using that chain of command means she's forcing the program to close up, or in other words, she's signing off. I type as fast as I can in case she disconnects completely.

Don't go yet. Truth? I'd rather chat with you. Thanks to three of my mates, you can now ask me *anything* about

wood screws versus nails. Even things you never knew you wanted to know.

lol. One too many screws loose between you?

Ha! You nailed it. One is living in a disaster waiting to happen, holding everything up with duct tape. One is building deep into the woods halfway through a two-year project using a wheelbarrow and a shovel. And the other is building a home as fast as he can get away with.

Building a home...

My mind goes a mile a minute in a quantum leap to next summer. And wood screws and nails no longer sound as boring as I wrote, all of a sudden. I sigh longingly, looking at the tip of Aurèle's cute hat covered head over Zac's shoulder. Sign me up on the Domesticated List, please. I sigh once more, deflating a bit. For now, I'll have to be content to stay put on the Waiting List.

"See anything of interest?" Zac asks me drily.

I jerk back, wrenching my attention from Aurèle. "Nope," I'm quick to deny, straightening from my slump. "I just thought someone looked familiar, that's all." A rush of heat spreads like wildfire on my cheeks that the wind chaffing at my skin has nothing to do with. Great. Just great.

Leo and Zac share a knowing look.

Oh, joy. Here it comes.

I fiddle with my cup and brace myself for a merciless ribbing that might even alert Aurèle. The guys can be kind of loud when it suits them. I should know. I'm one of them. Not to say, they're not above walking up to her table to invite her over on my behalf, charmingly insistent.

They've done it before.

Bloody hell.

"Wow. You normally would have flown them back to Boston if you weren't on call today?" Magali asks Zac, distracting his enquiring gaze away from me, wanting to confirm whatever Yann said to her just now, saving me in the nick of time. There goes my other kidney.

"*We* would have flown them back," he says to her. One arm draped casually over the top of her mustard-yellow bistro chair, Zac crosses his ankles. "And that's a big maybe. I want to be there for groundbreaking at the home site early tomorrow. Nice try, man." He smirks at Yann over his mug, taking a sip of his no-frills, regular black coffee while the fingers of his other hand brush Magali's arm in a slow back and forth, keeping her nestled to his side.

Upon witnessing their quiet intimacy, another shit load of envy hits me in the chest. In that moment, it's not so much that I want Aurèle to be mine but that I want to be hers. Leo arches a questioning brow at me that I ignore by fiddling some more with my cup, watching my coffee swirl.

Don't look at her.

Don't look at her.

Don't look at her.

I will my eyes to stay focused on the rich, dark color of what's left of my espresso. "You're pulling the plug now that we're used to being chauffeured around?" Yann grumbles to Zac.

"Porter Airline has a *direct* flight from Tremblant to Boston, I'm sure you'll recover well enough." Zac rolls his eyes at Yann.

My gaze keeps straying in Aurèle's general direction as I listen absently to the guys.

"Hell, I'll drink to Porter," Leo, our designated driver, says. "Saves me a trip to Montréal on the end of the weekend rush hour." Leo and Magali clink their white and blue earthenware coffee mugs in complete accord. I've never been to Montréal yet, but according to them, pretty atrocious road conditions prevail in and around the city, so much so as to be the stuff of legends among the locals.

I take another slow sip of coffee. My phone wiggles on the table, buzzing with an incoming reply. My chest pings right along, and a goofy grin spreads on my lips as I pick it up. Yann gives me a sidelong glance, quirking a surprised brow that says, *who's this guy?*

Can't blame him. I usually scowl darkly and curse at my phone, in no hurry to pick it up. But then again, the only texts I get usually spell trouble with a capital T, or in my case, in binary codes gone haywire. When test running a program, the code that is hardest to debug is the code that you know cannot possibly be wrong and finding it fucking kills me every time.

I put my phone back down, unwilling to give myself away by my eagerness.

My fingers itch to unlock the screen, but I scratch my scruff instead, willing Yann's attention away from me.

Resist. Resist. Resist. I repeat like a mantra.

"It's really a neat city but you need to go there without a specific timetable, otherwise you'll curse up and down," Magali concurs with Leo. Fuck resistance. Resistance is futile. I nod in silent agreement like I know the fuck what they're talking about, while discreetly sweeping my thumb over my screen, inching my phone away from the table and onto my thigh.

I look down.

"But, Yann, you really should come earlier next summer. The Montreal Jazz Fest starts at the end of June. You'd love it—"

Are you guys optioning for a remake of the Three Little Pigs?

I blame it on too much caffeine and not enough sleep, but I'm imagining them wearing pig suits and the resulting look on their faces. I slap my hand on the table, howling out an uncontainable bark of laughter loud enough that the conversation around me abruptly dies. I look up from my phone. All eyes are glued to mine.

Busted.

"Uh... Email. Inside joke," I mumble.

No one answers.

I slam back the remains of my espresso for countenance. I sit still, committing to not touching my phone for the next five minutes. Or, at the very least, until enough time has passed for me to go get a legitimate refill without raising suspicion. But instead, I fumble with the damn thing, sending it into orbit. Thankfully, Magali catches my phone just before it hits the floor deck and crashes to its untimely death.

I wipe my palms on my jeans before pocketing it with a sheepish look. "Good catch, thanks."

"You *like her* like her, don't you?" Magali asks me knowingly.

Is it that evident?

"Who?" I ask warily. If my ears had warmed earlier, now they're on fucking fire.

She cups her hands over her mouth and stage whispers, "The girl behind me you keep peeking at."

Shit, guess it is.

"No! Yes. Never mind." I rub the back of my neck. Is the sun getting warmer?

Zac checks behind his shoulder for the most likely suspect, making no bones about his intentions, and zeroes in on Aurèle right away. Great. I'm ready to jump him if he so much as moves a toe in her direction.

"Go and say hi," Magali encourages me.

"No way." I send her a quick, panicked look. Been there, done that. Anyway, if Aurèle gives me any real crumb of attention this time around, I think I'll be jealous of myself; the one who's here, not the one who's in Boston. How fucked up is that? Worse yet, knowing me, it's more than likely I'll give myself away in five seconds flat by tripping all over my tongue, saying something I shouldn't, letting on that I know more than I should. Might as well come out and be done with it. *Hi, I'm Olivier. But hey, don't mind me. I'm not really here. I'm in Boston right now having a private chat with you under—almost, but not quite—false pretenses.* Yeah, like that would go over well.

"Hey, maybe I know her. Do you want me to pass a note?" Magali says, her silver eyes flashing with a playful glint.

The cold wind buffeting the terrace does nothing to cool down my flaming cheeks. Hoping to disappear from sight, I promptly pull my charcoal-grey beanie down so low it now hides half my face.

"Shit," I mutter, slouching low in my chair. "Magali, do you really know her?" I whisper anxiously.

Magali is crazy outgoing. She knows half the people living in Les Laurentides and, at a guess, the other half probably knows her, so her threat is not an idle one. I'm so screwed.

"No, I don't. Relax." She pushes my beanie up my brow.

"You're panicking over nothing; she's not even looking this way, dude." Leo upturns his eyes.

"Please tell me it's the girl and not the laptop you're drooling over," Zac says drily. I give him my best shut-it-or-die expression.

There's no way I can keep up my conversation with her now. Not with all of them watching my every move. I shoot Zac one last lethal glare that bounces right off of him as I quickly type.

Something came up. Got to go.

"You know, women don't bite unless you ask for it," Magali deadpans, and Yann nearly spits coffee, thumping on his chest.

"A little warning next time, Magali," he coughs up.

Zac leans closer to her ear. "Really? Don't recall asking this morning..." The rest of what he says is lost somewhere in translation as Magali's elbow connects with his side.

"Behave," she mouths and Zac chuckles low.

I chance a quick peek over his shoulder. Fuck, she's gathering up her things.

I straighten in my chair, my hands fisting on my thighs underneath the table, fighting the urge to just up and grab Aurèle's arm to stop her from leaving. My eyes hungrily follow her every move as she gracefully walks by the terrace until she's out of sight. I blow out a breath, rubbing my chest, unsure if I feel relieved or tortured.

"No, really, guys, are women that terrifying as a species?" Magali asks.

We look at one another. "Duh," we all reply as one, fist bumping, and Magali shakes her head at us, complete with eye rolling.

With the imminent threat of discovery removed, I lean back, resting my ankle on my opposite knee, a smirk on my lips as gender-oriented quips fly high and low around our table for the next little while. Up until Coldplay's *Up & Up* chorus plays out of Magali's coat pocket, interrupting the flow.

"That's Amélie." Her brows dip as she fishes her phone out. "She'd text normally. I need to take this, sorry, guys." She walks down to the edge of the park, a frown etching on her face as she takes the call.

"Amélie, that's her friend from her Junior Freestyle ski team days who jumped off the ramp with her last winter, right? The one in the pictures she showed us?" Leo asks, scratching his chin.

"Yep, what about her?" Zac asks distractedly, keeping an eye on Magali, relaxing when he sees her face break into a soft smile.

"Heard Magali mention to Éolie last night that she's helping her with your home decor, and she seemed pretty enthused. Think Amélie can do something to tone down the duct tape at the farmstead?" Leo asks in all seriousness, staring at the bottom of his coffee mug as if it holds the answers to his impossible request.

Both Yann and I snicker. "Would take a miracle to tone that down," I mumble under my breath.

"Leo, come on, there's not much she can do on repairs. She deals with the finishing touches as a hobby of hers. Gut the place down or own the duct tape, man."

Leo cuts Zac a look. "Well, since I'm not gutting it down until our little twins move into their new house next year, I just thought Amélie could, I don't know, enliven it meanwhile."

I raise a disbelieving brow.

He shoves his dark-green beanie down his forehead. "Long winters, I've been warned enough," he grumbles.

"*Riiight.* That's what you call it now? Enlivening long winters," I say knowingly, glad to pass the puck.

"You're one to talk," Leo mutters, his chin pointing in the direction Aurèle went, effectively shutting my trap.

"I like Magali's suggestion of playing tic-tac-toe on the walls." Yann drains the last of his coffee.

"Actually, that's Amélie's suggestion, not mine." Magali drops a kiss on the top of Zac's head, before plopping back down on her chair.

"Really?" Leo visibly perks up. Curiouser and curiouser.

Magali gives Zac a sidelong glance.

"Don't look at me. I'm not touching this one." He holds his hands up.

Last month, Leo had a fit when we started *enlivening* the duct taped walls, cabinets, windows, you name it, with cheeky commentaries on life at the farmstead. His sense of humor didn't extend quite that far.

"Told you the idea would grow on you," she says to him. "But I'm sure Amélie can come up with other ones, if you're interested. I can ask her to drop by the farmstead and take a look. She hasn't been there in ages."

"Oh. Cool. Yeah. Sure. Anytime," Leo says, all the while nodding casually, as though pondering the matter at great length. He leans forward on his elbows, and asks, "Is tomorrow all right?"

Oh, man. Yann and I share a raised brow.

Interesting. Leo's crushing on the girl.

And Boston will be boring as shit in more ways than one.

Why am I going back again?

I'm not so sure anymore.

Eleven

P.O.

By the end of September, I'm totally hooked on Aurèle's handwritten letters. I crave them more than a crack addict would his next fix. Every morning I wake, hoping I'll get one. And every night, I hurry back to the condo, carried by the thought that one might be waiting for me.

And even though I didn't cave in yet and write her one, conceding defeat to her letter challenge, Aurèle was so right. I'm just not ready to admit it yet. Among other things.

"Thank you." I toss a quick smile to the uniformed man who holds open the heavy glass door for me on my way in.

Mister Johnson, our building concierge and all-around doorman, sends my heart into overdrive by producing a thick cream envelope from his breast pocket with a flourish. "You've got mail."

"Thanks." I pocket it and hasten over to the elevator banks. The dull sound of my haphazardly laced and scruffy engineer boots thumping on the marble floor echoes in the empty lobby. And close behind, the clip-clop of Mister J's hard soled, shiny dress shoes as he scrambles behind me.

Speaking in undertones, our concierge falls into step with me. "Such a rare thing these days, letters."

I nod once crisply, hitting the button for the thirty-sixth floor, hoping against hope for a swift escape, but no. He steps forward and places a gnarly hand over the retracted door to keep it from closing too quickly.

Mister J. is nimble on his feet and still going strong for a guy of his undetermined, but quite venerable, age. I'll give him that. He's probably ninety-five. I inwardly shake my head, amused by what just popped into my mind. Ninety-five... Aurèle would get it. I recall with fondness that particular discussion, the one at the heart of this writing challenge she wrestled out of me.

Mister J's three permanent grooves slashing the skin in between his white bushy eyebrows deepen. "A lost art, if you ask me," he insists.

An obsolete one if you ask me. "Yes, indeed." I sigh, resigned to the fact I'll have to hear the rest of his spiel before I can make good on my escape. A speech I get almost daily now, which is, overall, a small price to pay for his safekeeping of Aurèle's incoming letters, granted, but still. I can recite by heart what he'll say next.

"In my days, gentlemen courted their ladies with the might of their pen, not their penis! Think about it."

It's all I think about, and then some. "I most definitely will, Mister J. You have a nice evening now." Even though I know he's referring to wooing Aurèle with the might of my pen, I can't help my thoughts from straying to the might of my penis instead.

"You too, young man. You too. That Aurèle's a keeper, just like my Edith in her days, and I know these things." His faded brown eyes twinkling, he nudges his head back, pointing toward my coat pocket. He knows full well I'm not fooling him and that her letter is burning a hole twice the size of a zettabyte straight through my side and that I itch to read it. "Write her back tonight. A handwritten one, using thoughtful words. Real words." One wiry hand waves the air in front of him. "None of this emailing or texting mumbo jumbo you computer whiz kids use today." His voice grows aggravated like it does every time technology is mentioned in one form or another. And I'm not about to get him started on acronyms—the end of civilization and the return to the Dark Ages—according to him.

Wonder how I'll feel about it myself, seventy years down the road? Will I be harping about the lost art of emailing and texting while the young generation teleports away from unwanted speeches?

Bringing me out of my thoughts with an admonishing finger wagging in my direction, he punctuates, "Mark my words. Pen and paper will get you the girl, slowly but surely."

"I don't do any slower than a ninety's dial-up connection, Mister J."

I hide my grin behind a cough as he gives me a look. The same one I get anytime I deflect with a smartass reply. The one that says, "No wonder, poor sod, only has one oar in the water like the rest of his microchip generation." Aurèle's letters brighten more than my days; she lights a new fire in me.

"Like I said," he says with an exaggerated eye roll. "Instant gratification is ruining your generation. Where did anticipation go?"

Where indeed? He shakes his head like it doesn't even compute.

"You two should meet. You're of the same mind." I plaster a tight-lipped smile onto my face.

"Well, there you go," he points out, finally letting go of the door so I only get to hear half of his parting shot as it closes shut. "Knew I liked her for—"

"—a reason," I finish for him. On a swish, the elevator car shoots up with quiet efficiency. "Only one, Mister J.? Try one thousand and one unrequited reasons," I say, watching the bright blue digital numbers fly by on the control panel.

Inside, I drop my keys onto the trendy cement counter polished to a beeswax shine, and drape my coat on the back of one of the chic kitchen island stools, fully cognizant it will drive Yann's OCD tendencies up the wall when he comes back later tonight. And that he'll drive me bonkers in return by cleaning up behind me.

I fish out of my pocket Aurèle's letter and brush my fingers over my full name written in her neat, round cursive. A rush of warmth pumps through my veins, seeping into my soul as I imagine her, pen in hand, tracing those same letters my fingertip retraces now. A sense of deeper connection settles in out of nowhere.

"No shit." I sigh, running a hand through my hair. I stare at her handwriting. What started as a challenge, a dare, a line drawn in the sand pitting our wits one against the other, became more than that. Instead, the tables are flipped and I am the one constantly angling for another letter.

I tap the envelope on my open palm, deep in thought.

Would it be so bad to give in and write Aurèle an old-fashioned one instead of flicking a quick email, conceding the whole? Will she feel more connected to me?

I huff out a frustrated breath, giving myself a slight head shake.

Picking up Lucie's bag I left by the vestibule, I cross over the spectacular open floor plan. The added touch of floor-to-ceiling glass panes letting in the city lights like twinkling stars on a dark background makes it even more so. But the view doesn't captivate me tonight.

Staring at her return address, I slow to a stop, the envelope weighing in my hand.

The subdued and minimalist elegance of our rented condo, the magnificent view afforded over the city, none of it captures my attention like before. None of it matters. It's just a place to crash at night when I'd rather be sharing a small lake cottage somewhere in the back boonies of Val-David, fuck it all. So, why am I here, exactly?

Rubbing my temple, I sigh yet again. "Jesus. Get a grip. You've got a date with zeros and ones, and less than two semesters left before you walk away with your MIT master's," I tell myself. "It's what you need to do. That's why your ass is sitting here in Boston." The fact that I need the reminder is not sitting all that well with me, nor is the fact that I'm two breaths away from not giving a fuck about my degree anymore.

"You can do it," I encourage myself. "Focus, man, and get some shit done tonight."

With that in mind, I slip Aurèle's letter into my back pocket to read in the morning. "Here's to anticipation," I mumble into the semi-darkness. "And lack of enthusiasm," I self-mock under my breath, dragging Lucie with me.

If nothing else, I rationalize further, her letter will supply me with a much-needed boost that's not caffeine related for a change, and turbocharge my day.

To the muted sounds of a wailing siren coming from the street below, I walk past Yann's wide-open door, his empty bedroom confirming that he's not back from MIT yet.

Not two minutes later, I toe off my boots in the mess of my room, checking on my phone if Harry's connected, like I do a hundred times a day, even knowing that this late at night, he better not be...

"Good for you," I murmur.

More relieved than frustrated, I toss my phone and Lucie aside on the rumpled sheets of the king-size bed custom designed by the condo's owner. It's wide enough to double as a catchall clothes hamper and office desk. Not to say, as short as I am, I could probably go missing in there for a week if I had a mind to. Which wouldn't be so bad, come to think of it, if Aurèle came down here for a visit. Yeah, like that's likely to happen, I inwardly groan.

Fuck. Did I have to go there?

"Down, boy," I say to my twitching dick, but now, unless I rub one out, my priority reboot is shot to hell. Program not responding.

I curb a snort. Understatement of the year.

I sit up against the upholstered headboard, my fingers hesitating for a minute longer over Lucie. But the letter now burns a hole in my pocket.

Strings of linear codes and anticipation be damned.

My heart beating like bongo drums at a Santana concert, I rip open the envelope and unfold the sheaf of papers. I start to read, lapping up every word.

Chuckle du Jour. A Tee Chronicle. Now Showing. I read the title at the top of one page written inside a doodled marquee. I chuckle low, shaking my head. That girl really brings it, and me, to the next level. By now, it's kind of a running gag to send her a close-up picture of my one-liner tees attached to my emails. I kind of skirted around the no selfie rule with that one, but since it gives away nothing more than text, I got away with it. I figured if it entertains Éolie that much when I'm staying at the farmstead, it might do the trick with Aurèle too. Needless to say, it was a huge hit with her. Éolie doesn't know it yet but I owe her one for inspiring the Chuckle du Jour Chronicles just now.

Programmers are tools for converting coffee into code. I read on a drawn poster sitting underneath the marquee on a tripod easel stand. An accompanying text is written in photo caption like a newspaper article. She's cute.

Really (insert light sarcasm)? So far, as it's the only food group you officially recognize, I would never have guessed (insert tongue-in-cheek). Your endless supply of those is awe inspiring. And before you ask, it's unclear if I'm talking about the sheer amount of tees you own (genius way to avoid laundry?), or the cute one-liners that keep on coming. =D Probably both...

Lost in the collection of her every day anecdotes, I turn over the last of her ten page letter much too soon to my liking. I don't want it to end. Yet, here I am, racing to the finish line.

The sky is gorgeous here tonight. So many stars. The new moon is almost here. The waning crescent is just this tiny sliver of quicksilver dancing on the rippling water of the lake. At night, the firmament is not really all that dark up north, but rather white with stars, upon stars, upon stars. I've never really noticed before, living in Montréal, but up here, the night sky blankets me; its sheer vastness and quietness sucking me in. I wish I could capture it in pictures. So far, my efforts came out quite pathetic looking compared to the real deal. I think I'll stick with experimenting with daytime light for now, and maybe study constellations at night, instead. There's a textbook on them I found in the upstairs reading nook. What about you? Do you see stars at night where you live? Probably not. Boston must be suffering from light pollution just as much as Montréal, non?
To be continued...
Woke up early this morning, around five thirty, the left side of my face pressed against The Star Encyclopedia, a newly discovered Ursua Minoris printed on my cheek, Polaris by my earlobe. Oh, wait. It's freckles. False alarm!
This week we got into our fifth season with a vengeance. Indian Summer, which may last anywhere from a couple of days to a couple of weeks, bringing extreme temperature variations between night and day. With the resulting early morning mist as dense as a London fog running low to the

ground, it's like living in the midst of a medieval forest. Druidic, mystical, and ethereal up until the sun breaks striking the gossamer veil with arrows of light. Breathtaking just about sums it up. Again, all of my attempts to immortalize the moment in a picture look nowhere near the real deal, but I'll get there.

She's revealing so much about herself between the lines of her letters—her intelligence is obviously one of them.

Off to dress like an onion for my walk to the village where I'll post this letter. Wonder how many layers I'll shed getting there. =) Who knows, maybe it will get up to twenty-two Celsius in my little corner of the world today, and you'll be the one envying me for it.
See you (well, not see you, see you...Chat you?) down in the village—heavy-loaded MIT schedule permitting.

She's got that one right, and I'm not amused by it. We keep missing each other online due to my hectic MIT schedule, which does nothing to soothe my Instant Gratification Compulsive Disorder, or IGCD as Aurèle likes to call it.

If not, well, by all means, go postal... :D
Oh, and if your IGCD itches, don't scratch! Anticipate this letter. Almost there,
Aurèle
XXX ←cheek kissing three times @ la Suisse and not an X-rated option unlike someone I won't mention, mentioned. ;) Ciao!

Well, shit. I groan, flopping back against the pillows.

For the first time, Aurèle signed her last letter with three little kisses. A triple X that starred in all my fantasies these past three days and had me seriously debating whether or not to acknowledge them as more in my reply email sent two days ago.

In the end, slyness won over suavity—I simply asked where she wanted the kisses she sent delivered. Not that hard. Sly I can do. It's the hacker in me. Suave, well. . .not so much. Add to it that *better safe than sorry* is a sacrosanct motto every programmer lives by, and here I am, screwed solid. And in no way about to mess with something that saved my ass more than once.

So now I know. Firmly friend zoned.

Not disappointed. Nope.

But on that note, time to get some real work done. I boot up Lucie, determined to stick to ones and zeros for the rest of the night.

But where do I go, instead?

I zero in on that one specific Gmail account that's like a goddamn gravitational pull.

> **To:Aurèle not.even.alittle@gmail.com**
> **From:P.O.youvegottobejoking@gmail.com**
> **Subject:X-rated options for our Three Little Pigs not under discussion?**
>
> **Shame. It would hike up the ratings with a bang.**

Delete.

> **Shame. Don't you want to know where this little piggy went?**

Delete.

> **Shame. I'd be the big bad wolf to your little piggy, anywhere, anytime.**

Delete.

> ~~**Swine.**~~ **Fine. But it would have made such a porky ~~tail~~ tale, with a twist.**

Delete.

Lucie's screen glares back at me in the semi-darkness, almost mocking, her bluish glow highlighting my empty bedroom, taunting me.

I stare at my blinking cursor.

Write her back tonight. A handwritten one, using thoughtful words. Real words. You'll get the girl, slowly but surely.

The thought sticks and lengthens like a shadow at sunset.

I shoot out of bed before I change my mind and make a beeline for Yann's bedroom.

There, on his desk, two neat piles of hardcover notebooks sit underneath sticky notes on the wall labeled, **Used–Unused**. Like it's not apparent which is which.

I roll my eyes and snitch one of his new notebooks, grabbing a couple of pens from his metallic pencil cup only to scream bloody murder, spotting the big, ugly ass spider scurrying behind it.

I throw a bunch of notebooks at it from a safe distance, my skin crawling with the memory of a jarful of them poured down my back. Year seven was a bitch to the six of us at BIA as we had all skipped a few grades ahead by then. The Goddamn Geek Squad as we were called and bullied by the older crowd until we turned it around by owning our Great Geekiness Status, or GGS for short. Outsmarting them was our finest hour. I close Yann's door and seal it shut with a couple of towels, not taking any chances.

My heart still thudding in my throat, I shake my comforter a few times, double-checking my sheets.

Blessed nothing.

I huddle back against the headboard and crack "my" notebook's spine open.

Chère **Aurèle,** I start.

> **Star gazing brings back lots of good memories. I don't remember if it's Theo or Yann who started it all, but, once upon a time (we were twelve or so, back at BIA), the guys and I had this pretty cool telescope we shared. We used to wish upon Polaris, the North Star, on a nightly basis when younger, so, I guess we sort of fell into it in our preteen**

years. Studying astronomy felt way more mature at the time than wishing upon a star. We were know-it-all little shits, no doubt, and fully earned our Goddamned Geek Squad nickname or GGS for short by the end of primary school. Which, I might add, by the time high school rolled in, we had elevated to Geek God Status for the duration.

Anyway, star gazing is what honed our skills at stealthy missions past curfew under the nose of our dorm supervisor. Whole nights spent on our backs up in an alpine meadow, watching the Perseids. Spotting thirteen shooting stars in under an hour is my official and, as yet, unbroken record. Have you ever watched them? If not, you're in for a treat this upcoming summer.

"And maybe. Just maybe. We'll get to watch together next summer, and the next, and the next. If I have any say in this..." I say into the empty room like a long forgotten wish upon a star.

My fingers cramp from the unusual activity, and still, I write, and write some more about constellations and anything, and everything. And it's the beauty of it. There's something both freeing and intimate about handwriting a letter—something that goes beyond two friends just shooting up the breeze, chatting online.

Exhilaration fills me, a new lightness rooting in my chest as words pour out of me faster than I can write them, and I keep it up long into the night.

It's as though Aurèle is there, everywhere, inside me, beside me.

And maybe she is.

And maybe I get it now. The instant versus delayed gratification.

Some things are worth waiting for.

Twelve

AURÈLE

The pungent smell of fallen leaves wafts through the air, filling my nostrils with each step I take. If I were to ascribe a smell to October, this would be it.

I shuffle my feet playfully in the ankle-deep leaves lining the wood trail. It releases bursts of this particular aroma in the air, sending them dancing in my wake. I relish it, easily remembering the swooshing sound made by wading through a thick layer of dry leaves.

A lone maple leaf fluttering in the light morning breeze grabs my attention, still hanging on the tree's otherwise naked limbs. "Well, aren't you tenacious?"

The explosive colors of a Caribbean sunset, from the lightest gold to the deepest red, the sunlight piercing through renders it translucent, like the most delicate of watercolors. The sight of that leaf hanging on against all odds touches something deep inside me. I whip out my camera and shoot it from different angles until I'm satisfied with a few takes.

Maybe one of them will be artsy enough to share with Olivier. I grin up to the sky, happy. Today, the blue sky stretches on forever with just a few clouds pulled by the breeze, giving it form and depth. Already, a new letter starts in my head, sharing the moment with him in the only way I can.

Olivier.

His virtual presence accompanies me everywhere now, and I no longer feel so isolated. I take special notice of every little detail so that they pour out of me on paper. I never had as deep a friendship with anyone before, nor as organic. Writing him is as natural as breathing and the highlight of my days. And nights.

I skip to the community mailbox at the end of the avenue and drop my latest epistle into the slot for the three o'clock pickup as the instruction label says.

I've never seen the mailman, as the post is no longer delivered at home, and I'm not sure if I deplore the fact or not. On one hand, the whole process feels a bit disconnected. But on the other, it feels a bit like the fairies deliver it by magic, just as I imagined as a little girl when my mom sometimes wrote me cute notes she would post... Our one and only little secret, bonding on the side.

Taking out my key, I open the cottage's assigned mail slot and sift through the usual junk mail over the recycling bin.

Do I need music lessons? Not in this lifetime. And to think I used to hate my piano lessons. I sigh, a bit of despondency seeping through my happiness.

Pity party, table for one. I toss the publicity leaflet into the trash bin.

A new pair of alpine skis—leftovers from last season—at a forty percent discount. Nope. Bin.

A new shovel? Nope. Bin.

A new snowblower? Nope. Bin.

A new... I stare at the white business envelope with my name on it. My handwritten name and address scrawled in black ink.

I squint at the messy handwriting, peering closer.

Is that Olivier's return address?

My mouth opens wide and I nearly drop my camera.

Oh. Mon. Dieu.

It is! I bounce on the balls of my feet then twirl in circles, waving the envelope in the air like a lunatic. "He wrote me back. He wrote me back."

I press it close to my chest, still under the mild shock. Okay. More like utter shock. What happened to *over my dead body*?

Wait. Is he dying?

I tear it open, half terrified something bad has happened to warrant this communication, but I'm soon laughing at his opening line.

Cambridge, October 11

Humans and their snail mail.
In the amount of time it will undoubtedly take for this to reach
you, my apologies will be long overdue. So, I came up with a few
new adages:
- ASCII and you shall receive.
- ROM wasn't built in a day.
- Byte the bullet.

You were right.
Nothing feels quite like pen and paper, both, receiving from, and writing a letter to my favorite pen pal. So, turn the page.
And here I am.

Reassured that his familiar, self-deprecating humor is *au rendez-vous* and that he's not really dying, I read slowly while trekking back to the cottage.

I went through great lengths just to secure paper, I'll have you know. Not pretty. It went something like this:

"Arrgh," I yelled, startled by a bloody, ugly ass spider scurrying behind Yann's pencil cup only to have it stare me down from across his desk.
I threw a bunch of notebooks at it from a safe distance and missed by a mile. Not my finest hour.
"And if you don't want to see your last one, you better stay put," I barked the warning to the creepy crawler, barely suppressing a shudder. "And no inviting friends over either. There will be no partying in here. Got that?" If my blood curdling scream wasn't enough of a clue, safe to say, I hate those. Spiders. Not parties.
I closed Yann's door and sealed it shut with a couple of towels,

not taking any chances. "A word to the wise is enough. Your chosen roommate kills your kind on sight, just saying. I'll get my kick elsewhere," I exhorted the creature one last time. So far, so good, we left it at that and I haven't seen it since. Not sure if we're at an impasse or an understanding but just in case, I keep an eye out for the bloodthirsty eight-legged monster out there as I write.

And now, you know my darkest fear. In writing.

I chuckle more than once, reading about what he had to do in order to steal, at great risk, one of Yann's notebooks.

I'm touched beyond words by the dozen or so pages torn from a notebook filled with his messy, loopy handwriting, and his witty commentaries.

And by the time I'm done and home once again, I know just how to underscore that momentous, historic event.

I bend my head back in laughter, enjoying the kiss of the sun and breeze.

Thirteen

P.O.

"No, really. I have to ask." Theo raises a brow, pointing at my red shirt with the neck of his beer bottle. "What happened to your usual too corny pickup line ones? Besides, you do realize you're a dude, right?"

Can't blame him for wondering. In his shoes, I'd wonder just as much. As busy as our respective schedules are, we try to meet for a couple of beers once a month in one of the pubs lining the streets in the Old Boston district, and I invariably wear one of two shirts. Either the one that says: **Computer programmers know how to use their hardware.** Or the other that says: **Computer programmers don't byte—but they nybble a bit.**

Even though they're icebreakers more than pick-up lines, really, I cringe, finding them somewhat crude now. We couldn't find time to meet last month so the question of my change in wardrobe didn't arise. But tonight I'm busted. And I know I'll have to offer some sort of explanation.

I look down at my chest, entertained by Aurèle's witty *I told you so*, all over again. "What? Don't like my upgrade?" I smooth my hand over the inscription handwritten with a silver-colored Sharpie in her neat girly cursive. A present I've only just received this week along with her latest letter.

Man v1.0, Woman v1.5.
Any questions?

"Well, get this, Theo. Are you sitting tight? It just so happens that a *girl* dared him to wear it." Yann smirks at me. Balancing his seat on two legs, he takes a long pull of his draft, daring me to contradict him.

"A *girl*?" Theo asks him, eyes narrowing in doubt, making sure he heard right.

"For your info, she didn't have to dare me to," I say pointedly to Yann. "It so happens, it's well-deserved, and I volunteered."

Jerking his head back, Theo squints at me in disbelief. "What did I miss between September and November?"

"That." Yann points at my chest. "I swear he's been wearing that shirt for the past five days, ever since he received it. Your sense of smell is seriously lacking if you can't tell. Mine has been euthanized by now. Proceed with the interrogation, counsellor. I want to know why he volunteered."

Bugger.

Yann never notices anything outside math equations, usually.

Nerves tingling, blood rushes to my cheeks, rising my body temperature to an almost uncomfortable heat, making me sweat. But for the life of me, I can't do anything else than grin like a baboon, slowly shaking my head in amazement myself.

Over the girl, not the shirt.

Irresistible. Alluring. Magnetic.

This thing is about to go viral.

So be it.

I'll just have to pray Magali won't go knocking on Aurèle's door, introducing the gang before I can go back.

I throw a bunched up napkin at Yann. "I've washed it between wearings."

He throws it back and I catch it before it hits my chest. "News flash, dude. Only washing the armpits in the kitchen sink at night doesn't count."

Theo spews beer and spit, coughing up a lung. It's a toss-up as to who's the most surprised. Me, or Theo—in his impeccable charcoal-grey suit, red power tie, and crisp white shirt—eyeing the mess he made.

He whirls to Yann with an incredulous glance before mopping the worst of it with his cocktail napkin. Is that snot mixed in there? It is. "He what?" Theo asks him, somewhat more composed.

"Sharpie writing fades over time. I'm just preserving a piece of history." I chug the rest of my German import lager.

Yann snorts, tipping his chair back. "History? More like an alien abduction. His fingers are ink stained from constantly writing in notebooks. My stolen notebooks."

Wondered how long I could get away with it. Three weeks is longer than I'd hoped, honestly. "I prefer the term *borrowed*, and it's only one, you arse. Want to do something useful? Tell me where I can get fancy writing paper close by."

Theo's eyes flicker past me to Yann and then back to me. Here it comes, in three, two...

His eyebrows go up. "Say that again?"

I lean back in my chair, folding my arms behind my head, content with the world order I just messed with. "I'm corresponding with someone special. Get used to it."

"Corresponding?" Theo repeats, dumbfounded. "As in...real pens and paper?"

I grin at him, enjoying their shock more than I should. "Wonders never cease, right?"

Yann blinks owlishly. "Wow. This is more serious than I thought."

In the silence that follows, I signal the waitress for another round and she nods, the bartender deftly opening three more bottles of dark brew from behind the bar.

"Let me get this straight." Theo leans over, crossing his arms over the dark wood table, pewter-grey eyes drilling me with his infamous *don't fuck with me* lawyerly gaze. "You haven't touched a pen that isn't digital in some way or other in what, the last ten years or so, and now—" The waitress arrives with our refills, and he falls silent until she moves away. A lawyer thing. "*You're* corresponding as in, writing letters? And loving it?"

"That about sums it up, yeah." I salute him with my bottle and drink to that. "Did you miss the part where I mentioned she's someone special?"

"Must be to pry you away from linear codes. How's Lucie taking it?" Yann asks, clearly amused.

I scratch my sparse stubble on the underside of my chin as though deep in thought. "Boys, it's all about an-ti-ci-pa-tion," I drag each syllable in a slow drawl. "Lucie gets it the same way she gets my addiction to dark chocolate." I take a swig, an irrepressible grin forming behind my bottle.

I'm having more fun than I thought with this. Man, if they could only see the stunned look stamped all over their faces. Priceless.

Theo shakes his head slowly. "Your theory about alien abduction sounds more and more plausible, man," he says to Yann.

I snort. "Hey, whatever makes you sleep better at night." I shrug one shoulder. "Besides, Lucie met Harry when I met my girl. Lucie's good." I lean back, crossing my ankle over my knee to stop it from bouncing with unspent energy. Just talking about her is enough to spike my adrenaline. I itch to be back in my room writing to Aurèle.

It's dark out. No use checking if they're connected, but I quickly check anyway. I toss my cell phone onto the table, a stab of disappointment warring with a giddy sense of relief inside my chest, giving me whiplash. At least I know she's not into the bar scene.

Theo arches a brow at me.

"Uh... What?"

"Dude, we have no idea what that means."

They stare at me.

"Aren't you on a tight schedule?" Yann scrunches up his face like it doesn't add up. "Exactly when and where did you two meet, anyway, what with you working twenty-four-seven?"

"I'm almost afraid to ask who Harry is. Yann's right. Give it to us straight. How, when, and where?" Theo asks suspiciously.

I tick off my answers on my fingers as I explain. "Harry is her laptop. By way of her laptop. Last August. Val-David." Then I brace myself, already knowing what will come next.

"Christ, P.O." Theo swears a blue streak, rubbing a hand down his face. "Please tell me you didn't hack into her computer outside of MIT?"

"Chill, counsellor. I kind of outgrew dropping viruses as an attention getter." I roll my eyes. "What am I? Fourteen? I helped her out, troubleshooting from a distance."

Theo grunts, pinching the bridge of his nose. "Define 'distance.'"

"Bloody hell, Zac and Leo were right." Yann shoves his bottle back on the worn tabletop, his chair landing back on four legs with a thud. "It's not the promise of exceptionally good coffee that got your arse over there every morning," he grumbles, his green eyes shooting daggers at me from behind his lenses. "She's the girl you blushed all over that last day, the one from C'est la Vie Café, isn't she?"

"What if she is? What's got your boxers in a twist?"

Irritation clouds his features. "Thanks a lot, man. You just cost me a day of slaving, elbows planted deep in soil, at Leo's mercy. Not to mention what Zac will ask for his favor. Damn."

"Hold on." I shift my weight, leaning over the table which wobbles a bit on the uneven floorboards. "You took a bet on this?" I narrow my eyes at him, my neck bending forward, and I don't feel an ounce of sympathy for him on this one. "And you of all people couldn't figure the odds? Imagine that," I say, my voice oozing sarcasm.

He crosses his arm over his chest, huffing. "The coffee input threw me off my math."

"Enough," Theo cuts in, his sharp, courtroom voice slicing through this cross-examination the way a surgeon cuts through flesh with surgical precision. "The better question is, why the fuck did you act like you didn't know her then if you two met last August?"

I lean back, rubbing the back of my neck, wincing. This is the reason— this right here—that I didn't want to tell them the truth. But I can't keep it a secret anymore. Not when I'm wearing her shirts and stealing paper to write her letters. I take a deep breath. "Because she doesn't know she knows me," I mumble.

"Fuck me, he's in love with a computer after all," Yann mutters.

I shoot him a glare.

"You don't say," Theo mocks, brutal sarcasm bleeding from his tone. "Care to elaborate?"

I fiddle with my pint, scrutinizing the frothy beer collar resulting from it. "She had trouble with her laptop, but she blew me off when I offered my help in person, so..."

"Oh, man." Yann whistles low. "May the source code be with you when she finds out."

Theo, elbows bent over the table, rubs his temples. "Bloody hell, man. What were you thinking?"

"What was I thinking indeed?" My hands fist on my thighs and my jaw tightens with annoyance at Theo's harping. "Shit, you guys. I was thinking that hacking is like sex. You get in. You get out. And hope you didn't leave something that can be traced back to you. Did I leave something out of your usual warnings, *counsellor?*" I spit out and then breathe through my nose, calming the hell down.

They share a look.

I loosen my fists and unclench my jaw. Seeing her on that end of the summer day all over again, I swallow to wet my throat. "It just happened, man. There she was underneath that maple tree, gorgeous as all get out, and I couldn't resist making my presence known, engaging her from a distance, and she replied, and... I took the bait; hook, line, and sinker.

"To say it didn't go according to my initial plan to get in and get the hell out is an understatement. Guilty as charged, counsellor. Sue me." In an effort to get myself back under control, I stretch my legs out and take a swig of dark lager.

"Better me than her!" Theo argues further. "Christ Almighty, P.O. If she's so shallow as to pass you up at a glance, what the fuck piqued your interest in the first place, that's what I'd like to know?"

I straighten in my seat. Resting my elbows on the table, I rub my forehead, and sigh. "I wish I could explain, but I can't."

Yann snorts.

I ignore him and look Theo in the eye. "She's more than the pretty shell that brushed me off, man. She brushes everybody off from what I've seen. And no, before you ask, she's not in a relationship, married or otherwise. I got an unexpected 'in' with her and I ran away with it. I'm her only *friend*, as far as I know, and she lives alone in the back boonies of Val-David for the next year at least. No WiFi, no tech of any kind, and no real connection to the rest of the world. There's an untold story there I don't know about yet. All I know is that she's fascinating. What she writes, her thoughts and impressions, there's a hidden depth to her I want to keep on exploring." My voice grows thick with emotion. "Aurèle just blows me away until I no longer know up from down. I have no other choice but to believe in love at first sight, like Liam and Zac before me. Everything about her calls to me, the beauty of her mind, her wit, her charm, and don't get me started on her wacky sense of humor—"

"I hope it works out for you, man, I really do," Yann interjects with a slap on my back. "What if she Googles the hell out of you? Better come clean or you're screwed solid, whacky sense of humor or not."

"No, she won't." I shake my head adamantly, crossing my fingers underneath the table just in case, nevertheless. "See, she had this no talking rule in effect and I sort of added some of my own. No Googling, no social media, no selfies. Just us, getting to know each other from the inside out without outside influences thrown in the mix."

Theo raises a disbelieving brow. "And she agreed to that?"

"In a New York minute, man." My forehead puckers. "Want to know what I think? I think that, just like me, she got judged by appearances alone more than once."

Theo frowns. "Never bothered you before, dude, and it shouldn't now, either. Send a pic, tell her who you are."

"What do you think I've been doing for the past few months? Pretending I'm someone else?" But I know what he means, and that he means well. I sigh up to the ceiling, considering it anew for a brief moment, but everything in me rejects the very idea of doing it that way. "Look, this whole damn thing snowballed on me, okay. Is it ideal? Not even close. But it's too important to mess with, so I'll work with what I've got. I'm firmly friend zoned as it is, and I'm stuck here for another five months. Until I can get back there, I'm not about to do anything to rock the boat. When I come clean, it will be face-to-face, not in a letter or a text."

"You're playing with fire, man," Theo mutters.

"Sucks to be you," Yann says in a commiserating tone of voice.

"For now. But it's just until I can go back in person, for good. By then, we'll have some eight to nine months of honest sharing between us and maybe, just maybe, my initial deception won't matter anymore."

They stare at me with no comeback for once.

I look down at my bottle, tracing a bead of condensation with my index finger. "Aurèle... Aurèle is so much more..." I say with a shit load of conviction to back it up. "She's worth risking it all if only to have one shot at her."

I lift my head. Theo's fixing me with a thoughtful gaze. "That so?"

His stern features take on a faraway look and I wonder if he's thinking of giving it a go with Anaïs, the local custom jewelry maker he briefly met last winter. But Theo being Theo, we won't know what happened there until he's ready.

Not that I have room to talk...

I blow out a heavy breath. "She's the one, man."

Theo nods in understanding, and Yann scratches his jaw as though pondering what I just said at great lengths. "Now, you do realize this is too good to pass up, and in all fairness to the previous two, we're kind of obligated to never let you hear the end of it, right?"

"Ask me if I care."

"Yep, he's done for." Theo affirms, clicking his bottle with Yann's. "Another one bites the dust."

"I'll drink to that." Yann salutes me with his bottle, a slow grin spreading on his lips. "Three out of six; those odds are getting pretty interesting."

"Looks like Éolie's long ago visions are shaping up to come true." Theo high fives Yann before turning to me. "As for you? Do what you feel you need to do." He yanks me by the shirt collar, looking me in the eye before adding drily, "Within reason. Or I'll have your ass in a sling." He releases me, his lips twitching.

I curb a snort. "Sure. Like you don't enjoy your legal trips outside corporate law. We aim to please, counsellor. Where would you be without us?"

"Bored to death by corporate law, where else?" he says, dropping the half-grin curling his mouth. I search his eyes. Interesting. His face is now impassive, not a shred of evidence left that he's jesting. He fist bumps my shoulder, effectively bringing me out of my thoughts. "Go get her, man."

"We'll have your back." Yann goes for a high five, but a new thought stops him mid-motion.

"What?" I ask warily.

"Oh, not much. Just a little something that crossed my mind that's all."

He wipes his lenses with meticulous care with the hem of his green-plaid flannel shirt before pushing them back on his nose, adjusting them with slow, calculated moves, waiting to see who'll cave in first and ask. Theo hides a grin behind his bottle, the little shit, knowing that Yann is deliberately testing the limits of my patience. It's working.

"Just say it," I hiss impatiently.

The corners of his eyes crinkle behind his thick glasses. He raises a brow. "Think ZeeMan for the Impossible will be able to contain Magali's enthusiasm once she learns?" Hell. He's having way too much fun with this, but the bloody arse is right. "In my estimate, three out of five says he won't."

"Can't you figure out better odds with your time?" I accuse, slouching back in my chair. "I'm done for if not," I mumble to myself.

I'll have to call her personally. I'm not kidding. I'm ready to implore her not to do anything. At. All.

As though reading my mind, Yann waves my phone in front of my eyes with barely suppressed mirth. "Only one way to find out, dude."

I groan out loud. "That's what I'm afraid of."

"What are you afraid of?" Theo rolls his eyes.

He's the only one who never met Magali in person so he doesn't know the half of it. Video chats are nothing less than a watered-down version of her bubbly personality, in no way doing her full justice. In person, Magali is a force to reckon with, not unlike a steamroller when she gets going. Or the Energizer Bunny. Case in point, the Complementary Alternative Medicine, or CAM for short, a prenatal clinic they're building from scratch. Full speed ahead and damn the torpedoes, as Leo's fond of saying, is totally her speed. Her only speed.

"How long has it been since you went up north, again?" I ask Theo, speed dialing Magali's number.

"Too damn long," he replies wistfully before shaking himself out of it. "I'm willing to bet the girls will think it's the most romantic shit ever once you spill the details. They'll have your back."

"Yeah, and the rest of me taken hostage too just as soon as Magali learns about it. She can't pass up a challenge. And she will see it as such, man. I know she will."

Theo raises a quizzical brow.

"In person? Magali is Zac's carbon copy, give or take a few parts." Yann chuckles low. "She only has one speed, fast forward. And never, ever, dare her, or, you know, put down a challenge before her. She'll climb Mount Everest if she has to."

"She already thinks we're all girl challenged. She's not that wrong. But need I say more?" I ask, waiting for her to pick up the line. And as outgoing and scary creative as she is, it's not too farfetched for her to knock on Aurèle's door on a daily basis, extolling whatever virtues she thinks I possess like a persistent gnat snacking on a warm-blooded mammal, until she gives in or gives out. Not that Magali isn't charm personified, but still. A wild card is a wild card, and I want to be the one telling Aurèle, face to face. It's the only shot I've got.

Theo's brow shoots up. "Oh."

"Yeah, oh."

"Allo?"

"Hey, Magali. How's everything?"

"P.O.! You sound unusually chirpy. Good. So, so good. Must be pub night over there judging by the background noise. Are you with Yann and Theo?"

"I am."

"Zac's still at the hospital or he'd demand video, I'm sure. Put me on speaker phone, and *pleease* put me out of my misery. Tell me you're calling to spill the beans on your mystery girl and that she's the one I see from time to time at the café?" she says all in one long ass breath, her specialty.

I exchange awed looks with Theo and Yann at Magali's eerie sense of timing. We all video chat twice a month or so and the subject has never once come up—until now. "How did you guess?" I ask her. "No. Never mind. I don't want to know."

Éolie possesses preternatural senses, and among other things, she gets visions from time to time. Leo is still spooked by her quintuplets comment and the ten single beds found upstairs at the farmstead. Maybe she dropped a subtle hint on Magali.

"Knew it!" Magali exclaims joyously over the line. "The farmstead team rules. Go. Us."

"Did Éolie mention seeing anything?" I ask, noncommittal, but curious as fuck now.

Éolie's still quite shy, having grown up on a scientific sailboat in remote corners of the world, sheltered from human company as an added precaution due to her unusual gifts. To my knowledge, only the guys are privy to any of it, for now. Magali hasn't witnessed any of Éolie's weird, and Éolie isn't quite ready to come forward unless it becomes obvious. She has no control over that shit, so she can't demonstrate at will. And some of that shit, like self-healing at warp speed, needs to be seen to be believed.

"Pfft. Nope. Easiest guess ever for anyone with eyes at the café on that day. From then on, wasn't very hard to see coffee wasn't the real incentive," Magali says. "Think I'll go to that café more often now that it's officially out of the closet. Want me to say 'bonjour' for you next time I see her? Oh. And, Yann? You lose," she crows triumphantly over the line. "Prepare for a day's labor at the future clinic."

"Define labor in a prenatal clinic before I go into cardiac arrest," Yann deadpans.

"Be afraid. Be very afraid."

"Yeah, about that..." I say, taking a fortifying breath while Yann recovers from a fit of coughing, strangling on a laugh, and Theo chokes on his own suppressed laughter. "You don't get to meet her. You don't get to say 'hi' in any way, shape, or form. Not until I get back to the farmstead. Got it?"

"Five months from now? Are you serious?"

"As a heart attack," I say under my breath.

"Hey, I heard that," she sputters.

"Good," I intimate. "Should keep you out of trouble."

"P.O.'s saving all the trouble for himself," Yann says.

"What?" Magali demands.

"Our boy wonder here made contact by hacking his way through her computer." Theo steeples his fingers on a slow tap, enjoying a tad too much my squirming like a worm caught on a hook. And I know just what Zac meant when he said to me, "Remember payback's a bitch," last winter and again this summer. Theo doesn't know it yet, but when his time comes—and it will—I'll be there.

"Pass the message around, will you? Aurèle doesn't know she knows me," I admit, blowing out my cheeks on a lengthy sigh. "And I'm keeping it that way until I can tell her face-to-face."

"I'm not sure I like where this is going, Byte Man." Over the ambient noise, I can hear clear through the line the mixture of astonishment and wariness in her voice as she drops my old BIA nickname. There's a short beat of silence before she adds, "Why are you keeping it from her?" Her tone is now definitely this side of suspicious and, knowing her, she's preparing to hand my ass over to me on a silver platter to match the spoon I was born with if she doesn't like my answer.

Zac really met his match on that ski slope that night, I inwardly shake my head. Which is funny in its own way. But, man. That girl. Does she ever keep us in check, and humble, whenever we steer back towards entitlement. And we do once in a while. Unknowingly, but still.

"Look, Magali, it sort of happened that way, that's all. No premeditation on my part, no intentional deceit either, I swear. Let's just say I've recently been upgraded from friendly hacker to friend, and we're corresponding the old-fashioned way by letters as such. No outside influences."

She listens quietly as I give her the details of our agreement and how it came to be. "Which translates into no befriending her behind my back, otherwise, when I come clean she'll feel betrayed times seven, and I'll never be able to dig myself out of that hole. Steer clear. I've been granted this unforeseen 'in' with her, and I'll do *anything* for a shot at Aurèle. Name your price to sit on your hands and wait out."

There's another beat of silence.

"Anything?"

"Anything."

She finally sighs. "Want to computerize the clinic in the spring out of the goodness of your heart?"

"Done."

"Done," she echoes. "And well done, under the circumstances, I'll grant you that. Letters are so, so, romantic." I hear the smile in her voice and know that all is forgiven—for now. "We've got your back, until you're back. And if you ever need pointers, just ask Éolie or me. Even if you don't, ask anyway," she says without pause.

"Will do." And just like that, I breathe easier, knowing my chances just went from average to better than average. "And, Magali? Thanks..."

"Anytime," she replies, quiet conviction ringing through. "*Ciao*, P.O. Kiss the guys for me, will you?"

I snort. "Not happening in this lifetime. That's a definite do-it-yourself thing."

She hangs up on an airy laugh.

"Boys." I bring my bottle up. "To old-fashioned wooing."

"Hear, hear," Theo toasts, clicking his with mine.

"Amen to that," Yann joins in. "Tip the scales in favor, for the rest of us, man."

"Count on me," I vow.

I'll give it my all if it's the last thing I do.

Starting with the very next item now topping my must-do list.

Fourteen

Val-David, le 12 novembre

Cher Olivier,

Guess what the post delivered today? Yes. That's right. Harriet. Yours has to be the loveliest of revenge. You've got yourself a new convert for life (and as such, are hereby upgraded to Man,v.1.1.3).

There's nothing I don't love about my new tablet and I'll totally blame you tomorrow morning for my book hangover.

I can't begin to thank you enough for the thousand and one e-books already uploaded onto it. It's the most thoughtful thing anyone has ever done for me.

The photography books, especially, are magical. The colors in high definition, mesmerizing, and the artsy black-and-white ones, leaping out of the screen with light and depth... You've singlehandedly upped the ante for me, but now I know what to aim for. And of all of them, the ones by Anne Geddes are my ab-so-lute favorites and my biggest surprise; her babies are to die for.

And speaking of dying, I'm dying of curiosity now.

I didn't even know she existed, and I researched just about every type of photography on the net. How on earth did you come up with them? Not to mention a romance shelf containing four hundred books?!! You're a man of many, many surprises. Have you read any of them? If so, what's your absolute favorite? If not, I dare you to read some! Ha.

Harry will be jealous for sure; Harriet will never leave my side, we're in total sync.

Cambridge, November 20

Chère Aurèle,

You're very welcome.

Confession time. I cheated on the babies and the romances. You have Éolie and Magali—two of my best mates' ladies—to thank for those. I'm not sure if I mentioned it before, but Liam and Éolie have the cutest identical twins, Sébastien and Nicolas. Almost four months old now. So yeah, I know what cuteness to die for looks like. They're it.

Harriet, huh? I love it.

If you think I'm intimidated by your reading challenge, bring it on. Challenge accepted.

In all fairness, though, I should warn you that as one of the six members of the Goddamn Geek Squad—better known as GGS—I thrive on knowledge and conquering new dimensions. We didn't elevate it to Geek God Status for nothing. Just remember that! ;)

Side note: You didn't comment on the movie application uploaded with a ready selection of classics, nor the music one.

Need help figuring it out? Let me know via Harry and I'll walk you through it.

Favorite movie of all times? Share yours, I'll share mine.

Favorite music? Ditto.

Hey, speaking of. Want to share some music and movie nights with me? I double dare you.

Olivier,

My favorite movie: Prince Caspian – The Chronicles of Narnia. I had this huge crush on him. Still do. So for the sake of preserving my teenaged illusions, I will (absolutely) not Google the actor behind the character at the risk of shattering my heart. I like him just the way he is. Frozen in time (and character).

See? I'm good at following our "No-Googling" rule. (Helps, of course, that I don't have any internet signal at the cottage, but hey, details.)

Music? I'm more the quiet type. I no longer have any favorites but I remember with fondness my mom listening to Joe Dassin, Jean Ferrat, Simon and Garfunkel, the Monkees and the Beatles— her guilty pleasure—while I had to endure, at the time, endless classical recitals.

No need to help me with the applications.

Confession time.

I both feel terrible and touched beyond words that you went to so, so much trouble for me. But I'm afraid I'm not much of a movie fan in my old age. I no longer watch any. I read instead, preferring by far the unparalleled and undiluted images the stories bring forth in my head. If that makes me a book snob, so be it. And truthfully, neither am I a music fan. I don't listen to any ever, nowadays. Too many forced piano lessons, I suppose, are to blame…among other things.

I concede on your double dare.

Too many books, too little time.

What's my forfeit?

Aurèle,

I'll think about your forfeit, oh cruel one, and skip music and movie nights altogether. For now. But I'll be back.

Be warned, though; my own taste in music is www. In other words, pretty much, Wild. Whacky. Whatnot. Ditto for that movie thing you seem allergic to. For now.

Did I mention I thrive on conquering new dimensions and you're one of them? No?

I wish I could write it was really no trouble at all. But I can't anymore. I'm in deep shit, now. I better start reading those romances pronto, and put my

mind where my mouth is, or in this case, my pen.

You've had this crush since 2008? Jealous doesn't even begin to describe how Prince Caspian makes me feel right now.

As for my own, all-time favorite? Let's see. I'll go with The Lord of the Rings trilogy. A classic. Guess if you shared your all-time crush, it's only fair to share mine. The elf-maiden Arwen Undómiel gets my vote, hands down. So who am I to talk, really? She made my ten-year-old heart skip too many beats. How old were you in 2001 and what were you doing at the time?

> Olivier,
>
> Let's see. 2001? Seven years old. Living the curse of the über-upper-class only child. Ballet lessons. Piano lessons. Ski lessons. Horseback riding lessons—English of course, hunt seat. Diction and etiquette lessons. Highly exclusive, Westmount Prep School. And social events sandwiched in between. And, you know, some more of the three dreaded P's—Prestige, Power, Privilege—related activities. The usual, busy, busy schedule, performing every minute of every day.
>
> No excuses. Only results.
>
> Guess you know the drill, Tisserot. You went to Berlinger and belong to a dynasty even more dynastic than mine ever was.
>
> Yet, you're the single most, nicest person I know. What saved you?

Aurèle,

Yep. I know the drill. Contrary to popular belief, über-rich kids don't have it any better.

What saved me, you ask?

Boarding school, funnily enough, where the six of us guys embraced the "outcast" status for the duration—and a friendship with each other. Unbreakable bonds forged in the crucible by thirteen years shared in close captivity (aka the same bedroom). Which, by all rights, should have been a one-way ticket to the loony bin.

Want to know the secret sauce? Instead, Liam saved all of our sanities with his bedtime stories when he joined our ranks at seven years of age. His *Tales from the Enchanted Forest of Laure* sent us away on nightly quests for freedom in search of "Home" and the "Normal Kingdom." We were Knights of the Laure and had a grand time of it, cultivating our otherness. As a world-renowned Sci-Fi Fantasy author now, Liam's fantastical imagination is put to good use. But we were, dare I say, his first guinea pigs (yes, I went there). Not to mention, his prototypes. You really don't want to read some of our earlier versions.

You mentioned attending Meier for a year and a half. You didn't like the tiny bit of respite from the pressure cooker of your family?

> Olivier,
>
> No, it isn't that. I liked it well enough, I suppose. Over winter break on my second year of high school, my mom and I contracted a rare and virulent form of meningitis on a return trip from Southeast Asia on a commercial flight. My father, and his private jet, had stayed behind to conclude his business, no longer requiring us as props. We thought it was fatigue from jetlag at first. When we finally consulted, we were quarantined at the hospital for weeks. My mom didn't make it. And I almost didn't; took me quite a while to recover and to this day, I still have some lingering effects. I sort of got my respite there though. I was homeschooled (read: I tutored myself for the most part) from then on, mostly ignored. My father's heart (surprisingly, he had one...) gave up on him (not so surprisingly) close to eight months ago, and I renounced the succession, handing it instead to his handpicked son-in-law specifically groomed to his specs. I transferred all the shares into Laurent's name putting that life firmly behind me. He's welcome to it.
>
> Sometimes, I feel like a fairy tale character awakened after a long sleep. You can say I'm on a self-discovery journey in my small cottage in the woods by the lake, loving every minute of it. For the first time, I'm meeting me. The real me. And I met you along the way. You're more than just a best friend. You're the single most

very best friend a girl could ever have or wish for.

Thank you.

PS: Speaking of "friends" and "best," yours wouldn't happen to be Liam O'Shea by any chance? The author of Eiloe? If you hear a squeal, then a croak, it's me. Fangirling!

Aurèle,

I'm so sorry about your mom. I know you wrote earlier on you weren't all that close growing up, but still, it devastates me you went through this. As for you catching meningitis as well, I'd like to say I'm sorry, but I can't. It brought you, the real you, forth. We would have never met otherwise. And for that, I'll always be grateful. You're one beautiful soul, Aurèle. Special. Precious. Don't let anyone say differently.

PS: Will I earn brownie points if I confirm that, yes, my bud Liam is Liam O'Shea?

> Olivier,
>
> Okay, I'm done squealing. My two feet firmly planted back on the floor, staying put and no longer dancing on air. For now. You, sir, have earned all-you-can-eat brownies forevermore. But it's not for knowing Liam O'Shea. It's for knowing you. I'm privileged. My favorite word is your name, Olivier.

Aurèle,

I didn't really know what happiness was before. Not like this. Having you in my life makes me happy. Really happy. There are so many quotes from those silly romances that resonate within me, right now, when I think of you, it's not even funny. Happy is addictive as hell; I think I'm up to one book a night (and I have the squinty, red eyes and loony grin to prove it). You?

> Olivier,
>
> Then, we're neck-to-neck on the book hangovers. Or, maybe, it's heartbeat-to-heartbeat? Harry and I browsed the net the other day at C'est la Vie—waiting to see if you could make it and

connect—and we came across this line on a popular quotes website that we wanted to share: "I want to be your favorite hello and your hardest goodbye."

Aurèle,

You're my favorite hello when I wake and pick up where I left off the previous night, and my hardest goodbye when I turn off the light. And since we're sharing quotes from the net… I'd be happy to wear this one on a tee:

"If I could turn back the clock, I'd find you earlier so I could love you longer."

I love you, Aurèle.

Irrevocably love you.

Wait for me. I'm coming for you.

Aurèle,

Cambridge, March 22

I couldn't sleep last night, my previous letter replaying in my head on a loop.

See, I went for a long walk and dropped it in the mail before I fully realized what I'd done.

I never meant for you to first learn about how I really feel and all that you mean to me that way.

By letter.

I meant to wait until we met in person. For real. Mid-May. Did I mention I'm coming for you at the end of my last semester? If not, consider it done. I'll be there. That's a promise.

Maybe you'll receive both letters simultaneously.

A guy can hope.

Last night, impatient as all hell, too high on life, I sealed that envelope and dropped it in the mail (before I lost my nerve, I suppose). Even knowing deep down that it sealed my fate much too soon…

Guess there's no turning back now.

Be warned. I won't take back those words. They're pulsing into my heartbeats on their way to you.

Current status: Friends. Upgrading now. Please wait.

I need to tell you something in person. Face-to-face.

Please call and we'll set up a time for a video chat. 888.321.9876.

It's dawn. And I only want three things:

See you.

Hug you.

Kiss you.

No, I lie.

Deep down, I really only want one thing:

Love you.

Aurèle,

Cambridge, March 27

Not one word from you. It's been five days from hell.

Where are you?

Please, just tell me you're okay.

Call me at 888.321.9876, day or night. I'm waiting with my phone in my hand until I know you're okay.

Aurèle,

Express Post. Cambridge, March 29

Another two days in hell, Aurèle. You've got to have received my previous letters by now.

I love you. I won't unsay it. I won't say it enough.

If you need space, all you need to do is tell me and I'll stop.

Aurèle,

Express Post. Cambridge, March 30

I never meant to make you feel uncomfortable.

I will never, ever, pressure you if that's what you're worried about. And if it's all you have to give, you can just be my friend. My best friend. I'll take it...

If you won't call, please connect Harry and confirm you're okay. Just, please. I'm worried.

Aurèle,

Express Post. Cambridge, March 31

Remember music and movie nights you bypassed? Remember that you owed me?

Here's your forfeit.

Dial 888.321.9876.

I need to hear your voice. Bad.

Aurèle,

Express Post. Cambridge, April 3

My heart is still beating so I know that you're alive. Just confirm that you're well. Please.

If I erred, cut me some slack. It's all I ask.

But I'm not losing you over this. Do you hear me?

Fifteen

P.O.

Three hours after dropping at the post office my latest "express" plea to Aurèle finds me dragging my hands through my hair, resisting the urge to pull it all out. By my estimation, the tracking number on this one should be up and running by the time I'm out of here. Not that I'm obsessing or anything. Hell no. I'm way beyond that.

Sitting kitty-corner from me, Professor Abbasi, my dissertation supervisor, scrolls down Lucie's screen, commenting on some finer points of presentation I can't make heads or tails of. His lips move, but all I can hear are garbled words, not unlike holding a water polo strategizing session under water.

I bounce my knee while Abbasi triangulates lines of code on his notepad, double-checking mine, but even that doesn't hold my interest. One more hour to go before I can get out of here and check my mailbox. Again.

Suddenly, Lucie blares an air horn alert in the quiet of the room, startling us both.

My heart skips a few beats.

Harry.

Of course, Harry's connected for the first time in thirteen days, eight hours, twenty-two minutes, thirty-six seconds, when I'm in the middle of my appointment.

Correction. Thirteen days, eight hours, twenty-two minutes, forty-two seconds, and counting. Not that I am. But Lucie does with clockwork precision, doing the math on a loop, the widget preventing my useless ruminations.

My fingers itch to take over Lucie, right here, right now.

Hands fisting on my thighs, my gaze lands on my chest.

CAPS LOCK – Preventing Login Since 1980.

How ironic that I chose that shirt today, I can't help but think, considering caps lock has nothing on my current situation right now.

Abbasi squints at the emergency lights flashing in the middle of my screen, then raises a quizzical brow at me. "Mister Tisserot?" He clears his throat, readjusting his black and red polka dots bow tie. "Nice attempt at humor, but I fear you're not putting your *usual* focus into this meeting."

My pulse picks up, blood swishing in my ears.

"Professor Abbasi, I fear you're right." I unceremoniously flip Lucie's lid close, startling him just enough to cause him to jerk his hands out of the way, saving his fingers from a knuckle rap.

"Mister Tisserot...?"

"I need to take care of this," I say unapologetic, not waiting for his reply. My chair scrapes the floor as I shove away from the desk, uncaring if I'm being rude.

Thirteen days in hell will do that.

I step outside Professor Abbasi's office, my heartbeat in my throat, checking on my phone to see if Harry's still connected. Green dot. I send her a chat request and hold my breath.

I lean back on the wall, hands on my knees. I take a deep breath in. A deep exhale out.

And wait.

And wait.

And with a final, blinking light, my bloody phone dies on me. And I know Lucie's almost out of power herself.

"Holy fucking hell," I mutter. "What am I doing wasting time?" I run down the faculty corridor while wrestling with my coat and struggling to hang onto Lucie at the same time.

Emerging onto the landing, I dodge a few comrades hanging out in the stairwell.

I fumble through my bag and pull out Lucie. I power her up while I walk and send Aurèle another chat request, but it's not easy balancing my laptop without falling flat on my ass as I fly down the stairs.

Stepping out onto the sun-drenched sidewalk, I wonder if I'll make it in one piece to the nearest coffee shop, Bean Me Up, a Star Trek-themed coffee shop across the street—a caffeine haven like none other, catering to MIT geeks by offering electrical plugs every two feet. The closest place I can get to from here while ensuring Lucie will not die on me during the brief window I now have to reach out to Aurèle.

As I wait for her reply, I pray that she is ready to talk. And that she hasn't changed her mind.

Sixteen

AURÈLE

I really don't know why I thought it would be easier to do it down here, at the village mailbox. From my table at C'est la Vie, I stare across the street at the post office awning and I know I've been lying to myself. I want to take back the four Express Post letters I have just returned to him unopened.

How many more will it take?

I blow out a choppy breath and wipe excess moisture threatening to overspill at the corner of my eyes.

How much more can I take is the better question!

I blink at my screen, processing.

My heart beats erratically.

Olivier.

My fingers shake and it's unclear if it's from hunger or Olivier's chat request that's just popped up. By now, probably both.

A few black spots dance before my eyes.

It was supposed to be safe for me to come out. I timed it perfectly. What's he doing requesting a chat in the middle of his weekly appointment with his thesis supervisor?

My chest hollows out as I click on *access denied*, and click on *always,* blocking him for all eternity.

The bite of basil pesto and parmesan chicken panini I force myself to take sticks in my throat. I chew, and chew, but I can't swallow the food past the rock scraping my throat. My churning stomach, not faring any better, gives new meaning to rock bottom.

Trying not to gag, I discreetly unload the disgusting, lumpy mess into my napkin. C'est la Vie Café's specialty sandwich is no longer so appealing which is saying something after some eleven days of surviving on canned soup, holed up at the cottage.

I don't think I ever felt that overwhelming degree of wretched misery before, not even the interminable year and a half following my illness.

My heart's bleeding raw, and I wish I knew how to stop the hemorrhage. But what's the cure for a ripped-out heart when you're the one tearing it apart, one jagged piece at a time?

At least I got up this morning wanting to research website design templates. Eventually, I'd like to build one for an online gallery I've been thinking about and upload the pictures I've taken deemed worthy of such. Or that I will take, eventually worthy of such.

Olivier would get it, encouraging me along, I can't help but think.

Olivier.

I stare at my screen with unseeing eyes.

Not going there, Aurèle. You're here. On a date with Harry, and only Harry. It's a start. Progress. Keep to your resolution and purge temptation.

Do it. Now.

I click on my secondary Gmail account and grow wide-eyed as a huge bundle of incoming emails pile up before my eyes.

I rub my chest with one hand and absently right my thick, sage-green sweater with the other—its boat-neck collar, much too wide, keeps on falling over one or the other shoulder every time I lean over my keyboard. It's annoying. Even my fleece-lined grey leggings are hanging loose on my frame. All of my clothes are.

At this rate, I'll disappear into nothing before another eleven days goes by. Just like my deleted items.

Where do deleted emails go?

Olivier would know.

Olivier.

I say under my breath, "I don't know how to make you go away."

The fleeting image of the handsome stranger's face from last summer flits through my mind, his ghostly presence haunting C'est la Vie just as Olivier does Harry.

My throat tightens and I swallow the lump of emotion clogging me down as my fingers hover over my mouse pad, ready to close the app after deleting all twenty-six new emails unread.

My eyes water, wanting them back in my inbox the moment they're gone.

I take a shaky breath.

My unruly fingers click without permission on my email draft instead.

It's official.

I'm a masochist.

First drafted ten days ago, I kept deleting passages and adding to it along the way as I received one heart-wrenching letter after the other, breaking my heart just a bit more, one impossible request at a time.

I read over my unsent email for the hundredth time since receiving Olivier's letter, acknowledging out loud what I couldn't bring myself to admit.

I love you.

Irrevocably love you.

I could recite by heart all of his letters, each sentence etched on my soul for all eternity.

I wonder for the thousandth time if the clean break will ever stop hurting so much, or if I'll ever stop wishing for something that cannot be.

On my screen, the draft mocks me.

I can't delete it.

I can't send it.

I can't stop secretly wishing I had the guts to—even knowing that Olivier would, in all likelihood, sacrifice his shot at normal and happiness with someone else if I gave him the chance, and that it would kill me.

I resolutely shut the mail app and land on Harry's desktop background, the very first tee picture Olivier sent me. **COMMAND: A suggestion made to a computer.**

Only, now, it no longer brings a smile to my lips. I'll need to change it for something else.

A forlorn sigh escapes my lips as I quickly glance up from Harry, blinking my tears away. I hastily wipe the corner of my eyes with my fingertips before they spill over, the overflow of emotion too much.

My eyes meet the barista's. A guilty reflex I don't normally indulge in. And this is why. I'm caught like the proverbial deer in the headlights.

Clément, as his name tag proclaims, immediately comes my way, a frown etching on his face as he eyes my barely touched plate.

No no no no, I inwardly chant in the vain hope of warding him off. He's a talkative one, always trying to bring me out of my reserve by starting one-sided conversations over the counter. I never engage, always cutting him short with tight-lipped smiles and nods. And not for the reason he thinks. Well, maybe a bit of that too. Fortunately for me, the lanky guy acts pretty much the same towards every patron or he would definitely make me uncomfortable with his unwanted attentions and I'd have to stop coming here and secure another place.

But I like it here. It's where Harry and I met Olivier. And the stranger whose face is now a placeholder for him when I imagine his looks whether I like it or not.

My shoulders slump, discouraged by my wayward thoughts.

"It's not to your liking?" I read on Clément's lips, more or less interpreting. "Want something else?"

"No. Everything's perfect, *merci*." I fib, hastily focusing all of my attention back on the screen.

I pull out a web browser and get busy.

Too busy to talk.

Too busy to eat.

Too busy to think.

Too busy to keep falling in love.

Seventeen

P.O.

Access denied.

"H oly fucking shit," I curse below my breath, gripping two handfuls of hair.

In what parallel universe am I?

She blocked me.

Knife meets chest.

My heart squeezes so tight I think it might stop beating. For the barest of second, I don't care if it does.

I shift in my seat and lean forward to rest my forearms on my thighs. The background noise, the hustle and bustle of the busy café, everything recedes, leaving only one thought churning in my head.

What the bloody everlasting hell happened to make her shut me out like this?

I rest back on the chair and clench my jaw, a muscle contracting and releasing under my stubble-covered flesh.

I drum my fingers on the table, my bouncing knee rattling Lucie and my cup. My nerves are shot and I try to make sense of something that makes no sense to me. I know I was a little impulsive, but every vibe I got from her in every letter she sent made me feel like she might reciprocate my feelings. I'd never been more wrong, apparently. Her radio silence was just about killing me. But I also can't walk away without some sort of explanation.

I rake a flustered hand through my hair and then start typing codes into Lucie. Desperate times call for desperate measures. "Something's not right, Harry, and you better spill."

The notion that Theo will, no doubt, want to murder me for this decidedly stalkerish move flashes through my mind. "You'll have to stand in line, Theo," I mutter. "*This* might kill me first."

I stare at her screen, uncomprehending, my stomach bottoming out as I watch what she's currently doing on her end.

What the fuck...?

She's systematically deleting all twenty-six new emails, sight unseen.

I feel as though she just slapped me, right before delivering a sucker punch to my gut.

I am numb.

And once the initial shock begins to fade, I see red all of a sudden, my blood running molten like I swallowed a mouthful of hot coals.

"Oh, Aurèle. Don't you know some rules are meant to be broken?" I huff out some of the frustration that's boxed up inside as I prepare to blow up her no talking rule.

My head pounding, my pulse racing in my throat, my fingers fly over the keys as I encrypt furiously.

She'll never know what hit her when this little two-way video chat pops up full screen and she won't be able to block me out anymore.

If she's disregarding every murmuring of my heart and soul, she's going to do it to my goddamn face. "Then, and only then—" I freeze mid-rant.

On screen, she's pulled up an email she drafted dating back ten days ago, and just like that...

My heart forgets to beat.

My lungs forget to breathe.

My mind forgets everything else.

I draw a blank, blown away.

To:P.O.youvegottobejoking@gmail.com
Subject:Leave me be. For your own sake as well as mine...

Olivier,
I am so sorry.
I knew this would come. I ignored it too long, liking it too much.
Mea culpa a thousand times over. If only...
No. I can't do this to you.
I can't talk to you over the phone ever.
I can't write to you again.
I can't meet with you.
I'm not who you think I am.
I wish.
Lost in a world quilted by silence is who I am.
A world in which I remember the sounds of life, echoes of the
distant past.
A world in which I was whole; perfect for a short while.
A world now passing me by, soundlessly.
I've fallen in love with you.
Forgive me. I didn't mean to.

Operating on autopilot, I delve a bit further into Harry's entrails, and he yields the following gems. This file was last modified three days ago, on March 31st at ten sixteen p.m., and has been modified multiple times a day, every day since.

This time, she closes the app without modifying so much as a comma. And without sending it, either.

I lean back in my chair, pulling at my hair. Christ, she even has the very first tee pic I sent her set up as Harry's background.

I stare at her blinking cursor, unblinking, for who knows how long.

My thoughts spin round, and round, like test-tubes stuck in a centrifuge.

I shake myself out of my trance when she starts to browse the net, searching for website design templates with a newfound zeal, zipping from one site to the other. She's interested in setting up a gallery website?

"Go for it." I inwardly cheer, the ghost of a smile curling on my lips. But then again, with no internet where she currently lives...

My grin fades. *Shit, is she moving out?*

I scrub my hand over my face, trying to think clearly.

Nothing adds up.

But her, *I've fallen in love with you. I didn't mean to* echoes back at me. The words swirl in my mind in an endless loop, dizzying me, leaving my heart stewing like a bad martini, both shaken and stirred.

I didn't mean to. What the hell does that even mean?

This shit never happens in romance novels. Love happens. Not regrets.

Well, don't I feel special.

Working in the background so she can't see me, I dig up her draft file and upload a copy onto Lucie, rereading it one, two, five times, not any closer to understanding. To me, she's perfect as she is.

Why, then, clip our wings before we even had a chance to soar?

Frustrated and no closer to an answer, I shove my coffee cup aside, liquid spilling over the rim. Who needs coffee when you're dying inside?

I'm not who you think I am, snags at my consciousness. What does that mean? Did she lie this whole time? Is she really living up North full time or is it just a weekend retreat? Is she a bored Westmount socialite, then, playing a sick game of make the geek fall in love and see what happens when his legs are kicked out from under him? Is she really on her own, her father dead? Single? Did she run away, hiding from an even greater, abusive relationship? Having to keep quiet?

So many questions ricochet in my mind like a ball flipped left and right inside a pinball machine with all the bells and whistles, I can hardly wrap my head around them.

My gaze strays back to the unsent email, landing on the words:

I've fallen in love with you.
Forgive me.

And now, they're all I see.

My heart gallops into a fumbled sprint.

Maybe it's all those romances I've read so far. Maybe it's a brand-new insight. Who knows? The only thing I know for sure is that out of the chaos of my jumbled thoughts, a single one emerges, over and again.

Love will prevail.

"Fuck it," I declare out loud, uncaring of the weird looks I earn from the two dudes sitting at the café tables on either side of me.

I'm on a mission.

I'm not who you think I am, either, Aurèle, and you're about to find out I meant to fall in love with you.

Irrevocably.

Leo picks up on the first ring. "P.O.? What's up, man. Any news from Aurèle?"

"Leo, I need a favor," I say in earnest while confirming my ticket online. "Can one of you drop Volvo Number Three at Mont-Tremblant Airport?"

"Now?"

"Now."

"On it." He drops the call, my bud knowing that now is not the time for lengthy explanations.

Now is the time to go get the girl.

And I intend to.

Eighteen

P.O.

I cut the engine, my gaze sweeping over Aurèle's place.

At a glance, built on three feet high stilts, the blue and white cottage appears smaller than I imagined it would be against the scenery of forest and cliffs backlit from the last of the golden hour.

The shoveled pathways, the white column of smoke coming out of the chimney, and the single pair of snowshoes sticking out of the snow bank lining the front balcony are sure signs that at least one person lives here.

Aurèle.

So she wasn't lying about that at least.

It seems as if all the months of need distill to this one moment.

My nerves fire up in a frenzy with a desire that sings and a fear that stings.

I palm the keys and click the lock, climbing out of the car into the frosty late-afternoon air.

My entire being stalls in front of the car door, my mind focused on Aurèle.

Bracing my gloved hands on the silver Volvo's rooftop edge, I look to the sky for some kind of strength. The setting sun turns the puffy clouds a bright, opalescent pink.

I inhale deeply, letting the serenity of the place seep through my soul until I get a firm grip on my emotions.

This is it.

My breath fans out.

I shove away from the car, squaring my shoulders.

Moment of truth.

Blowing out my cheeks, I flex my fingers.

I've got this.

I round the front of the car and with each step feel slivers of that control stripping away.

My heart jackhammers in my chest, and my breath skips.

Suddenly, I'm no longer so sure what I should do when she answers the door. I know what I'd like to do... Kiss her until the world ceases to exist and there are no longer any questions in her mind that we belong together. But as far as what I *should* do? The hell if I know.

Rather than think it out, I rap my knuckles on the wooden door and stuff my hands in my pockets.

Agonizingly long minutes stretch by without any movements from inside.

I knock louder and wait, my hands bracketing the doorframe, bowing my head, listening.

Nothing.

Not a sound ripples through the silence muffling the cottage's snowy surroundings except for the haphazard rhythm of my heartbeat ringing in my ears.

I dismiss one possible reason after the other.

Sleeping in? At five something in the early evening, not likely.

Napping in front of the fire? I knocked loud enough and long enough to wake the dead.

Out for a walk? There's no evidence of a missing pair of snowshoes and without them? In three to four feet of snow, still? It would leave a trace the size of a canyon. And I hope to hell she knows better than to walk down to the village at this hour. Not with snow banks still more than twice her height and the crepuscular sun rays limiting visibility. Not to mention, in less than half an hour it will be pitch black up here, as in I won't even see my own fingers if I wave them in front of my face.

Headphones on, listening to music? Yeah, well. Music's not really her thing now, is it? At least, according to her letters—

Wait.

Now that I think of it, wasn't she wearing earbuds like a second skin last summer? *Christ.* I brush a hand over my mouth, blowing out a breath. That little fact didn't cross my mind once while reading about her emphatic dislike of music at the time, but am I unraveling the first of her lies, here?

With that possibility in mind, I hop over the railing and sink balls deep in melting snow. I trudge my way through to the nearest window, uncaring of the wet, biting cold soaking up my jeans.

This shit is cold as fuck and my jeans are freezing up solid, never mind that the beginning of April brings out tulips in Boston right now. I hope to hell my dick recovers and finds its way back out from who knows where it went hiding. I don't exactly relish the thought of doing the penguin walk in front of Aurèle, among other things.

But that's what I get for hopping on the first flight to Tremblant from MIT.

I wedge myself between the wall and the arched window frame, just wanting a quick peek inside, unwilling to freak the hell out of her if indeed she's there and we come face-to-face.

If not, I'll build an igloo and camp in front of her door if that's what it takes—though not before I suit up with my negative-fifty winter gear stowed in the station wagon's cargo bay, thanks to Éolie. And with my balls shrivelled up to nothing, guess it's something I should have had the foresight to wear from the airport.

"But then again, it's not like I anticipated being kept outside."

I swallow to wet my throat, all my current discomforts suddenly forgotten at all the possibilities opening up.

I peek inside and inhale sharply.

Aurèle.

She's there.

Nothing else registers, all of my senses overcome by the sight of her after so many months.

Right here, right now, she takes my breath away and I've never felt more alive.

The last rays of sunlight from the window pool around her. Haloed by the low light, she's more than beautiful, she's ethereal.

Meant to be.

Mine.

I feel it to the very marrow of my bones and the innermost recesses of my soul like a renewed vow, and I let myself free fall deeper into it.

Flattening my back against the wall, I exhale slowly to calm my racing heart. I need to regain focus, here, and fire up what's left of my frozen brain cells.

I take another peek.

No hallucination.

Aurèle's still sitting on the painted wood plank floor in front of the fireplace, flanked by two cozy armchairs overstuffed with cushions, her exquisite face shown in semi-profile. Like in most chalets up here, the main floor is one square room with no wall divisions between kitchen and living room. I can see right through the back windows to the small lake beyond. The shadow of the flames dapples the cream-colored walls and the scene exudes nothing less than a serene and pastoral feel.

I lean away. My reflection looks back at me, transparent as a ghost.

I frown. Something doesn't add up here.

My nose presses up to the glass, my warm breath fogging up the window. I wipe it clean and cup my hands on my forehead, squinting as I take in the scene in more details.

Wearing a faraway look on her face, seemingly without a care in the world, Aurèle's gaze is fixated on the fire. Her sylphlike arms encircle her drawn up knees with her chin resting on top as she quietly sits on the floor in her long thermal underwear less than twenty feet away from the front door and where I stand.

No bloody headphones anywhere to be seen, no TV, no blasting music to be heard throughout. Wouldn't she at least check who's knocking at the door through the window or something?

What the hell?

I squeeze my eyes shut a brief instant, knowing where this goes.

I turn away, the back of my head thudding on the wall.

Jesus Christ.

She's truly disregarding me. Disregarding me just the same as last summer while I freeze my balls out, bleeding my heart out.

I turn back to the window, slowly bracing one hand against the frame.

It's of no matter that my mind knows she doesn't know she knows me like no one else does. Déjà vu flares in my heart with a vengeance.

I can't get past the giant knot in my throat, the crippling sensation of complete paralysis.

And then my temper kicks in.

I didn't come all the way here to be dismissed so summarily without a single word exchanged. Not after all that we shared, heart-to-heart, in our letters.

No.

Just no.

I start banging on the window to make my presence known in what Theo would call his I'm-not-going-anywhere-might-as-well-give-in manner.

No reaction.

None. At. All.

What the fuck?

I tug my beanie down my brow with both hands and shove it back up. I shake my head slowly, incredulous.

Wow. Just wow.

I've got to give it to her, she's good.

Not that I wanted her to jump out of her skin, but at the very least, I would have turned around to see what the new commotion's all about if only to flip me off. Not even a shoulder twitch.

How in the bloody hell can she stay this stoic?

How is she so cold in person and so warm on the page?

I scowl and blow into my freezing hands before bracing them back on the window sill.

"Two can play at this stubborn crap, Aurèle."

I bang three more times for good measure, a tad beyond frustrated now.

To add insult to injury, for an answer, Aurèle stretches from side to side, arms above her head, before extending legs that go on forever, roasting the soles of her thick woollen socks in front of the bloody roaring fire, wiggling her toes.

I hit the window with my palm, irked to no end.

Jesus Christ! Is she deaf or something?!!

I freeze, except for my gaze, which travels over her in a burning sweep.

An involuntary shiver that has nothing to do with my slow transformation into Olaf slithers up my spine. Movies she no longer watches, music she no longer listens to…

A dark something teasing at the edge of my consciousness clicks into place and my blood runs cold.

Oh, fucking hell.

Deaf.

Aurèle's deaf.

For a moment, I don't breathe. I can't. The shock knocks the air right out my lungs.

I fall to my knees, my hands, chaffed by the cold and raw pounding, coming up to cover my face. The sting in my eyes overwhelms me as I recite in the lengthening shadows, word for word, what makes terrible sense to me now.

Lost in a world quilted by silence is who I am.
A world in which I remember the sounds of life, echoes of
the
distant past.
A world in which I was whole; perfect for a short while.
A world passing me by, soundlessly.

Holy Mother of God.

She wasn't being alliterative nor figurative but horrifyingly literal. I swallow a lump the size of the Matterhorn.

"Aurèle… You never brushed me off, did you?" I ask through a quiet rasp, looking her over. *You just didn't hear me. Or anyone…*

Her shoulders heave while her fingers fiddle with a loose thread on the toe of one of her socks. Is she crying?

I slap my palms on the glass, tempted to smash my fist right through.

Fuck me.

Pulling myself up on the balcony, I try the front door, rattling the knob, but it's locked tight.

I hang my head, my heart cut into ribbons.

Going back to the window, I feel so helpless outside, looking in. From where she sits, if she doesn't turn around, there's just no way to make my presence known if she can't hear me.

"Goddammit it all. Why didn't you just say so?" I shout all of my disquiet into the night over the unnecessary pain and frustrations inflicted.

But even as I yell out, my heart breaks for her.

A few early stars wink to life in the twilight. My lingering gaze absently takes in the frigid beauty of the night. The grounds transformed into an ice kingdom, dark but already sparkling in the dawning moonlight; hoarfrost coating the frozen trees like diamond dust.

I drop my forehead on the windowpane, the opening lines of her unsent email replaying in my mind in a whole new light.

> **I'm so sorry.**
> **I knew this would come. I ignored it too long, liking it too much.**
> **Mea culpa a thousand times over. If only...**
> **No. I can't do this to you.**

I feel as tall as a two-inch worm and as slimy as an amoeba for having thought even if briefly that she may have possibly played me.

My fingers press down so hard on the glass I'm afraid it will shatter.

There's so much implied in her letters that makes perfect sense now that I can read between the lines. All of that garbage about her father's disapproval and the way he treated her... If the bastard was still alive, I'd probably kill him myself for the systemic crushing of her true spirit and his almost succeeding.

I scrape my frozen fingertips over the window pane, wanting to scratch my way inside, wanting nothing more than to envelop her in my arms, letting her know that she's safe with me.

My fingers splay on the glass. "Come on, turn around, Aurèle. I'm right behind you."

My hungry gaze follows her every move, hypnotized. If I were a moth, I'd be toast by now.

She takes a few deep breaths before shuffling to the kitchen in the back without once looking over her shoulder.

At me.

Silhouetted in her front window like a serial killer stalking his next prey.

Bloody hell.

My heart pounds out of my chest with the sudden realization that, Christ, with her disability? She's so fucking vulnerable out here in the woods by herself.

I brace one hand on the house for support, bowing my head. Black spots dance in front of my eyes, reminding me that oxygen's not optional, but I can't seem to catch my breath, my lungs seized in a vise.

I know she has something to prove to herself but holy freaking hell. If I was a bit worried before, I'm a hell of a lot worried now, and not just by the bloody awful possibilities my fevered brain conjures up, either, but by everyday concerns.

Only two things keep my worry level less than pure panic—the reminder that she's been on her own for a few months and obviously lived to tell the tale, and the fact we always leave the doors unlocked at the old farmstead with no life-threatening consequences thus far.

I kick snow with the tip of my engineer boots, the leather soaked through, no longer feeling my feet, uncaring of it.

So now what? Convince her to move with the gang into the farmhouse?

Well, that's an awesome idea, man, especially considering you don't even have a foot in the door yet. Speaking of which…

I snap my neck back up so quickly that I give myself a head rush. And what I see gives me another.

From the open doorway, Aurèle is bent over, gathering a couple of fire logs from the covered porch, throwing them behind her on the kitchen floor before repeating the process all over again.

All rational thought escapes me and I turn and hit the trail, jogging around the side of her house.

The packed snow—sparkling like a lost constellation under the moonlight—crunches hard under my boots as I storm around to the back of the small cottage. My ears fine tuned to the creak of the door discreetly closing, I bound up the three steps and before she has the chance to lock it, I fling it open.

Nineteen

P.O.

I stand quickly, stamping the melting slush off my boots.

Looking up with a surprised yelp, Aurèle drops the logs she just picked up off the floor, coming face-to-face with me, her hands coming up to cover her mouth.

The two tear tracks wetting down her cheeks kill me.

Sapphire-blue eyes round with shock pierce me through, her bewildered gaze moving over my face. "You?" she murmurs so low her voice is barely audible.

She stares at me, blinking, unsure she's seeing right as though she recognizes me. *Does she?* To my knowledge, she never did spare me a glance. Well, maybe once, in passing, through C'est la Vie's bay window, but the contact was so brief I might as well have imagined it. And it certainly didn't earn me a second one.

Flying by the seat of my pants, I spread my arms wide and simply say, "Me."

Her disbelieving gaze roams down my body, burning a trail, singeing my heart. Her vivid blue eyes flash with something, maybe desire for all I know— or more aptly, wish—but she quickly masks it.

Channeling my inner Zac, I arch a telltale brow. A deep flush steals over her face. I could crow in equal relief and satisfaction that she'd been looking and liked what she saw.

We stare for the longest time or maybe, the shortest.

I want to kiss her so badly my lips throb.

My hands slide into my pockets—less I make an untimely grab for her—and I lean back on my heels.

Her eyes drop to the column of my throat, flashing with some unreadable emotion, and then flit back up to mine. Confusion flickers over her face. "Who are you and what are you doing here?" Aurèle asks with her nose all scrunched up, all sorts of adorable, ruining me a little more.

Holding her gaze steady, I say slowly, carefully, "You know who I am even more than I do." Thick emotion clogs my voice until it reaches a breaking point. "I'm Olivier."

"Olivier?" She blinks in surprise, gawking. "But, last summer I saw you at…" She shakes her head in slow disbelief. "How…?"

I rub my palm over my mouth, lifting my chin and dragging my hand down the stubble that's getting way too thick, to my throat that feels way too tight.

Time for me to come clean.

I shrug my coat off and look around for something to write on.

Twenty

AURÈLE

"You know who I am even more than I do."

I do?

I frown in concentration, staring at his enticing lips much too hard as he says, "I'm Olivier."

Eyes bugging out of my head, my stomach nearly drops to the floor for the third time in as many minutes.

The cute guy from the café is *Olivier*? And just like Alice in Wonderland, thrown into a new reality, so am I on the way to something new and foreign and dangerous.

Still in shock, I gawk as he shakes snow off his wet jeans, emphasizing his trim waist and...

Oh, so not going there, Aurèle.

But my traitorous eyes stay welded to his form as he shrugs off his leather bomber jacket. The reveal of a wrinkled, long-sleeved, cobalt-blue tee instantly tugs at my heartstrings.

CAPS LOCK – Preventing Login Since 1980.

A classic.

Remembering one of our first catchup sessions where he had to reset my password for that very reason—and how that shirt, then, came to be part of his extensive collection—the beginning of a smile curls on my lips.

It really is Olivier. Standing here in my cottage.

The golden-brown haired stranger I've been attracted to despite myself, and Olivier—my Olivier—are really one and the same. To think that all this time, in all the fantasies he starred into, I was right all along...

I hardly dare breathe, shocked into silence.

Thick-lashed, striking hazel eyes—in unusual shades of green moss and brown copper sprinkled with gold flecks—narrow slightly as his gaze sweeps the room, searching for something. He sucks his lower lip into his mouth, skimming his teeth over it.

I swallow, my skin tingling all over, imagining what he would do to my lower lip if I just had the courage to fling myself at him and wrap my arms tightly around his neck.

Which wouldn't be all that difficult as we're about the same height.

Not helping, I inwardly groan.

My stomach clenches and my hands press down on it as if I could contain the ecstatic flock of butterflies zooming around in my belly.

Maybe I've read one too many romance novels lately, but I can't seem to stop ogling him.

He's as lithe as I remember, but his muscles seem more defined than last summer and the gritty stubble peppering his angular jaw and high cheekbones appears to be a darker shade of blond now that his skin is no longer sun-kissed.

Olivier.

And he's standing here, in my kitchen, replying to my "how's that possible?" question on my blackboard—and as per our usual *modus operandi,* in the written form—with something akin to determination. And judging by his ramrod stance and clenched jaw, I get the distinct impression that whether I like it or not, he won't take my "I can't do this with you anymore" as an answer. And that *his* answer lies in the stuff *my* dreams are made of.

Involuntary hope flutters in the center of my chest—simple, simple dreams.

Olivier. Here. Now.

Even with thick socks on, the wooden floor is chilly under my feet, proof I'm not dreaming this.

And the temptation to just give in and throw my arms around him is so real, I can't breathe. My stomach cramps with knots of dread, and my earlier butterflies suffer from brutal mass extinction as I reason with myself.

I can't go there.

Not happening.

Not happening.

Not…

Muscles strain and flex on his back as he writes, exuding a quiet strength.

Not happening? Why is that again?

I'm holding on to my resolve by a thread.

I cross my arms under my breasts, well aware that I'm fidgeting. I'm still reeling, hardly able to wrap my head around the fact he's here. In my kitchen. Writing on my blackboard.

Why is he writing?

He doesn't know. No one does up here, and it's the closest to normal I'll ever get, and I just can't burden him with…me… I sternly point out the obvious.

He swivels, shoving his hands in his pockets, staring. He just stands there, an impenetrable expression hardening his face, unreadable, yet, anything but blank.

It's as though the universe is pitting my resolve not to give in against the temptation to just give in.

So far, the universe is winning.

He steps aside.

Just one little step.

And the reconstructed world I carved out for myself by living up here implodes with the words I read in pink chalk.

Twenty-One

P.O.

S potting a blackboard painted on the wall beside the kitchen cabinets with the beginnings of a grocery list in a familiar loopy handwriting, I quickly scribble:

Because my stubborn ass cheated twice by deliberately hacking into Harry. From MIT, earlier today…and…when, sitting by yourself underneath that maple tree last August, you initially refused my offer of help as I approached you in person. Or so I thought. I didn't know, Aurèle, that you couldn't hear me. And you didn't know I was spending my summer break last August in Val-David. Hence, we both lied by omission… I think that makes us even.

I wait, not breathing, while she reads my words. When she's done, her face leaches of all color. The crumpled expression slashing lines across that exquisite face tells me she hates herself for being defenseless against it. She squeezes her eyes shut, chest heaving. "And now, you know," she says, but it doesn't sound like a relief. More like she's lost.

She startles as I tuck a stray lock of silky hair behind her ear, but her expressive eyes remain stubbornly shut tight.

I tilt her chin up, feathering the back of my fingertips alongside her jaw, and she fights a shiver.

My pulse leaps, and my heart somersaults out of my chest as her Mediterranean-blue eyes reopen, piercing mine with such an intense, sorrowful look that I vow here and now to do whatever it takes to dispel it forever.

My right hand fists over my heart, thumping once before unfurling my fingers, inviting her in. "And now, I know… I love you," I enunciate each word slowly, hoping she'll understand all that she means to me.

A soft smile tugs at my lips as a look of incredulous wonder crosses over her face, warring with the infinite sadness lurking in her eyes.

My chest overflows with warmth and tenderness, the depth of which I didn't know I possessed. Until now.

I vow quietly, "And I'm not going anywhere."

Twenty-Two

AURÈLE

He knows.

I'm going under, swept at sea, as he takes three steps back, his eyes aglow with love and acceptance. Not a single drop of pity or repulsion swimming in their depth.

I swallow, my emotions so conflicted that I'm not sure how to respond or breathe.

He peers over at me with those gold-flecked, green hazel eyes of his—so warm and full of love. They slice right through me with their vibrant intensity, pulling me in.

How am I supposed to cut him loose?

I stand rooted—a war between *what should be* and *what could be* waging inside of me. Whoever said you've got to be cruel to be kind never had to.

Tingles spread across my skin, and I run my hands up my arms. The lines I drew in the sand are blurring with the receding tide. He is temptation incarnate. I want it so. Is that so wrong?

He slowly approaches me, causing my skin to heat and my blood to run molten.

A soft smile appears, popping a boyish dimple at the corner of his mouth as though he knows I don't know how to fight this anymore.

He pulls on my shoulders, drawing me into his strong embrace.

Overcome, I float, riding on a wave of warm sensations in an uncharted ocean. Unfamiliar, yet, safe. I feel safe.

His eyes touch upon mine for just a moment before he tucks me closer to his body.

Warmth wraps me tight, just as tight as the arms anchoring around me for a heartfelt hug.

His forehead drops to mine, his eyes falling closed. And mine follow.

We stand there, heartbeat-to-heartbeat. Neither one of us move for the longest time. This moment is bliss.

For now, I have no more fight left.

But I need to let go.

An eternity without him stretches before me. Dread fills my chest just at the thought.

Two more minutes.

Give me two more minutes.

Or an eternity of this…before I shore up my defenses and free him.

Twenty-Three

P.O.

M y fingers coil on her shoulders and I pull her gently towards me and she lets me.

A frisson races through me at her closeness.

I wade through the haze of longing and desire I see mirrored in her eyes, getting me high.

Her lips part on a whispered sigh as I capture a loose curl between my thumb and forefinger and gently rub, needing the tactile proof I'm not dreaming this.

Our eyes lock, hers filled with wonder, and my breath becomes pure energy in my lungs. My gut tightens, sending ripples into my stomach while rushing a strange chill through my limbs.

I step closer, my chest right up against her, so that if I inhale deeply, it will brush along hers.

My pulse thudding in my ears, I close my eyes and rest my forehead against hers, my hands coming up to frame her face.

I feel her breath stroking my chin. I feel the satiny softness of her cheeks beneath my palms.

I run the tip of my nose up the arch of her neck. The fragrant scent of lavender clings to her skin, wafting about my senses, flooding them with the rich, heady smells of summer.

I feel her everywhere, with my entire body, her scent in my nose and throat, her warmth sinking into me, seeping into the very essence of my soul.

And I let myself free fall into the moment for who knows how long before I pull back a fraction, our mouths a breath away.

My blood pounds with a wild potency.

I lower my gaze, watching as her chest rises and falls fast, her emotions raw. Mine, not far behind. Or too far ahead, I can't tell anymore.

Unable to help myself, I bring my lips closer, just below her ear, and brush a soft, reverent kiss. Her flesh puckers from my touch and she shudders. The realization that she's so receptive to me is almost my undoing. I still and lean in to inhale the delicate scent of her again, committing it to deeper memory. I'm drowning in her scent.

Her glance drops to my mouth and she swallows. Her eyes linger on my lips, and I'd like to think it's for something other than to read them.

Aurèle hesitates for just a second, then lifts her hand and places it right over my heart. She presses her palm to my chest like she is seeking a way to climb inside. I flex my hand over hers. "You are. In me. Right here."

Her expression turns soft and vulnerable. Deep blue eyes not leaving mine, she slowly leans down and my pulse jumps when she feathers a tender kiss on my chest right over my heart.

Her fingers flutter up to my jaw, tracing it, her eyes filled with quiet regret. "Forgive me. I didn't mean to—"

I cut her off with a light press of my finger on her lips. "Don't."

She holds my gaze, not shifting under the scrutiny. "You weren't supposed to happen, and now, I don't know how to stop loving you," she whispers, and it's unclear if she meant to say that out loud.

My heart hammers with new awareness. My blood pumps, rushing in my ears.

My hands splay on her back, her fingers flexing on my chest. "Good." I press a string of kisses alongside her temple down to her jaw and am rewarded by her sharp intake of breath. "So, so good." Leaning my head back so she gets to see my lips, I say with far more calm than I feel, "We won't know how to stop loving each other, together, from now on."

Her hands freeze right before her eyes slice to me. I see none of the joy I expected to see swimming in hers, reflecting mine. Only panic.

"Wait. No. Can't." She starts wiggling in my arms and I tighten my hold, my hands clamping on her waist, uncomprehending.

"Can't—?"

"You don't understand what you're in for. This is selfish, so selfish," she cries out, pushing on my chest, and caught by surprise, my arms drop.

I instantly mourn the loss of her warmth as she backs away from me until she bumps against the kitchen sink. She faces me from six steps away. Much too far.

My forehead puckers. "Selfish? Is that what you think?" I ask, incredulous as I take a step forward. This is one conversation that needs to be had, heart-to-heart.

She holds up her hands defensively, stopping me in my track. "Yes!"

I shift my weight to one side, my hands hanging low over my hips.

"Then, you know nothing." I flex my index finger, asking her to come back to me.

But she only shakes her head. "You'll only regret it in the end, and I can't bear it." She braces her hands on either side of the counter, clutching it in a white-knuckle grip.

My hands fist at my side, fighting the urge to make a grab for her. Or maybe shake some sense into her. I love her. She loves me. And the only thing standing between us is her disability?

Not happening.

No fucking way.

"Let me be the judge of that." I beckon her with a nod of my head. "Come over here."

She shakes her head again. In the forming shadows, agony blankets her eyes. "Can't you see?"

"No, actually." This conversation was going so much better when she was in my arms.

"All right. I'll spell it out for you." She turns around, her delicate fingers fidgeting on the back of her neck. She gazes out the window, refusing to look at me. "I'll never hear the sound of your voice. We can't even have a regular conversation, nor argue like normal people do, as I'll probably understand only half of what you're saying unless you speak very, very slow. Not to mention face-to-face!"

Crossing my arms, I lean against the wall, studying her profile, ready to wait her out. By turning her back on me, she's trying to prove a point that has no point.

She's right about one thing. And one thing only. We won't argue in quite the same way people usually do. Having to write it down in the heat of the moment should calm the hell out of me, though, so there goes another check on the plus side.

She peers at me over her shoulder, pursing her mouth at the unimpressed look I sport, reading it correctly. *Any more excuses?*

"We'll never talk over the phone."

I shrug, one eyebrow rising in sardonic disbelief. "People text now."

She whips her head back, her gaze sticking to the early night sky and silhouetted trees in the distance, effectively shutting me out again. Her voice cracks as she launches into a spiel about all the *good* reasons we can't happen. Her pitch is all over the place, and not as carefully modulated as she's scrambling to convince herself, as well as me, of something she'll never convince me of: that we're not happening.

We are. It's written all over me. If she'd only look, she'd see.

"And we'll never listen together to your favorite music or go to the movies or concerts or out on the town, dancing, or any of the other normal stuff you're entitled to share with your lover. I can't even ski anymore, something you love and that I used to just as well, without endangering myself and others! Can't you see it's so unfair to you?" Shaky fingers rub her temples. "I'll just bring you down."

"Enough already," I mutter. Shoving away from the wall, I stride towards Aurèle. Reaching out, I turn her around. "Don't. Decide. For. Me," I say vehemently as her startled gaze drops to my mouth. Purpose stamps all over me as I clamp my hands on her shoulders and give her a light shake. "Don't you dare decide for me! Who the hell cares about movies or concerts? Not me. We'll be stargazing instead. And we'll ski together, buddy system. We're happening, Aurèle. It'd. Be. An. Unfair. Crime. Not. To."

She stiffens, straightening her shoulders in a rigid stance, gaining half an inch on me.

Heat beats at my cheeks. Have I overplayed my hand?

But as she catches on to my words, her kissable lips part and her midnight-blue gaze drifts back to mine. "Stop tempting me," she says.

I hold my hands up, unthreatening. But my eyes cut to hers in an unrelenting stare. *Oh, I have every intention to tempt,* is the message they say, unremorseful and without an ounce of hesitation. "Stop grasping at straws."

Her tongue swipes across her lower lip and, as sexy as it is, it seems more like a nervous tic she's unaware of. Her gaze drops to the floor. "You really don't understand. I'm a burden whether I want to be or not. Just ask Laurent!"

My stomach bottoms out as she reveals some more details of her previous life, confirming what I already suspected from her letters. And I do get why, all too well, truth be known. In the stratospheric and rarefied air where perfect dynastic families dwell en masse, you can never be less than perfect, or else. I should know as the black sheep of mine.

She's never been allowed to disclose that she's deaf now. "I'm always second-guessing when people talk, and that's when I can see their lips. And talking? I hadn't even tried for the past eight years, not until I came here. I can't hear myself! And because I've been left with a permanent brain lesion, and you have to talk slow so I can understand, and I've had to relearn so many simple tasks for months and months afterwards, like tying shoe laces, don't you know I'm no longer sharp as a tack but dumb as a post on top of it?"

And not for one goddamn minute did they let you forget it? Oh, Aurèle.

"Or so I've been told too many times to count by my father and his immediate entourage, try daily... *Thankfully she's beautiful, but the less she's seen, the better!*"

My nostrils flare and I curse underneath my breath.

Christ.

Her father and what's-his-name really did a number on her.

Tempted to punch the wall, I breathe in, breathe out. Calming. Somewhat.

I slide a finger beneath her chin, nudging her to look at me.

Her troubled gaze meets mine. "I'm damaged goods."

I want to rip into anyone who made her feel like less of a woman just because she can't hear. But that will have to wait. Right now, I have to convince the love of my life that she belongs in it.

I give her a stern look. "Don't you ever, ever, say that again, do you hear—" I clench my jaw shut, realizing a second too late, wanting to swallow the word back in.

She arches a telltale brow in defiance but a world of sadness lurks in her eyes. *"Ce qu'il fallait démontrer."* The typical French expression she spits out—meaning what had to be proved—cleaving me in half, straight down the middle.

"No. You're not listening—" I pinch the bridge of my nose, inwardly slapping myself silly. Funny how so many expressions take a lot for granted... Things you never question, until, well, you do.

Her shoulders droop forward dejectedly, like she wants to curl in on herself. *Awesome, man. Way to go.*

"See, damaged. People act weird around me once they know. Never mind living it, day in, day out."

My palms come up and bracket her face, commanding her full attention. "Read. My. Lips," I order.

Her heavy sigh shreds my heart into ribbons. I wish I could take on her pain, dispel her doubts.

Her bottom lip quivers in protest, but she swallows her retort, her glance dropping to my mouth.

Good.

She needs to hear this once and for all.

And if it means I have to spend the rest of my life writing notes or talking slow, I will.

My fingertip taps against my lips a few times, illustrating what I'm about to say. "You hear differently, that's all."

Her breath hitches and she goes completely still.

I brush a loose strand of hair behind her ear. "Breathe, Aurèle. Just breathe. There's never been a day in your life that you weren't perfect just the way you are. You are not damaged. You are not chattel. You're an awesome human being. You made it this far, Sleeping Beauty." My thumb runs over her bottom lip once before I let go and arch a telltale brow, challenging her. "Don't let them win."

Twenty-Four

P.O.

H er mouth drops open the minute those words are out.

Her gaze collides with mine.

A small smile tugs at the corner of my lips as the back of my fingers tip her chin up, closing shut her gaping mouth.

"Is that what I've been doing?" She tilts her head to the side, a thoughtful look washing over her features, softening the angle of her jaw.

"Looks like it."

She ducks her head and looks at me from under heavy lashes.

My heart stutters against my ribs.

The glimmer of hope arising like a fragile new dawn in her eyes is a thing of beauty, telling me her heart and soul want in, all in, and her mind, though still cautious, is more than halfway there, now. As for body language...

Yeah, her body tells another story, one ripe for the reading.

Preferably in Braille.

And man, is it ever hard not to. Pressingly hard.

Visions of Aurèle underneath me in nothing but skin bombards my brain. My icy-wet jeans shrink on me and the only good news is that my dick no longer gives a damn about the cold-as-fuck material sticking to it like poured honey. *Aw, man, you just had to go there, didn't you?* I can hear Leo from here,

"I'm not touching this one with a ten-foot pole."

I involuntarily groan.

Great.

Now it's all I think about. Flowing honey and touching with a rigid pole thrown in there.

Fucking hell.

Not helping.

Screw your head on straight, now is not the time to think about worshiping her body, dude.

"I am letting them win, aren't I?" She nods slowly in understanding. Like the flip of a switch, I see the exact moment she shifts perception altogether.

Aurèle sighs breathily and turns her face so her cheek rests in the pocket on my shoulder. She hugs me tight, squeezing once, before stepping back. She takes a deep breath. "Thanks for kicking my butt. I needed that."

My hands drop to my side.

I shove my hands in my pocket, rocking on the balls of my feet. "Don't mention it."

She looks down at her feet, her fingers fidgeting with the hem of her glacier-blue thermal shirt dotted with silver white snowflakes. A rosy blush blooms on her cheeks, and she grows prettier by the minute—if that's possible.

Wonder what she's thinking about... Probably not what I'm thinking about, which is a one-way ticket into the gutter.

I sigh wryly, discreetly readjusting the steel pipe lodged in my jeans. Willing my pulse to calm down and my blood flow to circulate back to my brain, I square my shoulders and tip her chin up again. Tapping my lips, her translucent blue gaze drops to them.

We're about the same height, and who knew my being shorter than the average guy would turn out to be that relevant as we see eye-to-eye—literally.

I catch her hands and uncurl her fingers over my chest, covering them with my own.

My pulse picks up.

Christ, she's so gorgeous.

Even more so this close as I note a scattering of golden freckles on the bridge of her nose like a lost constellation waiting to be discovered, and the indent of a distinctive scar in the shape of a little O at the corner of one eyebrow. It matches the one I got on my chin, courtesy of chickenpox, and I wonder if she got it the same way.

We get lost in each other's eyes for a couple of heartbeats.

I itch to strain forward and kiss her.

Instead, playing it safe, I press down on her palms right over my heart. "Feel that?" She nods slowly, and I swallow. If this is karma, I don't rightly know what I did in a previous life to deserve someone like her in this one, but I'll take it. "It beats for you."

She stares at my hands safeguarding hers for the longest time.

Her smile starts in her eyes long before it hits her mouth but drops just as quickly on a wince—like swallowing a big mouthful of pure cranberry juice, the sharp tartness hitting you by surprise a few seconds after the fact.

Her fingers grasp my shirt, adding a few wrinkles to it. Something like sorrow flashes in her eyes with a dash of panic and a pinch of indecision thrown in now.

Aw, man.

Her breathing is choppy as she looks down at her feet, sending her high ponytail cascading over her shoulder—as well as sending my sense of smell in overdrive, her herbal shampoo mixed with the warm lavender fragrance of her skin where her neck meets her shoulder wafting through, filling my nostrils. All warm woman and clean, fresh innocence. A lethal combination.

I frame her face once again in my hands. I cup her cheeks, marveling at the satiny smoothness under my fingertips. "Don't be afraid. I'll follow where you lead."

"I lead nowhere," she mumbles, a tinge of sadness still lurking in her eyes as she stares off to the side. "That's the problem."

I nudge her chin back toward my face. "Not on this side of the equation." *Not on your life.* I brush her thick mane of strawberry-gold locks behind her shoulders.

"And which side is that?"

"Ours, Aurèle." I drop a soft kiss at the corner of her lips, mine lingering there for two or three or five heartbeats more than just a chaste peck between friends, definitely hedging toward lovers' territory.

She exhales on a shaky breath, trembling fingertips coming up to brush over the spot I just kissed, her eyes blinking in surprise, like she can't really believe what just happened. To her? Or to me? Hard to tell.

I force myself to take a few steps back—less I pounce on her caveman style and disprove what I claimed earlier; that I'll follow her lead. "Follow your heart; it knows the way."

Her fingertips brush over her lips, almost tentatively, as if discovering them. "I lost my heart to you," she says under her breath before catching my eyes. "It goes where you go. And it's scaring me. When you'll go, I'm afraid there will be nothing left of me but a hollowed shell."

Damn, she slays me.

Her bottomless blue eyes burn brighter than I've ever seen on anyone. At least, not while looking at me.

I see a raw yearning in her eyes echoing mine, and I feed on it.

My heart thuds. Hard.

I feel high on life. Hungry for more of the same.

I tap my lips and her glazed over gaze drops to my mouth, and I'm not entirely sure she's focused on what I'll say or what I'll do with said lips.

"I'm not going anywhere, Aurèle," I say, my eyes searching hers.

"You're not?" she asks imperceptibly.

I nod slowly, unable to take my eyes off of her.

And I'll do whatever it takes for you to see I'm not going anywhere, might as well give in.

Her clear blue eyes—their luminous color now reminiscent of the famed stained-glass-blue of la Cathédrale Notre-Dame de Chartres in Paris when the sun hits just right—search mine, gauging me, wondering if I'm for real. If this...us...is for real.

Is she testing me? My resolve?

Bracing my hands on the island counter backward, my fingers curved over the edge. I look over Aurèle. Do I bring it up? Do I ask?

Fuck it.

I walk over and cup the right side of her face with my hand. "Teach me sign language." I raise an eyebrow and tilt my chin up in clear challenge. Or pleading. I can't say anymore.

She shakes her head in a dazed fashion. "I don't know sign language."

I let my fingertips trail down her cheek to the curve of her jaw, regretfully taking a step back. "Then, we'll learn together or invent our own. Stop putting imagined obstacles in our way—"

I am interrupted mid-sentence as Aurèle flings herself at me and wraps her arms tightly around my neck.

"Okay." An inner glow brightens up her exquisite features, momentarily blinding me.

"Okay?" Jesus. I can hardly believe it. The moment is surreal.

"Okay."

I let out a pent-up breath and toss my head back, briefly closing my eyes on a quick, silent, *thank you, God.*

Twenty-Five

AURÈLE

All my good reasons why we shouldn't be together fly out the window. Inconsequential. He's so beautiful, inside and out, and willing to be with me? Insisting. *Surreal.*

Olivier holds me steady and I wrap my arms around his neck tighter, never wanting to let go.

He tilts his head back, his face cautiously optimistic, like he can't believe it. *Join the club.*

His clear hazel eyes lock with mine, seeming to spear right into the very essence of my soul. The feeling I get is pretty intense, bowling me over.

Involuntary hope flutters in my chest. Maybe, just maybe, it's okay to grab on to us, never letting go.

My heart catapults in my chest as my eyes race across his ruggedly handsome face. I don't want this moment to end, half afraid I'm dreaming it.

"We're really doing this?"

I nod. I do believe. *We're really doing this.*

I'm floating on a cloud, dancing on air. In equal part mesmerized and dazzled by all these wonderful sensations of light and warmth flooding me now, like the forgotten kiss of the sun bestowed on one's cheeks after a long winter.

We stare.

His eyes fill with a joy that burns brighter than the fiery glow of a thousand novas. The grin stretching his face intensifies, and so does mine in response. After what feels like forever, he breaks eye contact, his gaze dropping to my lips.

He dusts his knuckles down the line of my jaw, eliciting delicious sparks at the point of contact. I lean into his touch and rub my cheek onto his hand, like a kitten keenly seeking the warmth of a caress.

The scent of his skin dizzies me as I run my nose along the crook of his neck. He smells good, clean, like wintery mint and fresh air. Like endless possibilities and a million eternities.

My knees buckle. I hold on to him tighter, reflexively, my senses overwhelmed.

He runs his palm along the back of my head, his fingers threading in my hair, holding my face toward him in a firm grip as if afraid I'll look elsewhere. But I couldn't look away even if my life depended on it.

Doesn't he know he's all I see? All I want?

Simple, simple dreams.

A soft smile curves on his lips as I read on them, "I love you."

And I may swoon after all.

Twenty-Six

P.O.

I ward off a startling frisson as she rubs her cheek on mine—getting me so fired up, I'm nearly shaking with anticipation.

I stare into the deep ocean blue of her eyes, willingly drowning in their depth. I can't help it. Her whole face breaks into one hell of a dazzling smile.

Foudroyant.

A smile sending a warm wave of *happy* through my body, electrifying me.

My heart roars in my chest, my throat, my ears.

My hand fastens on the small of her back as my other sweeps back into her hair, holding her face towards me. "I love you," I mouth. *I love you. I love you. I love you.*

Her breathing hitches and she interlocks her fingers in a tighter grip on my nape, holding on to me as though afraid I might vanish into thin air. As if.

I kiss her brow and her eyelids flutter close on a sigh.

When she reopens her eyes, she gently brushes back my overgrown hair from my forehead and I swallow, lapping up the tender gesture. "I love you too," she whispers.

I still.

The words, nothing more than a breath of air from her parted lips, detonate in my chest, inflating my heart, engraving on my soul, flipping my world.

My mouth dries.

My throat thickens.

My mind blanks.

Straining forward, her mouth closes the remaining distance between us. A held breath hisses through my teeth, and my lashes lower halfway.

Oh, so softly, her warm, smooth lips feather over mine in a caress so sweet and caring it leaves me lightheaded and petrified, unable to process such tenderness.

A minute too long.

Mistaking my freeze-out for something other than utter delight and complete shock, she ducks her head, apologizing for going too fast, leaving me reeling from one extreme to the other. She squirms, pushing on my arms, blushing profusely. She never looked more adorable.

You're not going anywhere. No way.

I clench my arms around her back, anchoring her more solidly to my chest. When she stills, I cup the back of her head, bringing my mouth down to hers. Searing heat assaults me as our lips meet and part, melding together in a slow, earth-shattering kiss.

Yes, *this.*

Kissing her is like discovering a new landscape and coming home in the same breath.

Aurèle's small hands fist in my shirt, holding me to her as I sweep my tongue into her parted lips. She weaves her tongue against mine. Soft, pliant.

And it's all a blur of sensation from there.

Suddenly, I'm kissing her like crazy like I'd been dying to do for the past seven months.

Maybe for all my life.

Twenty-Seven

AURÈLE

His lips meet mine, softly, tentatively.

Rather gently, he sucks my lower lip into his mouth and scrapes his teeth against the sensitive skin there, his lips lightly brushing over the spot to soothe any hurts. His breath is now a chilled balm blowing over the spot his mouth had just been.

I've never been kissed before, I realize. Not like this. Not ever.

The quiet strength he exudes seethes beneath the surface, boosting my confidence. I fist my hands in his shirt, holding him to me as I slant my head to give him full access to my mouth.

His tongue entices mine to come out and play, and I revel in the velvety smooth glide as they dance with one another.

His hands move from my face and thread into my hair as we deepen the kiss.

Olivier's lips continue their sensual assault on mine and mine on them, in turn tasting, exploring, devouring, as time slows to a stop.

The feel of his body against mine is better than any novels out there ever written. I'm ruined for life. Addicted.

I arch into him.

And suddenly, he pins me to the wall with his body and crushes his mouth to mine. My heart pounds against my chest, the rhythm skyrocketing when he jerks his knee between my legs and I'm riding his thigh.

Our kiss is no longer tender, but hot and burning and needy in a way I didn't know existed.

Holy wow.

It's as if every missed kiss over these past few months fight to be had right here in this moment.

A moment I've been waiting my whole life for so it seems.

Twenty-Eight

AURÈLE

I lean into his chest, wanting more. Wanting to lick and taste him all over. Wanting to absorb him into me. Wanting to lose myself in sensations I never thought I'd live. Sensuality and all its promises of carnal delight swirling in my brain, frying my skin.

Until his body shifts and he drops his hands to my shoulders, his lips dancing away.

I whimper at the loss.

His lips move against my temple in a featherlight caress. I feel his chest vibrate against me as he catches his breath, mine long gone.

Tingling all over, I slowly reopen my eyes, lost in a brand-new world. An enhanced world where touch and taste reign supreme, and I no longer feel so apart.

He tucks strands of hair from my half undone ponytail behind my right ear, letting his fingertips glide down the column of my neck, something he seems fond of doing—not that I'm complaining—before he takes a reluctant step back.

He just continues to hold my gaze steadily.

My breath falters.

My thoughts scatter.

I press my fingers to my lips in wonder, testing their puffiness. "Why stop?"

Note to self: slack it on the romance novels.

His back slumps on the wall beside me. "I'm one minute away from taking advantage of you."

"Maybe I want to be taken advantage of."

He thumps his head on the wall, his face a mixture of amusement and frustration. "Jesus. You're killing me." He squeezes his eyes shut, his hands flexing at his sides.

I strain my neck forward and sneak a sniff right where his neck meets his shoulder.

His eyes pop open. "Are you sniffing my..?"

"Hmm. Hmmmm." I hum, my hands splaying on his chest. I feather my lips and run my nose along his collar, inhaling deeply. He quivers underneath my palms, holding me at arms' length. "Don't. My day-old tee must be smelly, I wasn't exactly expecting..."

The intoxicating musk drifting from his skin—all warm male and something indefinably Olivier—floods me and makes me woozy, knocking me off-balance.

"Whoa, there." He catches me easily, his fingers flexing on my waist, and gently, but firmly, he pulls me back to the side.

I turn toward him, furrowing my brow. "Huh?" I say stupidly, still riding my newly discovered olfactory high.

If I pay more attention, could I smell people coming instead of hearing them? But then it occurs to me just as quickly that I can't really go around sniffing people to imprint their unique smell on my brain. It might be perceived as kind of rude. Scratch that. It is rude.

"Give me a minute." Olivier slumps against the wall beside me and drags his hands through his shaggy hair, blowing out a breath.

"I'm too much?" I cringe, worrying my bottom lip, the message once more deafening in my head.

He shoots me a sideway look that says, *don't even go there.* "I need to bring it down a notch or else... In the words of infamous bygone rogues, you're two seconds away from being thoroughly ravished."

The strain leaves my body, and I relax against him. My gaze sweeps his face, a smile teasing at my lips.

"Is that so?" Enchanted, I can't hold in the happy bubble of laughter vibrating within my chest.

"Very much so. Thoroughly so."

"Promise?"

Olivier quirks a brow like he can't believe I just went there. He straightens from his slouch.

Hazel eyes search mine. "Aurèle, I need to read this correctly. I don't want to jumpstart an upgrade you're not ready for. This last week was pure hell for me, waiting for a letter—"

I put a finger on his mouth. The brief touch zings through me, electrifying my nerve endings, enthralling me. I don't want to fight these feelings anymore.

"We've been months in the making, I know that now. Sending back your letters unopened was the hardest thing I ever had to do. Falling for you, the easiest..." Tenderly, I brush back a lock of dark-blond hair from his forehead. "You asked for it. What are you going to do about it?"

I see a flash of his grin—dark and devilish—in the second before he moves close, pressing me flat against the wall.

"That, and..." He shakes his head, and thrusts his erection against me."... this."

His hot gaze roams over me.

"Don't look at me like that," I say. "It makes my knees wobbly."

His incredibly sexy grin widens. "Does it now?"

His free hand travels down my spine and stops on my ass as he grabs a handful. My lips part as I gasp, watching his eyes darken with a want mirroring mine.

Something like a growl rumbles in his chest.

He wraps both hands around my waist, hoisting me up so my legs wrap around him.

More, I silently beg. I can't begin to explain this crazy gravitational pull, like a buried part of me has been waiting for him all along.

"We're meant to be more," he says as if reading my mind. He leans in close, his face only a breath away from mine. "Now, you get it. All of it."

"All of what?"

"What I feel for you."

His lips slide against mine in an open-mouthed kiss to end all kisses, and I grind into him unable to help myself. I can feel every ridge and dip of his lean, wiry body as he thrusts his hips into me and my own meet every single one of his thrusts, surging forward.

His body burning. Mine on fire.

"It's the halfway mark in the romance novel, time to be ravished," I pant when we come up for air. "Take me to bed. Show me what it's like. All of it. For real."

"It is. I am. I will." His eyes scour mine before he adds, "Oh, and Aurèle? All those romances I've read?" His grin is slow, seductive, turning me to mush. "It will be worth your while."

I laugh, some giddy feeling sweeping through me as he tows me the rest of the way.

This.

This is what happy feels like.

Twenty-Nine

AURÈLE

O livier rolls me over and his tongue wets his lips as he shoots me an unfettered glance before looking back at me lying there in my panties. "So beautiful."

Fire licks under my skin.

Just the feel of his smooth fingers on my bare skin nearly sends me over.

He bends his head at length, pressing a series of kisses from my neck to my sternum. Olivier's mouth is there on the underside of my breast, his lips ever so gentle.

"Still okay?" he asks, fingers lightly trailing down my neck. I can only nod stupidly because I know, after this, I'll never be just okay ever again. But so much more.

Olivier kisses his way down my neck and chest, making my nipples perk up. He lowers his head and sucks one into his mouth.

A fresh shudder racks through my body at the foreignness of it and a dreamy smile curls on my lips at the rightness of it.

I thread my fingers into Olivier's hair as he moves his mouth to one breast and his hand to the other.

His tongue swirls on the tight bud before his teeth bite lightly and I cry out, surprised by the electric shock bolting through me, the sensation exquisite.

I hold onto his shoulders, the muscles shifting beneath my palms as he whips me into a frenzy of want as his teeth, his tongue, his mouth, in turn lick, nibble, suck, and bite on my nipples.

I whimper and thrash from side to side, hollowed out by unimaginable pleasure.

Hot hands splay wide, riding up the outside of my thighs, scraping over my hips and sides, gathering down my panties as he goes. I shift, but he reclines me back on the bed, close enough to the edge that I lay there, exposed.

When Olivier spreads my legs, my hands curl into fists, sucking in as much air as my lungs can hold.

He kisses the inside of my knee and fire rockets straight to my core.

I exhale toward the ceiling; my hands twist in the sheets and my hips jut in anticipation as if my sex already knows something I don't. I whimper as he kisses his way up one trembling leg. Olivier drags the tips of his fingers through my wet center, his lips and tongue traveling up the other leg.

Olivier's mouth moves over me as he places soft, delicate kisses on my sensitive skin. When he opens his mouth and traces his tongue along the contours of my folds, I jerk.

Oh, that feels good.

His mouth closes over my tight little pearl and sucks greedily while inserting one, then two fingers, pumping in, pumping out in a slow rhythm rendering me mad with lust.

I look down at Olivier through my eyelashes, an uncontainable moan slipping from my lips as he stares at me while swirling his tongue slowly in places that have never been stroked that way before.

So, so good.

I fist my hand in his hair, holding Olivier in place. My hips move, arching, bowing taut, my heels digging into the mattress. He picks up his pace, lapping, sucking, pumping, while my mind goes blank.

Just when I'm at the peak, he pulls his hand from me and slips his tongue inside. I gasp at the decadent heat of it, the startling intimacy.

My insides clench up so tight my feet come off the bed, all of my energies centering on one focal point.

And then…

I splinter into a thousand fragments of pure light, a constellation born.

Thirty

P.O.

God is she ever so beautiful, splayed out on the twisted sheets like the warmest fantasy. Making Aurèle come apart over and again under my mouth is, hands down, the hottest thing I've ever done… or seen.

Under my stroking she stretches like a pampered cat, and I can't get enough.

Shivers roll through her. Aurèle whimpers, mindlessly rubbing herself on me while my tongue traces her nipple, my mouth alternating between lapping, nibbling, biting, and sucking, whipping her from sated to all systems go. And I take a small moment to thank all the romance authors out there for their invaluable insight into the female psyche.

My balls drawn tight, I stroke the tip of my dick over the slick, warm, velvety smoothness of her folds. Teasing her.

That first touch sends bolts of lightning screaming down my guts, almost obliterating me.

I hiss a groan. "Fuck."

I squeeze my eyes shut, counting to ten, willing myself not to shoot my load in the next second.

Fuck.

I still.

She stills.

The tremors in my arms and both our chests heaving are now the only remaining moving parts. Aurèle's eyes flutter open. Her eyebrows squish together, and her gaze clouds over momentarily. It's like she's trying to figure out the reason for the interruption.

Fuck me to hell and back.

"Quick question." My gaze darts over her shoulder to the nightstand then back to her. "Condoms?" I wince out.

None of this was exactly planned beforehand, and I'm not carrying any.

I hang my head, trying to control my raging hormones and the urge to slide into her wet heat up to my balls.

Soft skin burns against mine, her pulse a thread heaving through.

This might kill me if Aurèle doesn't have any. And it will kill me if she does.

With the roar of my blood pumping in my ears and the few brain cells I still have firing up, I try to focus on what she tells me in her halting voice. Something about only one other guy a lifetime ago and that she's on the contraception shot—she's safe.

My breath hitches alongside my stuttering brain. *Does she mean what I think she means?* "I've never had sex without a condom." *Not to mention not having any in way too long.* "I'm safe, too."

She vibrates with interest, with need. "I want to feel all of you."

Fucking hell. I nearly lose it.

"You sure?" I ask one last time. My dick throbs in protest, wondering if I'm nuts to double-check.

She says everything with her eyes. *No holding back.*

Now I just need to hold it together.

The anticipation and excitement of what I'm about to do races through my veins, amping me up.

I need this so damn badly I can taste it. Will I last is another question altogether.

Grinding my teeth, I dip a finger, testing her readiness. So, so wet. Heavenly wet. Silky wet. Endlessly wet. For me. I close my eyes on a grunt as she whimpers, bucking her hips against my hand.

I draw her knees up and position myself. I pause, staring into her eyes, and then rock into her fully.

Aurèle's palms run over my back and her nails rake my skin, shudders wrack us both.

I rasp, pushed right up to the edge. "Still with me?"

"Yes. Please." Aurèle loops her arms around my neck, pulling me down for a kiss.

I thrust deeply once, and she surges forward, impaling herself more fully, meeting me.

"Olivier." My name on her lips parts her mouth on a soft sigh. Her eyes close, a blissful look blooming on her face as she surrenders completely. "I'm yours."

And I feel myself slipping a little deeper. And falling a little harder.

I haven't had something like this in my life before.

Not ever.

And it feels fucking amazing.

Thirty-One

AURÈLE

I'll never get enough of this, of him, or the way he pins me in place without a single ounce of effort.

Olivier's seductive touch, his lips and tongue on the most intimate parts of my body, is a revelation. He fills me with one solid thrust.

My breath shatters, his name on my lips.

I close my eyes in surrender, falling into the bliss of being owned in such a way. "I'm yours."

Intensity billows between us, wrapping us up, making us one.

There's a tightening in my core that intensifies with every rhythmic thrust of his hips. I chase it, digging my fingers into his ass, pulling him tighter to my body. Dropping his forehead to mine, he picks up his pace, hips snapping as his movements become frenzied and uncontrolled.

I cry out in ecstasy as the knots inside me unravel in glorious, pulsing pleasure. The climax seizes me, swirling in ever increasing circles until I'm dizzy and blind with rapture.

Olivier burrows his face in my neck, and his body goes rigid as he jerks and shakes.

I feel his orgasm echo my own as his cock throbs inside me, emptying, filling me up in the most mind-altering way.

Gasping for air, he collapses on me. I welcome his weight anchoring me. Heartbeat-to-heartbeat.

I'd been intimate with Laurent less than a handful of times. Boring times. Cold times. Rough times. But with Olivier, for this kind of fusion? Anytime.

Nothing compares. Not even romance novels.

He rolls to his back and pulls me on top of him. His hand floats toward my face, knuckles tracing down the angle of my jaw. "Not sure I'm ever going to be the same after that."

My thumb sketches along his bottom lip. "Can we do that again?"

"Again and again." Olivier quirks up his lips, his hand brushing my cheek.

An answering smile pulls at one side of my mouth before stretching into a full-on grin. In a fluid movement, he flips me over on the bed so I'm pressed beneath him. I am suddenly drowning beneath the stunning bulk of this man.

"Stay the night?" I whisper, running my hands up his chest.

His pulse quickens under my palm.

"Try to get rid of me." He swivels his hips in a maddeningly slow pattern, kissing his way down the column of my neck.

He thrusts, unhurriedly, maddeningly, and soon I'm undulating beneath him in a more frenzied fashion, but he refuses to pick up speed. Instead he gathers my wrists in one hand, pinning my arms over my head. "We have all night. What's the rush?"

Delicious tingles rain up and down my spine, showering me with a deep yearning for more of the same.

And well into the early hours of the morning, his magnetic touch teaches me another language.

One in which no sound is necessary.

One I hear perfectly.

With my heart.

And I let myself believe in simple, simple dreams.

Thirty-Two

P.O.

A fresh gust of wind howls shaking up the rafters, closely followed by the sound of a thousand fingernails scratching at the windowpane. Eerie.

I barely crack open an eye. My dream addled mind still swims in a residual sea of lust. If zombies are out there, they will have to wait. A mass of silky flesh is snuggled up close to me. The musky smell of sex and arousal still linger in the air, permeating the rumpled sheets.

Aurèle.

No dream.

Aurèle is facing away from me, curled in a ball. I move closer, tucking her into the crescent of my body, one arm around her stomach. Her breathing changes, and she hugs my arm. I kiss her shoulder, no longer so sleepy, but she only wiggles back against me before settling again, her body lax, her breathing deep and regular.

Not that I'm complaining, but now, I'm wide awake.

I stare through the window to the view beyond. The night sky is partly obscured by fast-moving clouds, but I see on and off the white brilliance of the waxing crescent moon sitting up there like a lopsided smirk and Jupiter dotting its corner like a well-placed beauty mark. From the opposite window, Polaris, my old friend, winks down at me. "Well done," I whisper in the dark, my wish upon a star sleeping next to me.

The door to the bathroom rests partially ajar and the bright overhead fixture we forgot to turn off after our late night shower—too spent to do more than tumble back into bed—bleeds a faint hue of light in a wedge across the floor. So does the moon illuminating the naked limbs of a young tree swaying against the window, the source of the god-awful noise grating on my ears like screeching banshees going to town.

Those things need pruning, stat. Or I need earplugs... Whichever comes first, I'm not choosy.

Aurèle sighs softly, turning in bed to face me.

At least one of us is sleeping through the earsplitting racket the wind engenders.

I kiss her temple, feeling like an arsehole for having entertained a thoughtless grumble about the irking noise and promise to be more careful in what I take for granted.

I skim the back of my fingers along the smoothness of her cheek, marveling. Over the past seven months, I fell in love with the beauty of her mind, her spirit, her soul…but meeting her in person blows me away.

I tuck my arm beneath my head, resting on my forearm, looking at her, thinking back. When have I ever felt this complete? This content?

Unquestionably, never.

I bring my fingers up to trail down the satiny smooth skin of her shoulder, her ribcage, her hips. The silkiness of her skin makes my heart beat faster and my dick twitch, lengthening at half-mast.

God almighty, what she does to me.

"Olivier," she murmurs in her sleep, and for a moment I think I'm busted.

In the low light, with her hands tucked beneath her cheek, she looks so young and vulnerable. And fuck me, but she is. More vulnerable than I ever thought. More vulnerable than she thinks. I brush away a few strands of hair from her forehead. She stirs slightly but settles again.

Pulling in a breath, I bring her flush with my body, and she mumbles. One of her hands flutters down to my chest, resting over my heart.

I trace it with my fingertips before cupping it within mine, protectively.

In that moment, I know without a shadow of a doubt that I won't be able to go back to MIT later on today if she stays behind in this isolated place where there's no bloody way I can reach her. Not with my sanity intact. Not unless she moves in at the farmstead. Or comes with me.

The question is, will she?

When my eyes open next, Aurèle lies down on her side, arm bent, resting her head in her hand, regarding me with a soft look of love in her eyes. *Me!*

"Good, you're up. Breakfast is almost served." She gives me a quick peck on the cheek, hopping out of bed, already fully dressed for the day.

"Then, where are you going?" I throw a pillow at her. "Missing a key player, here."

Catching it, she laughs and hugs it to her chest. "I meant real food, not me." She glances at me from beneath the thick veil of her lashes before casting me an adoring smile.

"Shame, I'd go for berry kissed lips. Berry, berry kissed." With a wolfish grin, I lunge for her, but she adroitly sidesteps my arms, stepping out of my reach.

"Was that…*berry* you just said?" Her nose wrinkles in adorable confusion.

I waggle my brow in confirmation, patting a place beside me. "Berry much so."

She chuckles low. "You're such a dork."

I don't think I've ever felt this lighthearted before. I'm so buoyed by happiness that I wouldn't be surprised to float up to the ceiling the minute my foot hits the floorboards.

"Yeah, but I'm your dork." I crack half a smile. I scoot back against the headboard, settling more comfortably with my hands behind my head.

Aurèle takes that as her cue and comes back to sit at the foot of the bed, her legs criss-crossing. She shakes her head at me with a world of affection warming her eyes.

"Do you have time for breakfast with me?" Her eyes trail the drop of the sheet to my waist, causing a slow burn in my guts, and a pop tent to rise in the sheets.

"How long have you got?"

"Depends." She plucks a thread off the comforter, twisting it in her hands. She looks down. "What time is your flight back today? You never said."

And just like that, I crash back down to earth with a loud thud.

I draw in a long breath before blowing out my cheeks.

I lean forward, pinching her big toe. She looks up. "That's because I'm not sure when exactly. No worries. None of the return flights departs Tremblant before three or four in the afternoon," I hedge, keeping it vague. *And we need to talk. Again.*

I check my watch before I turn back to her with a shrug. "It's early still." Not even seven a.m. "I'll look up the flights schedule after breakfast," I say. More of a question really, in a desultory tone she won't be able to catch.

"Sweet. Breakfast in five it is." She hops down. "We can walk down to the village together afterwards if you'd like. Lucie will get a good WiFi signal down at C'est la Vie, guaranteed," she says offhandedly, a twinkle in her eyes as she saunters off.

I sigh up to the ceiling, flopping back on the pillow. "Yeah, that's the problem," I say to the empty room. "No fucking signal, here, and you, more isolated than you're willing to admit."

With a strained sigh, I push myself up and sit on the edge of the bed. I scrub my face and force myself to stand.

I snag my underwear from the floor and pull them on as I fumble towards the adjoining bathroom.

I plod back out into her room and quickly dress. I grimace as I pull on my grubby shirt. I'm nowhere near as fastidious as our Swiss upbringing might imply, but, man, this might be a bit too much even for me. The clean effect of our late night shower is soon to be obliterated, overtaken by the smelly thing. Not that I would change a thing about last night and staying over.

Stepping into Aurèle's line of vision, a welcoming smile curls one corner of her mouth, and she tips her head to the side, inviting me to sit at the kitchen island.

An appetizing smell of eggs, melted cheese, and some type of vegetable frittata sizzling on the stove—enough to overtake every last one of my senses—permeates the room.

She plates the food and saliva pools in my mouth.

Tender fingers send chills racing down my spine when Aurèle flutters them along the base of my neck, leaning over my shoulder to place a mug filled with steaming black coffee down in front of me.

I'm done for.

"I like it out here." I lean into her and bump her shoulder playfully. "With you."

She ducks her head, but not before I see the joyful look blooming on her expressive face. She may not know this, but she talks eloquently with her whole body, and it's easier than she thinks to converse with her.

We dig in, and the silence stretching between us isn't awkward in the least, but as peaceful and comfortable as lazing around in a hammock on a Sunday afternoon, being rocked together by a gentle summer breeze.

Relaxing. Enveloping. Caressing.

Aurèle is all smiles and blushes at my obvious enjoyment of the food she prepared.

As we clear the table, I shift to the side to allow her to the sink. We work seamlessly in tandem, her rinsing, me stacking up the dishwasher as though we've done it together a thousand times before.

Add my name on top of the domesticated list, boys. In permanent ink.

"This omelet you whipped together can't possibly come from your full staff upbringing," I comment, flipping the frying pan over and drying it with a dish towel. "You have to tell me your secret for staving off starvation on your own with such brio. Talk slow, I'm taking notes."

Aurèle giggles, and I feel my smile deepen. "It's no laughing matter." I playfully smack her behind with my towel. "Left to our own devices and no available takeout? The guys and I eat cereal straight out the box more often than not. Sometimes with a Cheetos or two thrown in. And if we're lucky, we top it off with an unsweetened dark chocolate bar. Swiss, of course."

"Is there any other kind?" she deadpans.

I arch a telling brow. "Goes without saying." Leaning a hip against the counter, I cross my arms. "So? Give over."

A small, reminiscing smile curves on her lips. "No big secret." She rinses the last of the suds lying at the bottom of the sink, a ray of early morning sunlight transforming the tight bubbles into miniature rainbows tumbling down the drain. "At one point, I used to sit in one corner of the kitchen for hours on end, all but invisible, watching our chef gesturing wildly to the kitchen staff, demonstrating what he wanted," she says while she squirts a bottle of Burst of Citrus household cleaner all over the counter tiles and rips two sheets of paper towels. "It fascinated me." She shrugs impishly, wiping down the counter as she speaks. "Plus, bonus, I could no longer hear his yelling."

On the last bit, I blink in surprise, and a quick laugh escapes me at her unexpected joke.

I step behind her and wrap my arms around her middle, pulling her to my chest. I drop a kiss on the back of her head, giving her a gentle squeeze.

She squeezes my forearms, returning the hug, making me feel all warm and fuzzy inside.

Everything about her calls to me, and I want to savour every single minute of this all-encompassing pull.

I drop my hands to the counter on either side of her hips, close enough to touch but not quite.

Her unique fragrance, a blend of clean skin and fresh lavender, warm and all womanly, assails my nostrils, overtaking the lemony smell of the kitchen soap.

I close my eyes and inhale deeply.

Visions of her with the sun shining down and lighting up the lush lines of her body while I pound into the delicious warmth of it, engulf me.

Intimacy is bloody addictive.

I've never, ever, felt so insatiable before.

Quite the contrary. All my previous hookups—not that there were that many—were one and done. The girls were usually out of my hair so fast that if I had a fragile ego which I may have had, I'd have been wearing it around my ankles for days afterwards, which I may have done.

Meaningless sex. Meaningless girls. Just meaningless...

But now, with Aurèle, I can't help but ask myself, *what the fuck was I thinking back then, settling for hurried couplings not worth my time?*

"Can I get another hug?" she asks, her voice unconsciously dropping two octaves.

My eyes pop open.

Aurèle's head leans back to the side—her thick braid falling over one perky breast, exposing the graceful curve of her neck as she looks at me sideways. And fuck me if she isn't offering more with her parted lips and sultry look. A *more* I'm more than willing to supply.

A hug, really, now? My eyes ask.

I lean forward. Oh, so slowly.

Her eyes darken.

Her breath hitches.

She swallows.

Man, I just can't get enough of these reactions. Her. My slightest touch. Bringing her pleasure. She brings me to my knees. She makes me feel on top of the world.

"Is that all you want?" I tease before bending her over the counter. My hands unhurriedly run up beneath her thermal shirt, unclipping her bra.

Her head bows as I pin her down to the lower cabinet with my body and relish the shallowness of her breath, matching mine.

Dropping open-mouthed kisses along the back of her neck, I run my hands down, down, down the smooth skin of her taut stomach, eliciting a pleasured whimper from her.

Her forehead thumps on the ceramic-tiled counter, her breathing turning erratic as I maintain her into place, applying pressure so she can't move her hips by so much as an inch.

"No, it's not all I want," she says, panting.

I want nothing more than to prolong just about every fucking minute of this sweet, sweet torture. All kinds of erotic.

"What do you want?" My hands ask her as they slide inside her thermal underwear, pressing down on her, opening her. She whimpers.

One of her hands wedges between us, rubbing me through my jeans and robbing me of what's left of my breath, my control hanging by a thread.

"I want you inside me. Now." Her plea splinters my mind and any desire to take this slow and make it last.

Too late now—things are about to get dirty as fuck.

"That can be arranged." Shoving my thigh between her legs, I cup her ass, dragging her closer. "With pleasure." And even though she can't hear what I just said, I intend to show her.

Thirty-Three

AURÈLE

His breathing matches mine—hard, heavy, and hot.

Olivier's fingertips brushes the underside of my breasts, flattening his palms, going down, down, down, stopping short of the lacy edge of my panties. My gut tightens, pierced by arrows of pleasure as he mercilessly teases my lower belly with smooth fingertips without ever going under the elastic band.

My lower body hums, and I wonder if Olivier is as hard as I'm wet.

His upper body pins my torso against the ceramic tiled counter so I can't move. My nipples pebble behind my unhooked bra, every inch of Olivier's body in direct contact with mine, his erection snug against my ass.

I have my answer.

When I try to arch into him, Olivier's hands press down on me, and I welcome his weight arching into me and the coolness of the tiles underneath my flattened palms.

Too much. Not enough.

Olivier moves his hands over my ass in appreciation, squeezing gently.

I wedge my hand between us, my palm pressing down on Olivier's hard length, stroking him jerkily through his jeans as much as I can.

Need you inside me, now. I'm ready to beg.

A low growl vibrates in his chest and something in Olivier snaps.

He yanks me closer to him, quick to wedge his knee between my legs and force them apart.

My shirt and bra are pulled over my head in one fell swoop and tossed on the floor, and I whimper, panting with want.

My arms reach for him but my hands are planted back firmly on the counter before Olivier pulls down my thermal leggings and panties in one flick of his wrist, exposing me. I gasp in pleasured surprise as Olivier slips two fingers inside me, sliding one foot between mine, and kicks my legs out wider.

Flattening himself against me, Olivier's freed erection burns a trail stroking me from behind. He shudders, rubbing the engorged tip of his penis into my slick folds, slowly, teasingly. I jerk hard, the pleasure almost unbearable.

His hips thrust in small jerky movements, my hips arching just the same, wanting to absorb Olivier into me. I close my eyes, quivering, waiting for the bliss of him filling me up to the brim.

I bow into Olivier's touch, wanting, no, needing him to fill me up. My body tensing, tightening, already churning close to an explosive orgasm.

Olivier moves his fingers in and out of the silky wetness between my legs and rubs some of my flowing honey on my clit. The smell of our intermingling musk is quite enticing, causing a swell of lust in me. As though responding in kind, Olivier's cock bulges against my spine, and I tense in anticipation.

Now, now, now, I inwardly chant, and at last, Olivier surges forward, gliding in, impaling me so deep I can feel his balls pressed against my ass cheeks.

I hiss out a breath, overcome.

From this angle, Olivier fills me completely. Different than before, but good different.

Maintained on the very tip of my toes, I almost wilt at the knees, the only thing preventing me from folding into a puddle of goo on the floor is the kitchen counter I'm splayed against.

Olivier tugs my head back with my braid, sending tingles down my spine, his teeth scraping over the side of my neck in an open-mouth kiss.

I feel stretched, full, overflowing.

When Olivier pulls back out, I gasp and then whimper with his re-entry. Soon my hips are rocking with him as I moan against the counter.

Thrust. Retreat. Thrust.

My breathing picks up, and I chase my breath, panting like a blacksmith's bellows, trying to hold off my impending orgasm under Olivier's relentless hammering.

When he reaches around to massage me again, I groan, willing myself to last.

A rumble of pleasure vibrates from his chest as he slows down.

Instinctively, I rise up higher on my toes and arch my back, bracing my hands on the counter. His hands grip my hips hard, but still Olivier moves in a slow, agonizing rhythm.

My stomach feels weightless, my legs go numb.

"Olivier," I whisper his name in a litany.

"Olivier," I groan his name loudly as his thrusts speed up. He slams into me, and I can feel my orgasm rebuilding to its peak.

His thrusts come faster and faster, and I lose it, splintering on a burst of pleasure so sharp, I scream.

His body stills as he surges inside me, his hands tight on my hips.

My legs shake weakly, and my breath comes out choppy.

Olivier gathers me in his arms, the both of us slick with sweat, and we fold onto the floor in a boneless heap of flesh.

"Death by pleasure," I say, regaining my breath in a daze of happiness, my finger tracing his lips.

"Heaven?" he replies with a suggestive smile.

"What comes way after Heaven?"

"This." He rolls me over, and with his palms hitting the floorboards beside my head, he crushes his mouth to mine.

Thirty-Four

P.O.

"Found it."

"*Scène un, prise trois*," Aurèle says mischievously as I pick my shirt up off the floor for the third time in as many hours. Scrape it off the floor more like.

She's so cute, standing there already wearing Soft-shell pants, a knit hat, and scarf over a thick wool sweater in shades of white and blue in a Norwegian pattern. Maybe this time, we'll make it out the door.

"Yeah, think by now it'll start growing on me like mold on bread," I say, pulling my shirt on, the delicate scent of Aurèle's lavender soap clinging to my skin not enough to eliminate my wrinkled tee's fragrant *eau de sweat*. With more than twenty-four hours on the clock, the thing really went above and beyond the call of duty. Let's just say, doing a quick laundry hasn't even been a bleep on our radar and, now, it's kind of too late for that. Not that I'm really complaining, considering.

And if everything goes according to plan, the one Aurèle knows nothing about yet, Liam will have a fit if I come within five feet of the twins later on. I intend to drop by with her after our walk down to C'est la Vie. Just to show her around, ease her into staying over at the quack farm while I'm away. Preferably as of yesterday.

I wince at the whiff sneaking up my nose as I smooth the tee over my chest, shaking it in a last ditch effort to air it out some. No dice. Oh, well. Liam will either have to live with it or lend me a clean one. Or two. Or three.

I really don't feel like going back to Boston—even with Aurèle if she so chooses—but more and more like snuggling up to her here, away from cell phones and internet connections. My dick perks up, twitching in total agreement. My heart following close behind totally on board.

Have mercy.

I need to get my head back in the game. The other head. The other game. The one I don't feel like playing anymore even if just for another month or so. I know the end goal is a handful of weeks away but still. It's like what I've been reaching for is futile, shallow, not really worth the effort all of a sudden. Who the hell cares if I have a double Master's in software engineering and computer science from MIT? Who the hell needs another firewall app anyway with seventy-four already floating around?

"You don't know how sorry I am I don't have a shirt large enough to fit you," she pouts, brushing her hands over my chest and bringing me out my thoughts.

I tip her chin up. "Hey, you don't know how *not* sorry I am, you don't have a shirt large enough or male enough to fit me. I would hate to have to kill anyone."

She chuckles low before snuggling up to me, inhaling my collar, rubbing her nose in, fisting it. "Love that smell."

"Whoa. There." I hold her at arms' length. "Your sense of smell is seriously out of whack if you can withstand the whiff."

"It smells like you. It smells comforting. I would sleep in it, all wrapped up in you while you're gone." She backs away, giving me the once-over with a new confidence and a twinkle in her eyes. "Lucky for me, the memory of you is stamped all over this place now. Should be enough to keep me company when you're gone."

My stomach bottoms out, free falling like that one time I bungee jumped back at BIA—no thanks to Zac—or feels like it. "About that..." My hand darts towards her then halts in the air.

Bloody hell. *What have I been thinking?* Look at her, man. She glows. She's in her element and, furthermore, she's here, finding her footing. You can't ask her to come with you to a big city. Not if it's leaving her there alone for the better part of your days and evenings as crazy as your schedule is.

I stare, hard. *You're too precious. You're too vulnerable.*

That gripping feeling in my chest returns, and the thought of being away from her for weeks at a time doesn't settle well in my gut.

I'm so screwed.

"Hey," she says, gently pulling my arm, her brows creasing as she tries to decipher my expression. "What's wrong?"

I'm suddenly tongue-tied. Tied up in knots by this conundrum.

I swallow, tucking a stray hair behind her ear. "I'm missing you already."

"No one ever missed me before. I have to admit, I kind of enjoy it." She drops a sweet kiss on my cheek before pulling me by the arm. "Now, come on. We have an hour's walk in front of us down to Le P'tit Train du Nord Linear Park, and the light is just picture-perfect this time of day."

She plops my beanie on my head, playfully tugging it down so low it now covers my eyes. I shove it back up, but she's already halfway across the room, pulling her coat on and a camera bag over her shoulder before heading out the back door.

I scramble after her, wrestling with my leather bomber jacket with one of its sleeves still inside out from yesterday's quick stripping.

"Wait up," I call out from the balcony which, of course, is totally lost on her.

Man... Too early for bears, and I try to recall if there are wolves in this area, but I can't remember. Locked in her silence and already halfway to the lake, she could be toast without knowing it.

My heart held in a vise squeezes in my chest.

Chill, man. And I used to think Liam's imagination knew no bounds.

I listen to the quiet of nature, letting it seep in. The sound of white water rushes nearby. A few birds chirp in the trees. A light wind rustles in the conifers. Down the road, a car driving by in the distance is just about the only jarring sound disturbing the actual peacefulness of the place. But it's also a welcome thought to know civilization isn't so far from her doorstep after all.

Reassured, I make my way down the deck stairs to the driveway. The packed snow on the side trail—turning to slush under the late morning sun—makes wet sloppy noises underneath my boots, leaving behind deep footprints filling up with water, the cuff of my jeans already soaked through.

Aurèle, by now knee deep in snow, picks up her camera and starts shooting the nearby torrent gushing with melted snow spilling onto the still frozen lake, the frazil—or ice crystals formed in turbulent water as in swift streams—translucent under the sun's rays, forming dainty-as-lace ice sculptures. Pretty as a picture.

I debate joining her, but then, icy-wet jeans are not exactly high on my list of fun things to wear.

Even as I consider it, my stomach growls in protest.

I forage through the stuff we keep as standard emergency kits in the car doors' side pockets, like LED headlights and extra batteries, looking for the snacks I know I will find. I watch Aurèle crawl on her stomach on her quest for the perfect picture as I munch on a few raw almonds from a safe distance. Courtesy of Éolie's slight hypoglycemia, our fleet of Volvos all carry nuts. A pun Liam frequently uses against the rest of us.

I walk around, circling the driveway with my phone, checking the signal. Or lack thereof. I sigh heavily. Maybe by the main road I'll get a bar or two so I can text the guys. I unlock the rear passenger door and reach for Lucie's backpack, getting ready for our trek down to the village.

Jesus.

I didn't really notice yesterday, but it looks like a home improvement store threw up in there. I shove aside color samples, swatch samples, deco magazines, and tools littering the back. Magali and Amélie, her deco-crazy bestie, must have commandeered it recently on one of their missions. Between Zac and Magali's house nearly finished, the construction of their future clinic about to kick off, Liam and Éolie's house slowly taking shape, and Leo's effort to lessen the duct-tape effect, Amélie must be hopping. Makes me wonder how Leo's crush on her is doing. Man, I'm missing all the fun on that one… I've been gone too long.

When I straighten, Aurèle's lens is turned on me, and she's clicking away as she trudges back towards me. Feeling a bit uncomfortable under the barrage, I pop open the cargo bay of Volvo Number Three and fish around my winter coat for my sports shades. I pull them on, my eyes watering from the bright snow the convenient excuse I use to hide behind the mirrored lens.

"Sorry, you're my first essay in portrait," she says sheepishly, lowering her camera. "And you may be my new favorite subject."

As she leans on the side of the car to take a look inside from the open tailgate, I don't reply that I hope it will stay as such.

My answer would be lost anyway unless she looks my way or I turn her around, and that's if she's within touching distance never mind two hundred meters away. The point made all the more glaring by the fact that for the past eighteen some hours, closed-off from the outside world inside her little cottage, I've had her undivided attention, our conversation slow but fluent.

But here, out in the open, with her attention easily distracted and her focus elsewhere—way elsewhere—things are about to get real. And I get the impression I don't really know the half of what living with her disability entails daily as she pointed out in her initial rant. I have no real fucking clue, I realize, of what it feels like to live in a soundless world. Even my silence isn't silent. And the reality check hits me hard upside the head, knocking me on my arse, no longer confused about what to do with the anvil sitting on my chest just at the thought of leaving her behind later.

Forget the café. Forget reminiscing. She never asked, implying I was just a random tourist last summer, but she's about to know the real reason I was here for my summer break in August. And why I'll be here, well, from now on. And it won't be over coffee down at C'est la Vie. Nope. I'll be showing her.

Already, I breathe easier.

Leaning away from the car, Aurèle peeks up at me a question in her eyes. "Is that your winter gear? I must have misinterpreted. I thought you said you came straight from MIT?"

"I did."

"You did?" She scrunches up her nose in confusion. "What did you do? Highjack this car from a local on your way over?"

I laugh outright. "No, why?"

"That car looks well lived-in for an airport rental picked up on the go."

"That's because it's not. Remember our three little pigs?"

"Yes, of course, who could forget?"

I stow Lucie's backpack into the cargo bay and grab the tailgate door, swinging it shut. I look her over. "Well, change of plan. We're going to meet them in twenty. We're dropping in unannounced. Come on." I wave her over.

She grabs my arm. "Wait. You're telling me they're in Val-David and not in the Boston area?"

"Yep." I palm my keys.

"Whoa, wait. So, *they* were visiting you in Boston, then, on that September day? And what do you mean we're meeting them in twenty?" Her eyes grow wide as saucers, and she shakes her head vehemently. "No, we're not. We're walking down to the village. Flight schedules. Lucie. Internet connection."

I open my mouth then close it again, not quite sure whether to admit the truth straight up or ease her into it. I go with ripping the BandAid.

"No, we were here at the time. We were sitting behind you on C'est la Vie's terrace. I was flying back to Boston with Yann on that day." I brace my hands on the rooftop, caging her in.

"You were sitting behind me? You lied for two full weeks?" She squints at me like she can't believe.

"No, Aurèle. I just omitted a few truths…like you did." I arch a brow.

"I…" She stops, her cheeks flushing a deep crimson. She nods, looking down at her feet. "You're right."

I tip her chin up. "I never set out to deceive you, but I couldn't stay away, either. Last summer, I got this unexpected 'in' with you and I ran away with it. No lie. Ever since that first reply of yours, you've been pulling me in deeper, and deeper. And now, I'm madly in love with you."

"So am I, madly," she says, kissing the corner of my lips. "And I'm glad you did save me from Harry…" Her eyes twinkle as she adds, "Truth be known."

"Makes two of us." I open the passenger door and motion with my head. "Hop in."

She waves her hands in front of her for emphasis, warding me off. "I'll meet them some other time. You go say hello. I'll walk down to the village and we can meet back here. If you still have time. Or we can say goodbye right now," she says like it's a plan, a good one, nodding to herself convincingly. Good show, too, except for the flash of panic in her eyes.

"No way. I'm not leaving you right now."

Her face leaching of all color, she shakes her head, eyes wide. "I'm not ready to meet your friends," she says, aghast, like I'm the clueless one.

Oh, Aurèle. It only confirms to me that the best way to debunk her fears that she'll never fit in is to show her.

"What's this panic about? They've all been dying to meet you. And they're pretty damn cool, you'll like them. Liam is quite tickled you're a fan of his series, by the way."

"I'm sure they are. I'm sure I will. Eventually. Maybe. Not now. Not today. I can't do this."

"Well, that settles that. I'm staying here instead of over there." I can go without a high-speed internet connection without breaking into hives. Never tried it. But I'm sure I could.

Riiiight. I hear the guys collectively snort from up here.

Aurèle's eyes widen. "What do you mean you're staying? You can't. You're needed back at MIT."

"Who says?" I grab her arms to make sure I have her full attention. "Do you really think I can go back and leave you behind by yourself? With no fucking way to contact you at any given time? I'll go nuttier than nuts, so might as well stay and flunk for a good reason."

When I tug her along, she digs her heels in, refusing to budge. "That's what's nuttier than nuts. You have to go back!"

I sigh, looking up to the sky then back at her. "Look, Aurèle. My mind is made up. I'm staying."

"You can't," she splutters, gesturing. "As much as I like having you here by my side, I'll never forgive myself if you sacrifice all of your work, sabotaging yourself at the finish line, and for what? Me being incommunicado? I'll write letters, and we'll make chat appointments down at the café whenever your schedule permits. Daylight is getting longer. I can walk—"

I grasp her shoulders, shooting her a stern look. "Absolutely not. Don't you even get how vulnerable you are out here, out of touch, by yourself? Do you think I can live with myself knowing that?"

She rolls her shoulders back, jerking violently away. "What do you mean, vulnerable?" she asks suspiciously, but her knowing eyes drill me, shooting sparks, daring me to say it.

I shift my weight to one side, my hands coming over my hips. "Aurèle, don't play dumb. You're not daft. You're deaf." *There, I've said it,* my eyes say. *Satisfied?*

She clenches her jaw, breathing a couple of times through her nose. She nods at me. Whipping out a pen and a pocket notebook from her coat she scribbles angrily before shoving it in my face.

I'm deaf? No shit, Sherlock.

I swipe it out of her hands, my temper flaring. "Trying to prove a point, Aurèle? Read my lips—"

"Write it down. I can't hear you."

"Goddammit. Don't go there," I fume, scrunching the notepad in my fist. I lean into her face. "Can't you see it adds a whole new layer of worry?" No. Make that layers, upon layers, upon layers. "You're fucking isolated here."

"See what I mean? You're treating me differently like I told you *you* would!"

"Of course I do! I love you—"

"Knock it off. We wouldn't even have this discussion if it weren't for me being deaf. You'd be on your way back to MIT by now, back where you need to be." She pokes a finger in my chest, going toe-to-toe, not giving an inch.

"Newsflash. Moot point. You are. And no. I won't go back. Not unless you accept to stay at Leo's farmstead while I'm away. In a secured environment, civilized, among friends you not only can count on but high-speed internet and a bloody cell connection that actually has four bars!" I shout, furiously annoyed.

"Impressive. So that we can talk on the phone whenever you call?"

"Sarcasm will get you nowhere."

"And blackmailing me will get you somewhere? Or is that browbeating? Newsflash. Been there, done that. Escaped from it."

"Don't even fucking go there. I'm nothing like them."

She turns on her heels. I'm striding after her before I even realize I'm moving. I reach a hand out, but she stops and whirls around faster than I can touch her. "All this. Just because I'm deaf? Don't you see what I mean?"

"Sue me for caring."

"You're not caring, you're controlling. Don't do this to me!" she cries out.

I reach out to her, grabbing her arms. I search her troubled gaze. Can't she understand it's my decision? That she's my world, and if something were to happen… No. Not going there. "No. Don't do this to ME."

She shoves me away, and I stumble back a step. Stunned by her move, I'm slow to react, my hands only grasping a handful of air as she whirls out of my reach.

She sprints ahead of me like I'm a lion to her gazelle. Make that an out-of-shape lion and a sprightly gazelle in rubber-soled boots. With good traction.

Legs pumping, lagging behind, wheezing and coughing my lungs out, I call out to her. Like that would help even if she could hear me. Which she can't.

Fuck. I curse a blue streak, plumes of breath fogging in front of me as I chug along like an asthmatic choo-choo train.

She's running like the hounds of Hell are nipping at her heels.

Without slowing, she disappears round the last bend of the long winding driveway before it connects to the main road lined on both sides by snow banks twice her height.

Just as I wonder if I'll have to sprint all the way down to the village before catching up to her, the crunch of tires closely followed by the skid of a car accompanied by the dull thump of a blunt object hitting metal screech in my ears.

I vault through the underbrush.

"Aurèle!" Her name rips from my throat.

Thirty-Five

P.O.

Heart in my throat, I burst out of the woods to find a small Fiat 500 stopped in the middle of the road. I run up to it, my gaze darting from one side to the other, frantically searching for a sign of Aurèle but find none.

A sense of relief washes over me when I realize she must have made it to the Linear Park on the other side of the street, and she's probably halfway down to the village by now.

I'm out of breath. I lean forward and put my hands on my knees.

There's a small indent on the hood of the car, facing me. I glance back at the driver of the bright-red Fiat, a young woman staring straight ahead, visibly shaken, and I wonder if she hit a deer.

She pays me no attention. I tap on her window. She startles before lowering it. "Are you all right? Want me to call for road assistance?" I ask.

"Is she... Is she dead?" she asks, wide-eyed.

I almost rip her car door open. "What the fuck happened?" I ask, also growing wild-eyed.

"A deer. There was a deer I kept looking for. It jumped out of the snowbank to cross the road further up, and I was driving well below the speed limit looking for others," she says, and I almost weep. *A deer. Everything's going to be all right.* "But even driving at a crawl, I swear I never saw the flash of pale blue coming. I swear," she babbles, repeating it on a loop, just frozen there, doing nothing.

Aurèle. Aurèle is wearing a glacier-blue coat.

"Aurèle!" I scream her name, turning in a circle.

"Is that her?" the driver asks in a hopeful voice, pointing behind me.

I whirl around so fast I almost lose my balance. Spotting her up ahead sliding over the snow bank, I yell her name, breaking into a full sprint. She gingerly gets up and freezes upon seeing me running up the hill.

She takes a few wobbling steps on the road and vaguely points behind her at the undergrowth of saplings growing by the side of the road before her knees buckle, and she folds.

I skid to a stop in the snow next to her. *She's okay. She's going to be okay.* "Christ, Aurèle. You just shaved ten years off my life."

She huffs breaths and blinks up at me in confusion. I touch her face. It's cold. She's so cold. As soon as I put my hand under her shoulders to pull her into my lap, she cries out in pain.

"Hurts...." She holds her shoulder, grimacing.

I scoop her up in my arms from the left side, mindful of her right shoulder, whispering, "Let's get you checked up by Zac."

"Who...?" she asks faintly just before collapsing in my arms, her head lolling to the side, a red stain blooming on the back of her shredded coat. Blood drips on the road, a goose egg swelling on the side of her head, a trickle of blood wetting her hair.

I fall to my knees. "Call 911," I bark, tearing my jacket off.

"Aurèle! No, no, no. Stay with me." I staunch the flow of blood with my shirt from the worst of her lacerations, my only thought to keep the blood from seeping out of her.

Blood everywhere. So much blood, turning the white snow crimson.

Funny that I'm not passing out, I'm thinking. I can't stand the sight of blood without turning green. Both Yann and I can't, and we're infamous for it.

Soon, though, her bleeding stops from the applied pressure and cold combined, but she's so still, lying there in the snow on my jacket.

I touch her face, trying to get some sort of reaction. When I get none, I start to panic and press my fingers to her neck, checking her pulse. It's there, beating a slow rhythm. I close my eyes briefly. "Thank you," I exhale on a long breath that plumes in front of me.

"The operator says help is on the way, and not to move her," the driver says and her presence barely registers. "I'll go wait on the crest of the hill to flag them down."

I don't reply. I can't.

I tap her cheeks to revive her. She doesn't respond.

I rub some snow on her forehead. She still doesn't respond.

I lie down beside her. I'm shaking. My whole body is shaking. "Aurèle, stay with me," I repeat over and over, kissing the pulse point at her wrist, but she's lying there with her eyes closed.

Everything slows down to a standstill and becomes blurry until I hear the wail of sirens in the distance.

Someone pulls me back and asks me to move aside so that they can help her.

Paramedics swarm her, their movements quick and efficient.

They're moving her onto a gurney.

I can't speak. I can't breathe. It's my fault. It's my goddamn fault.

"Sir, we need to go. Are you riding with her?" one of the paramedics asks as the others carry her to the ambulance. They don't wait for my reply, loading her up, the driver already cranking up the engine.

Shaking some of my numbness out, I scramble after them before they can close the cargo bay on Aurèle and leave me by the side of the road.

I call out, "I need in there!" I climb in. They shut the doors, and the ambulance pulls away. I hold her hand the entire ride.

"Stay with me," I repeat over and over, but she never regains consciousness.

Thirty-Six

P.O.

Feeling like a caged animal, I pace the length of the waiting room several times, breathing hard, but trying to calm down.

All I can hear is the sound of my breathing.

The antiseptic smell mixing with my nerves is getting to me; I feel nauseated.

I scrub my hands over my face, my pulse spiking with each minute I'm kept in the dark. I need to calm the hell down for Aurèle. She doesn't need to see me like this.

What's taking so long?

This is my fault. She has to be okay. She *has* to.

Fuck. I try to breathe through another bout of nausea, but, Christ, just remembering what spurred her on to run blindly onward...

I clutch my chest, seeing all over again the round Fiat 500 seemingly intact, its metallic red paint glittering in the sun but sitting askew on the road like an oversized butterball turkey.

And now, just thinking about it I break into a cold sweat.

Christ. Not again. I scramble back into the men's room and bend over the sink in the nick of time. I double over and puke my guts out. Dry retching. No puke left this second go-round.

I feel a swish of fresh air as the heavy door opens and closes just as quickly with a resounding click. Good. I'm to be left alone. Let them think I'm carrying a dreadful virus like the plague.

I wipe my forehead with the back of my hand and brace my hands on the lip of the counter, neck bowed, waiting for the merry-go-round in my head to stop swirling. When the room stops spinning, I splash cold water on my face with trembling hands and stumble back out into the waiting room. The torture room. Where fellow inmates are waiting, barred from the other side, kept from what's happening behind closed doors. Behind the nurses' station. Where I'm also bloody barred from now.

I lean against the wall, too restless to sit but too weak to pace the floor. That's where Zac finds me, closely followed by Magali, Leo, and Liam. I must have called, or texted, at one point, but for the life of me, I can't quite remember doing it.

"Any news?" Magali asks hurriedly, a worried frown marring her features. *Not good*, my mind screams. That girl is usually the poster child for good cheers and optimism. And as a midwife, she has medical training. She knows something I don't.

I straighten from my slouch, pulling at my hair.

"They're not telling me anything! Not a damn thing," I tell her. My head snaps back to Zac and I ask, close to unraveling, "Zac, man. It's been hours. Why aren't they telling me anything?"

His fingers curl on my shoulder, and he squeezes reassuringly. "It doesn't mean it's necessarily bad."

I shake my head, breathing through my nose. "Doesn't mean it's necessarily good..." I can't finish the sentence, and Zac doesn't refute me either. I take a deep breath, trying to maintain my composure. "Not only that. She's deaf, Zac, and she thinks she's defective as it is. Just before passing out she grew more and more confused. What if she wakes and tries to understand what's going on? She needs me in there. I'm the only one she has."

I pinch the bridge of my nose, my eyes burning with the hot sting of tears. Fuck. I'm losing it.

"Hang on. I'll go find what news I can, but you've got to let them do their jobs without breathing down their necks. It's not helping Aurèle." Zac and Magali exchange a look I can't begin to decipher before Zac disappears beyond the nurses' station into no-man's-land.

"You heard the man." Leo grabs me by the arm, shoving me in a seat to stop me from following. His head tips in the direction I want to go. "Keep it together. They're doing all they can."

I don't bother to answer.

"Come on, man. Drink up before you pass out." Liam gives me a sports drink. I just stare at the glacier-blue liquid, the same color as Aurèle's coat.

My throat thickens, closing up.

"Can't." I shake my head no.

Magali uncaps it, urging me on. "P.O., sip."

"Later."

Her hand comes to rest on my back. "Do it. Now."

"Are you always this bossy?"

"Only when giving orders." She arches a brow, staring me down.

Despite myself, I snort. Zac has his hands full with this one, all right. I take a small sip, making a face. It tastes like shit but I welcome the distraction. "Remind me again why I'm drinking antifreeze?" I ask flatly.

"Because you've got to cool your jets and chill down a notch?" Liam says pointedly, one eyebrow angling up.

"Easy for you to say…" I trail off into silence, running a hand down my face.

"Hey." Liam drops in the seat next to mine and turns his head towards me, crossing his arms over his chest. "Running all the worst-case scenarios in your head is not helping either of you. Trust me."

If there's one person in this room who knows what I feel right now, it's Liam who went through his own hellish wait on Éolie and the twins not that many months ago. I lean forward and rest my elbows on my thighs, looking at my black engineer boots, aged and worse for wear, splattered with blood, the darker stains, diluted by slush, tracking down the sides like teardrops.

I swallow. "It's my own goddamn fault she got run over."

"How do you figure?" Leo asks, coming to stand in front of me, hands on his hips. I sigh heavily.

I feel the combined weight of their disapproving stares. I know what they think. And yet, despite what they think, I am guilty.

"This, I've got to hear," Magali huffs, shooting me a stern look.

I wipe my hand over my face. "I pushed her too hard, too soon…" I stare at the tempest stirred in the neon-blue liquid I'm supposed to sip. Is the bottle shaking, or is it me? "She was so intent on getting away from me, she ran headlong straight into incoming traffic. And I couldn't even warn her."

They all exchange glances.

Leo pins me with a direct look. "Man, she's deaf. How's that your fault?"

I glare at Leo.

"Leo's right, man. Stop blaming yourself for something that's not even close to being your fault, and start being grateful she wasn't run over by the snow plow, instead," Liam says caustically.

"Not helping." I squeeze my eyes shut to ward off the visual.

"Your misplaced guilt isn't either." Magali plops down on my other side, offering me a steaming cardboard cup of dark brew that I refuse. Just the aromatic smell of that hot coffee is enough to turn my stomach.

She curls my fingers over it. "You can always drink it. But at your own peril. The waiting room coffee is known to be thicker than rubber soles with the flavor to match. But it should thaw the ten icicles you now sport back into regular digits and keep your hands warm. If you want the good stuff, we'll go to the cafeteria," she says coaxingly.

I take a deep breath, and I'm not sure if it's to tell her off or thank her just the same, but before I can reply, she pats my knee. "I know, I know. No way."

Several long minutes pass without a word exchanged between the four of us.

I eye dispassionately the solid cream color of the synthetic floor beneath my feet, wondering absently how they achieved seamless skirting in a room that wide. What kind of a big-ass roll of vinyl does it take—?

"Maybe what she needs is a wristband with motion detectors and sound recognition that would jolt her attention to a possible danger when she's distracted?" Magali says quietly in the lull. "You're the computer whiz—"

Wait wait wait. I jump out of my seat and whirl on her. *Why didn't I think of that?* "Magali, you're a genius!"

"Agreed," Zac says from behind me, and I whirl on him, everything else forgotten. His face is impassive, not a shred of evidence left there to give me a hint of what's coming.

"Is she okay?" we all ask at once, surrounding him.

"As okay as can be expected." Magali exchanges a quick, worried glance with him before smoothing out her expression. I feel the strands of my body hair stand up as my skin pricks with goosebumps. I narrow my eyes, but Zac's in doc mode and not giving anything away. Serious. Too serious. "She's being set up in a room as I speak," he reassures us, relenting a bit.

"That's good, right?" Liam asks the question burning on my tongue.

Zac holds up his hand, staving them off. "Hold your questions. I'll brief P.O. first, if you don't mind." He motions for me to follow him. "Come with me."

I stay close to him, trailing right behind him like his shadow, down one busy corridor and up a flight of stairs. His jaw tight, he nods in passing to a few colleagues, knocks on a door and, when no one answers, he ushers me into a small conference room and into a swivel chair.

"When can I see her?"

He crosses his arms over his chest and leans against the doorframe. Is he afraid I'll make a run for it and find Aurèle by myself? He should be. I might do just that.

"Do you know any of Aurèle's past medical history?" The out of left field question brings me out of my thoughts.

"Depends," I answer cautiously. "I know she caught a particularly virulent strain of meningitis some eight years ago, and it was rough going at the time. She never said in as many words, but I can add up that it left her deaf, why?"

"Because what I'm about to tell you is confidential. I wouldn't normally share without her prior consent, but since I know you're in it for the long haul..." He straightens and walks around the table, pulling out a chair before plopping down across from me. "Makes it a hell of a lot easier to explain and, for the record, with no next of kin listed anywhere, I vouched that you two are getting married, or as good as already."

"Do you see me complaining? It's as good as done as far as I'm concerned. Now, spill, I'm worried enough as it is."

He clicks a pen on and off with his thumb before tapping it on the edge of the table, one of his tells when faced with an unpleasant task. "Good news is the gash on her head is superficial. She has a fractured clavicle, a dislocated shoulder, and some lacerations on her side sustained when she was thrown into the undergrowth, and some of those required sutures."

I lean forward over the table. "*That's* good news?" I ask, frowning darkly.

"Yes, actually. She's pretty damn lucky that the snow cushioned her fall and that the saplings were young enough she wasn't impaled—" I gag, holding a hand over my mouth, and he stops mid-sentence, pinching the bridge of his nose. He breathes in. He breathes out. Another tell of his. "Well, you get the gist," he says quietly.

"Don't you think I know?" I breathe in. I breathe out. "Christ," I curse under my breath, holding my forehead in my hands, my neck weighing a ton and a half, while my gut churns. "I'm sorry. You're right."

"Look..." He sighs, massaging the back of his neck. "I didn't mean it quite that way."

"And yet, it is what it is. If that list of injuries is the bloody good news, what's the bad news?" I ask in a monotone.

He clicks his pen then, realizing he's doing it, he throws it across the table, getting up to pace only to plop his ass back down on the seat opposite mine. He steeples his fingers in front of his mouth. "Keep in mind that the human brain is all at once resilient and fragile. It's a delicate balance to maintain, and still pretty much unchartered territory in so many aspects—"

"Cut the crap, man," I urge. "Give it to me straight."

"No shit, P.O." He looks up to the ceiling then leans on his elbows, crossing his arms over the table. "Her brain scans came out clear, no internal bleeding, nor swelling, and they show signs of normal activity. But it confirms an older, permanent lesion of her medial periaqueductal gray running through the right side of the lateral hypothalamus, or the medial geniculate nucleus where the center for hearing is located. Just to give you an example on how intricate and vital the brain is to each and every one of our senses, if the worst of the inflammation and swelling from the meningitis viral fever had damaged the lateral geniculate nucleus of the thalamus which relays visual information to the primary visual cortex—a thin sheet of tissue less than one-tenth of an inch thick located in the occipital lobe in the back of the brain—she'd have been blind instead of—"

"When I said *give it to me straight*, I meant in plain English..."

He leans back in his chair, eyeing me. "The ears by themselves are just transmitters and with her wiring screwed to hell, her brain is cut off and can no longer process any auditory sound waves."

"Whoa. Back up." I scrunch up my face, brow creasing in concentration. "Are you telling me Aurèle's deaf because her hardware is no longer connected to a runnable software?"

He strokes his chin, a speculative glint entering his eyes. Is he thinking what I'm thinking? All sorts of crazy ideas about developing a microchip implant spin in my head.

I bob my head, lost in thoughts. Maybe that's my true calling as a software engineer; my incentive sure is there.

Zac clears his throat bringing me back to the here and now.

"Well, seen that way. Yes, your computing is spot on," he confirms to me. "As it is—"

"Hold on." While my mind goes a mile a minute in every direction, not the least of which branching out in my research and software development, I realize something belatedly. "If her scan came back in all clear, why is that considered bad news, exactly?" I ask suspiciously.

"I was getting to that..." He sighs heavily, brushing a hand down his face. "Not having any plausible causes as to why she's not waking up leaves us with a bunch of speculations and nothing tangible to fix. All we know at this point is that Aurèle is still inexplicably unconscious, and the damaged side of her brain got the brunt of the knock on her head, even as minor as it was."

"In other words, we know jack about the ramifications of that."

He nods grimly. "I'm not going to sugar coat it, man. The next forty-eight hours will be determining. Her injuries as a whole are not life-threatening in the least but if she slips into a deeper coma, the hospital may need your signature somewhere down the road... She might never wake up."

Thirty-Seven

P.O.

Bursting out of the cloud cover, the crepuscular sunrays bounce off the white sterile walls of Aurèle's private room bathing it in soft, natural light one last time before the sun sets, dropping out of sight behind the mountains.

Zac flips on the fluorescent light fixtures as he walks out, answering a call from his clinic. "She's six weeks early. Have you ruled out Braxton-Hicks?" he says to whoever's on the other end.

I wish he hadn't done that. It was easier to pretend in the low light that this wasn't a hospital room. Now, Aurèle's too-pale complexion appears waxy and much too still under the harsh brightness, the only spot of color on her face is the dark bruise at her right temple.

I sit by her bed, interlocking my fingers with hers. Her hand is cold. So cold.

She might never wake up.

I take deep breaths, and stare at the LED screens on the beeping monitors hooked on her lifeline mapping her heartbeats, her brain waves, her every breath—my only focal point.

All I can do is wait. And listen. And helpless doesn't even begin to describe how I feel.

It's excruciating.

"I'm already at the hospital. How far apart are her contractions?" I hear Zac ask the caller. He looks at me from the doorway like I might shatter any minute. *Too late for that*, I'd like to say, *my heart's already splintered into a thousand fragments of regret.* But I keep quiet, in no mood for another lecture on misplaced guilt.

"What? You mean to say she came in four centimeters shy of fully dilated not knowing what was going on?" Zac's voice rises.

Magali went back to the farmstead to pick up Éolie, promising to stay with Aurèle until Zac's shift, officially starting in thirty minutes, is over, while Liam and Leo left earlier to babysit the twins—unlike Éolie, they need both set of arms to keep up with them. Can't blame them, I would too. But now, it feels like the changing of the guard as they, too, promised to be back later after the girls' turn. I briefly wonder how Zac got them all extended visiting hours especially when they aren't immediate family. Then I wonder why. It's not like I'm going anywhere anytime soon, despite what they think.

Who cares if I'm not going back to MIT? Who cares if I'm looking at two years down the drain with only five weeks remaining? Who cares if Aurèle won't even know the difference if I'm here or they are in my stead? I'll know. That's what counts.

"I'm on my way," I hear him say from a distance.

Guess outside Aurèle's room, life goes on. Just not hers. Or mine.

She might never wake up.

I stare at the monitors with unseeing eyes, the beeps of her heart beating fills my ears like a roar. My chest hollows out.

I no longer know how to live without you in this world. I don't want to know.

"Hang in there, man." Zac pats me on the shoulder. "I'll be back as soon as I can."

"Take your time," I say flatly. "I'll be here."

Zac gives me one last look before he hurries off.

I turn her hand over and kiss her palm, then press it against my cheek. "Come back to me. I'm here," I whisper over and over again, minutes ticking by, eating away at this forty-eight-hour window relentlessly. I wish I could stop time until she wakes up. Or at the very least, reset the clock every hour on the hour. We're already down by ten hours on this countdown.

With the dried blood washed out of her hair, the strands spread on the pillow like poured honey touched with cinnamon and hide the angry bruise on her scalp extending to her right temple.

She looks so peaceful, like she's just taking a nap. *Sleeping Beauty.*

I stand up and kiss her forehead, her brow, her cheek, her lips, whispering words of love, hoping against hope that she'll magically wake from my true love's kiss.

Minutes go by, slipping away like sand through my fingers.

She doesn't stir.

Then again, this is no fairy tale. This is real life.

She might never wake up.

I stroke her cheek, careful not to disturb her nasal cannula. The supplemental oxygen helps her breathe easier, I know, but that she needs it at all kills me. "I'm so fucking sorry."

I just want to lie down with her and lay my cheek on her chest. I want to listen to the steady thrum of her heart beating. I want my head to rise and fall with her every breath. I want my arms to hold her. But there are too many wires and tubes and cords running everywhere.

I kiss her forehead again. And again. I know she can't hear me, either way, but I talk to her, anyway. And maybe one day, she will hear me. No, scratch that. No maybe. I vow here and now that one day it *will be* possible. But first, she has to wake up.

She might never wake up.

I shake my head against my own fears. "You have to pull through. You have to come back to me. There's so much we have yet to do together, you and I," I murmur, sudden tears overwhelming me. Seven months boiling down to eighteen hours of bliss, is that all we'll get? I wipe my eyes with the back of my hand, taking a deep breath, holding it in.

I tilt my head against the back of the chair and stare up, swallowing, blinking away extra moisture. Futile. Hot tears track down my cheeks, wetting my neck. My hands press down on my chest in a vain attempt to alleviate the pressure. Useless. Still feels like an eighteen-wheeler is bloody parked on it, and I'll never fucking breathe freely ever again.

I take her hand in mine bringing it up to my lips. I kiss her and keep my lips pressed to her hand, breathing her in. I close my eyes...

"P.O.," Magali says, and I jerk my eyes open.

"Hey," I greet both Éolie and her quietly.

I can sense them behind me, hovering and building up the courage to ask me a question. I feel like they're waiting on me. To what? Cry, maybe? Yell? Hit something? It's Aurèle we're waiting for. To wake the hell up. Not me.

Please wake up, I inwardly entreat, beg, pray, dropping one last kiss on her hand before gently depositing it back on the coarse material of the thin hospital blanket, careful of the IV drip on her wrist, afraid she might break. Or that I might.

"No change?" Magali asks softly.

She might never wake up.

I shake my head, brushing back a strand of hair from her cheek, my throat aching and my eyes burning with unshed tears.

I look back. They exchange a quick, worried look before smoothing out their facial expression into a cheerful one.

Éolie hugs my shoulders and kisses my cheek warmly, offering me an encouraging smile. "I brought you a change of clothes and other goodies from the farmstead. We also stopped by Aurèle's and grabbed her toiletries along with a more comfy flannel nightgown," she says, picking an overnight bag off of the floor before tilting her head towards the bathroom adjacent to Aurèle's private room. "Why don't you take a shower while we sit with her?"

I know it's irrational and that technically, the bathroom's in the same room, but I can't help it. I shake my head. "I'm good, thanks."

From the corner of my eye, I see Magali check the readouts on the machines. Then she studies the nails of Aurèle's right hand and the sling of her bandaged shoulder wrapped tightly around her chest. Is it too tight? Catching my worried frown, she smiles reassuringly, but too brightly, smoothing over Aurèle's blanket. "Hey, don't mind me. Bad habit."

"Would you tell me if you saw a worsening sign?"

"Absolutely." She pats my chest. "Not," she mumbles under her breath.

"Heard that."

"Meant you to. She's in good hands."

She waves her hand in front of her nose. "Also, you stink." Her face screws up like she's just sucked on a lemon.

Éolie grabs my hand, tugging me up, or trying to, I'm not budging. "P.O., come on. I brought your favorite handmade soap and shampoo from the farmers' market. You'll feel so much better once you shower and change..."

"Tempting, but no. I'm not changing my shirt until she wakes." Not while there's still a faint trace of her smell on it. They stare at me, unimpressed. "She wouldn't want me to, she thinks it smells comforting. And I... I..."

It smells like you. I would sleep in it, all wrapped up in you while you're gone, she'd said, not even an hour before I sent her running headlong into traffic.

In a quick move I don't see coming, Éolie whips the shirt right off my back. I blink in surprise then wonder no more how she handles both the twins at the same time with only one set of arms.

"All right. Here's the deal," Éolie says sweetly, folding my shirt with care. How can such a soft voice carry so much authority behind it? "You shower, and while you shower, I'll give your shirt to Aurèle to cuddle with. You can put it back on once you're done. Deal?"

Not that a scalding hot shower doesn't sound appealing, but... "Do I have a choice?" I grumble, snatching the duffel she holds up to me by the strap.

"*Non,*" they both say in unison.

I sigh. "Figured."

"Now that that's settled, I'll go see what I can scrounge up at the cafeteria while you shower so you can eat something," Magali says over her shoulder, already halfway out the door. Before I can so much as protest that I'm not hungry, she swivels round and point a finger at me. "No argument, we see your ribs."

I hold my hands up in surrender. "*Me* argue with you?" I ask wryly, my tone of voice somewhere in between are-you-crazy or do-you-think-I'm-stupid. Even Theo knows better than to debate with her.

"See, that wasn't so hard."

Less than ten minutes later, I walk back into Aurèle's room, dry towelling my hair, more refreshed than I thought possible. Wearing Liam's borrowed jeans turned at the cuff and clean socks and underwear, I feel like a new man. Almost.

"Any change?" I ask Éolie, draping the damp towel on the back of a chair by the foot of the bed. She doesn't twitch so much as a finger, leaning over Aurèle, her forehead resting on the left side of her face.

No answer.

"Éolie?" I frown. "What's the matter?"

But she remains as still as a salt pillar with my shirt bunched in her hands, holding it like a prized teddy bear between her and the crook of Aurèle's neck. I round the bed, coming to a stop in front of her, waving my hand in front of her face, but she doesn't react in the least, her unblinking eyes turned inward.

Fucking hell. Not another one gone on my watch.

I stretch out my hand and try to loosen her death grip on my shirt and Aurèle's arm as gently as I can to get her into a more comfortable position, debating whether or not I should call Liam to come get her before a nurse comes in and gets alarmed.

"Sébastien!" Without warning, she straightens, gasping for air as she yells her son's name. I jump backward, fear giving way to relief when I see she's coming out of it.

With wide eyes, she grasps me by the forearms, swaying on her feet, digging her fingers in.

"Hey, hey, I've got you, sweet, no worries."

"P.O.?" She blinks, looking around as if she's forgotten where she is.

I lower her into my chair and she blinks up at me, still clutching my shirt over my arm. "You can let go now." She looks at her hands, the shirt, the bed, the chair, then me. "Care to tell me what that was about?"

"Sorry," she winces, her eyes clearing. "I get a bit disoriented and dizzy when I'm yanked away from a vision while in the midst of it."

She was having a vision while leaning over Aurèle, all but hugging her and cuddling my shirt? Bloody hell. And I pulled her out? I rub a hand down my face. *Can this day get any worse?*

"You don't know how sorry I am right now. But fuck, Éolie. I've never seen you have one, I thought you were having some sort of seizure, you were so still and unresponsive." I curse underneath my breath, angry at myself for inadvertently interrupting her. "Was it about Aurèle?" I take her shoulders and search her eyes beyond hopeful. Éolie may not control any of the shit she sees, but so far, she's only ever had visions of happiness somewhere down the line.

"Please tell me."

"P.O.," she says gently. She looks at me with sad, understanding eyes. "It's not foretelling in the sense that it will happen no matter what. There's no guarantee in what I see; it's just a glimpse of happiness in the making. And even though it's rooted in the now, it won't happen by itself."

"I don't care. Give me something, anything to grab on to."

She stares at my shirt with a faraway look in her eyes. "Have you ever been to the small clearing on top of the bluff overlooking the farmstead?"

I furrow my brow, trying to see. "Can't say that I have, but I intend to now. What about it?" I grab a chair, scooting closer. I lean forward, my forearms resting on my thighs, intent on listening to each and every word Éolie will utter.

"I think…it's where you'll live." She hands over my shirt.

My fingers fist in the goddamn shirt that has seen more action in the past thirty-four hours than a Marvel hero in a year. "With Aurèle?" I ask anxiously.

"Although I didn't get the impression you lived there alone, I really can't say…" Her face twists in sympathy. "I didn't see her at all before being zapped out of it. I'm so, so sorry."

I blow a breath through my cheeks and lean back in my chair. She leans forward, touching my knee. "But if it helps any, Liam and I had just arrived at your place to pick up Nicolas and Sébastien, three or so, on a balmy summer evening at the height of Les Perséides. And they couldn't stop talking about a telescope and shooting stars. They wanted to stay for the night and go with you, stargazing."

I do the math. Nicolas and Sébastien will turn one in three months, so, some two years from now. I hold out my shirt, offering it back to her. "Can you go back?" I ask urgently, impatience simmering in my veins.

She shakes her head slowly, commiserating. "You don't know how many times I've tried before. I never get the same vision twice, but even more irking, I never know when I'll get one nor when and where it will take place and with whom."

Awesome. Way to go, man, nice save you did there. "Well, that answers that."

I sigh heavily pulling my shirt on, and, despite myself, sniff the collar where Aurèle nuzzled me. Was it just twelve hours ago? Feels like forever.

I grab my head in my hands and stare at my feet, settling in to wait.

Thirty-Eight

AURÈLE

Silence.

Deep silence.

Stark blankness.

I can't orient.

I feel the weight of my body. Yet, I feel strangely disconnected, as though held in suspended animation.

Darkness dances on the edge of my consciousness.

Shaky fingers cover my hand, squeezing mine repeatedly. A thumb brushes back-and-forth. The gesture, oddly comforting, brings a burst of warmth and happiness. I want to squeeze back in appreciation but can't, my body weirdly unresponsive, try as I might.

I can't help the anxiety that swims rivers through my mind.

Why can't I move? Where am I?

I struggle with a bout of panic, attempting to open my eyes. But my eyelids are sealed as tight as a bank vault and as heavy as lead.

The effort exhausts me, making my head pound fiercely.

The darkness gains on me. I let it catch me and pull me under.

I float in between realities as if I'm in a dream. In this moment, my surroundings are so sharply defined that I can't be sure this isn't real.

I don't really know where I am.

It's night.

The firmament is such a profound indigo blue that it's almost surreal in color.

Moonlight beams adorn the evergreens with silver highlights like tinsel on a Christmas tree. The small woodland meadow I'm sitting in shimmers in the low light as though sprinkled with fairy dust, enchanting me.

A sultry summer breeze ruffles my hair and caresses my skin while carrying the fragrant smell of wild berries in bloom and fresh wintergreen mint so sharp I can almost taste it on my tongue. I breathe in deeply, peacefulness descending upon me.

When did I ever dream a dream this aware, experiencing such exquisite stimulation flooding me with warm sensations of well-being? Never. That's when...

There's a house at my back that looks familiar, yet, one I've never seen before. The angles are minimalist and modern, not something I would normally go for. But as the entire façade is made of glass, a twin moon reflecting in it like on the surface of a quiet lake, I can't help but envy whoever lives there. I wish it were me.

The view. Everywhere. It's breathtaking.

I itch for my camera, snapping one mental picture after the other.

Down in the valley, the windows of an old farmstead give off a cheerful glow. Not far from the vintage house, there's a roaring bonfire. Its bright flames burning high up, illuminate from behind an old barn with its roof caved in. The dark silhouette of a man drops another log in, igniting sparks in an incandescent spiral like will-o'-the-wisps enticing one to come closer and watch the dancing flames.

Entranced, I see hundreds of fireflies frolicking in the small meadow. It's magical to watch, not unlike stardust falling from the sky in a shower of dazzling confetti.

I sit back in a comfortable lounge chair under a canopy of twinkling stars on top of a rounded hill. On the horizon, outlined against the deep blue of the velvety sky, other forested hills surround me as far as my eye can see. Well-rounded, hundreds of millions of years old, they're not quite mountains anymore. Les Laurentides. I would recognize their unique, rolling shape anywhere. They call to me like a pulse line pounding in my blood. Like I belong here. Still, my surroundings are new to me.

It feels like I live here, but I've never been here in this exact spot before. But if I could just stay here indefinitely, I would. I grin up to the sky, shaking my head. Not that any of this makes sense.

I feel like I sit on top of the world, witnessing three shooting stars streak across the heavens in quick succession.

Leaning forward into my seat, I dig my toes into the warm sod beneath my feet, wanting to anchor myself that much deeper in the delightful moment. Wasn't I knee deep in snow this morning? Where am I?

I breathe in a lungful of the fresh air out there.

The prickly needles of tall conifer trees and odorous cones bear the pungent fragrance of the forest. I even catch the hint of wild chicory from down the valley. The bittersweet perfume of the flower gets carried by the mild breeze with the hint of something else. Warm. Familiar. Precious. Reassuring.

Olivier.

"No clouds tonight. We couldn't have asked for a more perfect peak to watch Les Perséides this year." His voice—deep and magnetizing—carries across as he saunters up to me, mentioning the mid-August peak of the famed meteor summer showers. "I saw four just on my way over."

I jolt, my entire body snapping to face his. "I can hear your voice?"

My eyebrows arch and I gape in astonishment. I hear the crunch of his boots stepping over a thick carpet of pine needles. Olivier's headlight bobs a few feet away on a foot trail meandering from the house between wild blueberry bushes growing low to the ground. He's grinning from ear-to-ear as he holds up a telescope.

In the backdrop, a symphony of crickets chirps to the accompanying concerto of leaves swishing in the wind. A night bursting with sounds? Am I hallucinating? I absently ponder as I lose myself in the relaxing sounds. Or am I dreaming a vivid dream?

Remembering sounds I heard many times before is one thing, hearing new ones is quite another. *Non?*

"Where have you gone to? Come back to me." Olivier's urgent voice brings me out of my thoughts.

"I really can hear you."

His mouth hooks up in a slow, sexy grin.

He drops down in front of me, balancing on the balls of his feet, his finger tilting my chin up, effectively closing my wide-open mouth. His gaze steady on mine, he kisses my palm before tenderly placing it over my heart. "In here, you do."

He pulls me to my feet, and I stare, listening to his voice, mesmerized by the gravelly sound of it as he tells me how much I mean to him.

I lean into the curve of Olivier's arm, and he immediately tightens his hold on me.

"I think I'll just stay here forever," I say wistfully.

"I can be persuaded," he says before resting his chin on top of my shoulder.

"I love you. So much..." I say, the beginning of a tremulous smile dancing on my lips. *Can this be for real? Please, let it be real.*

He kisses me like he wants to remove every bit of doubt crowding my mind. Like he is proving me wrong. And it's so, so right.

"Love you more." His lean, capable hand picks up mine to deposit yet another tender kiss on my palm, his lips quivering as they stay there for a long minute.

"Not possible," I say adoringly.

"Don't bet on it."

I nestle back into his arms and lay my cheek against his warm chest, listening to his quickening heartbeats, his pulse skyrocketing. Or is it mine?

My hand is weirdly cold and shakes with deep tremors as his thumb brushes over my knuckles in a slow back-and-forth, even though the gesture, quietly reassuring, calms me. Strange. I get an obscure impression of déjà vu, like someone comforted me the exact same way a few minutes ago—just before I looked up into the starry night. But didn't Olivier just get here?

I try to squeeze his hand back, but a grey mist appears out of nowhere, and I can no longer see through its density. "Olivier," I call out.

"Stay with me," he says in a fading voice, almost pleading. From afar, I hear Olivier begging me to come back to him. I want to, but I can't find my way through the opaque haze surrounding me.

My right shoulder pulsates with a lancing burning pain. I feel a firm pressure on my wrist at my pulse point before warm fingers deposit my hand back on a coarse material. I can't move my hand over it, nor move my arm.

All of my limbs refuse to obey.

I flutter open my eyes for a second. The lights above me are so bright, way too bright white, blinding me.

Where's my night sky?

Where's Olivier?

Am I at the house on the hill?

The effort of trying to make sense of it all wears me out. I give in to the exhaustion, closing my eyes on a sigh.

Underneath my eyelids, all I see are waves of grey in a sea of nothingness that swallows me whole.

I let it.

Thirty-Nine

AURÈLE

I open my eyes into a white, sterile world.

Much too bright.

I blink furiously, willing my eyes to adjust to the white ceiling with fluorescent lights above.

It is once again silent, but after the contrast of my dream, the silence is eerie. Sad.

I want to go back to Olivier and that house on top of the hill, my whole being consumed by the vibrant sounds of life I heard perfectly there.

Why can't I get back there?

A wave of nausea grips me. I close my eyes, waiting for the room to stop spinning.

When I reopen them, the too bright room from earlier is darker, not as hurtful to my eyes.

I'm lying flat on a narrow cot with metal railings, tucked beneath a white blanket. I try to move my arms, but it's as though they are stuck, pressed close to my body. From the corner of my eye, I can see part of a familiar green and yellow plaid sleeve sticking out. Why am I wearing my favorite flannel nightgown in a strange bed?

Soft, natural light spills onto the room from the large window to my right. It's daylight. The sky, awash in various shades of grey, is soothing. A wave of peacefulness washes over me, bringing forth images of huddling under a blanket, reading in my pajamas to the accompanying pitter-patter of raindrops playing in the background. It has always been music. It's always called to me in ways I cannot explain.

Fat raindrops splatter on the windowpane and my gaze tracks down the droplets of moisture gathering in rivulets.

No pitter-patter.

Quiet.

So quiet.

My weary glance sweeps the room slowly. A tower of machines stands beside me. A tangled bundle of tubing seems to connect them to me and me to them. The sight is strangely familiar.

I've been here before. Or somewhere similar.

I feel a strange disorientation as if my brain can't connect what it sees to what's happening to me.

I rest my tired eyes for a short while, my mind in a haze. Where am I? How did I get here?

When I blink my eyes back into focus, three people crowd together by the foot of the bed on the other side of the room.

Two stunning women I don't recognize.

On the left, is a brunette with striking silver eyes and a creamy complexion. The woman on the right is light blonde with unusual eyes, their color a translucent turquoise framed by dramatic, naturally dark eyelashes and a caramel, sun-kissed complexion.

They're both crouching low beside the hunched figure of a man sitting in a pastel-blue plastic chair.

Their features are soft with compassion as they rub his back and try to coax him to drink from a Tim Horton's cup. On the small table beside him, is a sandwich wrapper. A memory tugs at me. Wasn't I going out for lunch down in the village myself just now? But then, I really don't feel hungry, and the fleeting thought floats away.

I observe them quietly, fascinated by their apparent nurture of the man.

I wish I could capture the moment behind the lens of my camera. "Portraits of Love," it would be called. Maybe I'll start a collection of those someday.

They cajole and persist but the guy sits unmoving. Both his hands are tunneled through his golden-brown hair as he cradles his head in his hands. His elbows rest on his spread knees. His long sleeves, cuffed well above his wrists, show off his lithe sinewy forearms.

I squint.

I know those arms.

I know that cobalt-blue tee.

CAP LOCKS, preventing login since 1980. I'm sure I would read on that shirt if only he'd straighten in his chair...

I know him.

Awareness sings through me, and I jolt inwardly.

Olivier.

He looks sad whereas I'm so happy to see him.

I shouldn't be.

My stomach churns as the sentiment tiptoes on the fringe of my memory, spinning in my head.

I frown, closing my eyes in thought.

He's not supposed to be here.

Olivier would, no doubt, tease me mercilessly if I were to ask. He'd probably joke that my CPU has more holes than a slice of Emmental cheese.

I inwardly grin.

Funny, that. Olivier is Swiss and a computer whiz.

And it pops into my head.

MIT! That's it. He's supposed to be in Boston.

Why isn't he? And why does he look so distraught?

My eyes flutter open wider.

What am I missing?

The girls are talking to Olivier but, try as I might, I can't hear them. A strange feeling of disappointed hope crashes down on me. Where is that place I went to? It felt so real.

I tug my bottom lip between my teeth, pulling it taut. The taste of my chamomile and calendula lip balm bursts on my tongue. I swipe it over the creamy smoothness underlying the rough edges of my cracked lips.

Weird.

I don't recall putting it on, or using it for an age. In fact, I don't recall having dry, chapped lips...or how I came to be here for that matter, wherever "here" is.

The edges of panic begin to creep around me. Why can't I remember getting here? The blonde beauty straightens away from Olivier, wrapping up the sandwich and affording me a clearer view of the other woman's lips. I narrow my eyes in concentration, hoping to pick out some clue.

"P.O., this isn't doing you any good," the brunette seems to be saying as she puts the lid back on the coffee cup. "She might be in the hospital for a long—"

"Don't say it." The girls look at each other over Olivier's head, a worried look now marring their features.

So, I'm in the hospital?

I eye the tubes running through me, my nose, my arm. It finally clicks.

Duh.

What happened?

So many questions my fogged up brain has no answers to.

I need to ask.

I swallow to wet my throat. It hurts, as if I just swallowed a mouthful of thistles.

"Olivier?" I croak.

They all jump as if they heard a gunshot. And in unison, they all look over at me. Olivier leaps from his chair, and my glance darts between him and the girls as they all talk at once.

All I hear is silence.

Not one sound.

An all too familiar void...

The blonde stays back, a soft, knowing smile playing on her lips while the brunette gestures excitedly in the doorway, hailing someone in the corridor, but Olivier is at my side in a split second. Cupping the side of my face, his eyes search mine, his so troubled, a paradox of joy and sorrow swimming in their depths. "Hey, you."

Why are you so sad? Why am I here? I want to ask. "Why are you here?" I ask instead.

The lost look washing over his face guts me.

"It's where you are." He swallows hard, and my eyes trail the bob of his lean, wiry throat. One side of his mouth curls up in a semblance of a smile but doesn't quite make it. "What do you remember—?"

The dark-haired girl nudges Olivier hard, stopping him mid-sentence, telling him something, like he needs to wait.

For what?

I don't get it.

The two girls surround Olivier for a talking to. I squint at them, my face scrunching up in concentration, but even as brief as it is—with their three similar heights and their heads huddled close—I can't see their moving lips.

I inwardly cringe. It's so easy for everyone to forget I can't hear a thing, myself included.

My glance darts between them, but all I see is Olivier shaking his head adamantly and the two girls gesturing before the brunette takes charge, pushing a button on the intercom by the wall.

I move my head to the side too quickly and a bout of nausea washes over me.

I can't keep up.

The effort to make sense of it all is too much.

My eyelids flutter close.

I feel I should know who those two are, somehow, but I can't quite place them. Which in itself is bizarre. Aside from Olivier, I don't know anyone up north. But it's like we had this conversation before.

A faint recollection of Olivier and I straining against each other at my cottage flits through my mind. Hot, sweaty sex against the wall, on the kitchen counter, in the shower, and occasionally on the bed.

My pulse picks up as warm sensations flood my lower belly. The sensuality of those fleeting images slices through the haze swimming through my mind, leaving behind traces of well-being and happiness like I've never known before…and a tingle or three. I strain, pushing on the memories. But I can't recall what was said before, during, after. It sits at the edge of my consciousness, tauntingly.

My thoughts spin round and round or maybe it's the room?

My head throbs.

I try rubbing my fingertips over my temple, but I only drag along the IV line attached to my wrist.

My hand plops back down.

Clammy fingers catch mine, clasping them repeatedly, anxiously. I squeeze back and reopen my eyes slowly to Olivier's concerned ones. "Stay with me," I read on his lips.

My brain is pudding. "At the house on the hill, you mean?"

Olivier shakes his head. "What house—?"

The brunette interrupts him mid-sentence by poking on his chest. "Don't force any of it," she seems to be saying. She shoots him a stern look and his lips flatten. "She probably has a killer headache and if not, you'll give her one. Her doctor is coming by shortly, wait for him." He looks down at his feet, and she fills a small cup with ice chips from a thermos carafe by the bedside.

Water. I'm so parched all of a sudden.

She puts the cup firmly into Olivier's hand and pads over to me before reaching up on her toes to give *me* a quick kiss on the head. "Your mouth is probably as dry as the Mojave Desert, but take small sips or you might get sick," she admonishes, waiting to speak until my eyes are on her lips. "I know things feel foggy right now, but don't worry about your memory. It will all come back to you in your own time. Don't sweat it." She rubs my shoulder in encouragement, then shuffles towards the door, leaving me a bigger mass of confusion, my thirst all but forgotten.

"Don't overdo it," she warns Olivier, pointing a finger at him.

He gives her an indecipherable look before his gaze drops to his fingers, which are now clasped on the plastic cup, squishing it. "Too late for that now, isn't it?"

From where she stands in the doorway, the girl pitches me an apologetic smile, her eyes pleading with me.

For what, exactly? I can't tell.

"We'll come back later," the gorgeous blonde one says, leaning over me, smoothing my blanket. "When you feel a little less muddled and up for company."

"No need." Olivier's back visibly stiffens. "Docteur Tremblay will most likely discharge her into *my* care soon, now that she's awake. Pass the message along, will you?" His lips purse mulishly, and he crosses his arms over his chest as if challenging the entire universe to say otherwise. I get the impression that it's a familiar argument between them all.

She says something to him, and his shoulders relax by a fraction.

Undeterred by his soured mood, she hugs him goodbye and beams at me the loveliest of smiles before slipping out.

I watch the empty doorway, touched and befuddled by their inclusion in equal parts. Finally, I look back at Olivier.

"They know me?"

"They know of you, and you know of them. That was Magali and Éolie." Olivier reaches out and tucks a stray hair behind my ear.

Magali and Éolie?

It jogs my memory. Snippets of our conversations as we chatted well into the night and over breakfast trickle back in.

Of course.

Magali and Éolie.

They live in Val-David, just like me. C'est la Vie! That's how Olivier came to be into my life in the first place. Purely by coincidence. A chance encounter at the café from afar last summer as he stayed over at his friend Leo's farmhouse.

I wonder what it would feel like to have lifelong friends, ones you can count on to be there for you, come what may… A chosen family.

I smile, but I guess a tear slides down my cheek because he wipes it away.

Pain flashes in his eyes. "I'm so fucking sorry, Aurèle. If I could take it back, I would." He presses a soft kiss to my hair.

Just then, an image of Olivier's face tightly drawn in anger flashes through my mind as he decreed that I go live at his friend Leo's farmstead, a perfect stranger, if I wanted him to go back to MIT, or else… Some of the lingering cobwebs clear, the gist of our argument and my volatile accusations following close behind, the rest tumbling back in helter-skelter.

An achy soreness starts in the middle of my chest and spreads outward.

I instinctively recoil as I recollect feeling betrayed, or validated in my long held beliefs, whichever, and my headlong flight, recklessly running ahead, blinded by tears of fury and despair, uncaring of my surroundings, something I'm well aware I can't afford in my condition. But the need to outrun the suffocating heartache closing in on me at the time annihilated everything else on the way.

I look at the IV drip and the blinking machines. *What have I done?*

The sting of tears prick my eyelids, and I blink furiously as my vision blurs.

An older nurse comes into my line of vision, smiling encouragingly. "You will feel better in no time. Docteur Tremblay will be here any minute, don't fret."

Olivier leans over. "She's been awake for the past few minutes. What's taking him so long?"

"There's no cause for alarm. He's getting out of surgery." I don't say a word as she checks my vital signs, and Olivier says something to her or she says something to him, I'm not sure; they're both talking over my head. She leaves, offering me a sympathy smile on her way out.

Olivier takes my free hand, and he runs his fingers over the back of my hand and then my palm, over and over as if reassuring himself that I'm here, awake.

How bad off am I? For the first time since fully waking, I take stock. Real stock.

I don't feel any discomfort nor aches. But my right shoulder is bandaged, my arm immobilized, strapped to my chest. I wiggle my fingers, a residual twinge of pain shooting up to my neck. I must be on some sort of pain meds then. I shift my legs a bit from side to side, feeling stiff and sore all over like I've been flattened by a truck carrying a ton of bricks. Was I?

"Am I okay?"

"Shhh, you're okay, now," Olivier calms me.

His fingers graze my cheek and send a shiver down my spine. "You're okay," he repeats over and over while helping me sip from the cup of melted ice chips.

Dark circles under his gold-flecked hazel eyes emphasize their dull shine, their usual sparkle absent. His shaggy hair is matted to his skull in places and sticking out in others. His clothes are all stretched out and wrinkled, his shirt stained over his chest by what looks like dark smears of ketchup. I narrow my eyes. Or is that blood?

"Are you okay?" I turn his words around on him. I brush my hand over his cheek, the need to touch him—a living, breathing thing.

He nods, torment crowding his tired eyes. He squeezes them shut as he exhales on a slow breath. "I will be... You made it back."

Back from the house on the hill where I think I heard what his voice sounds like? He was there with me before I slipped into a grey nothingness. "How long was I out?"

Olivier's face hovers above mine, inhaling deeply, as if he can't breathe without me.

He closes his eyes briefly before straightening. "You stayed unconscious twenty-nine hours." He checks his watch, blowing out his cheeks. "Forty-two minutes..."

And another snippet of memory comes back to me. We're in bed, teasing and joking late into the night, and I had never felt that level of intimacy ever before. He had checked his watch then, too. An old-fashioned Philippe-Tisserot. "Guess an indestructible Tisserot really goes with everything as naked as I am," Olivier had smirked, checking the time.

I deadpanned, "No wonder their slogan is, *Tisserot. Timeless, bare essential.*" To which he had choked on laughter, his chest vibrating from it underneath my fingertips.

"Always was an oxymoron to begin with, timeless, really, for a watch?" We had dissolved into fits of infectious laughs, just feeling silly and giddy from happiness. *What happened?*

Straining forward, he strokes my hair before softly pressing his lips to my brow. "All in all, both the slowest and fastest one thousand seven hundred eighty-two minutes of my life," he confesses as we stare at each other. He touches my cheek, his thumb brushing across my lips. His eyes swim with so much emotion that it makes my heart turn over and my blood roar. "But now that you're awake and recognize me? I will be okay, and so will you." He kisses my palm, before laying it back down over the blanket, covering my hand with his own.

We stay quiet for some time, the gentle stroking of his thumb over my hand soothing.

"Can you tell me what happened?" I finally ask, ready to find out.

Taking a look around, he rubs at his chest, swallowing a couple of times, and my heart goes out to him. He swallows a couple of times before his glance catches mine. I force a smile with closed lips, but it comes out weak.

"You're okay... Discounting a minor concussion, dislocated shoulder, and fractured clavicle as well as a few lacerations on your right side and quite a few bruises sustained when you pitched into saplings growing by the ditch after you rolled over the hood of a small Fiat 500...”

As I catch on to what he says, horror and distress wash over me.

Olivier takes a few deep breaths, his nostrils flaring. “And I couldn’t…and you didn’t...” His eyes glisten, tears spill over and track down his cheeks, and he pinches the bridge of his nose, swallowing. “Jesus, give me a minute.”

I blanch, filling in the blanks.

My throat thickens. My breath escapes in an unsteady hiccup.

It must have been awful for him to witness.

“You couldn’t warn me away from a car I didn’t hear coming...” I finally manage to say, my eyes swimming in unshed tears as I look at my surroundings. Obviously, I’ve been deluding myself into a false sense of normalcy over the past seven months… I endangered everyone as a result.

My stomach drops. “The people in the car. Are they...?” I can’t finish the thought, one catastrophic scenario after the other flashing through my mind.

I squeeze my eyes shut.

Please, let them be all right.

Olivier nabs my fingers with his longer ones. My eyes snap to his.

He rubs his thumb over the back of my hand. “Not a scratch. Just a small dent on the hood and a mild shock.”

Overcome by relief, I slump back against the pillow.

He hovers, brushing a kiss on my forehead before leaning away. “I will eternally be grateful those Fiats are low to the ground and round as a beach ball. Thankfully, the woman was driving well below the speed limit having just encountered a pack of deer further up the road.”

His devastated gaze holds mine for a long heartbeat before he looks over his shoulder at two men now standing just inside my room. Doctors, at a guess from their white lab coats, which, no surprise, I didn’t hear coming.

One of them looks to be around Olivier’s age. Lean, athletic built, bronze skin, sculpted face, pulpy lips. At a guess, Italian, or Greek. The guy certainly has enviable genetics, but I prefer by far the cute wholesomeness of Olivier— less intimidating, much more real. He has the kindest copper-colored eyes, though, as he leans over so I’ll see his lips. “Hi. I’m Docteur di Fiori. And you’ll be fine in no time, Aurèle," he reassures me.

I nod with a tight-lipped smile, both abashed by the trouble I caused and relieved it won't cause any lasting damages. A lesson I'm not likely to forget.

I blow out a self-conscious breath.

He holds my gaze as he gives a little chin nod toward Olivier who didn't budge from his place beside me. "And my mate, P.O., here, will be as well." He clamps one hand on Olivier's shoulder in quiet support. "Right, man?"

His mate, P.O.? He must be Zac, then, his doctor friend, the one who's madly in love with Magali and building a home as fast as he can get away with, I remember now.

"Riiiight," Olivier says to him on a long exhale. He plays with a lock of my hair and tips his chin towards his pal, confirming my guess. "This one's Zac, in case you're wondering."

One of our three little pigs...

The nonsensical thought catches me by surprise and brings a soft smile to my lips. A pang of nostalgia hits me next. I really enjoyed this special time when we corresponded, Olivier and I. For the first time, I felt "normal" was within my reach with none the wiser about my handicap.

I look back at them, trying to decipher the rest of the conversation, but they're turned away and I miss it.

I suppress a sigh, dropping my gaze to the catheter taped to the back of my left wrist, hooked on a drip. I watch a bead of clear liquid drop at regular intervals into the tube connecting me to the IV bag.

Given the chance of a do-over would I make the same decisions and pretend I was normal for a while, like I did? I'd like to think I'd be more courageous, but the truth is, I'm not really sure. While it lasted, it tasted so, so good... Addictive. Like meeting *me* after a long separation. Or at least, an undamaged version of me. One I could have been before meningitis left its indelible mark.

Olivier's earnest face as he stood in my kitchen writing his own confession on my blackboard pops into my head. He never faltered in his convictions that we are meant to be. Not once. Even after knowing my limitations and my own lies by omission.

He loves me, regardless. The real me. Not the one I pretended to be.

Isn't it time I do the same leap of faith? All in. Not halfway in.

I sneak a sideways look at him but his attention is now divided between Zac, who's talking, and the other doctor. A barrel-chested middle-aged man with a receding hairline who nods absently once in a while, squinting behind reading glasses as he types something into my chart.

My head darts between the three men, but I can't follow the exchange all that clearly. Another bout of nausea grips me, the effort simply too much. I keep my eyes on Olivier until my dizziness recedes.

After a short while, his lips thin in a straight line as he crosses his arms over his chest glaring at Zac. His eyes cut to mine, one finger tapping on his lips to get my full attention. "Zac," he says, his intent eyes never once wavering away from my face even though I know he's not talking to me. "I'm not leaving."

I let out a breath, tearing up. Of course he will leave. Soon. If it weren't for me, I remind myself, he'd be back at MIT where he should be right this minute. Where he should have stayed all along. But for now, he's here, with me and, somehow, that's all that registers. My chest expands with a mixture of gratitude and relief. And love.

Zac nudges his head back towards the door. "Can I talk to you outside for a minute?" he says to Olivier.

"No can do, man."

But before I can thank Olivier for being there for me as well as tell him how very sorry I am for the mess I made of things, Zac grabs his arm and tugs him away from my bedside, all the while talking to him through closed teeth.

Despite myself, my chest caves in. "You're leaving?" I croak, panicky, even though I know he shouldn't even be here at all.

Olivier shoves away from Zac with a downward pull but placates him with both hands up. He locks eyes with me. "Not in this lifetime. I'll be just outside the door while they run a few tests."

Promise? "Okay..." I nod at them both, swallowing. A few tests... I know the drill, and it wearies me. I really could have done without another hospital stay in this lifetime. But this time around, I only have myself to blame.

A look passes between them.

"I'll stay with you, Aurèle," Zac says.

"Okay," I repeat, giving him a tired smile.

I stare at the empty doorway, wishing I could follow Olivier out.

Forty

AURÈLE

"I'm Docteur Tremblay, your attending physician," the older man says, his round-cheeked face coming into my line of vision as he elevates the bed into a half-sitting position. "Good to see you awake. I understand you gave everyone quite a fright for a little while there."

I pluck at a loose thread on my blanket, hoping if I focus on it hard enough it will keep the tears at bay. "It's entirely my fault, and I'll never be sorry enough."

Zac fastens his hand on my good shoulder in a gentle squeeze. I look up.

He searches my eyes giving me one last comforting squeeze in reassurance. "Hey, no more blaming yourself."

"Easier said than done," I mumble under my breath. "It really was a stupid thing I did."

Zac nods a few times, his expression sympathetic. "We all do stupid stuff at some point, and yours isn't the worst, trust me. You won't win that contest." He shifts his weight, his hands on his hips. "But I need you to stop worrying about that and focus on getting better. My bud is counting on you to pull through. So am I, and the rest of us."

He raises a brow in clear challenge, his facial expression so like Olivier's in that moment that I can't help but wonder how many other quirks the six of them share, perfected through their years of growing up together. Sharing a room for thirteen years? As a unified group, misfits or not, they must have been formidable when not taking no for an answer. "Deal?" he asks, cocking his head to the side, eyes narrowed, waiting.

Effective. Case in point. "Deal." I give him a small, albeit weary, smile.

Zac gives me a thumbs-up.

My smile dims as I go through a series of standard hospital tests. A throwback to a harrowing time I'd rather not live again. I rub absently at my chest, my heart aching as the memory of that hospital visit mixes with this one.

Lastly, Docteur Tremblay checks my pupils. "Any headache? Pain? Dizziness? Sensitivity to sound and light?" I read on his lips.

I let out a lengthy sigh.

Yes. An over sensitivity to sound, or the absence thereof. One I need to shed permanently...

I take a deep breath and forge ahead. "No pain. A throb in my head that comes and goes," I answer truthfully. "Same for dizziness and sensitivity to light but not to sound." I lift my good shoulder into a half-shrug.

"Right, right. Of course. Not to sound." He nods to himself, reading over my chart. "Not with those permanent lesions to the medial forebrain and your connective tissues."

"Right. Permanent." *Deal with it, Aurèle,* I remind myself. Besides, it's not the first nor is it the last time you'll encounter a doctor with an insensitive bedside manner.

"Yes, well..." Docteur Tremblay's ruby cheeks flush a darker shade of red seeing the look on my face, and he coughs behind his fist for countenance before typing into my chart.

Zac offers me an understanding smile from behind him, rolling his eyes heavenward, and I appreciate more than I can say his friendly ones filled with nothing but acceptance. No pity. No discomfort. No repulsion. *Same as Olivier.*

I like him.

"For your headache, we'll try solid pills and unplug you from all of these," the older man says, waving in dismissal to the machines a young nurse is already turning off.

She shoots Zac a flirty look from beneath thick eyelashes that's totally lost on him, I notice, before she's on her way out the door, wheeling the larger machine with her as she goes.

I like him more and more.

"Can I get rid of this too?" I raise my wrist with the catheter taped on. It's annoying the way it sticks out now that my good arm is no longer connected to the IV line and can move more freely.

"No, this stays until you're discharged, I'm afraid," Docteur Tremblay says, the stout man's face still florid in color. I raise an enquiring eyebrow. He eyes me over the rim of his reading glasses. "Nothing to be alarmed about. Just standard procedures in case we need to re-administer fluids expediently." He rolls the tubing of his stethoscope, stuffing it into one of the deep pockets of his lab coat, the headset popping out.

Zac puts his hand on my arm, and I look up. "Here you go." He gives me a shallow paper cup containing two bright orange capsules the nurse brought over.

I take the pills and wash them down with the remaining water. The glass is refilled seconds later. I finish off that one too.

Docteur Tremblay squints behind his half-moon glasses, typing one last thing into my computerized chart before logging out. "Excellent news overall. I'll see you back after your next MRI in a couple of hours then. Docteur di Fiori." He inclines his head in Zac's direction and scurries out without a backward glance.

Another test? I stare at the empty doorway. *When will I be able to leave this place? No one says the important stuff around here.*

Zac tilts his head to the side, grabbing my attention. "No one? That bad, hey?"

I grow wide-eyed. It goes to show. I haven't talked in eight years and now, after months of living alone, practicing my voice and pitch seems like I can't stop babbling without knowing it. *Awkward much.* "I really said that out loud?" I wince, my face heating up, probably flushing to the roots of my hair.

He shakes his head, amused. "Don't fret. Magali says it all the time, so I'd say you walked right into this one."

I gape at him. Did he just crack a joke at my expense?

"Sorry, my bad. I couldn't resist messing with you." His eyes twinkle with suppressed mirth.

I look on with wonder and a bit of bafflement by the good-natured teasing that includes me without one trace of embarrassment, or condescension, or sneer, or nothing else.

"If your vital signs hold and your newest brain scans are still showing clear, you could be discharged as early as tonight if you accept to be released under my care."

I furrow my brow into a deeper V. "Your care?"

"You'll need constant supervision for the next few days, Aurèle. So, yes. You could be released tonight, but under my care. You shouldn't be alone with your type of injuries and medical history for the next couple of weeks at least. And at the risk of driving you batty under a week, you're quite welcome to stay with us at Leo's quack farm while you recover."

Behind him, someone grabs his attention and I see Olivier frowning at Zac. I glance between them, and Zac says to me, "Just until P.O.'s back from MIT, mind you." He dips his chin, gesturing to the side. "Then he'll take over."

P.O. reaches out, folding his hand on mine. "Don't listen to him. He knows I'm not going back. You'll be released into my care."

My eyes grow wide. *What?* I frown, filled with dismay. "No. You have to get back to school. You have to finish."

He scowls, crossing his arms over his chest. "Wanting you safe at the farmstead is what landed you here in the first place. I'm not repeating the same mistake twice. I'll take you to the cottage and stay with you there."

I grab his shirt by the hem, yanking him close so he knows I'm serious. "And I'm not repeating mine, either. I'm here because I let my fears get the better of me, and I'm so very sorry. It was so careless of me but I'll deal. You're graduating in less than five weeks. You have to go back to MIT!"

Behind him, Zac holds his prescription pad over Olivier's head with an arrow pointing down. **(One hell of a stubborn arse.) My offer stands. Take as prescribed. No substitution**, he wrote in block letters.

I curb a snort of surprise and a laugh bubbles in my chest as I realize I do, in fact, want to accept Zac's offer and stay at the farmstead.

I don't know what it feels like to be part of a family. A large one. A boisterous one. A real one.

But I'm ready to find out.

Olivier gives me a quizzical glance before catching on. He snatches the notepad, skewering Zac alive with a lethal look. "Don't you have babies to deliver?"

"Don't you have to be at MIT?" Zac arches a telling brow.

"What he says," I say to Olivier and, to my utmost delight, Zac high fives me. Me!

"Welcome to the dark side, Aurèle. We have cookies. And not the login kind."

"Real smooth, man." Olivier looks up at him, one eyebrow raised in sardonic disbelief. "So suave."

"I know," Zac says, shooting me a conspiratorial wink before heading out the door.

Olivier leans over and strokes my cheek. "I don't give a fuck about the diploma, Aurèle. It's just a piece of paper when all is said and done." His warm breath tickles my chin. "You're way more important."

I brush the pad of my thumb over the shredded skin of his lips. His teeth really did a number on them. Too-serious, moss-green hazel eyes peppered with whiskey gold flecks meet mine.

"It's too much, Olivier. Please, if not for you, then for me." I plead with my eyes. "I'm sorry enough as it is." *I'm ruining your life...*

His head jerks back in surprise like he received an unexpected slap on the face. I frown. Did I yell?

Before I can ask, he turns away, grabbing his neck with both hands. His shoulders tense with frustration? Aggravation? Disgust?

I cringe, the words I just dropped on him replaying in my head. *If not for you, then for me?* Looks like I'm not above using emotional blackmail, myself.

His jaw clenching, he drags both hands through his shaggy hair as he starts pacing the room, having a one-sided conversation as I see his lips move but he's not even looking my way... I can't make heads or tails of what he's trying to say. I try again.

"I'm so sorry."

He turns around, scowling. "Don't." He stops at the foot of the bed, shifting his weight to one side, hands on his waist. "You're right about one thing. And one thing only. *This* is too much."

My heart hammers with apprehension. "This...?"

He sighs heavily, looking at his feet. "Look. We need to talk."

We need to... "Talk?" I ask, making sure that's what he said.

His jaw clenched, he stares off at the wall over my head.

Just stares... His eyes unseeing.

His reaction sends an icy chill down my spine. The reality of what my disability entails on a day-to-day is probably catching up to him.

My chest hollows out.

My heart pounds.

Crickets chirp in my head.

Is this where he tells me I was right? I'm too much for him after all?

Forty-One

P.O.

uining her life? Christ almighty.

"Look. We need to talk." I scrub a shaky hand through the mess on top of my head.

She nods a few times. "Talk...?" she asks with a slight edge of panic to her voice.

I stare at the intercom on the wall, contemplating the best way to make her understand how it makes me feel, how to explain... Maybe if I write it down, instead, she'll have a better go at processing what I'm about to say if she reads it along, as I don't want her to miss one word. Not one fucking word.

I catch her eye. "Give me a minute to write this down and organize my thoughts, it's too important."

This shit needs to be redressed once and for all before it gets the better of us. And I need to hustle it up on a sound recognition bracelet before I wither and die from constant worry. Who cares about a firewall app! It's meaningless, it's...

She swallows, her throat working up and down as she slowly nods.

I root around her bedside table, knowing Éolie left a pen and pocket notebook in there as she wasn't sure Aurèle could read lips. I find both articles underneath her toiletry bag and send a silent thank you to Éolie.

I lower myself to the floor and lean against the wall, not bothering to pull up one of the chairs sitting empty by the foot of the bed. I pull my knees up and start writing, using my thighs for support.

"It was easier to pretend," she offers softly.

I stop my scribbling. My gaze cuts back to her, my gut twisting. "To pretend what, exactly?" I ask cautiously.

She shakes her head and rubs her palm over her eyes. "That I'm whole."

My chest does funny things.

With slow, methodical movements that belie my urgency, I uncover her eyes and bring her hand to my mouth, tenderly kissing her palm before bringing it over my heart. "Why are you saying this?"

I want her to spell it out.

"Because reality can't be ignored." Aurèle holds on to me by the shirt as tears slide soundlessly down her cheeks. "Isn't that what you're about to say? That you've realized I'm too much of a burden?"

I hate that that's the first thing that still pops into her head.

"Trust me, not even close." I strain forward until our breaths mingle. Mindful of her right shoulder, I kiss her deeply, thoroughly, outlining the bow of her lips before pulling away to stare intently at her. I want to kiss those tears goodbye. No. What I want is to kiss her doubts away, dispel the reason behind those tears.

"Does this looks like I'm pretending you're something you're not?" I kiss her brow but don't wait for her answer.

"You." I gently kiss the bruise at her temple.

"Are." I kiss the side of her jaw, tasting in my lips the saltiness of her tears, my words whispering on her skin, showing, more than telling.

"Not." I kiss the dimple on her chin.

"Damaged." I kiss one corner of her lips. "But so very." Then the other.

"Very, special." And then my lips pounce on hers, and I kiss the fuck out of her like I've been dying to ever since she whispered my name upon waking, all of my fears of the past two days pouring out of me and into it. Then I ease up the forceful bruising of her mouth and stroke my tongue over hers, velvety rough and warm. My kiss turns from frustration to shivery seduction as her lips melt onto mine, replying with the sweetest of touches. So soft and beautiful. Delicate and feminine. My lips tremble.

God almighty, what she does to me. But here and now is not exactly the place nor the time to show her the rest.

It takes everything in me not to though.

"So, so special. To me," I whisper, my fingers splaying out over her face as I drop a string of light kisses on her mouth. My lips linger one last time before I straighten away, only to bend over and steal another one, unable to resist her upturned face.

She sighs breathily as her eyes slowly reopen, their depth filled with wonder.

"Convinced?" I flick the tip of her nose to lighten up a bit. "I can always go another round if not."

She cracks half a smile. "In that case, I may never be convinced enough..." she says dreamily, doing wonders for my ego on one hand, but on the other...

Cocking my head to the side, I arch a brow. "Yeah, that's the problem."

Her own furrowing, she frowns in thought before her eyes widen, the double meaning behind her words washing all over her face. She turns her head on the pillow, looking out the window.

I scoot closer and hold her chin, pulling her face toward me. "If you could change one thing about me, would you?"

Her expression softens and I trail one finger down the side of her cheek. "No," she murmurs, reaching up to touch the hard lines of my face.

"No? Interesting," I say quietly. I pull a hand through the strands of her hair, gently stroking her. "Neither would I."

She stares at me for a long moment.

Then she chews at that plump pink bottom lip, and a blush creeps up her neck. Oh, what I'd give to read her mind right now. She looks down then peeks at me through her eyelashes, looking adorable as fuck.

"Well, except for your ego, which is clearly out of control," she says.

"Smart-ass," I reply.

She grins and smoothes her thumb over my lips. Her fingertips trace down my jaw, her expression sobering. "Bear with me. Eight years of intense conditioning won't go overnight, but I'll work on it. Don't give up on me."

I kiss her brow. "Easiest promise I've ever made." Her eyes light up the place, warmth spreading in my chest.

I lower the guardrail and sit by her side, one ankle crossing over my knee, facing her. Aurèle's hand slips into mine and she pulls it onto her lap. I squeeze her hand and she squeezes back. I interlace our fingers as I finish scribbling what I'd started to a few minutes ago before I got sidetracked, bracing the notepad on my bended leg, frequently shooting her a sideways look as she tries to read as I write.

When I'm done, I kiss her knuckles, catching her eye. "You need to read this over many times a day, any chance you get, until you absorb it in its entirety. Inside and out."

She smiles tremulously and nods.

I wrap her fingers around the notepad. In her half-sitting position, I brace my hands on the mattress on either side of her hips and say by heart what I just wrote down. "Aurèle, your hearing loss is a part of who you are and we deal with it, that's all. No lie. I do see you differently now. I'll worry more, and you can't hold it against me. But disability or not, without a shadow of a doubt, I'd see you differently just as well, tomorrow and the next day, and the next. I love you, and every bloody minute my feelings for you grow more intense, more profound, more permanent and in turn, you become more precious, more vital, more compelling. Does it scare me? Hell, yes. A helluva lot. Just the thought of living without you in this world decimates me. But I'd rather be scared of that than live without you in my world. My love for you is worth the risk. *You* are worth the risk. There will be many times when I only take you into consideration. Not me. You. It's still my decision and mine only. In other circumstances, would I go back to MIT for the five weeks I have left before getting my two degrees? Sure, I'm no idiot. But things are what they are and if it comes down to your well-being and safety (insert my sanity right here), nothing is worth risking that. You're not ruining my life, you hear. You're enhancing it. You're inspiring me to be more, and that is addictive and makes me high on life. Easiest choice, ever, Aurèle. I choose you. I always will."

"No one has ever chosen me before." She stares at my words with watery eyes.

I tip her chin up. "About time someone did. Besides, you made me see that I don't want to be tied down to a firewall app that will need constant updates." I take her wrist in my hands, staring at the catheter sticking out.

"What do you want?"

"For starters, I want to develop a sound recognition wristlet that will alert you in advance to any dangers like that Fiat if you're about to step blindly onto its path." She tilts her head, pleasantly intrigued. I kiss her knuckles all the while keeping her in my sight. "I'm not trying to clip your wings, Aurèle, I want you to soar. I just need you to wear a bloody parachute while doing so, so I don't die in the process. Got that?"

"Got it..." She holds up the paper. "In writing." Her smile is slow, creasing her cheeks. "What's this about a wristlet? Am I to be your guinea pig then?"

"Damn straight." I touch her face. "You're special that way."

I'll work my way to the microchip implant—that I promise, I inwardly vow. But for now, I don't want to build up her hopes on what could very well be just a chimera. But the wristlet that's a given.

"You know what I think?"

I lift an eyebrow. "What's that?"

"I think you're pretty damn special yourself."

I have no idea how to respond, but she gives me no real chance to as she motions me closer. I lean over, and she cups my cheek so she can kiss me. Her eyes soft with love, she says, "I choose you too. Now when are you springing me out of this place? Heard this morning the quack farm's recruiting roommates. They really follow through over there, and I'd like to apply for a family membership."

I throw my head back, laughing, delighted by the prospect and the easygoing way she said she'd *heard* this morning... "Now that I can arrange." I kiss her forehead.

Aurèle reaches up and brushes back my hair. "Good. Because as soon as I'm settled in, you and I will have a talk about finishing your degrees."

My eyes find Aurèle's as she speaks, and her warm gaze strokes gently over my face.

"Why do I get the impression that comes Sunday night, I'll be on a plane back to Boston?" I lean down to feather a kiss at the corner of her mouth.

"Hmmm. Maybe..." She sprinkles light kisses over my jaw. "Because I'll do my very, very best to convince you to?"

My lips melt into hers.

"Convinced?" She smiles against my lips.

I lean back so she can see my lips. "Not yet. I like this convincing thing we have going on." I say before nibbling playfully on her lips.

Soft and so gentle, she deepens the kiss, her fingers thrusting upward into my hair, tangling as she pulls me even closer until I'm halfway in and halfway out the bed. Without breaking our kiss, I blindly swat around for the switch, lowering the bed until I lay beside her on her left side, quite mindful of her injuries.

Fingertips splay across my chest, and she leans her head back. "Convinced now?"

"Hmmm. Maybe I can be persuaded…but just to make sure." I lean up on my elbow, looking at her. "Can you go another round?"

Her twinkling laugh fills up the room. "Convince me."

"How long have you got?" I grin, brushing back her hair.

"As long as it takes."

"In that case, forever sounds about right." I shift my weight slightly and scoot lower into the bed until our noses are just a breath apart.

"Music to my ears," she replies deliberately. The intrinsic acceptance uttered behind the casual words certainly not lost on me, I nod my understanding. God, in this moment, I have never loved her more.

"You ready for the next chapter?" she asks softly, her fingertips lovingly tracing down my cheek.

Oh, am I ever.

And this time, I don't mind at all being shooed out of her room as a nurse preps her for her last MRI before being discharged.

We exchange a soft look just before I close the door behind me.

The next chapter? Bring it on. Our story is just beginning.

Forty-Two

(Or, as P.O. asked for, the next chapter...)

AURÈLE

"But—" I try to argue.

"No buts, doctor's orders. You stay put on bed rest for another day or two and then, we'll see how it goes." Zac snaps his medical bag shut. "Besides, without any painkillers, you'll need it. That kitchen brings mayhem down on us on the best of days. I'd enjoy couch surfing while it lasts if I were you." He smirks at Leo coming round.

"Hey, no dissing my house. She's sensitive," Leo says to Zac while offering me a bowl of red grapes.

I thank him, snagging a small bunch. "Sensitive?" I repeat, confused. *Is that what he said?*

"Vindictive more like," Zac says to me, tipping his chin towards Leo.

"Forgiving more like." Hands on his hips, Leo rolls his eyes heavenward.

"Forgiving, my ass. You're not the one who almost fell through the floor and into the kitchen sink."

Oh, that explains the newly cracked ceiling planks over the sink.

"Shouldn't rattle her old bones going at it like rabbits," Leo smirks at him before stoking the fire.

My glance darts between them, enjoying their interaction.

"You know, Leo, there's a reason behind those ten single beds you found upstairs. They didn't appear by magic," Zac says unfazed, leaning against the kitchen doorjamb.

"Yeah, but do notice the master bedroom's located on the main floor. There's a reason for that and it lies within the cracks you made over the kitchen sink," Liam says, coming into my line of vision and handing me my refilled water bottle, the reason behind my argument with Zac. Not only do I have to drink plenty of fluids, but I can't get my own refills... My butt has to stay put on the couch, and I need to holler for assistance just to walk to the bathroom, giving new meaning to couch potato.

"Good point." Zac slaps Liam on the shoulder. "When are you moving into your new house again?"

"You'll have to stand in line," Liam says to him. "P.O. made a bid for our empty room before you, man." He arches a telling brow at me.

I gape, a flush of heat warming my neck and crawling up to my hairline. I stare wide-eyed into two sets of eyes watching me with barely restrained mirth.

I roll my eyes and shake my head at them, but in truth, I'm delighted by their teasing.

"Don't mind them," Leo says to me. "They were raised by wolves." He waves them off. "As for you two, I don't care if Éolie saw quintuplets in there, I'm nowhere near ready to fill those up yet."

"Riiiight. Keep telling yourself, that," Zac says with a knowing look. According to P.O., Leo is seriously, but secretly, crushing on Amélie, Magali's closest friend.

"Yeah, how's that working for you, man?" Liam smirks.

"Isn't that the twins waking up?" Leo narrows his eyes at him.

Éolie and Magali are on grocery shopping detail and should be back shortly. Liam is in charge of his two rambunctious little twins currently down for a nap, both too adorable for words.

"I didn't hear a thing, you?" I ask Liam all innocent like.

Leo's mouth drops open but his blue-grey eyes flash silver, glinting with approval and a hint of suppressed merriment. "She really went there?"

Liam thumps on his chest in a fit of coughing, choking on laughter. "Oh, you'll do, Aurèle. You'll do just fine."

Leo shoots me an amused glare. "Hey, I brought you grapes, didn't I? That means you should be on my side here."

"What can I say?" I shrug my good shoulder. "I like the dark side. They have cookies."

Zac chuckles, fist bumping me. "Speaking of which… Want some dark chocolate and macadamia ones?"

"You really need to ask?" I say enthusiastically, my mouth watering. There's still a faint trace of melted chocolate and baked vanilla lingering in the air from last night.

"Hey, there's some left?" Leo asks, perking up.

Éolie, Magali, and Amélie-of-the-Secret-Crush baked some yesterday, inducing a feeding frenzy the likes of which I had never seen, just before Olivier had to leave for Tremblant's airport. The girls ended up stashing an impressive loot into an overnight bag for Olivier to share with Yann and Theo. But judging by the look that passed between Leo, the designated driver, and Olivier, I'm not sure the cookies made it to Boston.

"Your secret crush," Liam air quoted in an attempt to explain, "may or may not have—"

"What are you, thirteen? I don't do crushes," Leo scoffs, sauntering off to the kitchen after Liam.

"Watch this," Zac mouths to me behind his back. "Too bad. She may have left a crumb trail for you to follow…" he baits Leo. I grin.

He whirls on Zac before crossing over. "She did?"

"Wouldn't you like to know?" Zac nudges him aside with his shoulder, bypassing him into the kitchen.

The living room empties, leaving behind a new form of quiet into the silence of my world. The place is usually hopping with people and something going on. Unusual for me, but not at all unpleasant.

I pick Harriet up from the huge slice of a once-mossy maple tree trunk flanking the couch and used as a coffee table, intent on browsing through photography books, one of the many perks of having high-speed internet at the touch of my finger. And I must admit, browsing through libraries anytime or working on my photo gallery whenever the mood strikes me is spoiling me. I don't mind admitting Olivier's right on that one.

Olivier.

I sigh, the dull ache in my chest from missing him more present than the associated aches and pains from the soreness of my body.

Still, only four more days before the weekend and the possibility of Olivier flying back here for a visit. I frown slightly. Olivier is up to his neck in meetings at MIT right now, and I shouldn't count on it, nor count the days.

Meanwhile, I remind myself, I can keep in touch "live" whenever…and it really makes a difference in the size of the hole his absence left behind after being with him constantly for the past few days.

While my left hand holds on to my three-day-old state-of-the-art smartphone, I type like an arthritic little old lady with the fingertips of my right hand, my arm immobilized by the sling.

A grin a kilometer wide stretches on my face while I type, thinking about last weekend and Olivier's attempts at teaching me how to use it before he flew back to Boston. We may have become distracted by making out a few times. But thanks to Magali, Harold and I have come to an understanding this morning.

> Me: Just to let you know Harry is jealous I find it easier to text one-handed with Harold now that we're better acquainted. And if I get a good read on Harriet? We're all missing you. xxxx

My gaze sweeps the cozy room strewn with toys, books and magazines, throw blankets, and cushions, echoes of silent laughter bouncing back at me everywhere I look. I watch the shadowy glow of the flames dancing on the walls, highlighting the duct-tape gracing them here and there filled with witty quips and games of tic-tac-toe.

For the first time in forever, I feel connected, included, exactly where I'm supposed to be. Loving. Loved.

I press send, warmth seeping through my chest. It sings through my blood and causes my nerve endings to tingle.

This.

This is what happy sounds like.

And the next...but who's counting?

AURÈLE

You wouldn't know it's the second week of May just by looking out the window, snow mixed with sleet falling almost horizontally, spewed from a slate-grey sky. Hard to believe that just yesterday temperatures hovered in the upper-twenty Celsius and it felt like summer.

Rain or shine. No one cares up here really. Well, aside from tourists wearing long faces at the café when we get unseasonal temperatures, which is sort of funny as unseasonal is kind of seasonal up here anyway. There's something unpredictable, beautiful, and breathtaking in every type of weather we get in Les Laurentides, I can't help but think, snapping one picture after the other, getting the feel of my new digital camera.

Harold vibrates with an incoming text message, and I pick him up from my belt clip, a smile already forming on my face.

> **Good morning. Did I mention recently how much I love you, and how much I miss the bloody everlasting hell out of you? If not, consider this your warning. Be ready. xxxxx**

Good morning, love. And yes, you did. Only five minutes

ago, but who's counting? Only five more days by the way...
And duly warned and ready. ;) xxxxxxxxxxxxxxxx

I press send with a silly grin that feels permanently etched on my face nowadays.

Aside from one visit two weeks ago that flew by much too quickly, we're on the final countdown. Only five more days before Olivier flies back here for good this time, the next chapter left wide open for discussion.

I can wait...and can't wait. I hug myself with both arms, feeling another silly grin sprout on my lips. My sling officially came off yesterday after receiving the all clear from Docteur Tremblay. Now I just need to regain the full span of my shoulder arch, and the strength in my dominant hand. Both are already much improved, thanks to the physiotherapy exercises Magali suggested I start ahead of schedule a couple of weeks ago.

Chubby little fingers snag the back of my knee, bringing me out of my thoughts. I twist around and find ten-month-old Nicolas-the-Intrepid trying to bear his weight by holding on to me, but when he catches my eyes on him, he plops back down, holding up his arms. They know how to get their message across without a sound. I smile down on him, kneeling, unsure if he'll be safe in my arms and unwilling to take any risk. He doesn't seem to mind, instantly climbing his way up my lap. I catch him up and he wraps his chubby little arms around my neck, cuddling me. I smile my delight up to Éolie, who's helping Sébastien toddling along on unsteady legs as he holds on to her fingers, and she smiles in reply.

"I never get tired of this," I say, nuzzling Nicolas's neck, inhaling his sweet baby scent.

This.

This is what happy smells like.

"You're kind of irresistible," I say, looking down into the most extraordinary pale turquoise eyes I've ever seen framed by black eyelashes, never mind that their particular color comes in triplicate. Except for their eyes—the exact same shade as Éolie's. Sébastien and Nicolas are Liam's carbon copy, right up to the dimpled chin and dark locks the color of rich espresso coffee. I never tire at looking at the twins. I'm itching to capture them on camera, and now that my sling came off, I'll be able to.

"I know, right." Éolie smiles softly, lovingly, ruffling Sébastien's mop of dark curls as he snuggles up next to me, joining Nicolas on my lap.

"Still sleepy, huh," I say to Nicolas playfully, in connivance as I'm no longer taking long naps myself. I don't tire as easily now and may even venture out more this week. I'd like to go on longer treks armed with my new camera. "I know the feeling," I tell him with a tickle in his ribs that sends him into a fit of giggles I so wish I could hear. But at least… "I know the feel," I whisper in his ear, letting his little chest vibrate against mine. All-knowing eyes so like Éolie's blink up at me, and I swear he pats my cheek consolingly in understanding.

Éolie rubs my arm. "I'm sure he does too," she says to me, a world of compassion passing through her eyes. "They have this innate awareness of our moods, and he felt your sadness just now."

"Sometimes," I find myself saying to her, "I don't know if I feel blessed or cursed for having heard before." I kiss the top of Nicolas's head before setting him down, both now engrossed in a colorful cubic activity center.

Éolie shoots me an indecipherable look. "I won't pretend to know what it's like for you because I really don't. So please don't take this the wrong way if I say, I know what you mean. You can't miss what you've never known. Sometimes, I don't know myself if I feel blessed or cursed for having seen."

"Seen?" I ask, unsure I interpreted correctly. She looks at her little twins with such love that I can't resist taking a snapshot.

"Seen." She looks up and I lower my camera. "Happiness unfolding," she says with a long speculative look my way. In the space of an instant her face takes on a faraway look, and if eyes are truly windows to the soul, hers is otherworldly. I get the impression she's deliberately omitting something, but I don't press her for details even though I really want to. Sébastien imperiously offers her a wooden block and she shakes out of it. She smiles down on him, accepting it, and he rewards her with a lethal toothy grin proudly showing off his six little pearly whites.

"Happiness irresistibly follows them," I say with a quiet smile as Sébastien and Nicolas take turns stacking a few blocks and gleefully knocking them over while I start my own, ending up perilously close to the Leaning Tower of Pisa. "And I should count my blessings instead of feeling sad about my hearing loss, but, unfortunately, it still hits me hard sometimes, and it makes me feel ungrateful when really I'm anything but." Just then my block tower topples over, tumbling to the floor with my latest addition. Nicolas blinks in surprise, glancing from the mess on the floor to the block in his hand.

"All gone!" I chuckle as he waves it madly at Sébastien as if to say, *did you see that?*

Éolie puts her hand on my arm. I look up. "It's okay to be saddened by it." She tilts her head my way. "But no matter how sad your hearing loss makes you feel at times, never lose sight that happiness blooms everywhere in your wake, Aurèle. I see it. P.O. lives it. We all love you for it." She takes my hands, squeezing, her eyes in earnest. "Happy follows you too. Don't let anyone tell you differently. Not even the voice in your head that tells you otherwise." She squeezes my hand tighter and I squeeze hers back. "You hear?"

I nod quietly. "I hear you." I grin softly, hugging her. "Thanks."

She leans away, shaking her head slowly, her face aglow. "I haven't done anything. You did." A dimple pops up in her cheek, and she hugs me back. And again, I get the impression there's more to it she leaves unsaid. More she has "seen."

But before I can ask, Sébastien and Nicolas crawl up on our laps, wanting in on the hugging fest and for the next little while, we end up sprawled on the floor, the twins shaking with mirth as we play peek-a-boo and tickling monster.

"No wonder you're in such good shape. The Energizer Bunny has nothing on them." Éolie chuckles while I catch my breath, leaning my back against the couch. A burst of sunlight streams in like a flamboyant guest, not waiting for an invitation. I reach for my camera wedged between the couch cushions. "While we have the place to ourselves, would you mind terribly if I experiment on you three?"

Magali and Zac are spending the afternoon painting at their new house. Liam and Leo are giving them a hand so their official moving day can take place over the weekend.

"Knock yourself out," she jokes as Sébastien swipes off the latest pile of blocks, sending them across the floor and Nicolas into gales of laughter, and for the next little while, I do. As Éolie plays with her little ones, I capture the moment for all eternity. I'm in the zone.

We're all gathered in the living room—except for Leo, who's not back yet from an errand.

It's early evening, even though it's hard to tell looking out the window. It's so black out it could just as well be the middle of the night.

I check Harold, making sure I don't have any missed texts.

None.

Weird.

I haven't heard from Olivier in the past few hours. It's not like him. I frown slightly. I hope the ironing out of the last kinks and wrinkles of his thesis presentation went smoothly.

All your ones and zeros behaving as they should? xx I press send, glancing up to find the focused gaze of Zac still scrolling down Harry, a wide-eyed Magali peeking over his shoulder, gaping.

"You really got an eye for it," Zac says to me, handing over Harry. "How long have you studied the art?"

"Huh… Just a few months, and studied is stretching it a bit," I say and they stare in disbelief. "It's just a hobby for now," I continue, giving them a look. "Like scrapbooking." Other than sharing some occasionally with Olivier, I've never showed anyone else the pictures I've taken before. But they wouldn't take no for an answer after seeing today's crop.

"Aurèle, no shit. I can't even decide. I want them all framed," Liam says as he scrolls through the pictures I took earlier this afternoon and sent to his phone.

"You took these and you think it's just a hobby?" Magali exclaims, plopping back down beside me on the couch. She takes Harry from me, scrolling down my photo gallery once more. "Aurèle, no. Just no."

Éolie straightens the footie pajamas on Nicolas's toes as nonchalantly as possible before shifting him on her hip a little higher. She gives me this *I told you so look*, her eyes sparkling.

"You captured their very essence in every single one," Liam says, eyebrows raised, staring at his screen. "I have no words which sucks for a writer." He absently rubs Sébastien's back who, nestled in the crook of his neck, sucks his thumb, completely abandoned.

His little cherubic face tilts my way, and he grins sleepily around his thumb, drooling, cracking my heart wide open. Where's my camera when I need it?

Across the room, Zac takes a sip of his drink and appraises me over the rim of his mug. He leans back in his chair, draping one arm over the back rest. "Ever thought of opening a studio?"

Magali's head pops back up, and her eyes widen with excitement. "You're brilliant," she says to Zac. "This is absolutely brilliant."

"I knew you'd think so." Zac hides a satisfied grin behind his mug.

"Aurèle, you have to say yes, please say yes," Magali pleads. "We've been planning on offering unique baby pictures as part of the gift shop at the clinic and we've been looking for a portrait photographer of your caliber," she says while admiring one I took of the twins sharing a book, an arrow of sunlight beaming down on them. "Liam's right. These are too perfect for words."

"You're serious?" I ask her, exuberance catching.

"Never more so." Magali nods, scrolling down Harry. "You'll fit right in."

"You really think so?" I tilt my head in question.

In six months from now they'll be opening a prenatal Complementary Alternative Medicine clinic, or CAM for short, a place where prenatal state-of-the-art medicine will meet holistic medicine head on. Magali envisions it more like a resort stay than a private hospital one.

"Yes, yes, and yes." Magali joins her hands in supplication. "Just say yes." She hands over Harry.

"Yes..." I shake my head, a bit dazed as I imagine what this wonderful opportunity could be like, to be there, encapsulating these intense and special moments when life welcomes new life.

"Brilliant!" Magali jumps up, crossing over to Zac on the other side of the room. More like waltzes her way across. I can't help but grin.

My head's swimming with possibilities, my thoughts swirling, when Harold vibrates on my hip.

You're too perfect for words. And you'll fit right in. Brilliant.
Magali's words, not mine.

Wait, what? How does he...? I swivel round and there he is, leaning against the front door. "Olivier!" I jump up and he meets me halfway, swinging me up into his arms and in a circle. He kisses me hard and long, leaving me breathless.

When he leans away, I hug him tight before asking. "I'm just too happy you're visiting to scold you even though I should. But really, what are you doing here at your busiest?"

"You're looking at my latest errand," Leo says, coming into my line of vision. "And MIT's newest graduate."

"What?" I ask, unsure I read his lips right.

"You pulled it off, man," Liam high fives a beaming Olivier. "Welcome home."

"About time, too," Zac says, slapping him on the back. "We were afraid we'd spill the beans and spoil your surprise."

"How on earth were you able to...?"

"Come here," Olivier says as he pulls me into his arms. "I doubled down at MIT so I could get back here sooner. Missing you helped as an incentive to fast forward everything." He leans down and kisses my healed shoulder meaningfully. "Feel good having both arms back?"

"Not as good as having you back." Olivier's hands creep over my shoulders, and I turn instinctively into the shelter of his arms. "This is the nicest surprise. I can't believe you're here for good."

A sandy-blond guy comes up from behind haloed by the porch light and ruffles Olivier's mop of hair, earning a glare and a few choice words he ignores. "Thank the fuck, he's been nothing but a pain in the arse. He's all yours, now, Aurèle."

Olivier flips him off and I peek over his shoulder, catching the pewter-grey eyes of the chiseled-face guy I recognize as Theo standing in the open doorway, watching me. We never met in person but Olivier FaceTimed me on their last monthly Tuesday-Night-Beer-Fest a couple of weeks ago, and I virtually met him and Yann then, briefly.

"Theo, right?"

I extend my hand but, instead of shaking it, his grin widens before he takes my hand, kissing my knuckles, then, bringing me flush in his arms, he hugs and kisses me on both cheeks, taking his sweet time. Theo winks at me. "Now that I see all that he was missing, hell, I would have complained too."

Olivier shakes his head at him, nudging him aside. "Quit hitting on my girl, and go find your own." He wraps his arm around my shoulders, resting on my opposite arm, his fingers lazily tracing lines up and down my skin.

They exchange a look I can't begin to decipher.

"Don't mind if I do," Theo says to him on a wry grin.

Olivier nods, tenderly dropping a kiss on my temple. "It's worth everything, man," he says to him while looking at me. "I'd take Zac's offer into serious consideration if I were you."

"I will." Theo slaps P.O. on the shoulder, diverting my attention to his lips and what he says. "Ready to announce yours?"

"Yep. Listen up, guys," Olivier says to the room at large, his hands framing my face so I can follow on his lips. "Theo sold the intellectual property on my firewall app to one of the big five, and you're looking at Tisserot Médical virtual head of research and development, a brand-new affiliate company of the mothership." I grow round-eyed, and his whole face lights up from within, brushing back a strand of hair behind my ear. "I'll be developing this pretty cool sound recognition watch with Aurèle's input."

"I love you," I mouth, overcome.

"Love you more." Never dropping his gaze from mine, he kisses my palm.

I shake my head slowly. "Not possible."

"Don't bet on it." He kisses my forehead.

"You'd lose. Every time I think I can't possibly love you more, you go and do something that makes me fall harder." I kiss his cheek. "I'll show you later."

"I'll hold you to it," Olivier says, his eyes soft.

"You won't have to."

Amidst the happy expressions fusing on faces left and right, I lay my head on his shoulder and absorb his warmth and strength. Contented, I let the good vibes of Olivier's and Theo's reunion with the others wash over me. I let it flow. Watching. Just watching.

This.

This is what happy looks like.

"Thought you might be interested in knowing Anaïs from Cutting Edge Designs will hold a permanent exhibit at the clinic," Zac says to Theo, bumping his shoulder on his way out to the kitchen, draining the last of his hot chocolate along the way.

Theo stills. "She is?"

Magali pats his chest. "She is," she says to him, straight-faced, following Zac.

"Ah, yes. Lovely, lovely Anaïs," Leo says, eyes turning upward, seemingly lost in thought. He scratches the stubble on his chin, giving Theo a side-glance. "I've been thinking of asking her to etch that granite boulder by my future barn lab. It would so improve my view...in very fine details," he drops before sauntering away.

"Wait a goddamn minute, here. That boulder is at least fifty feet tall, she'll be at it forever. No way, man," Theo thunders in Leo's wake disappearing into the kitchen.

"I take it whoever Anaïs is, Theo likes her?" I ask the only other two left besides us. Éolie shoots me an effervescent grin, nodding enthusiastically.

"Yep. Leo and Theo. Man, two clueless peas in a pod. And on that note, bedtime." Liam's arm snakes around Éolie's waist before dragging her and Nicolas to his side. "Later," he says to us over his shoulder. "Much later."

"Much, much later," Olivier replies to him, looking at me wolfishly. Alone at last, Olivier pulls me flush against the hard wall of his body, trailing his lips down my neck and grinding his burgeoning erection against my backside.

"Sounds like a plan." I tilt my head to the side, offering my mouth. Olivier glides his fingertips from my shoulder inward along the line of my collarbone, and I sigh in pleasure. He skims his palm down my arm and at my elbow he diverts his explorations, turning me around.

He takes my hands and pulls them around his lower back, only letting go when I fist my hands in the hem of his tee. He then takes my face in his hands, tilting it up. "A good one, too." He lowers his lips to mine and softly strokes them with his tongue. His mouth moves down the side of my throat, making me shiver. A delicious swarm of butterflies spreads their wings and takes flight within my belly. My blood is thrumming while my body grooves with remembered bliss.

"Want to hear a better one?" I wipe his dark-blond hair across his brow and out of his eyes.

"Only if it involves me having my wicked way with you until we lie in bed in a pile of relaxed mush for the next day or two."

We are so close, mouths only inches apart, but neither one of us makes a move as anticipation begins as a buzz in the back of my head and floods me.

"That's a wicked plan." I trail my fingers down his pecs and rake my nails over his nipples through his shirt. "I'm so in. You?"

His chest vibrates with a growl. "Oh, I plan to be so *in*, you won't know where you end and where I start," he says with a wolfish gleam in his eyes, advancing on me while I back away.

"Is that so?" I take off running for our bedroom. Something like joy takes over every cell in my body with each pounded step. He catches up to me just past the threshold, his arms wrapping around me from behind. Olivier tugs me back so I stand with my back to his chest.

Deep laughter rolls from him, vibrating from his chest.

He pushes the door closed with his foot and the next thing I know, my back meets the coolness of the downy comforter. I twist to evade him, rolling once, twice; he dives for the hem of my shirt. I somehow manage to clamber over him and gasp at the feel of his arousal. He wrestles with me until he flips me over with ease, pinning my wrists. Lowering his head, he kisses and licks at my smile as if he could taste it.

I take a couple of deep breaths, a laugh bubbling in my chest.

He rolls onto his back, bringing me flush to his side. "I will never get tired of this."

I rub a circle on his chest over his heart. It thumps strong and steady under my fingers, so I lean in and set my lips to the precious spot, sealing the moment with a kiss.

This.

This is what happy tastes like.

And the next...or an epilogue in disguise

P.O.

Over breakfast the next morning, I absently listen to Magali and Aurèle discuss hiking trails behind Leo's fields while I demolish the rest of my meal.

Zac left earlier for the hospital, and as for Theo and Leo, who knows what they're up to, but the rest of the house is pretty quiet. Liam, Éolie, and the twins are on their midmorning nap.

Hmmm. Napping twice a day. I scratch my jaw, shooting Aurèle a sideway glance. Liam might be on to something.

I bite into my second croissant dipped into a thick, rich chocolate nougat spread and chew, going into a dark chocolate induced coma.

Magali waves her hand in dismissal. "No, no, no. No worries," she says to Aurèle, her elbows coming to rest on the table. "Yesterday's blizzard is so passé, there are only small pockets of snow left from last winter in the underbrush. You'll have a good time exploring. It's truly magical in there, and I can't wait to see the pictures you'll take."

"I've been wanting to see it forever." Aurèle sighs dreamily. "I'll probably lose it and take hundreds. Feels so good to have the sling off." Aurèle exercises her arm and shoulder under Magali's watchful eye, discussing at-home physio techniques and shoulder arch exercises for a few minutes.

"Weren't you meeting the architect at the clinic's site this morning?" Leo asks Magali as he walks by on his way out the back, his rubber boots trailing mud tracks all over the wood plank floor.

I eye the mess. *And I speculated on what he was up to not two minutes ago?* I roll my eyes. "Well, there's a clue. Leo's having a field day."

Aurèle giggles, and I grin at her over my cup, my chest expanding with warmth. I thrill at the sound of her tinkling laugh, ready to crow, *I did that. I made her do it.*

"*Zut de flûte*," Magali exclaims, wide-eyed, checking her phone, surging from her seat. "Late again. Zac will have my head on a platter."

"Likely story," I snort around my last mouthful of chocolate croissant.

"You're right. It won't be my head on the platter," she laughs, pulling on her coat.

Aurèle and I exchange an amused look. "Ever heard of too much information?" I ask drily.

"No such thing," Magali replies cheekily before stopping halfway through pulling on one of her sleeves. "Okay, well, maybe," she says, a reluctant smile lurking at the corner of her lips as she zips her coat up. "I concede."

"Wonders never cease." I salute her with my cup.

"Don't let it go to your head." She chuckles low, pulling on a rainbow beanie. "Have fun, you two." She blows us kisses over her shoulder, and a second later I hear the front door slam shut.

I push my plate away, asking Aurèle, who's diligently pumping her fingers, "Refueled and ready for more physical therapy?" I waggle my eyebrows suggestively.

"Not that kind." Aurèle shakes her head at me. "I'd take a hike if I were you," she says mischievously.

"All right, all right." I hold my hands up. "Finish up the other kind, and we'll go." My voice thickens with amusement, and I reach for my cup.

Theo shuffles into the kitchen with the worst case of bed hair I've seen him with in years, not since our Cambridge University years, anyway. There's nothing even remotely lawyerly about him this morning. Not in his holey grey tee, a gym relic from our BIA days, and old sweatpants riding dangerously low. He's scratching his unshaven chin, stifling a yawn promising to be the size of the Grand Canyon.

Spotting us, he glares at me over Aurèle's head. "You're dead," he says. His voice is controlled, raspy as he replies to Aurèle's chirpy *"bonjour"* with a grunt that may or may not pass for a "good morning."

I blow ripples into my third cup of instant crap coffee as I watch him wrestling with the coffee jar on the other side of the room, inwardly snickering. Poor sod. Guess we kept him awake for the better part of the night, and I'm not about to tell Aurèle what racket the headboard banging against Theo's wall caused either.

Aurèle shifts beside me, turning so she faces him. "Yesterday, I didn't catch what the offer was Olivier referred to?"

The bonehead is not yet awake. He's mumbling, cursing the jar on the counter with his back still turned away.

I place a hand on her upper arm and lean down to place a kiss on her shoulder. She looks at me. "Zac offered Theo a full-time position as legal counsel for the clinic, and he's here on a month hiatus to evaluate his options," I say to her.

She straightens in her chair. "That's—" Aurèle exclaims before Theo swoops over.

"Awesome? Amazing? Wonderful? You can say it." He winks at her, swiping out of my hands my mug of coffee before walking around the table, a second later plopping his ass down on a chair across from us.

"Theo, you're a pain in my ass," I mutter, plunking down another mug and refilling the water pot.

"Right back at you," he says, undeterred, while slathering an obscene amount of crunchy peanut butter onto a slice of freshly baked baguette.

I wince in disgust. "You're the only one I know who readily admits crunchy PB looks like shit and can stomach to eat it, too."

Aurèle scrunches up her nose. "Thanks for the visual."

"That's why, right there. No one messes with it," Theo says, biting into it with gusto. He has a point. No one touched that jar since his last visit.

I sling my arm over the back of Aurèle's chair, and twist a strand of her hair around my fingers. "Don't mind him. He brings weird shit up all the time."

Aurèle has her elbows on the rustic kitchen table, and her chin propped up on one hand, her vivid blue eyes wide with interest. "Weird shit," she repeats in all seriousness while the fingers of her right-hand flex and squeeze a pair of squishy blue balls.

"Speaking of weird, scary, crazy shit..." A laugh bubbles in my chest. "There's something quite disturbing in watching you do that."

"Really?" she deadpans, squeezing harder.

"Really," Theo jokes, slouching down in his chair. "Takes a sadist to design those in a blue color if you're asking," he mutters, and Aurèle flushes a becoming pink.

"You suffering from a case of it?" I snicker at Theo outright, brushing the back of my finger on her warm cheek.

"Ha. Good one," Theo grunts around a mouthful of lumpy bits, glaring balefully at my fingers stroking Aurèle's skin. "I'd say get a room but then again, no!"

"And on that note..." Rising, I wrap an arm around Aurèle, and lift her from the seat before he has a chance to drop on me another little sarcastic remark that she might catch on to. No way in hell I'll let him inhibit her and risk blue balls myself. "Ready to take a hike?" I ask Aurèle and her face lights up the room.

She gives me a quick peck on the cheek. "Just let me get my camera, and I'm all yours." I nod stupidly, stricken mute.

"Man, what I'd give," I hear Theo mutter wistfully from behind me, but before I can expand on that, not that he would anyway, kind of Theo thing, he picks up his phone, effectively shutting me out. "Maitland," he answers on a frown, sauntering off to the living room.

Ten minutes later, I wrap my arm around Aurèle's waist, pulling her into the warmth radiating from my body as we walk past the fields and into the forest beyond.

A loose plan is forming as I walk.

The few times I've been hiking in here was either to get to Zac and Magali's new house site, all but a five-minute walk from the farmstead if we cut across the fields, a little longer by road, or to Liam and Éolie's meadow farther up by another ten minutes' walk from Zee's place.

I pull her to a stop. She turns around as I drop my arm, tilting her face to look directly into my eyes as she wraps her arms around my neck.

"Trust me?" I ask.

"No, not at all," she deadpans.

"Hey!" I poke her in the ribs and she laughs, sidestepping me.

"I, Aurèle de Grandpré!" she shouts out with her arms wide open. "Do trust, Philippe-Olivier Tisserot, with her life." She leans into my chest, kissing me on the chin. "Better?"

"Much." I take her hand and lace our fingers, tugging her along. I eye her askance. "Want to go check the construction sites? I want to show you something," I say, wanting to show her what it could be like, wanting to put ideas into her head because I sure have them.

"Lead on." She squeezes my hand, and we're off.

The trail is wide enough, thankfully, and we can walk side by side and talk. "Did you know Magali used to play house as a little girl in the woods where their home now stands?"

"No, that's such a cute story," she says, eyes soft, wonder lacing her tone of voice.

"I know," I say slyly. "Imagine that." *Please do...*

The main trail separates into two a few hundred meters in, and Aurèle makes a right instead of left and into unexplored territory for me.

I tug her to a stop, motioning with my head. "It's that way."

She points right. "Have you ever been that way?"

"Nope."

"Then let's go explore," she says excitedly, pointing her camera on the cluster of birch trees growing straight from a moss-covered boulder up ahead, their roots like claws digging into the rock.

"Lead on." I sigh conceding defeat. For now.

Soon, we have to walk in single file, the trail narrowing on a steep incline. "Whose bright idea was it again to agree to this?" I mutter under my breath. "Oh, yes, mine," I grumble, both at the missed opportunity to show Aurèle the other two homes right away and that we can no longer talk. Well, not unless I want a one-sided conversation.

A torrent, gorged up on melting snow, roars nearby. Aurèle, her camera glued to her face, stops every few meters, snapping pictures, engrossed in mossy trunks and boulders against patches of immaculate snow, evergreens in the backdrop, dripping wet, glowing iridescent in the sun.

And just like that, I forget everything else but this moment in time.

"Look," she says every few minutes from behind her lens. And I look. She's so gorgeous, her face resplendent lit up from within.

"Come on, we're almost at the top," she says excitedly. "Pretty sure the view from up there will be even more breathtaking."

"From down here, too," I say to her back, climbing behind her, enjoying the view of her round ass filling up her Soft-shell pants from another angle all right. "Breathtaking." *And all mine...*

She inhales deeply on her way up. "Breathe that fragrant air."

And I do. Breathe her in, feeling like the luckiest guy on earth.

Near the top, she stops dead in her tracks. *"Oh mon dieu,"* she whispers in awe. "You won't believe this!" She invites me to follow with a pleading look behind her, her thick, loose braid sliding against her shoulder. "This is eerily familiar."

"It is?" I ask the wind as I follow her.

"It's like I've been here before," she continues, her voice hesitant. She slowly turns around. "Only, there's supposed to be a house with an entire façade made of windowpanes sitting over there." She points behind me.

"You've been here?" My heart slows, my breath catches in my chest. "When?" I ask sharply.

"You'll think I'm crazy." I see her eyes at once unsure and imploring. "But I came here, before I woke up in the hospital."

"If you're crazy, we'll be crazy together. What were you doing here?" I ask, my chest tight with hope—for what exactly, I don't even know yet.

But instead of replying right away she walks down a faint trail meandering between wild blueberry shrubs until she reaches the bluff overlooking the farmstead below. She's standing so still.

I go to her, sinking to the ground and plunking her between my knees. Her back to my front, I wrap my arms around her and drop my chin on the top of her head. Her scent of warm lavender collides with nature and settles inside me.

"It was the most beautiful, velvety summer night at the height of Les

Perséides, and you brought out a telescope."

She holds her hands out, trying to catch the wind as she retells every minute detail of the night she lived with me, ahead of us.

Kneeling before her, I take her by the shoulders and look deep into her eyes. "I will make it happen. We will live in that house, and you will hear again, Aurèle. Just like you experienced before you came back to me," I vow quietly, promising to thank Éolie first thing for that glimpse she gave her.

"It's of no matter. I know that now." She takes my hand and turns it over, pressing my palm over her heart. "Because in here, I hear you perfectly."

Incandescently
(Liam's story)

By Design
(Theo's story)

Indigenous
(Leo's story)

Exposure
(P.O.'s story)

Apprehension
(Zac's story)

Gravity
(Yann's story)

Journey Into the Incandescent World
of Sylvie Parizeau...

The Forest of Laure

Note From Aurèle

Dear Reader,

A little more than a month ago, I never would have dreamed that this love story could be mine for the taking. But, thanks to Olivier and his unfailing faith in us and stout devotion to the cause, here I am. Living proof that *Love* happens, ready or not. And I couldn't be happier. You'll see ;). And now, you ask? Now I can't wait for Yann, Theo and Leo to find and hold onto that someone special too. And something tells me that Theo is next to fall under the spell. This is not the end. This is just the beginning for all of us. Want to bet?

See you soon,

Aurèle

By Design
(Theo's story)
in the works

Name:
Theodore Edward Barclay-Maitland

Nationality:
British

Current status:
Frustrated by a girl he can't forget.
Bored to tears by corporate law.
Final verdict. Move on or move in,
but make a move, man.

cold,
smooth
& tasty.

Continue on, and get a sneak peek at Zac's story, Book 2 in the Incandescent Series, if you haven't yet.

Apprehension

INCANDESCENT SERIES
BOOK 2

One

ZAC

Apprehension

noun

1. anticipation of adversity or misfortune; suspicion or fear of future trouble.

"Oh. *Mon. Dieu. That's it.*"

The girl's blissful cry reverberates throughout the ski chalet over the gurgling sound of the industrial coffee machine I'm milking for all its worth.

I blink.

For a reason I can't explain, that voice elicits a weird flutter in my chest.

With a will of its own, my finger slackens pressure upon the coffee lever. A trickling of smoldering dark brew inches its way up into my fifth cup to go, stopping at the three-quarter mark.

I tip my head to the side.

"Spot on," the voluptuous voice moans to the high ceiling of the café in what I'd call orgasmic enthusiasm. I look right and left, glad no other patrons are witnessing me...witnessing her. And then I see her. Or rather, her appendages.

A nimble tongue licks a slender index finger, greedily lapping it up in an exaggerated wet sucking sound.

My gut tightens.

I stare, torn between *what the fuck*, and *please don't stop.*

I give the girl the once-over. Facing away from me but bending low over the counter, her tight little body's hot all right. Her black turtleneck and soft-shell ski racers showcasing curves I'd like to palm. Interestingly enough, the fact that we're standing in the middle of a ski resort cafeteria, or that, no shit, it's probably colder than absolute zero tonight up in Québec's Laurentian Mountains, barely registers. Right this minute, I don't really care. My fingers twitch and warm up instantly, and so does my dick.

It's been a little while…

Lost in a steamy daydream, I find myself standing at the counter, coffees in hand.

"Will that be all?" the elderly cashier rudely interrupts me mid-fantasy, ringing up my five coffees to go, stowing them in a disposable cardboard tray.

"I'd like to have some of what she's having," I deadpan as I hand over some money to the sugarplum fairy manning the cash register.

"You totally should. Mireille outdid herself. Here, have a taste." The splendid specimen of a girl turns to me, offering me half her cupcake.

I quirk one eyebrow, and her gaze tracks mine to the icing that's just about swiped clean. She shrugs sheepishly. "Tell me one of your guilty secrets, and we'll be even," the enchanting grey-eyed creature says, looking me straight in the eye. Her expression is guileless, which only adds to the tease in her words. My heart picks up its pace.

"I think I will," I quip, bending low, trapping her gaze into mine. "Have a taste that is." I take a bite out of the offered cupcake still cupped in her hand without breaking our stare. Her impossibly large eyes grow by a fraction, and she stills. Well, that certainly caught her attention. *Good.* I shift, pinned by the clear silver of her unwavering eyes. And suddenly, I'm the one who's caught.

Her creamy complexion stains rosy under my scrutiny, eyes wide and full of wonder locked on mine.

My pulse jumps in my throat.

That look. Those eyes. A déjà vu sensation washes over me.

We stare. Just stare. The space of an instant or an eternity, not sure which.

Why do I feel like I know you, like we've met before?

I reel back. Where in the bloody everlasting hell is that shit coming from?

I don't do involved. Ever. My usual type has a universal itch in need of scratching, and not much else.

My best friend Liam's new normality is messing with my head. It must be. After a lifetime of wandering, he's finally—and only recently—settled down with his new wife up here in these mountains. His pregnant wife. And all he can talk about is "normal." Maybe this is me being jealous. I have a sudden yearning for his brand of happiness, yet I have this feeling that I've just bitten off more than I can chew here.

The cupcake is delicious though.

The girl's wondrous eyes flicker past me and then back to me. "See? Definitely a keeper," she says with aplomb.

Damn, her smile is enough to knock a bloke off his feet.

"Are you sure?" a middle-aged woman asks from behind the counter, her tone of voice floundering.

"Yeah, pretty much," I say dumbfounded. She knocked years of suave right off me, so it seems, and scrambled my brains by the same token.

The girl who's too lovely by half, studies me in the space of a second, before answering the timidly voiced question, addressed to her in the first place. "Told you so. A keeper."

Wait, *what?*

A keeper? Me? I inwardly scoff. "Worst pick ever, sweetheart," I say under my breath.

Shifting my weight on one leg, I cross my arms, feigning bored disinterest as I finish my taste of her baked concoction. Curiosity burns a hole in my gut, wondering what this bizarre conversation is all about. "What was that?" I angle a brow, challenging her.

The girl's exquisite face tilts in my direction. She raises her brow, challenging me right back. "A taste of something addictive. So worth keeping."

The woman's audible gasp from behind the counter pops our newest staring contest bubble. "Magali, seriously?" Blonde-haired and of the indeterminate age variety, her eyes dart between us, plump fingers fidgeting with her apron, clearly uncertain.

Ma Ga Lee, I murmur to myself, testing the French musicality of her name on my tongue, and liking it. A tad too much.

The girl stretches over the counter. Long locks of her dark-brown hair stick out every which way from underneath a rainbow-colored wool beanie. Adorable comes to mind. One of her hands clasps the other woman's fidgety fingers, giving them a gentle squeeze. "Seriously. This one above all the others."

I still. Six words. Like a vow. Unheard of. *This one above all the others.* What would it be like to be so chosen? My breath catches in my throat. She can't possibly be talking about me?

Magali. Soft lips...soft words ...the voice of an angel.

"And which one would that be?" I ask, a bit reeling from my wayward thoughts.

A small, delighted chuckle escapes Magali's lips, and I'm strangely pleased to be responsible for eliciting it. Mireille gives her a weird look, but Magali looks down before I catch her eyes.

"This one," Mireille informs me, motioning to the blackboard behind her where an elegant penmanship conveys the cafeteria's treat of the day under the heading *Decadent Bliss du Jour.* A damp spot underneath leaves the blank space wide open to interpretation. She points to Magali's half-eaten cupcake. "I just gave you a leftover diet cupcake I baked for Yolande and me." She points at the elderly cashier. "It's not meant as a special treat... It's so bland, *non*?" the middle-aged woman says in a hushed tone as though confessing to a great sin.

Bloody hell. My breath swooshes out, and I'm strangely disappointed. Of course, she'd been talking about the dessert. *Get over yourself why don't you?*

"You did?" Magali's brow scrunches up in disbelief while her pearly whites take a tentative bite of the cake where a bit of frosting remains. "I don't know where you've put the diet in there. It melts in my mouth. The moist center is pure decadence with that frosting, and you know I can eat my weight in sugar. I'm telling you, this is your Avalanche Cupcake to top them all, and you'll have everyone coming back for more, guaranteed. *Definitely* worth keeping," she says.

"Don't you agree?" Her pale silver eyes land on me as she smiles the most brilliant smile I've ever seen. Two dimples, cute as all hell, dance at the corner of her full lips.

My pulse jumps. Killer dimples. Kissable lips. *Definitely.*

"Definitely," I parrot. You'll have me coming back for more, I inwardly vow. *Where the fuck did that come from?*

Magali cranes her head above my shoulder. "Yolande, don't you agree as well?"

Three pairs of eyes swivel to the white-haired cashier. She grunts something that can pass for a yes. Not quite meeting anyone's eyes, she starts fussing with the display baskets of whole-grain muffins and homemade energy bars arrayed temptingly next to the coffee machine beside the cash register.

I lean back against the counter, crossing my ankles, my ski boots at an angle, waiting for the outcome of this nonsensical debate about plain old vanilla cupcakes. In reality, I can't seem to make myself just up and go before I know more about this girl. She's fascinating.

"I'll be back for more," I say before I can stop myself.

Magali's eyes flick to my night ticket affixed to my left sleeve and the tray with five cups resting on the counter beside me. "See, Mireille? Everyone agrees on your newest treat, even visitors just passing through."

Just passing through. My chest constricts painfully upon hearing the words. What's with that? I've said them myself with a shit ton of relief to back them up more than a thousand times before.

Mireille twists her hands on her apron. "I'm not really sure that cake makes the cut for *l'ardoise.*"

Magali leans closer, putting her hand on my sleeve. A fresh citrus scent worms its way to my nose and I inhale deeply. "Mireille's been trying to come up with the perfect Avalanche Cupcake ever since a local blog post mentioned that her *Bliss du Jour* wasn't worth the detour. Very bad form."

I'd like to wax lyrical on the goddamn cake if just to get on her good side, but for the life of me I can't think of any words; my mind's a blank slate. "Indeed." I rub my jaw, unnerved by the heady rush of warmth her nearness sends zipping through my nerve endings, firing me up. *Does she feel it too? This thing between us.*

"You can say it's a matter of pride now to prove that blogger wrong by the end of the season, and Mireille gets my vote on this one." Magali leans away, and I mourn the loss of her hand on my sleeve. *Who's this guy?*

Mireille clucks her tongue on a soft head shake. "I'm still not convinced this afternoon's whipped chocolate berry mousse cupcakes topped with lemony frosting, weren't, I don't know, more...*it?*" She dips a spoon into a stainless steel bowl, handing it over.

Magali's luscious lips part and she hums while her tongue takes a slow swipe of frosting, licking off the spoon.

Fuck, I can't breathe. I clutch the counter.

"That's funny." Magali's forehead furrows, her tongue getting in another slow lick. "I could have sworn I tasted this, plus a mix of maple and vanilla there, at the end, on mine. You know, less tart. Sweeter."

The grandmotherly cashier, Yolande, clears her throat, looking down at the floor. "I sort of...spread another layer of frosting on Magali's cupcake."

Spread another layer of frosting on Magali's cupcake? The visual, man.

"Yolande," gasps Mireille.

Yolande shrugs both shoulders. "What can I say? It needed a boost."

Jesus. I don't need a boost. I'm sporting a boner from hell that not even the concept of a negative forty-something wind-chill factor awaiting me outside deflates. Never mind micro-fleece thermal layers stretched to the limits of endurance.

For an answer, Magali's eyes dance with something akin to mirth looking me over, and I wonder for a minute if I voiced my thoughts aloud. I grab the coffee tray, making sure it provides adequate coverage over strategic areas. The guys are probably freezing to death waiting on their coffees, and I can't stand here much longer without making a complete fool of myself.

"Time's up, Magaliiii. You coming, or what?" one of the ski resort dudes, in full patrol gear, hollers from the cafeteria doors, a few feet away from where I stand rooted in the quasi-deserted room, a huge bonfire keeping everyone on a ski break tonight out-of-doors.

Magali hands the bowl back over the counter. "Have to go. Cédric will have my head for sure but it was totally worth it. Here's to one of your tastiest collabs." Magali salutes both women with what's left of her cupcake before opening wide and shoveling it down in one swallow. "Keep it up," she says around a full mouth of baked goods.

Yeah, that's the problem.

My brain's stuck in neutral, my testis drawn tight, and my stomach's clenching in knots.

Great times ahead skiing this off.

"It's off the chart with frosting, you really should try it," she says to me in all seriousness, wiping crumbs from the corner of her lips as she spins on one heel.

"Off the chart with—" I choke, my voice barely audible. I'm struck stupid. What the bloody hell? I don't do tongue-tied. Ever.

"Enough. Come on, already," the hulking patrol guy shouts at Magali, grating on my nerves. My eyes narrow.

"I'm coming. I'm coming. I'm coming," Magali chants away.

Christ above, what's left of me to harden stiffens in a nanosecond. My blood pumps wildly, churning in my ears. The dude spares me a burning glance before pushing back out on his poles and skis, presumably on his way to the lifts.

My hands fist at my side. "Your boyfriend doesn't like you having treats?" I call out to her. I may have something against him if he gives her a hard time for enjoying herself. I may have something against him, period.

"Boyfriend?" She shakes her head on a small laugh. "Won't Cédric have a hoot over that one?" The rhythmic thumps of her coordinated moves, heel to toe, make walking in these things sound effortlessly easy, which I know for a fact, is far from being so. "Guess I'll never hear the end of it now, will I?" she adds cryptically.

I clump my way over to her in my ski boots, managing to balance the coffees and myself in an effort to keep pace. "Meaning?"

Reaching one of the long tables a bit farther down, she shrugs on a bright-red jacket labeled Mont Saint-Sauveur Ski Patrol in reflective white letterings, before grabbing her helmet, sporting the resort logo in front, with her name, Magali, tagged on the back of it.

She's a ski patroller too? Nice... Maybe not a boyfriend, then. Even better.

She shoots me a smile that turns her from gorgeous to flat-out devastating. A direct hit to the solar plexus. "You owe me one."

"What—?"

"Guilty secret," she says over her shoulder.

For the space of a moment, we fall into each other's eyes, a meeting of souls. "Just so you know. What I said earlier on wasn't just about the cupcakes, either." She winks.

I stare, slack-jawed, as she disappears in a blur of red, pushing her way out, past Leo and P.O., who whistle low.

"Won't ask what's been keeping you." P.O. takes the lid off one of the cups I've almost forgotten I'm carrying. His muddy, green-hazel eyes glint with suppressed merriment, giving me the once-over.

"He shoots! He scores!" Leo smirks, quoting the saying on the long-sleeved tee I wore this afternoon at Liam's courthouse wedding. He ties back his shoulder-length sandy brown hair before shoving back down his dark beanie. I give him a look, unimpressed. Liam and Éolie are expecting twins, and the shirt's only funny within context.

"I'd say it was just the usual shit," P.O. says, vastly amused, "but the mouth hanging open's a new one. What'd she do? Say no?"

I shoot him a glare. "*She*," I uncharacteristically bark at P.O., "has a name."

Magali. Her name is Magali, I'd like to say, but refrain. I'm not ready to share any details yet. I'm still reeling from the encounter and my unusual reaction to her.

"I'm sure *she* does." P.O. smirks.

"Give over, man." Leo plucks the coffee tray from my unresisting hand.

"It's not like that," I grumble as I follow them out. I blink.

Shit. It's worse than that.

My eyes scan the crowd of skiers, dismissing one red coat after the other, realizing too late that I've let her disappear on me.

"Of course it's not," P.O. says in an offhand manner, watching me.

"So, tell me again why you're *not* looking for a bright-red coat, and a pretty fucking hot patroller wearing it," Leo says, annoyingly smug, and P.O. low fives him.

I grit my teeth, my gut weirdly churning. "She's a friendly sort, that's all," I finally manage, irked to no end by Leo's comment as we approach Theo and Yann waiting by the bonfire.

"Who's a friendly sort?" Yann asks, picking one of the disposable cups. P.O. sips from his, hiding a smirk.

"A girl, apparently," Leo says knowingly.

"Friendly as in 'just friends?' That's a new one." Yann's face scrunches up as though the notion does not even add up, his bright-green eyes blinking behind his wire-framed glasses. "Girls up here are a different species altogether if Zac can't even score one."

Theo scratches his blond scruff, his mouth twisting, fighting a laugh.

"Want a shot at me, stand in line," I mutter, my fingers gripping my own cup.

"About time," Theo says, snatching a cup. "Level out the playing field for the rest of us."

I cut them a look. "Aren't you guys regular comedians tonight?"

"I could have made two more runs down the slope, man," Theo comments, struggling to keep a straight face. "Took you that long to wipe out in there."

The three others chuckle under their breath, and I'd normally join in the ribbing, dishing it right back, but for some unfathomable reason I have no wish to explore right now, they're pissing me off instead. Big time.

"Wipe out, my ass." I guzzle down the lukewarm coffee before squishing the cup into a ball, pitching it into the bonfire. It lands dead center of the roaring flames.

Transfixed, I watch my cup crash and burn, a strange sense of apprehension washing over me.

Acknowledgements

Curious about the pretty amazing people who contribute to my story-telling journey behind the scenes? Take a look :

http://www.sylvieparizeau.com/behind-the-scenes/

Book cover design provided *By Hang Le* ♥

Copy editing provided by *Red Road Editing* ♥

Proofreading provided by *Avanturine Press Author Services* ♥

Coaching, story development editing, insights and SO much more provided by *Heather Hildenbrand*. ♥ you. xoxo

Grégoire, you know why. . .and I'll always remember it. *Je t'aime pour les prochains mille ans.* xx

Melleny, Melleny, Melleny. You've been, throughout, my go get. Your unfailing faith in me, P.O., and Aurèle, brought their story to life. Readers from all over owe you and so do I. Just to let you know, we are beyond privileged to have you in our lives. Love you. xoxo

My heartfelt thanks to all the wonderful bloggers out there who took a chance on me; I have no words (and for an author, as Liam would say; that sucks big time ;)!

And to you, dear reader: *You* make this story-telling journey, extraordinary.

If I did pique your curiosity and you'd like to know just a little bit more about me? Feel free to peek inside my head by exploring this website: www.sylvieparizeau.com

Curious about the real village my characters live in?

Feel free to explore right here:

http://www.sylvieparizeau.com/sylvies-chronicles/

Fall in love with a book and share it with the world; leave reviews. It matters. You matter.

STAY IN TOUCH. Spread the love. ♥

Sign in to my newsletter and get both, the Forest of Laure Map as a gift screensaver and your first email-tribe-only bonus scene, featuring Liam and darling little Sébastien.

Warning: May contain traces of Zac and become addictive.

Gift map, excerpts, teasers, bonus scenes, village news, upcoming releases, hugs.

Don't miss out!

My e-mail tribe gets it all. So can you.

http://www.sylvieparizeau.com/link-to-newsletter/

Ready to meet the guys? Check them out.

https://www.sylvieparizeau.com/meet-guys-incandescent-series/

About the Author:

Incurable romantic. Obsessive daydreamer. Happily Ever After devotee. Epilogue activist. Fairy tale enthusiast. Unicorn believer. Romance novelist the rest of the time.

Author of the up and coming Incandescent Series, Sylvie lives her own Happily Ever After in the beautiful mountains of Les Laurentides in Northern Quebec alongside her whole set of characters. In between treks in their backyard wilderness, you can find them hanging out over at:

https://www.sylvieparizeau.com

Come and say hello. They'd love to hear from you.